ALIX JAMES

THE MEASURE OF LOVE

THE MEASURE OF A MAN COLLECTION, BOOK ONE

A PRIDE AND PREJUDICE VARIATION

Cover Design by GetCovers.com
Cover Image Licensed by Period Images
Background image licensed by Shutterstock

Blog and Website: https://alixjames.com/
Newsletter: https://subscribepage.io/alix-james
Book Bub: https://www.bookbub.com/authors/alix-james
Facebook: https://www.facebook.com/ShortSweetNovellas
Twitter: https://twitter.com/N_Clarkston
Amazon: https://www.amazon.com/stores/Alix-James/author/B07Z1BWFF3
Austen Variations: http://austenvariations.com/

Contents

Dedication

I don't know how, but he still loves me.
I'll spend my last breath loving him back.

Chapter One

DARCY POUNDED HIS FIST furiously on the weathered door, rattling the nearby shutters. This ramshackle "rooming house" in London's East End was no better than a brothel—exactly the sort of place Wickham would frequent. Desperation had chased Darcy to the city's filthy underbelly once before, but the viper had slipped his grasp. Not this time, though. The street lad who had taken Darcy's coin said that George Wickham was back, and he was not alone.

The door creaked open, and a pinch-faced woman in garish rouge peered out. "You, sir! State your business or be off!"

"I am here to see George Wickham." Darcy shouldered past her into the dim, smoky foyer, hand drifting toward the pistol holstered under his coat. "Where is he?"

The Madame crossed her arms. "Don't know any. Now, see here, I run a reputable—"

"Do not trouble yourself to conceal him." Darcy grasped her arm, pressing several coins into her palm and curling her trembling fingers over them. "Wickham is upstairs, is he not?"

The Madame licked her thin lips, eyeing the money. After a moment, she jerked her head at the stairs. Darcy took them three at a time, his boots pounding up the rickety steps, his breath coming in heated puffs. The Madame's shrill cries echoed after him, demanding he behave "civil-like", but he heeded her not. His fury would not be contained a moment longer.

Wickham was here. After weeks of relentless searching, justice would be served. No more innocent lives ruined by that blackguard's selfish whims. Darcy ground his teeth, an image of his dear sister Georgiana's anguished face flashing before his eyes. *Never again.*

He took the last few steps in a single leap, the old wood groaning under his weight. This was the room—he could hear a feminine voice fretting softly from within. Gathering himself, he kicked the door with an echoing crack. The lock splintered apart, opening on a dingy room wreathed in opium smoke and illuminated by one rusted oil lamp.

Wickham lounged on the bed like a sultan, shock melting into his trademark wolfish grin. But it was the girl who drew Darcy's blazing eyes—for all her buxom déshabillé, hers was the face of a child—a child with tumbling golden curls who couldn't be more than fifteen years old. She tugged the thin chemise around her shoulders, her mouth opened in protest... but Darcy's voice thundered first.

"Wickham!" he roared.

With nostrils flared like an enraged bull, Darcy seized the front of Wickham's shirt and slammed him against the wall hard enough to make the mirror rattle dangerously. Out of the corner of his eye, he glimpsed the girl fleeing from the room but paid her no further mind. His full fury was reserved for the hateful villain before him, now twisting and writhing in his tight grasp.

"Well, well, if it isn't Mr High and Mighty," Wickham choked out. "Wasn't expecting to see you in a den of iniquity. Don't tell me you've finally come to your senses and sampled the wares for—"

Darcy cut him off with a swift right hook to Wickham's sharp jaw, sending him sprawling to the warped floorboards. "That was for Georgiana, you bastard," he spat. As quick as a jungle cat, he pounced, hauling Wickham up once more by the shirtfront. "Now, you dog, you are going to pay for what you've done!"

Wickham coughed wetly as Darcy threw him against the stained mattress. Yet as he swiped blood from his mouth, his cracked lips twisted in a jeering grin.

"Come now, what's all this about? Can't blame a fellow for enjoying a willing girl's company. Why, your delightful sister was the one who threw herself into my arms. Begged me to run away with her, she did! How is dear Georgiana?"

With a roar of outrage, Darcy seized Wickham by the shirtfront once more, hauling him up and slamming him into the headboard so hard his teeth clacked together.

"You will not speak her name!" he thundered, cocking his fist back again with murder in his eyes.

Wickham held up his hands, still grinning his infuriating, insolent grin even as twin trails of blood leaked from his flared nostrils. "Very well, very well. But tell me, Darcy, however do you propose I 'pay' for my indiscretion, as you call it? Will you take a cheque?

For I dare say the entertainment was well worth more than you'd get from flogging a dead horse." His grin turned positively vulpine. "Why, I imagine your dear sister still misses my affections. Jealous now, is she?"

Darcy trembled with rage as he gripped Wickham by the shirtfront, his fist raised and ready to explode against that foul, sneering face once more. How easy it would be to beat this blackguard within an inch of his life, to feel the satisfying crunch of bone and flesh yielding to his revenge. Blood for blood.

With Herculean effort, Darcy regained a shred of control. He was no street ruffian, and Wickham was hardly worth dirtying his hands over further. Breathing hard through flared nostrils, Darcy released his foe and stepped back. Wickham collapsed against the mattress, face swelling grotesquely from Darcy's fury. "I have better plans for you."

Wickham spit crimson through his ruined grin. "What's this? The high and mighty Darcy gone squeamish at the sight of blood? You ought to have sent your attack dog cousin if you didn't have the stomach to see this through. Fitzwilliam would have happily finished the job."

Curling his lip in disgust, Darcy replied in a deadly soft tone, "Be grateful Colonel Fitzwilliam is not here. For your brutality against innocents, he would tear you limb from limb without hesitation." He flexed his aching, blood-stained knuckles. "Fortunately for you, some semblance of reason still governs my actions. But test that fraying thread further at your own peril."

Wickham leered up at Darcy through swollen lips. "Come now, old boy, no need for this unpleasantness. Why not relax and sample the wares? I've a tasty little tart just downstairs, ripe for the picking. Pretty as a picture, with fire in her blood—just how you nobles like them. Still innocent in all the ways that matter, too."

He licked the blood from his teeth, eyes fever-bright. "How about it, Darcy? Care to take her off my hands and school her in the ways of men?"

Revulsion churned Darcy's stomach. He hauled Wickham up by the throat, shoving him brutally against the stained wall. "Have you no shred of decency or conscience left? She is but a child! Ruining innocents for sport—you disgust me."

Wickham just chuckled. "Innocent? That one was born wild. Why, Miss Lydia is a gentlewoman in name only. She makes most London whores look saintly."

At this casual besmirching of yet another young lady's reputation, Darcy slammed Wickham back again, arm pressing viciously across his windpipe. "I'll see you rot."

Wickham just leered, undaunted. "Oh, I hardly spoiled anything. But sweet Georgiana, now there was a tender lamb ripe for the plucking. So softly yielding, so deliciously willing to be taught and shown and taken..."

With a savage roar, Darcy seized Wickham about the neck and began raining blow after brutal blow upon his fiendish, grinning face. In the distance, he was dimly aware of violent shouts and pounding footsteps on the stairs over the roaring in his ears, but all his world had narrowed to crushing the life out of the blackguard who had hurt Georgiana.

They grappled violently, crashing into the furniture and shattering some sort of bottle. Darcy deftly avoided a knife-handed strike at his throat, but missed the knee rocketing upwards into his groin. He staggered, and Wickham slammed into him full force. They tumbled out of the shattered doorway, teetering together on the landing's edge with flailing arms.

Wickham managed to grab the splintered railing, steadying himself. But Darcy was already overbalanced—he felt nothing but sick terror as the stairs rushed up to meet him. His head cracked against the wooden floorboards, and pain exploded through his back like a gunshot. Still, he tumbled limply down, every edge and nail of the crude staircase gashed his flesh until all went black.

Far off, a familiar voice cried out. "Good God... Darcy!" Strong hands rolled him onto his back. Darcy struggled toward consciousness, and pain—blinding pain—returned in nauseating darkness. Colonel Fitzwilliam's familiar face hovered above him, creased in horror. "Darcy! Can you hear me?"

He tried to stand, but there was... nothing. No response or sensation where his legs should have been. Fighting panic, he gasped, "My legs... oh God, I cannot feel my legs!"

ELIZABETH PACED THE WORN carpet of Longbourn's sitting room, twisting a handkerchief between anxious fingers. The family had gathered here each evening for the past fortnight—waiting, praying, as her father searched London's seedy underbelly for their lost Lydia. Thus far, his letters had told of naught but failure. Yet when the creak of carriage wheels echoed outside in the twilight, Elizabeth's heart seized in her chest. Papa had returned, and his journey ended. She steeled herself against a surge of hope as Jane gripped her wrist, eyes round with shared trepidation.

They hurried to the entrance hall as Mr Bennet entered, travel-stained hat in hand. One look at his haggard face, the grim set of his jaw, and Elizabeth's fragile hope guttered out. The news would not be good. They had not found Lydia.

At this confirmation of her deepest fears, Mrs Bennet collapsed into the same hysterics that had provoked her since that express came from Colonel Forster. "Ruined... my poor girls are ruined!" she wailed, dampening her handkerchief with tears. "And my sweet Lydia gone who knows where with what sort of man?"

Mary crossed her arms, rage smouldering beneath her sullen expression. "What does it matter whether she comes home at this point? Papa not finding her changes nothing. The loss of reputation in a sister is a stain upon us all."

"Oh, how could you, Mary?" Kitty wailed.

"Yes, yes, how could you, Mary?" Papa asked tiredly. "You ought to rejoice, at least, that I did *not* find her with the constable or bring her home in a box. Jane, have some tea sent to my study." He braced his hand on the door leading out of the drawing room, hesitating slightly as his eyes found Elizabeth and Jane. Then he quit the room.

Kitty clung to Mama, weeping and hiccoughing. "It's all so h—horrid! I cannot endure it. I wish I had gone to Brighton too! I could have stopped her... or at least gone so that we might be together—"

"Oh, such a state I am in. Oh, where is Hill?" Mama demanded. "My salts, I need my salts!"

Jane rolled her eyes at Elizabeth as Mama's lamentations rose to near-ear-splitting volumes. "We should speak with Papa," Jane urged softly.

Elizabeth nodded. Their father's drooping shoulders and faded eyes terrified her like nothing had ever done. With a fortifying breath, she followed Jane to the study. Pausing at the door, Elizabeth steeled herself and knocked.

There was no answer for a moment, but at Elizabeth's second knock, they heard, "You may as well come in and hear the worst of it." Elizabeth spared Jane a glance. Then, biting her lip, she pushed the door open.

Mr Bennet raised his head from weary hands, his eyes bloodshot and posture stooped. "Lizzy... Jane." He attempted and failed at an encouraging smile for his eldest daughters. "I am relieved to see your compassionate faces, at least amidst the turmoil out there. Please sit, though I fear I have little to offer besides empty hands."

Elizabeth took the chair opposite her father as Jane perched beside her. The silver scattering his temples seemed so much more pronounced after even a fortnight away. Guilt and regret lined his face as deeply as grief.

He ran a trembling hand down his jaw. "Forgive me, girls—I've failed you all..."

"No, Papa." Elizabeth reached across the desk to grasp her father's other hand. "We must hope. Tell us, what did you learn in London?"

With a shuddering sigh, Mr Bennet related the scant crumbs of intelligence gathered. Tracking the carriage bearing Lydia and this Mr Wickham she had met in Brighton through several coaching inns... Hiring Gardiner's private investigator to navigate London's less savoury districts without success... Long days pounding grimy streets and haunted nights plagued by visions of his youngest daughter's peril and ruin...

Jane's eyes shone with tears as he haltingly relayed it all. Even Elizabeth harboured little hope left untainted by dread after learning how thoroughly this man had disappeared into the urban labyrinth with her sister.

"...I confess my imagination torments me, supplying endless possibilities for why a scoundrel like Forster claims Wickham to be would run off with a gentleman's fifteen-year-old daughter," Mr Bennet eventually finished in a bleak voice. "Would that I had been a better father..."

Elizabeth squeezed his hand. "The fault lies with the man's wicked intentions... and Lydia's own recklessness. We must not abandon hope."

"Had I but put something by for you all! Then my most deserving daughters need not be without all hope of a respectable future!" He dropped his head into his hands, his fists tugging at the tufts of hair above his ears.

"Papa!" Elizabeth cried. "There must be something to be done. You said Uncle hired a private investigator. Surely, there is hope! Why..." she tugged her lower lip to the side of her teeth. "No one could hide Lydia for long. She is too loud."

Her papa snorted, shaking his head. "Aye, and what I would give to hear her carrying on about her bonnet just now. Leave me, girls. Let me soak in my shame alone—I surely deserve it."

Elizabeth sighed as she nodded. "Hill ought to have your tea ready soon, and then you must rest, Papa. Surely, we will have some word tomorrow."

Yet despite her steadfast words, sick fear slithered in Elizabeth's heart. What horrors could Lydia be facing now at this strange man's mercy?

Chapter Two

Fire lanced through Darcy's body, dragging him cruelly back to wakefulness. He suppressed a pained groan as the ornate ceiling of his London townhome swam into focus over him. Panicked memories filtered back—Wickham's sneering face... a desperate struggle... plunging down the stairs... then sickening blackness.

Low voices filtered through, muffled by the pounding ache in Darcy's skull. He struggled to focus on the hushed exchange between a grim-faced stranger and his cousin Richard hovering behind.

"...spinal damage may be catastrophic... too early to determine full severity..."

Anxiety prickled sharply as Darcy stirred.

"What... what has happened?" He rasped weakly.

The colonel grasped Darcy's hand. "Thank God you're awake. Lie still—there, breathe easily."

Darcy's throat went dry as he struggled to order swirling memories. Why could he not will his legs to move?

Sensing Darcy's rising panic, the doctor leaned over him. "We have kept you sedated for two days. You suffered a rather serious fall, Mr Darcy."

"Why can I not feel my legs?" he barked.

The doctor traded a significant glance with Richard. Darcy stared at his cousin, but Richard shook his head and covered his mouth with his hand. Then he turned away, leaving the doctor to answer.

"There has been a great deal of damage, Mr Darcy. We... we cannot yet determine if... if you shall walk again."

"Cannot determine?" Darcy erupted hoarsely. "Blast it, when can I move my legs? I've matters to attend. Are you a doctor or not?"

The doctor held up a placating hand. "Please try to calm yourself, Mr Darcy. It is still very early. The swelling may yet—"

"Calm myself and wait helplessly abed? When will you be able to answer me?" Darcy thundered.

"Now, surely, Mr Darcy, you must know that these things take time."

"My back cannot be broken. It cannot be! I can..." He grunted, trying to sit up, but was only able to crunch his stomach muscles, and that, not without pain.

"I cannot say for sure, Mr Darcy, but I am not entirely without hope for—"

He tried forcing himself upright, face purpling, but found his chest fettered and bound against such efforts. "I'll have no platitudes or false hope! Summon more doctors, if you must, until one gives me honesty!"

"See here, Darcy, be reasonable!" Richard grasped his shoulders as Darcy struggled. "Dr James is already the third physician we have brought in."

"And what did the others say?"

Richard dropped his eyes.

"Blast and damn you. They inspect me while I am knocked unconscious with laudanum and are shocked when I do not respond? Find one who can repair my legs!"

Richard clasped the hand Darcy was waving around and anchored it to the bed. "Now see here, raving like a lunatic will not aid your recovery."

Chest heaving, Darcy's head collapsed against the pillows as his wrecked body betrayed his swirling, impotent fury. As enraged denial slowly spiralled into panic, the doctor tried urging more laudanum on him to dull the pain.

"Pain, what pain? That is precisely the problem, is it not? I cannot feel anything!"

"Sir, your head... the shock of it all—"

Darcy swept out a quaking hand, sending the glass vial flying. "Get out!"

The doctor sighed regretfully. "As you wish. But I must insist you take the drought for your recovery, if you refuse to rest."

He hesitated before withdrawing, but Darcy speared him with a molten glare. "I said get out. Now!"

Only when they were alone did Colonel Fitzwilliam cautiously approach the bedside chair. "The doctor only means to help ease your torment, Darcy."

Darcy turned his face away, shame burning his cheeks at this helpless, invalid state laid bare even to his cousin. As panic's cold talons sank deeper, his breath came in ragged gasps. "Richard... you must help me. I cannot bear this! I cannot be... Tell that doctor he is a fool. I shall walk!"

He grasped Richard's sleeve with fervent desperation, all traces of his customary stoic strength vanished. "Help me... in God's name, find someone who can make me whole again!"

Pity shone brightly in the colonel's eyes as he grasped Darcy's trembling hand. "Here, now... peace. You must rest and gather your strength."

He gently pressed the discarded vial of laudanum back into Darcy's palm, closing his fingers over it. Darcy eyed him with a scalding glare, then sloshed the bitter liquid down his throat.

"Let this draught soothe your mind so your body may heal. I will do everything under heaven, Cousin. And one or two things under hell, if I must."

"PERHAPS TODAY WILL FINALLY bring word from Lydia," Elizabeth mused as her slippers whispered through the quiet garden. Dapples of afternoon sunlight shifted over the path where she walked arm in arm with Jane, both their faces etched with worry.

"Or Uncle's investigator will have new information after scouring London's streets another day," Jane murmured back. "I know the chances seem slimmer each day, but we must keep faith."

Elizabeth sighed uneasily, eyes following a butterfly flitting among the roses. "I cannot bear imagining where that thoughtless girl is now. You do not suppose that Mr Wickham might have abandoned her, do you? Anything might have... wait, do you hear hoofbeats?"

Both sisters turned sharply as the unmistakable thunder of a galloping horse echoed from beyond the garden hedge. Exchanging an anxious glance, they gathered their skirts and hastened through the rustic gate onto the lawn. An unfamiliar rider drew rein just before them, his horse lathered and heaving breathlessly.

"Excuse me, ladies!" The rider pulled off his cap, wiping sweat from his brow with a grubby handkerchief "I've an express letter for a Mr Bennet!"

Hope and foreboding warred in Elizabeth's breast as she turned to the house. "I shall fetch him at once!"

Jane led the rider round while Elizabeth rushed inside, gathering her startled sisters. Soon, Mr Bennet stood scanning the mysterious letter, brow furrowed. His daughters crowded anxiously behind him, breaths bated for whatever revelation lay inside.

The rider touched his cap. "I'll be off then, sir."

Mr Bennet looked up bemusedly from the unfolded pages. "Oh yes... of course, your payment."

"Already rendered, sir." With that, the rider wheeled his mount, galloping down the drive as Mr Bennet's outstretched payment faltered.

"Well, Papa? Oh, what does it say?" Elizabeth pressed tremulously.

Mr Bennet turned the pages over once more before his shoulders slumped. "Thank God." He exhaled something unintelligible, then refolded the letter and handed it to Elizabeth, and went inside without another word.

Kitty craned her neck to see while Mary strained impatiently beside her. Jane nodded, and, hands trembling, Elizabeth unfolded the missive. She drew a sharp breath as her eyes scanned the first lines.

"It... it says here that Lydia is safe." She clutched Jane's hand, joyful tears pricking both sisters' eyes at this first glimmer of hope.

Elizabeth read on haltingly, "The letter writer, a Colonel Fitzwilliam, says he... no, his cousin... how very strange, they almost share a name. He discovered her still in the company of... of Mr Wickham." Shocked gasps met this revelation. Kitty's hands flew to her mouth while Mary pursed her lips disapprovingly.

Collecting herself, Elizabeth continued, "...she will be returning home in this gentleman's carriage, with a maid sent to keep her company and the colonel riding alongside to act as her escort."

"Thank the Lord!" breathed Jane.

"A colonel!" Kitty pressed her hand to her chest in a near-swoon. "Do you suppose he is handsome?"

Haltingly, Elizabeth finished, "It says here... she is expected on the morrow."

"Tomorrow!" Kitty trilled. "Oh, but what shall she tell us? Perhaps they were secretly married this whole while!"

Mary cut her off. "Foolish girl! If Colonel Whoever-he-is went through such efforts, likely there is shame yet to be unveiled." She shook her head ominously. "Mark my words."

But Elizabeth was too suffused with glad relief to heed Mary's cynicism just now. She squeezed Jane's hands, both sisters' eyes shining with gratitude. Against all hope, their dear, wayward Lydia was returning home.

S UNLIGHT FILTERING THROUGH THE window stirred Darcy to wakefulness. For one merciful moment, as the chirping of sparrows filled his ears, he forgot. Then, full memory crashed down with all its bleak despair.

He was still numb below the waist. Even the slight shift of his head ignited fresh waves of agony from the stitches crossing his scalp. Darcy explored them with tentative fingers, then hesitantly slid a hand under the blankets. He focused every fibre of his being on willing his toes to move, tears pricking fiercely as only lifeless numbness answered.

There was a quiet knock, and then his valet, Giles, entered. "Thank the Lord you are awake at last, sir. Can I fetch you anything?"

"I am not hungry."

"Of course, sir. I beg your pardon, but I ought to..." Giles cleared his throat and dipped his head toward Darcy's bed.

Confused, Darcy searched the man's carefully schooled features. Then, with dawning horror, it struck him. Mortified heat flooded Darcy's cheeks.

"I... my person... I fear I cannot..." he stammered haltingly, desperation choking his strained voice.

Giles flushed but nodded in understanding. "Of course, sir. Allow me to assist you."

Mute with shame, Darcy stared blindly out the window as his faithful valet's gentle hands tended to his most private needs. He was now fully at the mercy of his traitorous body and the kindness of others! Like a helpless babe... or a cripple. Was this to be his life now under others' care?

The ignominy threatened to crush what fleeting dignity remained until Giles finished. Darcy rasped into the laden silence, "Where is Colonel Fitzwilliam?"

Giles tidied the discarded linens, his gaze averted. "He set out before dawn, sir, escorting the young miss back to her family."

"Who?" Darcy's brow furrowed. "What young lady?"

"The girl found with Mr Wickham. You rescued her, I believe?"

"I... I cannot recall her face," Darcy admitted after a frustrated pause. His memories of those frenzied moments were but shards of visceral panic and pain.

Giles nodded. "Well, sir, I am happy to see you returned to us, against all odds, by God's grace. Shall I fetch some tea? A book, perhaps?"

"No! Leave me be."

Giles thinned his lips and dipped his head. "As you wish, sir."

Once alone, Darcy indulged in a torrent of frustrated tears. Even victory over Wickham tasted as bitter ashes while he lay imprisoned in useless limbs. And he hardly spared a thought for the nameless damsel now making her happy return to her family under Fitzwilliam's protective wing.

A NERVOUS KIND OF busyness filled the drawing room where all the Bennet sisters waited in tense silence. Though breakfast was long past, each daughter wore her finest dress as if expecting fashionable morning callers. Not that they had been troubled by *that* sort of business lately. No one was calling, save Charlotte Lucas when her mother did not catch her, and no one was likely to receive them, either.

While the daughters of Longbourn waited in the drawing room, Mrs Bennet, however, had not yet left her bedchamber, claiming she felt faint and dizzy every time she thought of stirring. She would not feel well again until her dear Lydia was back under her roof, and until then, she would nurse her nerves in the quiet of her room.

Every stray whinny from the barnyard or clatter of wheels from the farm wagon set their hearts pounding anew... until the clock crept past eleven and restlessness replaced fraught anticipation.

"It is very fine of this Colonel What's-his-name to return Lydia, I grant." Kitty smoothed her skirts for the dozenth time. "But the least he could do is be punctual about it!"

"Hush now; be grateful if they arrive at all." Jane laid a calming hand on Elizabeth's, where she clenched her handkerchief into a tense knot with her skirts. "The roads are still muddy, and surely..."

Jane's gentle chidings broke off as an unfamiliar carriage swept grandly up the drive, appointed with a liveried rider and accompanied by a sharp-looking gentleman in a red coat.

"La! So, that is a colonel's carriage!" exclaimed Kitty, wide-eyed. It is positively enormous!"

"Kitty, the letter said the carriage belonged to the colonel's cousin, a Mr Darcy," Elizabeth reminded her. Not that Kitty was listening.

"Why, it has gilded trim and scarlet wool upholstery! Oh look, is that Lydia?"

Elizabeth pressed herself against the glass, wondering what sort of shattered shell remained of her fifteen-year-old sister. Would she be frightened? Ashamed? Repentant? Bruised and misused?

All gazes fixed eagerly as a familiar giggling figure stepped down, assisted by the stone-faced maid. Even at a distance, Lydia looked thrilled, casting admiring glances back at the elegant equipage and saying something to the maid behind her.

Turning back to the house, Lydia paused only to adjust her jaunty bonnet before sailing toward the front door, chin raised as though returning from a grand tour rather than narrowly escaping ruination.

Jane and Elizabeth traded doubting glances. "Well! At least she appears unharmed," murmured Elizabeth with more optimism than confidence.

Chapter Three

As Lydia flounced through the door, Elizabeth felt the first hopeful stirring that perhaps all was not irrevocably ruined. Her wayward sister appeared healthy, at least, if shamelessly buoyant. Surely, if matters had gone... too far... Lydia would not seem so cheerful.

"My dear sisters! La, I have missed you all dreadfully." Lydia breezed right by Elizabeth and Jane's tentative embrace to air-kiss each before turning expectantly.

"Come, Kitty, you must hear absolutely everything about gay Brighton and the splendid officers—"

"A moment, Lydia!" Jane interrupted, casting an uneasy look at the stern countenance of the colonel who had entered behind her. "Surely, you have had a fright. Are you well?"

Lydia laughed. "Do I not look it? Oh, and do not you look at me like that, Lizzy. Is that pity or disgust in your eye? I am perfectly well, as you see."

"Lydia, Jane is right," Elizabeth said. "This is no light matter. Are you not hurt? Where were you these few weeks?"

Lydia sighed. "Oh, Lizzy, *you* ought to go to Brighton. I know all the officers would find you agreeable. Mama always says the men fancy Jane because she is so beautiful, but it's the lively dancers the officers like, and you—Well! Why did Mary just stomp away? I am sure I said nothing to upset her. Oh! Mama!"

Cheeks aflame, Elizabeth was shielding her face from their visitors—even the maid who had accompanied Lydia in the carriage could not keep the shock from her expression. Elizabeth had begun silently formulating further excuses for Lydia when Mrs Bennet burst from her room and down the stairs.

"My darling girl! Oh, you live to flutter Mama's poor nerves once again!" Mrs Bennet nearly dragged Lydia bodily toward the stairs through helpless, mortified Elizabeth's fingers. "My sweet girl is restored to me! Come along, Kitty, let us take dear Lydia upstairs to rest herself."

But Lydia laughed that off airily. "La, Mama, I simply must tell you all about my adventures first! There were balls every night with such refined company—why, with a bit of effort, we will all have officer husbands with splendid uniforms before the summer—"

Each foolish boast twinged painfully in Elizabeth's breast as she watched the stoic Colonel Fitzwilliam bristle. Lydia's childish antics were an added trial after his evident ordeal—and by all appearances, their father's worried prayers and London's finest investigators had done far less to recover her than this weary soldier.

Must they now also bear the mortification of Lydia casting aside any pretence of remorse for the havoc unleashed? With sinking dismay, Elizabeth read worlds of censure in the colonel's tightened jaw as her sister obliviously prattled on.

The awkwardness intensified as even the flighty lady of Longbourn now abandoned propriety for elation at Lydia's miraculous return. Elizabeth's eyes beseeched the colonel not to judge them all too harshly by silly Lydia's obliviousness and her mother's caprice in indulging it—she dearly hoped his understanding would be their saving grace.

Jane hastily interrupted, "We have missed you dearly, Lydia. Thank heaven the good colonel and his cousin went to such lengths to return you safely home. You must be famished."

At his politely reserved expression behind Lydia, Elizabeth added, "Perhaps we could remove to the drawing room for refreshments and... privacy."

"Drawing room, nonsense!" Mrs Bennet scoffed. "My dearest girl, you will come and rest yourself upstairs, and tell me everything! Kitty, you come, too. Lizzy? Jane?"

Jane and Elizabeth shared a glance, then shook their heads slightly and stepped backwards.

"Oh, well, then! Come, my dears. Hill just brought me a fresh pot of tea before you arrived!" Mrs Bennet turned in a flutter of lace and beckoned her two younger daughters to follow her back up the stairs. Seconds later, they were all gone amid a cloud of giggles and squeals.

Elizabeth winced, glancing first at the colonel, then at the maid. They had not even been introduced to the gentleman who had brought Lydia home, and for him to be treated to such a display! Would he now judge the entire Bennet line by silly Lydia's irresponsible escapades? She sent her father a pained look. Would he say nothing?

Mr Bennet at last stirred himself from his stupefied silence, exerting enough willpower to compose himself somewhat, though his voice was raspy and faint. "I do not believe we have been introduced, sir. Thomas Bennet, at your service."

The colonel bowed slightly. "Colonel Fitzwilliam, lately of His Majesty's First Regiment of Foot, at yours."

Mr Bennet blinked, then offered a bow in return. "I suppose I should thank you, Colonel, for restoring my daughter... undeserved as that mercy may be." He sighed, suddenly looking all of his fifty-odd years. "Please join me in my study while I await the true tale."

Elizabeth exchanged a weighted glance with her father as he held the door for the colonel. Surely, their strained hopes rested on whatever revelations Colonel Fitzwilliam had brought... and by his flinty gaze, they would not be glad tidings.

Elizabeth paced the Longbourn drawing room, too unsettled to sit, though Jane perched anxiously on the settee. The only sound was Mary mournfully plonking away at the pianoforte, though her wounded mien betrayed she had little true absorption in the music.

At an off-key note that set Elizabeth's teeth jangling, she finally turned to her glowering sister by the instrument. "Please, Mary, you play beautifully, but perhaps something less... funereal... would better suit the occasion?" At Mary's baleful glare, she amended gently, "We all share your vexation, but take comfort. Lydia is returned to us, however undeserved fortune smiling upon vice may be."

Mary's fists crashed discordantly onto the keys. "Indeed, it is a perverse fortune when my tedious devotion to proper conduct has earned me nought but this public disgrace! I am universally shunned, yet silly Lydia is rewarded—no doubt she will have an officer husband before Michaelmas!"

"We must not rejoice in our sister's folly," Jane put in, "even so, we have much to be thankful for."

"Thankful! You will hate me, Jane, but I would be more thankful if she had never come home. Better to have the neighbourhood's pity than their censure."

"Mary!" Elizabeth cried.

"Don't you scold me, Lizzy. You know it as well as I do. We were on tenuous enough footing already, and now none of us shall ever get a husband. Mama is right. We shall be starving in the hedgerows as soon as Papa dies."

Elizabeth shared an exasperated glance with Jane. "*You* speak to her. Perhaps some of your goodness will rub off." She started for the hallway, then stopped and looked at Mary once more, then back at Jane. "And perhaps some of Mary's practicality would do you a bit of good, too."

"Well, where are you going?" Jane protested.

"I am going to find out why poor Colonel Fitzwilliam has sat unattended for so long. Where is Hill?"

Jane grimaced and pointed up the stairs. "With Mama still."

"Then I will fetch her." Elizabeth dusted off her skirts and started for the stairs. But as soon as she was out of sight of the drawing room, she paused. Braving that den of females was more than she could countenance. And robbing her mother of her housekeeper just now, when Hill's presence likely kept Mama at least somewhat more sedate, was not politic.

But regardless of Mama's hysterics, *someone* must offer basic hospitality. "Well, Lizzy, you have two legs," she muttered to herself. "And you need something to do, anyway."

As soon as she pushed open the kitchen door, she found a plain-faced girl perched at the worktable sharing the scullery maid's nuncheon. Elizabeth paused for a moment to study her. This was the maid who had ridden with Lydia. 'Plain' was not quite the right description for her. Her features were attractive enough, but there was something about her face that reminded her of Charlotte. Perhaps 'plain-speaking' was a better way to explain the girl's clear, direct gaze before she dropped her eyes at Elizabeth's inspection.

Elizabeth drew closer. "I hope you have been able to refresh yourself, Miss..."

The girl scrambled to her feet. "Beg pardon, Miss. Beth Reynolds at your service. I accompanied Miss Lydia home."

"Yes, I know. I hope my sister was not too trying of a companion for you."

The girl's eyes shifted up to Elizabeth's, then back to the floor. "That would not be my place to say, Miss."

Elizabeth thinned her lips. "Well, I, for one, am grateful that my sister had a respectable escort, and I thank you, Beth. We share a name! I am Elizabeth Bennet."

Beth's throat bobbed and she risked a longer look at Elizabeth. A faint smile even touched her lips. "It's a right fine name, Miss."

"I suppose it must be. Please seat yourself and finish your tea before it oversteeps. Sarah?" Elizabeth glanced at the scullery maid. "Papa and his guest have not yet been... oh, dear."

Sarah turned around from the kettle at the stove—her apron splattered in blood and feathers poking out of her hair. "I'm sorry, Miss Elizabeth! Hill said if I did not get this chicken ready for dinner, she'd have my head."

Elizabeth sighed. "Well, I suppose I can put the tray together on my own. You oughtn't be making tea with your hands covered in poultry innards."

The scullery maid nodded her thanks, and Elizabeth poured a pot of hot water and assembled some pastries on a tray. Gathering her courage, she set off down the hall before she could lose her nerve... or drop her mother's fine porcelain.

The pungent aroma of steeping tea leaves filled the hallway as Elizabeth gingerly made her way towards the half-open study door. She knocked and heard the voices within cease. "Come," her father called. Elizabeth steadied her rattled nerves before nudging the door open with her shoulder.

"Excuse me, Papa, but I thought the colonel would like something to refresh himself."

The colonel stood and cleared the path to her father's desk for her to set the tray down. "Your father has already lubricated my throat with something a bit stronger, but I will take the tea as well, and gladly."

Elizabeth offered him a taut smile and set to work. Under the weight of the two men's searching gazes, she carefully doled out cups and saucers before, at last, curtsying to take her leave.

But her father's weary voice gave her pause. "You may as well stay, Lizzy. No doubt you shall pester the details out of me, regardless." He took a long draught of tea before continuing wryly. "Please, Colonel Fitzwilliam, permit my daughter any further questions your forbearance will allow."

"Oh, but I do not think—"

"Come, Lizzy, my head has withstood all it can of the particulars. Surely, you will think of something that I have not done yet." To the colonel, Mr Bennet merely gestured. "Lizzy helps me with a great deal that she probably ought not. You may speak freely before her, Colonel."

Mortification flooding her cheeks, Elizabeth sank onto the very edge of the seat across from the colonel. He gaped openly back at her, glancing occasionally at her father as if to ascertain that the gentleman had truly asked one daughter to sit party to the description of another's disgrace.

Colonel Fitzwilliam had a pleasant face, if not a handsome one. His were features formed by hardship and duty, but there was a kindness in his eyes that she liked. He allowed her to study him, his lips twitching faintly into a smile as she did so. Mustering her courage, she inquired softly, "Where did you find Lydia, if I may ask?"

The colonel set aside his barely-touched tea. "I did not find her. My cousin, Darcy, did."

"Then please convey my—*our family's* deepest gratitude for his efforts when next you see him."

At this, Colonel Fitzwilliam seemed to withdraw into himself, staring at the floor with sudden haunted regret.

Alarmed, Elizabeth ventured gently, "Forgive me, have I misspoken? You seem very distressed, Colonel."

He drew a breath and shook his head. "I must beg your indulgence. Darcy... endured a very great deal... in his endeavours." He reached for his cup and appeared to have to force a swallow of his tea down his throat.

"And you wonder if my sister deserved such an effort," Elizabeth guessed.

The colonel's weathered features creased into lines of empathy. "Your sister hardly acts as one narrowly escaping ruination."

"I beg you not to mistake her callousness for our family's true sentiments. Mama has always indulged Lydia's wild humours too readily. The rest of us are sensible of our debt." She cleared her throat delicately. "Ah... I noticed that you did not disclose *where* he discovered her."

The colonel glanced at Mr Bennet, who gave a tired nod. Fitzwilliam took another sip of his tea and looked down. "At a brothel."

It was a very good thing that Elizabeth was not holding a teacup herself, or it surely would have been shattered when her fingers went suddenly nerveless. "No! Oh, please... No! Is she... Can she be..."

"I cannot vouch for her virtue," he supplied. "But she was with him for well over a fortnight, and knowing Wickham as I do... I understand you are not acquainted with him yourself? I cannot say you have missed anything by the oversight."

"No." Elizabeth stared at her father, the blood running from her cheeks into her shoes. "Lydia wrote of him, of course, but she wrote about several officers she knew. There was no particular evidence of regard for Mr Wickham more than any others in her letters. She said he joined the regiment shortly after they arrived in Brighton. All the ladies were charmed by him, and... oh, Colonel, a brothel?"

"I am afraid so. Darcy learned through... various sources... that Wickham is friends with the Madame and has on previous occasions taken girls to that... establishment... and then left them there when he had done with them."

Elizabeth gasped, covering her mouth with her hand. "You mean that she was almost... almost..."

"Take heart, Miss Elizabeth," he interrupted kindly. "Your sister is safe now."

"But from what? Oh, what she must have done... how can she be so damned *cheerful* about it?" She swallowed and bit her tongue, her cheeks heating all over again. "Forgive my language, sir. I do not normally..."

"I would say in this situation, it is warranted. You will hear no censure from me on the matter." He smiled tiredly and continued. "The one comfort I can offer you is the intelligence that... well, I hardly think I ought to be discussing such things, especially in the presence of a lady, but Mr Bennet, I had not finished—"

Mr Bennet pinched the bridge of his nose, then waved a hand. "Please."

The colonel chewed his lip and braced his hands on his thighs. "I took her to Darcy's house immediately to secure her safety. That was full three days ago. I would have brought her to you sooner, but matters there... Well, there were several points of crisis, not the least of them being the disposition of Mr Wickham himself. But I questioned the housemaids attending Miss Lydia closely, and it would appear that... there is evidence that..."

"She has had her courses," Elizabeth supplied bluntly.

He looked up at her and flicked a hand her way. "Thank you for sparing me the admission. Yes. I believe your family has cause to hope for a complete restoration of her prospects."

Elizabeth hesitated before confessing in a small voice, "I am afraid it is too late for that, Colonel. The whole town learned of that express from Colonel Forster when Lydia vanished... I know not how. I suspect Kitty told Maria Lucas, but whatever the source of the gossip, the end result is that we are now universally shunned. My own aunt and uncle Philips shut their doors to us."

"I am sorry, Miss Elizabeth," he sighed heavily. "I fear they may not be the last, if this is known."

She withdrew a handkerchief from her pocket and dabbed her nose, for it seemed suddenly inclined to betray her. "Even Papa's silly cousin Mr Collins wrote us a letter of... condolences. But he was far more concerned with congratulating himself that such disgrace had not befallen him. It seems that he had given some thought to presenting himself here this autumn and inspecting each of us for a potential bride because he is to inherit Longbourn. Happy circumstance for him that he had not yet come!" She tried to laugh, but her voice shook. "As if any of us would have the odious little sycophant in any case!"

Colonel Fitzwilliam's eyes darkened with compassion. "Vicious tongues indeed, to turn on innocents. You have endured much, and now stand to lose your family legacy when your father passes. I am deeply moved by your trials, Miss Elizabeth."

She composed herself and put the handkerchief away. "Thank you for being so frank with us, Colonel. I suppose you have already informed my father, but... exactly where is this Mr Wickham now? Is Lydia quite safe from him?"

"Newgate. Awaiting the Assizes."

Elizabeth blinked. "Newgate! For absconding with a foolish girl who ought to have known better?"

The colonel stirred uncomfortably. "That was not his only crime. If you are a praying woman, Miss Bennet, you may pray that when he is brought to trial, justice is done." He glanced at her father. "If you will both forgive me, I am wanted back in London at once. I regret to say that I have told you all I know. If there is anything more I can do..."

"No, thank you." Mr Bennet waved a hand, then heaved himself from his chair to offer the colonel his hand. "I daresay you have already done more than enough."

Chapter Four

SHADOWS CREPT TO THE far edges of Darcy's bedchamber, playing over elegant furnishings now feeling more like prison bars with every interminable minute. Still unable to move his own useless legs, he'd slept little, wracked by tormenting dreams soon banished by harsh waking.

Now he could only stare bitterly at the plaster whorls patterning the ceiling, denied even the relief of pacing off his frustrated energy. As the light outside crept higher, Darcy's brooding thoughts spiralled deeper into a well of enraged helplessness.

Giles eased open the door. "I see you are awake, sir. Is there anything I can do for your comfort?"

The tentative hope in his eyes was soon crushed by Darcy's waspish demand. "Leave me be. I've no need of anything."

Undaunted, Giles gently persisted. "Cook has sent up a hearty breakfast tray..." He gestured hopefully to some unseen maid behind him, but Darcy sliced a hand through the air.

"I've no appetite. Take it away."

His stomach growled betrayal at this bald-faced lie, but Darcy ignored it. Like everything now, hunger and such base needs were no longer his own to manage. Soon enough, they would have to humiliate him further with their wretched ministrations... bile burned in his throat at this humiliating dependency.

Alone again, all Darcy could do was brood hatefully over Wickham's smirking face as his dreams and hopes crashed down those filthy boarding house stairs. What more could the blackguard have robbed him of? Even dearest Georgiana still bore scars from her own foolish trust in that demon's silver lies...

Memory unwillingly swept him back to that same shabby room just over a month earlier, where a trembling Georgiana with red-rimmed eyes and tangled golden curls spilt out her naïve dreams and bitter shattering...

No! Darcy's fists clenched helplessly in the bedclothes as molten tears of rage and grief boiled over. The guttural howl of an enraged beast echoed through his sumptuous prison.

The door crashed open without warning, admitting Colonel Fitzwilliam's imposing frame, carrying a tray like a housemaid. Ignoring Darcy's baleful glare, he set the tray down and crossed both arms with a stern glower.

"I could hear your bellowing clear down the hall, Cousin. If you've breath to spare on such theatrics, surely food is not entirely beyond your strength."

His meaningful glance took in the untouched breakfast tray. Before Darcy could snarl a retort, Richard leaned over the bed in entreaty.

"Come, man, you must keep up your health. Not only for your own recovery, think of your sister. Georgiana needs you..."

At this, Darcy jerked his head away, unable to shield the sheen of anguish in his eyes. "She is better off without an invalid brother who could not protect her."

Richard sighed and poured a cup of tea, then carried it on a saucer to the table beside Darcy's bed. He drew up a chair and sat down. "How is your head?"

"It might as well be cannon-shot," Darcy growled. "Where were you yesterday?"

"Surely Giles told you. I escorted Wickham's latest conquest back to the bosom of her family."

"She *has* family?" Darcy snorted. "I assumed she was another of his street tarts."

"Unfortunately not. She is a gentleman's daughter—a child of fifteen, permitted to go to Brighton with the regiment as a guest of the colonel's wife."

"Preposterous," Darcy hissed. "Her father must be the veriest fool."

"No more so than we," Richard mused quietly.

Darcy shot him a glare. "The two situations are nothing alike!"

"Of course not." Richard shifted in his chair. "I... I have not yet told you why I came back to London when I did. Why I came immediately to your townhouse looking for you, and how I found you after I discovered you had already gone."

Darcy stared at the ceiling. "Prescience. Good luck. Whatever it was, I care not."

"Darcy, you must listen... here." He grabbed another pillow and lifted Darcy's cheek to cram the pillow behind him, letting him rest his neck with his head pointed at the chair beside the bed.

Darcy growled in pain and glared at his cousin. "What? Make it quick and leave me be."

Richard sat back and looked at his hands, clearly choosing his next words with care. "Darcy... there are tidings you must know."

"Wickham is in gaol. You told me. Why did you not shoot the bloody bastard?"

"It is not that. I could not tell you until you were more lucid, but there is something else."

As Darcy glowered at the wall, Richard tried again, more firmly.

"Darcy. Darcy, look at me, damn it all!"

Grudgingly Darcy complied, arrested by his cousin's grave expression. Richard took a bracing breath, then gripped Darcy's hand with sudden force.

"Georgiana is with child."

Disbelieving horror dawned slowly, but when understanding crashed over him, he wrenched savagely at the bedclothes until they tore free from the mattress seams.

"No! God, not her, too... he has taken everything from me!"

"Enough!" Richard's sharp command cut Darcy's anguished tirade short. "Spare your self-pity and attend to your sister's welfare first. There will be time enough later to curse Wickham's name."

But Darcy only turned his devastated face to the wall once more.

"What possible good can a useless wretch like me do her?" he whispered harshly. "Georgiana's ruin falls squarely on my head... I failed her, as I did you, Richard."

"There is no point in thrashing ourselves over what is past. There is only one thing to be done now."

Darcy shook his head. "No. I will not see her forced to marry some man we have paid to take her. She is but sixteen!"

Richard raked a hand through his hair. "That is not what I was going to suggest. Indeed, there must be a marriage, but not her."

Cold horror crept over Darcy as comprehension sank its claws in. Richard was fixing him with a steady gaze, just waiting for Darcy to blurt out the words.

"You cannot mean you think *I* should claim her child as my own? To hide Wickham's bastard?" Revulsion twisted his features. "I would rather see Pemberley burn!"

Richard held up placating hands as Darcy spat curses, his battered body trembling violently.

"Peace, Darcy! Surely, claiming her child is the only way to salvage your sister's future!"

Darcy bared his teeth, incensed past reason. "You expect Georgiana to endure Wickham's child under her own roof? No!" He slashed the air weakly. "I will send the babe off to some tenant family, far from her sight!" His chest heaved from exertion and swirling emotion.

"Think, man, think!" He searched Darcy's face intently. "What of Pemberley's legacy?"

At this, Darcy attempted to lever himself higher, his lip curled scornfully, though the effort clearly pained him. "Do not mock me. After everything else! It is too much. Georgiana faces ruin enough without the insult of me claiming that bastard child!"

"Darcy, you must listen, for just—"

"No. I refuse." He turned his face into the pillow, blinking hard against throbbing agony and rising emotion.

Richard passed a weary hand over his eyes, marshalling his arguments. When Darcy finally opened one eye toward him, Richard gently grasped his hand.

"Cousin, forgive my indelicacy... but in your current state, you may be unable..." He gestured vaguely to the inert legs beneath the blankets, unable to give voice to the harsh truth.

Horrified disbelief flashed across Darcy's face. With a strangled sound, he tried wrenching away. "Damn you, I've no wish to hear—"

"Darcy!" Richard captured his forearm, stilling his agitated motions. Quietly but relentlessly, he continued. "You may not father an heir of your own now, and Pemberley is entailed. Georgiana's child, born under the Darcy name, could secure Pemberley's legacy." He held his cousin's tortured gaze. "And consider—it would spare your sister from facing the consequences alone. Please... reflect on it."

Bitter laughter erupted from Darcy, grating on his raw throat. "Kindly answer me two questions then, oh wise Solon. First, what woman alive would consent to pledge herself to a crippled wreck?" He flung a shaky hand out. "Second, who could believe I sired an heir in this worthless body?"

Richard studied his own clasped hands. "The second is simpler. We shall keep knowledge of your... infirmity contained for now. At least until matters are secure. We move you to the country—perhaps to Mother's lands in Scotland as soon as you are well enough."

"Poppycock. You cannot keep such a thing quiet. Do you think that endless parade of doctors you marched through here is not bandying gossip all over London even now?"

"The physicians will greedily guard that secret for the right purse, and I have offered it. Well... *you* have, I suppose. With my family's influence, a special licence could be quietly procured. Father is friends with the bishop. No questions from that quarter."

At Darcy's continued caustic laughter, Richard raised his voice. "It would secure Pemberley for Georgiana's son—legitimate him!"

"If it is even a boy! And who is the child's mother supposed to be? Hmm? Which of the empty-headed single females of your acquaintance would you have me yoke myself to... no, better yet. Which one would *have* me now? Vultures, every last one of them. I would not trust them with my home before, and now, when I have so little ability to contain such a woman, you would let her run my house? Insupportable."

Richard sighed heavily, as if the weight of the world lay upon his shoulders. "It is the only way, Darcy. Are you even listening if I try to explain?"

At Darcy's sullen glare, Richard braced his hands on his knees and took a deep breath. "There is... one young lady I could suggest as a prospective wife. She would understand the necessities." He hesitated delicately. "And I believe she would accept you, to save her family's honour."

"Really," Darcy retorted drily. "So, she is ruined herself. What a jewel you have procured."

"Not she... not the lady herself, but her family. Her father's estate is entailed, and she has four sisters, one of whom has brought a stain upon the others."

"And this is the woman you would make the mistress of Pemberley! I suppose she even has relatives in trade."

"As a matter of fact, she does. I met her uncle already—a merchant in Cheapside."

"Leave me, Richard. I'll hear no more of this. Bad enough you want me to raise Wickham's bastard as my own, right in front of poor Georgiana. Now you want me to take a woman no other man would have in order to do it!"

"The last thing you need is a woman of fashion and fortune. You need—*Georgiana* needs someone you can trust. Someone who can manage."

"And you think this stranger is she?"

"I do."

Darcy strained his chest muscles and twisted his arm to yank the additional pillow out from under his head. It was a tedious task, made all the more so because he could not fully lift himself off the offending thing to pull it away. He had to tug it free by measures until he had worked it loose enough to throw it across the room. Then he lay back, staring at the ceiling.

He heard Richard growl, and his cousin got up. Finally, he was going! Darcy closed his eyes and gripped the torn sheets, waiting for the door to click. So he could pretend for a moment he had not heard...

"She is a kind woman, Darcy."

His eyes popped open again. Damn them. "What?"

He heard Richard's steps turn back to the bed. "And an intelligent one. Compassionate, but tempered with a strong sense of justice. Clever enough to think two steps ahead of her circumstances, practical enough to do what must be done, even when others fail. And she was gentle enough to stop and speak with a mere maid—a stranger in her home—and offer her comfort."

"What care I for any of that?"

"But best of all..." Richard wandered over until he was leaning over him, staring directly into Darcy's face. "She can find a way to laugh when she really wants to weep."

Darcy stared back, swallowing hard. "And why is this a virtue?"

"Because, Cousin... that may be the quality you need more than any other in a wife."

"I do not need a wife at all. Least of all, one who is desperate."

"I am afraid, Darcy, that you no longer have the luxury of choice. And as Georgiana is now more than six weeks gone, you have no time, either." Darcy heard Richard sigh. "I will speak to Father on the matter this very evening."

Chapter Five

T HE SIMPLE ERRAND OF visiting Meryton's shops had turned into a humiliating trial of running the gauntlet for Elizabeth and Jane. No sooner had they stepped onto the village's main thoroughfare than a gang of boys came barrelling out of garden gates and alleys to surround them.

"If it ain't the trollops of Longbourn come visiting!" shouted one towheaded lad. Before Elizabeth could react, a rotting apple core burst wetly against her shoulder. Raucous laughter followed more small missiles sailing through the air toward the cringing sisters.

Then, from the corner of her eye, Elizabeth spotted Mrs Purvis—formerly one of her mother's bosom friends until Lydia's disgrace—looking on with pursed lips. Did she mean merely to stand there? Outrage propelling her forward a step, Elizabeth rebuked sharply, "Mrs Purvis, kindly have your son stop this loutish harassment at once!"

But the matron only laughed with her companion before turning away in a flounce of skirts.

As more refuse pelted their cloak hems, Jane tugged imploringly on Elizabeth's clenched fist. "Please, Lizzy, let us get home quickly. You will only make it worse by confronting them."

"They *need* to be confronted!" Elizabeth shook off her pleading grip, weariness and resentment boiling into fury within her breast. "Do you think this behaviour will stop merely because we turned the other cheek? Nay, it will grow worse until it is unbearable."

Wheeling on young Toby Purvis, she scolded hotly, "Have you nought better to do, sir, than waylay two ladies going quietly about their business? Where is the decent upbringing your mother so proudly nattered on about over tea not three months past?"

Toby and his cohorts only hooted rudely. "Ain't no ladies here! Just the trollops what run off with rakes n' get what comes to 'em!" With that, he sprinted away before Elizabeth's hand could connect with his filthy ear for such insolence.

Quiet tears slipping down her cheeks, Jane tugged Elizabeth's arm. "Come away, Lizzy... he's not wrong."

Before Elizabeth could form another indignant retort, a stern, cultured voice carried over the rancorous laughter. "That is quite enough, young sirs!" At the command, every boy scattered.

Elizabeth's furious tears halted in shock as she beheld Colonel Fitzwilliam glowering through his town coach's window at the fleeing boys. Relief nearly buckled her knees when he stepped lightly down and hurried across the manure-spattered street.

"Miss Elizabeth, Miss Bennet—forgive the crude manners of that ill-bred youth." His concerned eyes sought the smears marring Elizabeth's spencer and Jane's downturned face. "Are you quite well?"

Dabbing her furious tears hastily away, Elizabeth managed with as much dignity as she could muster, "Perfectly well, sir, but I thank you. Your interference was most timely."

The colonel hesitated, seeming to wrestle with some inner decision. Then he offered politely, "Well, I am just on my way to call at Longbourn. May I offer you ladies transport there?"

Exchanging a wordless glance, the bedraggled sisters nodded gratefully. As the town coach started smoothly off, Elizabeth studied her grimy, ruined hem before inquiring, "Kind sir, to what do we owe the pleasure of this visit?"

The colonel removed his hat and ran a distracted hand through his hair. "I wished to ask after your sister Miss Lydia's... progress settling in, and to call upon your father." His grave eyes darted from Jane to Elizabeth. "And in truth, I had rather critical matters I hoped to discuss with you ladies, as well."

LYDIA RAN UPSTAIRS TO primp her hair when Elizabeth and Jane returned in Colonel Fitzwilliam's carriage with him. "There now, did I not tell you he would come to call? La! The officers always return for me."

Before she could rush out of her room again to greet him, Elizabeth stood to block the door. "No, Lydia, you shall wait up here." At Mrs Bennet's offended gasp, she continued firmly, "Until we understand the colonel's purpose, prudence dictates you keep out of sight. Or have you forgot how direly your actions have endangered this entire family?"

"But Lizzy!" Lydia gripped her shoulders beseechingly. "Surely, any gentleman caller now should be encouraged! You cannot lock me away forever when our only hope is advantageous matches before Papa d—"

"Stop it, Lydia!" Elizabeth hissed. "Your childish fixation on your marital prospects so soon after an escapade that proved utterly ruinous shows that you are too stubborn to have any contrition or sense! For all our sakes, I must insist you remain here with Mama until the colonel leaves."

"Lizzy, how can you speak this way?" Mrs Bennet burst into tears as she shepherded the spluttering Lydia from the room. "She is perfectly right, you know. The colonel may well have come to ask after her hand! She is so very lively and pretty. Oh! My poor nerves... To be so cruelly tried by my own daughters!"

Though Lydia's self-absorbed carelessness roused Elizabeth's resentment anew, guilt gnawed as their mother's sobs faded down the hall. Had she been overly harsh? Jane slipped a bracing arm around her tense shoulders, murmuring, "You were right to curb her. Appearances must be salvaged if we are ever to show our faces in society again."

"I know." Elizabeth sighed, deflating. "Yet I feel wretched to cause Mama pain."

"Your kind intentions excuse the manner," Jane soothed, squeezing Elizabeth's knotted hands gently where they still twisted her handkerchief. "Here, take some tea to soothe—"

Jane's soft reassurances broke off as Mr Bennet emerged solemnly from his refuge. "Lizzy, Jane... Come to my study, please."

Stomach in fluttering knots, Elizabeth wordlessly followed Jane after their father's sullen look. Had they guessed false? Had the colonel come to deliver more shame upon the Bennets?

The heavy door thudded closed with an air of grim finality. Their father sank as one resigned into his desk chair without preamble, appearing another decade older.

"Best get it over quickly, Colonel. Pray, impart your purpose to my daughters." Defeated eyes still avoided meeting the girls' startled queries.

Discomfited, Colonel Fitzwilliam cleared his throat several times before beginning awkwardly. "As you ladies have no doubt surmised, I came today to discuss something of utmost import..."

He trailed off under Elizabeth and Jane's apprehensively arched brows. Fidgeting with his coat buttons he finally resumed, almost wincing, "An offer of marriage... for one of you."

Elizabeth blinked in bafflement between the colonel's mottled complexion and her own sister's similar stunned disbelief. "I... beg your pardon, Colonel. Did you say... marriage? You hardly know either of us. Surely, you needn't apply to a stranger, and..." She cleared her throat. "Apart from a rather... embarrassing stigma attached to our family, we have very little to bring to a marriage."

The colonel plucked his empty teacup from the saucer and tipped it distractedly to his lips before frowning in disappointment and setting it back. "I appreciate your candour, Miss Elizabeth, but, well... perhaps I ought to further explain. The offer comes not directly from myself, but my cousin, Mr Darcy."

Jane stirred, roused from shock. "Mr Darcy, sir? We are eternally grateful for his chivalry regarding Lydia but... you cannot mean for one of us to marry someone we have never met!"

The colonel's pained grimace deepened. "I'm afraid that is precisely the case needed. It is a matter of some urgency."

"I... there seems to be some misunderstanding, Colonel." Elizabeth's brow furrowed in bewilderment. "I am sorry for the gentleman's... urgency... but what could this possibly have to do with us?"

The colonel drew a pained breath before carefully relating a most delicate situation—how Mr Darcy's beloved sister Georgiana had nearly fled to Scotland with fortune-hunting Wickham before her brother intervened... but not soon enough to spare the tender innocent from a vicious assault at Wickham's hands.

Jane uttered a dismayed, "Oh!" as sympathetic tears trembled in Elizabeth's eyes once more.

"Poor Miss Darcy!" Elizabeth breathed. "My heart aches for her! Was she very young, then?"

"About the same age as your sister, Miss Lydia. Or scarcely older." He fingered that empty cup again, his gaze flicking between the two. "And now there will be lasting consequences."

"*Oh*," Jane sighed.

Elizabeth closed her eyes and groaned. All her relief at Lydia's safe recovery, the evidence that, whatever else had happened, at least there was no pregnancy to carry... What if matters had gone differently? "I am so... so sorry," she whispered.

"Wickham's vile work, not yours," the colonel dismissed heavily, his features taking on a haunted look. "But it does leave Miss Darcy in an impossible predicament now that there is a child. Though we have concealed it so far, soon her... delicate condition shall be impossible to hide."

Understanding crashed over Elizabeth like a frigid wave. With rising panic constricting her throat, she rasped, "You... you cannot then mean that Mr Darcy, to salvage his sister's reputation..."

"Must claim her child as his own heir, yes. And to do so convincingly requires him to take a wife rather urgently."

"But why come to us? I have seen Mr Darcy's carriage. Heard of his heroism, his stature, his house and his wealth. Surely, such a man could crook his finger and summon a dozen heiresses willing to take his name. Why would you come to us, of all people? Is Mr Darcy..." she swallowed. "Is he such a terrible person that no other would have him?"

An oppressive silence hung after Elizabeth's blunt questions, stifling in a room grown suddenly too warm. The colonel ran a finger under his collar before glancing to Mr Bennet, perhaps for guidance or a reprieve. But her father only brooded over his untouched whisky, staunchly avoiding his daughters' disbelieving stares.

"My cousin is... not a man of misfortune, typically." The colonel floundered at last under Elizabeth's hawkish, entreating gaze. "Nor does he lack for... prospects. He is conscientious almost to a fault, and highly respected. But his standards for a partner have always exceeded mere... monetary or social qualifications..."

His speech faltered again to anxious hemming. Elizabeth felt Jane's grip unconsciously tighten on her arm.

"Forgive me, Colonel, but you have only illustrated more reasons why it would be fantastical for the gentleman to apply to either of us."

Finally, with a rush, the colonel continued hoarsely, as though ripping off a bandage in one tear. "The situation has changed drastically. He is now paralyzed below the waist, confined to his rooms."

Elizabeth rocked back, struck utterly breathless by such shocking cruelty. Then her logic reasserted itself, and heat rose to her cheeks. "But... Lydia said he burst angrily into their room to tear her away from that rogue. He cannot be so very paralyzed as you claim!"

The colonel appeared almost relieved at this resistance, any argument better than hollow silence. "Your sister had already fled from the chamber to the kitchens when the struggle commenced. She did not see Darcy topple down the stairs during their violent altercation afterwards. How he has suffered since..."

He passed a shaking hand down his face, lines of torment carved into his weathered visage to mirror Elizabeth's inner turmoil. She turned beseeching eyes on Jane, wordlessly imploring her rational sister for some plausible answer, some wise morsel of encouragement. But for once, even Jane's lips found no hopeful words.

The colonel squared his shoulders as though bracing for battle. "When I brought your sister home, I was most struck by Miss Bennet and... and by you, Miss Elizabeth." He nodded respectfully towards each of them in turn. "I saw gentle hearts and good sense; the qualities Darcy needs now in his confined state."

Swallowing hard, he added, "My cousin no longer requires fawning debutantes vying for Pemberley. He needs strength, patience... love, truly." The colonel shifted in discomfort. "I will be frank—my initial plan was to offer specifically for your hand, Miss Elizabeth."

Mr Bennet roused from his bleak study to pierce the colonel with a protective glare before growling, "Colonel, I insisted you not exert undue pressure on Elizabeth alone. You must present the offer to both eldest girls if you had the audacity to tender it at all."

The colonel looked abashed even as Elizabeth felt Jane's convulsive gasp through their linked hands. Seeking to gentle her reaction, Elizabeth asked, "But even with such extenuating circumstances, surely men of Mr Darcy's standing have... options, Colonel, which preclude stooping to disgraced strangers."

Sombre understanding weighted the colonel's words. "The choice remains yours, of course. But there are few families now that I trust enough to ally with the Darcy name. You understand and respect, as few would, that in order for the plan to succeed, there must be absolute secrecy regarding Miss Darcy's... condition. As well as Darcy's. Naturally, his injury cannot be hidden forever, but it must remain quiet just long enough for... Well, I can see that you understand."

Elizabeth caught her father's eye as panic began to rise in her breast. Marry a perfect stranger! A man confined to his bed, who could never be a proper husband... who needed a nursemaid more than a wife. And who would require her to live a lie, raising someone else's child as her own...

"I know you owe them nought," the colonel broke into her thoughts. "But my cousin is one of the best men alive. And it is not merely the matter of saving Miss Darcy's reputation. Darcy, too..." He drew a breath. "His estate is entailed. If he fails to produce an heir, the consequences... Well, they do not bear thinking of, Miss Elizabeth. I am not the man to beg, but I am begging you to consider. Please. You have a chance to save the family of the man who saved yours." He leaned forward and stared gravely. "And to secure everyone's future."

Before Elizabeth could rally her scattered thoughts, Jane cried in quiet desperation, "Lizzy, no!"

She turned, and Jane was shaking her head, white to the lips. "I see the look on your face, Lizzy. You've got that stubborn look about you again. Please, you cannot seriously accept. We do not know this gentleman, paralysed or not!"

But Elizabeth read the colonel's sincerity... and her father's silent pleading. He knew as well as she did that this offer was something they could not afford to reject out of hand, but at what cost? It might be dearer than any of them were willing to pay. Squaring her shoulders, she turned to address the uneasy officer.

"If possible, Colonel, I should wish to meet Mr Darcy before giving any answer. I must know something of the man himself first."

A flood of tension eased from the colonel's face. "That is precisely what I was hoping you would say, Miss Elizabeth. I would have been less optimistic if you had given me a direct answer without asking leave to consider more carefully. Mr Bennet? What say you, sir?"

Elizabeth held her father's gaze—hers begging some sort of encouragement, one way or the other... and his simply filled with dread. Finally, he heaved a sigh. "We will leave for Town in the morning, Colonel."

Chapter Six

SUNLIGHT CREEPING INTO DARCY'S bedchamber illuminated floating dust motes... and little else to occupy his gaze. Doctors' orders still kept him flat on his back, the hated bell rope dangling uselessly as his only means of summoning assistance.

He was thirsty. And hungry, but a burning in his throat and stomach overpowered both sensations. Never had he been so attuned to his body's every function, yet never had its workings been so completely beyond his domain. Darcy swallowed back rising bile at his helplessness under even basic needs.

The door creaked open, and Giles entered with that forced cheer Darcy had grown to despise. Darcy bore with Giles' ministrations, his mind disconnected from the ignominy of it all. Once Giles had done, he moved to the door and took a hot kettle from some maid outside, then went to the basin to pour it. He turned around then, a towel over his left arm and a razor in his right hand. "Let us make you more comfortable, sir, starting with a shave, shall we?"

As Giles calmly prepared hot water and a blade, incredulous fury tightened Darcy's unshaven jaw. "Have you lost all faculty of reason? Unable to even sit upright, do you expect me to tilt my head back at your command?"

Giles hesitated. "Perhaps if we employ a pillow, to keep you comfortable, while I—"

"I am sick to death of being 'comfortable.' Leave me untidy. At least I can feel my face itching."

"Sir, if you will permit me, I believe that I can..." But he fell silent under his master's molten glower before reluctantly bowing out.

Some minutes later, the bedchamber door clicked open again, ushering in Richard bearing comb and scissors. Taking in Darcy's wild glare and scruffy beard with dismay, he shook his head.

"Darcy, really, your stubbornness tries the servants. Letting yourself go will hardly make you feel better. Come, let us make you a little more respectable."

Before Darcy could snarl an objection, Richard had fetched the basin of hot water and a straight razor. But when he lifted the sharpened blade to his cousin's overgrown cheek, Darcy twisted furiously away.

"I'll suffer no more fussing or primping! Let me be." He slashed the air with one limp hand.

Clucking under his breath, Richard set aside the razor to take up comb and scissors instead. With gentle but insistent fingers, he tamed Darcy's lank, unwashed curls. Darcy endured these further ministrations in brooding silence until suspicion kindled anew. Turning his head with effort, he fixed Richard with a piercing stare.

"Confound it, man, out with it! Why this sudden obsession over my looks?" He winced as Richard's comb caught a painful snarl. "It's not as though I prepare to receive visitors reclining on my deathbed."

Ignoring his cousin's baleful glare, Richard gently worked fragrant oil into Darcy's tangled curls and began combing and snipping. But at this presumptuous overfamiliarity, Darcy snarled and jerked his head sharply away.

Undeterred, his cousin brushed stray hairs off his neck before dabbing more rosewater onto the comb with a placating smile. "Come now, Cousin, permit me to tame this mane just a little. Surely it brings some relief to be tidy again?"

His good-natured cajoling slowly penetrated Darcy's irascible temper. Grudgingly, he remained still under the comb's soothing rhythm. As two long weeks of being bedridden weighed heavier on his mind, even simple grooming kindled a reminder of the vigorous man he'd been... the man now lost forever.

"Why bother primping me?" he bit out hoarsely. "As if I've callers awaiting my company."

The colonel paused, meeting Darcy's wary eye. Discomfited colour rose as he turned aside under that piercing stare. "Well... in truth, your situation has aroused some gentle sympathy."

Hopeful outrage sharpened Darcy's breath. "Sympathy? Dare you mean some opportunistic debutante aiming to shackle a helpless cripple—"

"No!" Richard interrupted sharply. Softening again, he continued, "But I have found a compassionate young lady who... may yet provide you a chance to offer marriage."

He slammed his eyes furiously shut, but Richard pressed insistently, "They have come all the way from Hertfordshire! At least allow her the courtesy of an introduction."

"And why should I endure inspection from strangers?" Darcy demanded querulously. "I gather no mould nor sprout fungus! Leave off fussing over my looks."

"Come now, Cousin, indulge me in this? She may prove your saving grace. "

Memory sparked then, quickening Darcy's contemptuous tone. "This is the mysterious Miss Bennet, is it not? Of the supposedly 'disgraced' family you mentioned." His eyes narrowed. "The ones from... Hertfordshire, was it not?"

Richard looked doubly uncomfortable even as dawning horror and outrage overtook Darcy's expression.

"*Hertfordshire?* You traitor! Have you tried ensnaring me with that trollop's own sister?"

"Now, Darcy—"

"You would saddle me with the sister of Wickham's leavings? Out, out at once with the chit!" Darcy roared. "Disgraced family, indeed. I'll warrant no respectable man within fifty miles will even speak to them!"

"It is because of their misery that Miss Elizabeth would consider accepting you!" Richard shot back. Then in more placating tones, "At least allow the lady basic courtesy, since she astonishingly still gives you consideration. And if you ask me, the greater miracle will not be *you* accepting *her*, but the reverse. You might endeavour to impress her with those noble manners you keep tucked under your pillow."

When Darcy only scowled blackly at the far wall, Richard tried gently wheedling once more. "I beg you, Cousin, for your sister's sake and your own pride, be civil."

A curt nod was the most response he could wrest from Darcy's mulish temper. With a resigned sigh, Richard straightened his shoulders and quit the room to fetch the mysterious Miss Elizabeth Bennet.

E

LIZABETH KNOTTED HER FINGERS until they ached as her eyes fixed on the clock.

Its relentless ticking filled her ears like the countdown to an executioner's axe striking its blow.

She couldn't stop staring at the lavish furnishings surrounding them: a grand piano of deepest mahogany that must have cost a year of even Longbourn's revenue... silver heirloom candlesticks taller than a toddler and polished to a reflective gleam... a landscape of Pemberley's famed natural lake and garden—the ones Colonel Fitzwilliam had told her about—worth at least a month's work for any accomplished portraitist. She felt almost an interloper surveying this luxurious world so far removed from her own experience.

As the silence stretched, Mr Bennet finally whispered tersely, "I insist, Lizzy, you mustn't feel beholden to this man out of misplaced guilt for his injury. It was none of our doing, now, was it?"

"But how can Lizzy ignore the stark reality of our circumstances?" Jane whispered back. "Were it not for Mr Darcy's selfless recovery of Lydia, we would likely still not know where she was! She might be abandoned by now, or... or worse."

"All I am saying is that Lydia did not ask to be saved... much to my chagrin... and you cannot pay for your sister's folly with your own future."

"What future?" Elizabeth asked in a hushed voice. "I begin to think Mama is being a little too optimistic when she says the hedgerows will shelter us."

Her father covered his eyes and ground his teeth. "And you think this wealthy, handsome man will prove your salvation, do you?"

Elizabeth slid her gaze to her father. "I do not know what I think."

"I tell you, Lizzy." He leaned forward, a bit of urgency sparking in his expression for the first time in many weeks. "Strong, healthy men do not take well to being struck down in such a way. He may well be a changed man from what you were led to expect by his cousin's glowing description. He may even hold you responsible for his indisposition, connected to Lydia as you are."

Elizabeth's mouth opened slightly. "Oh, surely not. He is a reasonable man. You heard what the housekeeper said when she brought our tea. She has never had a cross word from him in over twenty years. He is kind and fair and... and perhaps I can be of some help to him."

Her father studied her gravely for some seconds. Then he turned back to the window, staring out at the London street. "You are very cheerful, my child. I pray you never have cause to part with your optimism."

Elizabeth closed her eyes and prayed the same thing. She felt the lavish chamber slowly closing around her, the formidable weight of centuries pressing down with almost palpable force. Never had the humble comforts of Longbourn felt quite so threadbare and inadequate as under this room's haughty grandeur.

What claim did she truly have to even contemplate aligning their soiled name to all this ancient legacy? An unbroken line from William the Conqueror, Colonel Fitzwilliam had said—as matter-of-factly as if he were ordering butter for his bread. Nobility and power were second-nature here. No hint of individual quirks or fading imperfections softened those imposing family portraits glaring judgement down their long patrician noses.

Jane was looking paler by the minute. Rallying herself inwardly, Elizabeth smoothed her skirt's sweat-dampened fabric. She was Elizabeth Bennet still, whatever came. With effort, she manufactured brittle laughter.

"Truly, I only hope any potential alliance spares our loved ones further hardship... of course, nothing is yet fixed. If it is only his legs that are wounded and not his eyes, the gentleman may yet prefer Jane to me as his bride."

But even as she said it, Elizabeth knew that for a hollow bit of cheer. Jane truly was the one who looked as though she fit in with the opulent surroundings, with her classical looks and serene manners... until one looked at her waxen complexion and dilated eyes. No, Elizabeth could not possibly let Jane take this burden on. It must be Elizabeth, or neither of them. And the heavy stare her father levelled at her in response to her jest told her that he knew this as well as she did.

The renewed silence sat heavier moment to moment, until Colonel Fitzwilliam finally re-entered, some forty minutes later, with profuse apologies. The strain had etched new lines around his forced smile.

"Mr Darcy will receive you now."

Elizabeth rose on trembling limbs that nonetheless carried her forward steadily. Trepidation roiling her stomach, Elizabeth smoothed her skirts with clammy palms. Steeling herself, she rose bravely to discover just what manner of man awaited—paralysed protector or indifferent tyrant?

Darcy lay stiffly unmoving as the door opened to admit Colonel Fitzwilliam and the mysterious Miss Bennet at last. He kept his sharp gaze upon the far corner of the ceiling even as he sensed awkward figures shuffling uncertainly closer in his periphery. He could not bear meeting the mingled revulsion or saccharine pity he would see writ clearly in their expressions. Another humiliating inspection of this bedridden wreck of the former Fitzwilliam Darcy, Esquire.

"My cousin, Mr Fitzwilliam Darcy." Richard waved toward the hesitant party. "This is Mr Bennet and his eldest daughters, Miss Jane Bennet and Miss Elizabeth Bennet."

"Daughters... plural?" Darcy jerked his head with an effort to better see the hovering group, instantly wishing he'd left well enough alone. The fairer of the two women wore such a look of sickly horror that he feared she would faint outright onto him at any moment.

The other—Elizabeth, was it?—eyed him keenly, despite the colour riding high in her own cheeks. Her bold gaze piercing him like a hawk its prey stirred prickly heat under Darcy's collar. With effort, he strove to salvage nonchalance as he twisted his lip into a sneer. "Richard? You make it sound as though I intend to establish a veritable harem—did you have trouble choosing only two?"

Pale Miss Bennet flinched. Miss Elizabeth stiffened, eyes sparking dangerously even as her tight jaw prevented an immediate retort.

"The Bennets have agreed to *meet* you, Darcy," Richard growled, his voice cracking menacingly. "*Both* ladies are lovely and accomplished."

Darcy rolled his eyes and tucked his chin into his chest to view them a little better. So, this was his cousin's idea of angels of mercy—two common girls clearly out of their depths and an equally uncomfortable, stooped patriarch apparently all too willing to sell their flesh for security. Some angels! Apparently, he merited little better. Well, might as well have a look at them.

The pale one, he dismissed out of hand. The knee-watering pity he could see twisting her face and filling her eyes was enough to make him ill. Instead, he turned his full attention to the dark-haired Elizabeth Bennet, forcing an impassive expression. It was bitterly satisfying to stare at her, unflinching, even as she searched his face for some sign of hope. He gave her none.

Her return scrutiny at least revealed a keen mind behind those too-generous lips and finely arched brows. Minute flickers of thought and feeling danced in her eyes, and she tilted her head slightly when he locked his gaze on hers.

No pity in those eyes. No, more like... daring. And her features were rather interesting, the longer he studied them. Darcy wagered he would have found this woman almost handsome, even if she was not classically beautiful, in another life. But what need had he any longer for a handsome woman?

Richard cleared his throat, probably already reading the direction of Darcy's thoughts. "You may speak frankly to Miss Elizabeth. She is—"

"She is tolerable, I suppose, but not handsome enough to tempt me—"

Indignant fire blazed in Elizabeth Bennet's eyes, and when she looked like that, she was... well, she was *very* tempting. But what was the use? Darcy blinked back up to the ceiling. "—were I in any condition to act, let alone walk her down the proverbial aisle. Do we understand each other, Miss Bennet?"

Before she could storm a retort, her withered sire did an astonishing thing and found his long-atrophied backbone at last, though his reedy voice trembled with each word. "See here, sir, you have no cause to offend my girls when we have only come at the summons of your family."

Lowering his contemptuous stare from the plaster overhead, Darcy cut in, "And I see you finally take an interest in your daughters' reputations—now that you believe a fortune within your grasp. What a serendipitous epiphany!"

Richard was covering his face and shaking his head, and poor, quaking Miss Bennet's cheeks were already flooded with tears. But Miss Elizabeth whirled on him, her face flushed with blistering ire and her voice ringing with passion. "No fortune can compensate for such arrogance, sir! Were you the last man in all England, I would never consent. Not only are you clearly fractious and bitter, but spectacularly ungentlemanly!"

Turning on her heel, deaf to Richard's calls begging her to stay, Miss Elizabeth quit the room—chin set at a mutinous angle and cheeks flaming brighter than the red drapes over the windows. At least the others had the sense to follow her out.

As soon as the heavy door thudded shut, Richard rounded furiously on him. "Confound it, Darcy, I have never witnessed such deplorably boorish behaviour! What demon possessed you to malign those ladies so, particularly Miss Elizabeth?"

Darcy only scowled. "You cannot seriously insist those awkward creatures were 'ladies of quality' as you claimed! The one quailed like a lamb before slaughter, and the other wore her pretensions far too openly."

With an inarticulate growl, Richard began aggressively tidying the already fastidious room, sending small decorative items flying helter-skelter. "I credited you with more discernment! Did you not perceive Miss Elizabeth's ready wit and composure despite your insults? She was prepared to look beyond the invalid to the man's true nature. Few women of our world possess such generous intellect..."

He trailed off, the fight leaving his frame. "But why am I stunned when you resent the Bennets for unintentionally burdening you so? There never was a lady born good enough for you."

"My objections are not solely selfish, believe it or not." Darcy clenched his fists against the sheets. "You cannot throw a young woman of little exposure into these unfamiliar shark-infested waters and call it a kindness! She will be eaten alive, no matter my protection. Did you see how that pale one crumbled with her first look at me?"

"It is not Jane Bennet I chose for you. I hand-picked Elizabeth Bennet when she... are you even listening?"

Darcy ground his teeth and dragged in a sigh. "So why bring the other one at all?"

"Because both are eligible. Both are sweet and caring and you ought to count yourself lucky if either of them would have you. And..." he leaned back, almost in defeat, "...because Mr Bennet forbade me to single out Miss Elizabeth and let her feel the sole responsibility for saving her family... and yours." Richard's lips twitched. "He would not say it, of course, but it seems clear that she is his favourite daughter. And you have done precious little to persuade the man to trust you with that which he holds dearest."

Darcy studied his cousin, a sinking conviction weighing his chest. He *had* been a brute and a churl. But better to warn the lady off now than to wheedle her with sweet words and promises he could not keep. He swallowed and let his head sink into the pillow. "No woman could endure this. Not if her motives be pure. She can only be a mercenary, or worse, a fool—thinking she is better than others, that she can bear up where the rest would falter."

Richard rounded on him again, though his tone turned beseeching. "Darcy, Elizabeth Bennet, at least, is no trembling debutante to wilt under a few sidelong glances. I feel it in my bones—she sees you as a man of honour dragged low by happenstance, not merely an invalid, and not merely as an opportunity. How many women are there of whom that could be said?"

When Darcy only scowled stubbornly up at the bed hangings, Richard grunted and moved to the door. "I shall go make what apology I can and try to convince the lady you are merely overwhelmed and unwilling to bind her unfairly. But so help me, Darcy, if Miss Elizabeth Bennet walks out that door today, I doubt any other will deign to walk back in."

Chapter Seven

"MY BONNET AND PELISSE, please!" Elizabeth rushed to the waiting footman, cheeks still burning. Never had she endured such rabid indignities from man or beast. "We can go to Uncle Gardiner's in Cheapside until we have recovered our wits."

She turned around to find her father and Jane trailing after her, looking shocked and wan. "Papa! Surely, you are not dragging your feet?" she whispered. "I cannot abide another minute in this house." Shame and fury clashed to overthrow her tenuous composure with each memory of that vile man's abusive remarks.

"No, no," he rasped. "But have a care, my dear. My old bones can hardly keep up with you."

Elizabeth wrapped her arm through her father's and fairly marched him toward the door. "Please have our carriage brought directly," she implored the butler, who stood rigidly by the door.

He opened his mouth as if he meant to say something, but then reshaped his words to utter something completely different. "Of—of course, Miss Bennet." He snapped his fingers to a young footman, who bolted for a side door while the butler uncomfortably shuffled his feet. "I shall speed preparations, but I am afraid it may yet be some ten minutes before your carriage can be brought round from the mews. If you will allow me..." He rang the bell pull for the housekeeper. "Pray, Miss Bennet, at least permit us to make you comfortable while you wait."

"No, thank you, that is quite..." she began, but Jane cleared her throat.

Elizabeth's vision swam scarlet at the thought of enduring ten more seconds under the same roof with that hateful scoundrel. But Jane was right... they could not very well march out the door and wait on the street for their carriage. "Actually, yes, thank you." She forced a smile for the butler and allowed him to escort them to the drawing room and close the door. Her shoulders sagged, and she gushed out a sigh at the ceiling.

"Perhaps Mr Darcy is only feeling put upon," Jane suggested. "Surely, it has all been very difficult for him, and doubtless, he is in much pain."

"And what excuse is that? Many people are in difficult straits, but they do not abuse others."

"But Lizzy—"

"I am sorry, Jane, but I cannot possibly countenance—" Before she could release the scathing diatribe on the tip of her tongue, Mrs Hodges, the housekeeper, knocked at the door. The woman must have been waiting in the hall to appear so quickly! At Elizabeth's invitation, she entered with an apologetic face. Her eyes tripped over Mr Bennet and Jane, then landed squarely on Elizabeth as she made a curtsy.

"I am sorry to hear you are going so soon. Perhaps a small nuncheon while you wait? Some brandy, Mr Bennet? A blanket against any chill, dear?" Addressing the footman again, she ordered, "Stoke the fire here at once!"

Exchanging defeated looks, the Bennets reluctantly submitted to her attentions, though Elizabeth felt her threadbare composure unravelling by the second. But when the housekeeper herself brought in a tray, one that came so quickly it must have been ready-assembled and waiting for them, she drew the line.

"Thank you, Mrs Hodges, but I require nothing. You are too kind, but my aunt and uncle will surely receive us as soon as we can be away."

"Oh, Miss! Surely you will not leave so soon, without even a morsel to sustain you on the road back?" The housekeeper's hands twisted over her apron, creases lining her worn face.

But it was not only she, for a maid stood behind her, pale and tense, and the footman who came to tend the fire kept sending indiscreet glances toward Elizabeth as if waiting for her to give some indication of her pleasure. Seeing them all so undone turned the knife further into Elizabeth's chest.

They needed to leave. This instant, before Elizabeth could permit herself to have second thoughts... but that was before the first tears streaked freely down the housekeeper's face. Oh, this was too much! First, Colonel Fitzwilliam nearly guilted her into coming to meet this Mr Darcy, and then, the man's entire household seemed to be conspiring to add burning coals to her head.

But there was nothing artificial about the way Mrs Hodges was struggling to hold herself together to act like the proper housekeeper she was. And perhaps there was nothing else for it—Elizabeth acted on tender instinct, reaching to clasp her work-worn hand.

"Please do not take on so," she murmured gently, a lump swelling in her throat. "You cannot be faulted for worrying about your master. Truly, you have all extended graciousness itself to strangers, even in this painful hour, and for that, I thank you most humbly."

But Mrs Hodges shook her grey head miserably, face crumpling like wet parchment as she sobbed openly into her apron. "Oh, Miss Elizabeth, you cannot understand our relief when Colonel Fitzwilliam said you would come! So cheerful and steady he described you, the beautiful angel to chase Mr Darcy's demons away..."

Acid clawed Elizabeth's innards with dawning horror. Clearly, the colonel had sung her praises, and word had spread below stairs. These good souls had conjured romantic fantasies of Mr Darcy's redemption at her hands. And like overeager readers, they had collectively written the next chapter of his heroic revival without consulting the key players.

Now she was forced to play the villain, crushing innocent dreams under her slippered heel along with her own as she spurned the designated hero. The role sat wretchedly. Face flaming, she tried consoling Mrs Hodge's crest-fallen hopes between shooting Jane pleading glances.

"Alas, it appears I was not the angel you wished for. But take heart, Mrs Hodges. Your master is an intelligent man, I've no doubt, and he shall yet find some contentment and purpose."

Mrs Hodges sniffed and shook her head. "Aye, and look at me, carrying on so! Forgive me, Miss Elizabeth. Never once have I lost my head, but you see, we all think so well of the master, and we hoped... Well! Millie, will you warm up Miss Bennet's tea?" Mrs Hodges stood back and dipped a deferential curtsey. "I hope we can make you comfortable until your carriage arrives, Miss."

After the woman had gone, Elizabeth remained staring at the door, all the breath gone from her lungs. "Papa?" she murmured. "Is it possible I have misjudged Mr Darcy?" She turned around. "Everyone seems practically to worship the man! Have I done wrongly?"

"After such an uncivil address? Any lady with sense would flee!" Mr Bennet huffed before his eldest daughter's quelling glare moderated his tongue. "Can you honestly fancy yourself married to such a brute as that?"

"No," Elizabeth agreed. "You are quite right. I would do well to forget Mr Darcy and this... strange mischance. Oh, where is the carriage?"

Not ten seconds later, the drawing-room door burst open to reveal Colonel Fitzwilliam, and Elizabeth's last frail thread of composure snapped like an over-tuned piano wire. Grim satisfaction tightened his anxious features as he noted all three Bennets still uncomfortably situated among the lavish furnishings.

"Thank God you have not gone. I had the deuce of a time soothing Darcy's temper and feared you might have quit the premises entirely by now!" Doffing his hat, the colonel mopped his ruddy forehead before turning earnestly to Elizabeth.

"Please accept my abject apologies for Darcy's atrocious lapse of decorum, Miss Bennet. I can only imagine how shocked you must be after I regrettably inflated your expectations."

Elizabeth forced her pinched social smile. "While the unfortunate display was... unexpected to me, I understand it might have been doubly so to you. Given his faithful servants' glowing accounts of their amiable master, I expect you thought we would be received graciously. Pray, think no more of it." Gathering her dignity, she subtly angled her body away in a clear dismissal.

The colonel, however, was not so easily deterred. Switching tactics, he dropped to perch awkwardly on a silk brocade ottoman practically under Elizabeth's nose.

"I must beg you to reconsider. Darcy endures agony you cannot conceive. Consider, a once healthy, active man now living under threat of lifelong infirmity—not remotely an excuse for abuse, yet perhaps grounds for mercy?" His battle-scarred countenance turned pleading. "Might you grant one further interview before abandoning all possibility between you?"

Elizabeth rolled her eyes up to the ceiling, praying for just enough civility for the kind colonel but sufficient condemnation for the man upstairs. But before she could deliver a scathing setdown, Jane touched her wrist, blue eyes awash in sisterly concern. Drat it all, even Jane's tender heart would not withstand watching her kick this well-meaning officer any further while he was down!

Smoothing her features, Elizabeth replied through gritted teeth. "While your dedication speaks highly, sir, I assure you nothing further remains requiring my input."

"I should perhaps have advised you before—Darcy has never been strong in creating first impressions. He is too much on his guard, do you see, and he has never been in a position where others were not prepared to put up with his nonsense."

She thinned her lips. "I shall take your word for it, Colonel, but you are mistaken if you believe I am eager to form a second impression of him."

Fitzwilliam ran a frustrated hand down his face before leaning intently nearer still, voice lowered cajolingly. "Miss Elizabeth, please, at least speak with Darcy once more. Alone, if I can persuade you to it, for—"

"Alone! You *are* mad."

"Not so, for with no one else in the room, you will hear his true sentiments, unvarnished by watchfulness for what everyone else thinks."

"Oh! I think I have had quite enough of Mr Darcy's true sentiments. Unvarnished, indeed!"

"Then, if nothing else, set him straight on his boorish misjudgements—surely you cannot let such foul slights pass unchallenged? He deserves to hear it from your own lips, the rascal, with no one else present to whom he can deflect his protests."

Elizabeth nearly launched upright from her seat. "Colonel Fitzwilliam! Whatever are you implying, sir? That I ought to sneak off alone to a strange gentleman's private quarters to... to... set him about?" She stumbled, cheeks flaming scarlet at his arched brow. "That is wholly inappropriate, whatever my feelings on the matter!"

The audacious colonel at least had grace left to look slightly abashed under her outraged stare. Clearing his throat awkwardly, he tried one last desperate gambit, though his eyes sparked with dawning hope at catching her interest. "Forgive me. I merely thought you seemed a lady of particular spirit. One not to suffer insult silently." He paused meaningfully before adding, "Unless, of course, you worry you have misjudged Darcy's character... or your own strength in facing him thus vulnerable?"

Elizabeth sucked in fury like dragon flame. How dare this presumptuous, officious, conniving...! With monumental restraint, she managed thinly. "I'll remind you, sir, that whatever you might have been given to believe about my family after my sister's behaviour, I do know something about proper comportment. I shall not be tempted to have words with the man alone in his bedroom."

The colonel sat back, equal measures frustration and grim amusement sparking his reply. "I confess myself bested, then. For it is obvious that I was wrong, and in asking your courage to rise to the occasion, I have quite overstepped both my bounds and your limits. I will see you to your carriage without further delay."

Elizabeth stared at the arm he offered, then flicked her eyes coldly back to his face. "I begin to see now why Mr Darcy is so frustrated. Do you always see such success at manipulating people to your liking, sir?"

A corner of his mouth lifted. "Have I offended you, Miss Elizabeth?"

"You have issued a challenge to my dignity, sir. One I ought to refuse out of hand."

His smile grew a little bolder now. "But you will not."

Elizabeth swallowed and narrowed her eyes. From somewhere near the periphery of her awareness, she heard Jane's indrawn breath, but she would not glance at her sister. Instead, she gathered her skirts in one hand and hiked her chin yet one measure higher.

"Let me to this boor, then. He shall hear my mind one last time."

Elizabeth felt as though someone hooked a finger down her throat and physically dragged her all the grudging way back up the grand staircase after Colonel Fitzwilliam's smug retreating figure. She vowed to meet Mr Darcy's eye once with steady civility, relay her farewells, then escape forever... never to be goaded again by dreams unfulfilled or guilted by doleful dark eyes. Steeling herself, she crossed the threshold alone.

The sounds of harsh, ragged breathing drew Elizabeth's eye to a slumbering Mr Darcy as she crept nearer. From this vexing man's heroic—and frankly intimidating—physique, to his proud profile now softened by sleep... the entire tableau before her whispered of virility and power that made his present helplessness doubly cruel by contrast.

Darcy shifted slightly, though apparently unaware of her presence yet. His formidable chest and forearms still declared him nature's favoured son, but he lacked any outlet to expend that restless energy now confined in his useless lower limbs, like a mighty draught horse shackled by only one errant hoof.

Elizabeth approached nearer still, studying him, cataloguing impressions that guarded eyes and waking alertness might obscure. One of his large, aristocratic hands restlessly clenching and unclenching in sleep drew her gaze. What pursuits would those strong fingers never grip—a fencing foil or billiard cue—to master again? His aquiline features were all chiselled edges and sharp intelligence—and currently gaunt with bitter despair, if Mrs Hodges was to be believed.

Elizabeth's wayward appraisal wandered along the blankets shrouding Darcy's useless thighs and calves. Until that deep voice, clipped yet honeyed, nearly made her jump out of her own skin: "You may as well come closer. It's hardly as though I plan to ravish you." Beneath the sarcasm, anguished bitterness etched his tone. "And I've not even shoes to fling—only words left as weapons against beauty's arsenal."

Elizabeth flushed guilty scarlet at being caught out, hand flying self-consciously to her throat. Forcing starch back into her tone, she countered, "Or against what small virtues I possess. As I am 'not handsome enough to tempt you,' I imagine you must be quite immune to whatever power I do have."

Some emotion flickered over Mr Darcy's countenance. With a visible effort, he rasped, "Well, you may sit down, at least. Else Richard can brag about conquering the great Darcy's savage temper with a mere slip of a girl standing over me."

Elizabeth eyed the bedside chair reluctantly, instinct urging her to bolt back out the door and recover some semblance of her pride. But the man before her now seemed deflated more than threateningly temperamental. Stomach churning with trepidation, Elizabeth gingerly lowered herself into the chair angled near Darcy's elbow. Judging by his pinched features, whatever poison he had worked up to spew would come momentarily.

The gentleman turned his head with effort upon the pillow to regard her directly. In profile, she had missed the sharp intelligence in those heavily lashed eyes, shards of ice crystal though they were.

"So. You are the unfortunate creature Richard thought to leg shackle to a crippled man." He grimaced. "What do you there in the savagery of... Meryton, is it? Play mistress of the house while your mother instead fusses over ribbons and lace?"

Affront jerked Elizabeth more rigidly upright, though she bit back a scalding retort with effort. Clearly, still waters of disdain ran deep here. And murky.

At her continued silence, something like chagrin flickered across Darcy's brow. "You must think me beyond the pale. I fear misery has corroded my tongue... along with everything else beneficial." He looked aside, jaw working. "The degradation seems never-ending."

Against her will, pity whispered traitorously through Elizabeth. She leaned fractionally nearer, searching features shuttered once more. "Does it... pain you very much?"

A brittle facsimile of a smile cracked Darcy's granite façade. "The laudanum helps... sometimes. Other times, not even a narcotic euphoria can numb whatever remains sensible in this useless carcass." His eyes squeezed shut briefly in naked agony that wrenched Elizabeth's breath.

But his next sullen glare headed off tender sympathy. Like a turtle retreating under its shell, all traces of vulnerability vanished. "Can you even imagine what it means, to have one's entire being confined thus? Helpless? To never seize freedom on horseback or dance floor again until death drags you under?"

The raw agony bleeding through Darcy's bitterness pierced Elizabeth's heart. Haltingly, she whispered, "I cannot profess to fully understand being thus chained. Yet, I have faced the anguish of seeing my own small hopes and dreams wrecked through no fault of my own... and had to find purpose again from the ashes."

Was that brief, arrested look in Darcy's eye the dawn of grudging connexion? But all too soon, his darkened façade reasserted itself with hardened contempt. "Pretty phrases cannot fathom this existence! Do not pretend any true comprehension with your girlish platitudes. If there is one thing I cannot stomach, it is pity." He flicked a biting hand as though to banish her from his sight.

Stubbornness coiled Elizabeth's spine. "Indeed, I do begin to pity you, sir— though not for your unfortunate injury."

Darcy barked caustic laughter. "Is that so? Pray to enlighten me about what deserves your philanthropic sympathies, then!"

Squaring her shoulders, Elizabeth met his scorn steadily. "I pity your hopelessness. Your inability to envision any worthwhile future, thus, you lock yourself in your own mental prison. There are worse fates than yours, sir. A mind or heart permanently paralyzed to possibility remains far more crippled."

Throat tightening unbearably, Elizabeth rose on trembling limbs, palms clammy within the gloves she had already pulled on in preparation for a quick departure. She had witnessed enough unguarded torment here. "I thank you again, sir, for Lydia's restoration. And... I am sorry. But I am clearly not what you need. Farewell, Mr Darcy. I wish you... peace."

Hand upon the door frame, she hesitated once more under the accusation in those wintry eyes. But the still form turned away without further remark or entreaty. Disappointment tinged with relief flooded Elizabeth's veins as she gained the hall at last... until Darcy's broken tones sounded behind her.

"Miss Elizabeth?"

She turned back, her fingers still on the door latch. "Sir?"

His eyes were closed, his fists clenched as his nostrils fluttered. "Perhaps... Perhaps we could... help each other."

She let her hand fall from the latch. "I am listening."

Chapter Eight

H IS HEART WAS RACING after calling the intriguing Miss Elizabeth Bennet back. It was a miracle that she had even stopped to hear him, let alone turned to consider his request. And now she was standing over him again, those full and eloquent eyes resting on his face. Waiting.

Darcy shifted uncomfortably on the pillow, shame heating his cheeks. Devil take it, what could he even say after practically throwing the lady out moments before? "Do... have a seat again, if you please."

She glanced at the chair, as if truly deliberating, then perched carefully upon it. Darcy's fingers fidgeted on the blanket. "Forgive my ungallant attitude. Contrary to what you might believe, my father *did* instil proper manners in me, including standing for a lady, as proper etiquette dictates." He offered a shadow of a rueful smile. "Civilised manners have gone out the window some days, I fear."

To his immense relief, Miss Elizabeth's brief answering smile felt far less forced. "I never quite understood that rule, anyway. If we are showing deference to a person, why do ladies not stand when gentlemen enter the room, as well?"

He could think of nothing to say to that. Was she... serious? She could not be. Could she be teasing him? He tried to return some airy quip, but this seemed not the time for that sort of levity. For several leaden moments, only the crackling hearth broke the desolate silence, and her eyes began to shift uncomfortably.

Oh, hang it all. This was no way to begin. Fighting past the paralysing bitterness, Darcy forced out in low, rough tones, "Why did you return? Surely, my foul temper gave you sufficient reason to leave." He searched her face. "What madness permitted me another chance?"

Miss Bennet clasped her hands tightly in her lap as if to brace herself. "In truth, I know not for certain. Only... I think perhaps behind the anger and despair still resides the honourable gentleman who rescued my sister." She drew a shaking breath, risking greater vulnerability in turn, though her discomfort screamed in every line of her body. "If he yet breathes behind that caustic veil of yours... that is a man I should be proud to know."

He turned his face away. "I did not go there to rescue your sister."

"But you did, all the same."

"And what have I rescued her to? A shamed existence? A future of uncertainty and disgrace?"

She was silent... silent long enough that he turned to look at her once more and found her expressive eyes focused on his hand on the blanket. "You do not understand. My father and uncle searched for a fortnight but could not find her. You were able to do what they could not—you discovered her. We thought her lost forever."

"She *is* lost, and your family ruined."

Miss Bennet blinked up at him. "And you think that to be a fate worse than death, do you? I know some do. Perhaps I should, as well."

"It is your own prospects she ruined. Are you not angry at her foolishness?"

"Of course, I am. I am outraged at how careless she was, not only for her own safety but the fears of her family... and the welfare of her sisters. I am furious that my mother indulged her every whim and mortified that my father failed to correct her when she was younger. But that does not mean that I wish she had been left to the mercies of the brothel... or worse."

"Then you claim you can separate your concern for your sister from your indignation over her actions?" He scoffed and turned to look back at the ceiling. "Pretty words, Miss Bennet. I wonder if there is any truth in them."

"Mr Darcy, I see no point in arguing with you. You may choose to credit me with whatever feeling you wish, but that does not affect the truth whatsoever. I do not care to put myself in the way of your scorn any longer, so if you will excuse me..."

His head snapped back around, sending a shock of agony through what he could feel of his back. It was his unconscious hiss of pain that stilled her, and she anchored herself back to the seat with widened eyes.

"Are you well, sir? Should I call for someone?"

His teeth clenched as the pain subsided, and he forced a breath. "Yes... I mean, no. I do not require anything. But I would not have you go thinking that I scorn you." He swallowed and studied her face. Intelligent eyes that seemed like they could pierce to his marrow, barely tamed ringlets of shining chocolate framing a face that was sprinkled with sun-kissed freckles, and a mouth that... Well, there was hardly any point in imagining *that* anymore. "In fact, Miss Bennet, I find you rather remarkable."

A sharp chuckle left her. "Colonel Fitzwilliam took great care to impress me with your honesty. As well as your gentlemanly sensibilities. I see he has exaggerated again."

"I am perfectly in earnest. It is rather something to meet a lady whose future has been blighted by a heedless sister, who can yet care for that sister's welfare."

Her rigid spine softened, and she folded her hands more easily in her lap as if she were settling in for a moment. "May I ask you about your own sister, Mr Darcy?"

"Ah, yes." He loosed a bitter laugh. "The reason you are here."

"You must love her very much."

He gazed at her, his eyes sweeping her from forehead to her folded hands, and sighed. "I have raised her for the last five years. She has been wholly my concern... well, and Richard's. But we hardly saw him for four of those years, as he was away with his regiment. Tell me, Miss Bennet—you said that your parents erred in the raising of your younger sister, but at least they had the advantage of maturity and experience to aid them. What chance, do you think, has a bachelor only just come into his inheritance at the age of two and twenty? What odds would you give him of shepherding his ten-year-old sister with wisdom?"

She glanced down at her hands again. "Mr Darcy, not all mistakes can be laid at the feet of the guardian. Some are a person's own to claim. I cannot speak to this case, of course, but why do you feel her fate was your fault?"

"How could it not be? I placed her in the care of that woman. I sent her away to Ramsgate."

"And did you send Mr Wickham to meet them there? Did you conspire toward your own sister's ruin?"

"I failed to warn her about him. I know him, Miss Bennet."

She lifted her shoulders. "Knowing him and knowing what he means to do are two different things. I am sure you gave her good principles, and she chose selfishness instead. She would not be the first."

He sighed and thought about staring at the ceiling again... but he had been staring at it for weeks. Elizabeth Bennet was, if nothing else, far more appealing to look at than the plaster over his head.

What was he to say to that? If anyone else had the audacity to call his sister selfish, he would have thrashed them. But there was no recrimination in her tones... if anything, there was absolution for him, if he chose to hear it. How did a man respond to that? And would anything he said even matter to her? She had made her mind up about him already, and he had given her all the reason she needed to walk away this instant.

But she was still sitting there.

Inwardly, Darcy cursed his clumsy helplessness—what could a lady of such striking cleverness and dignity want with an embittered wreck like him? Money was the obvious answer, but she had already declared that all his wealth could not gild the pig he had made of himself. Yet, she had come back, and had spoken gently to him.

Desperate, he seized on answering the mystery of Elizabeth Bennet herself... and whether she truly was as artless as she appeared. Carefully keeping any note of accusation from his tone, Darcy ventured into small talk. "Your father... seems quite... devoted to you. Tell me, have you any other siblings besides the elder one I just met and the notorious Miss Lydia?"

And that proved a beginning. She detailed her family for him, including her relations in trade and her father's cousin, who was to inherit their small estate. None of that was a surprise to him, for Richard had already made her prospects, lot lack thereof, plain. But he liked hearing it in her words. It made her a person to him, rather than a number.

"And... what do you do for leisure?"

"Nothing I shall be likely to enjoy again soon," was her tart response. At his questioning look, she explained that she adored walking out of doors, taking the air and communing with the sweet earth and sky... but of late, it had become nearly unsafe for her to do so. And she loved to dance... *why* did she have to love dancing, of all things? But again, recent events had determined that she would not be showing her face at any balls in Hertfordshire in the future.

Well, he could no longer walk out or go to balls, either. Thus far, they were equal, but for entirely different reasons.

Then, somehow, they got on the subject of their favourite books, and Darcy felt himself on somewhat safer ground to prod and examine her thoughts. Beneath her genteel composure at his mundane inquiries, quick intelligence sparked in her eyes. Each answer revealed her bright mind and staunch loyalties further, easing his disbelief any gently-born woman would willingly swear her lot to a useless millstone around her neck.

After some fifteen minutes, she arched one delicate brow mischievously. "Come, sir, surely, as interrogations go, this all seems rather one-sided? Having secured my entire family history and my thoughts on everything from Cervantes to milk cows, from lace to Sophocles, it is your turn to speak. What of your own expectations regarding this proposed union?"

Brought up short, Darcy wilted against his pillows once more. What did he truly expect anymore? Raising his eyes to the distant ceiling, he admitted lowly, "In truth, I hardly know. I cannot expect to seize what I once took for granted ever again."

Silence swelled between them once more, yet this quiet, shared commiseration felt strangely... comforting. Until slender fingers chanced a feather's weight on his knuckles. Startled from his dark reverie, Darcy sought her face anew. Yes, there was trepidation there. Compassion—he would have expected no less—and curiosity, but something else, too... It looked for all the world like hope. Perhaps they two lost souls might find a safe harbour together, after all.

Tentatively returning her sympathetic touch, Darcy rasped, "Miss Elizabeth, think you that you could find some manner of... contentment, facing permanent ties to a bedridden husband and all his black humours?"

She met his vulnerability with a crooked smile. "I think between my naturally impertinent temper and your dour moods, we may likely send each other to Bedlam some days. What say you to that prospect, sir?"

A hint of an answering smile cracked Darcy's granite façade. "I cannot think why we would let Fitzwilliam talk us into this... but I am not afraid of you."

Her smile widened. "Nor I of you."

T HE ECHO OF MISS Elizabeth Bennet's hesitant agreement had not even faded before Darcy snapped at his hovering cousin, "Richard! I know you are outside. In here at once."

His cousin poked his head in within seconds. "I say, that's a marked improvement in temper already. Why, the furnishings are still intact, and..." He glanced around warily. "Am I given to understand that Miss Elizabeth is not bolting for the door as expected?"

Darcy grimaced. "The lady has permitted herself to 'reconsider,' thanks to your blasted interference. Though what good may come, I've little notion."

Richard clapped his hands together, sagging against the bedpost in profound relief. "Oh, capital! Knew you had it in you, Darcy. My most ecstatic congratulations, and now—" Breaking off, he rushed eagerly for the door again. "Now, I must send an urgent word to Father. Thank Heaven he insisted we order the licence already, on my recommendation. He sent me a message that the bishop authorised it only this afternoon."

"What?" Elizabeth yelped, leaping to her feet. Two flags of offended colour flew high on her sculpted cheekbones. "Excuse me, Colonel, but did I hear correctly? You took improper liberties preparing a marriage document without my consent or my father's blessing. When did you have this ordered?"

"A special licence takes three days, at minimum," Darcy supplied. At Elizabeth's swift glance, he offered a wry twist of his mouth. "And he only told me about it two days ago."

Darcy quite liked the way her chin lifted as she stared his cousin down. "That is highly irregular, Colonel, given that Mr Darcy and I barely made one another's acquaintance an hour ago. You planned this before you spoke to either of us about it? Is *my name* on that document?"

Mischief and satisfaction battled in Darcy's expression. Elizabeth Bennet might just prove to have some mettle of her own. "If that shocks you, my dear, best accustom yourself sooner than later to this presumptuous fellow organising your life to his way of thinking." He cast an ironic look at his unrepentant cousin. "All in the name of expediency."

"True expediency in this!" Richard held up protesting hands. "I swear, every step was meant to aid you both through these straits. I counted on the good sense of each of you, and you have vindicated me." He turned earnestly back to Elizabeth. "You shall find my parents to be stalwart allies too, ready to lend all assistance getting you comfortably situated."

Elizabeth struggled visibly to collect herself, colour still high. "Be that as it may, such casual disregard over legalities cannot continue. I absolutely protest any further such meddling."

"I would expect no less. I have done my bit, and now, I feel you will suit one another as you please."

Elizabeth let go of a strained breath and forced her features to smooth. "If we manage not to kill each other, perhaps we will get on well enough. Colonel, my father and Jane—"

"Already settled in comfortable rooms, and another is being made up for you, Miss Elizabeth."

Her mouth dropped open. "Rooms! Indeed, you are a presumptuous rogue! I thought we made it plain to you that we intended to stop in Cheapside with my aunt and uncle."

"Forgive me, but I thought it best... and your father did not disagree... that if you *did* decide to accept Darcy's proposal, we should avoid drawing attention to the house for now. The more unfamiliar carriages are seen outside the home of Fitzwilliam Darcy... Well, I am sure you can appreciate that my cousin often attracts much notice, and we would rather not draw attention at this moment."

"But our carriage—it will have been waiting nearly an hour outside already."

"Not at all, for I stopped the footman before he ever sent word to the stables to have it readied."

Shocked indignation flashed over Elizabeth's features before she slumped back into her seat, struggling not to betray reluctant amusement. "Colonel, what else have you not told me?"

Richard puckered his lips and cast his eye to the ceiling that had been Darcy's only entertainment this fortnight past. "Did I mention that my father is the Earl of Matlock?"

Her brows arched. "Little wonder you are accustomed to ordering people around."

"No, no. I learned that skill in the Army. In all honesty, Miss Elizabeth, I wager there remains a great deal I have not yet told you, but only because I did not wish to overwhelm you. You have enough to bother with just now." Richard opened the door and made them each a short bow. "I will make arrangements for the ceremony to take place tomorrow morning at ten. Miss Elizabeth, I will send a maid in ten minutes to show you to your room."

As the door closed again, leaving them quite alone, Darcy watched in fascination as a myriad of emotions flashed across the lady's expressive face—the face of his bride-to-be. Odd, that, how quickly he had reconciled himself to the idea. How swiftly his notions of the proper wife for Fitzwilliam Darcy of Pemberley had been thrown over in preference for a woman willing to play nursemaid and surrogate mother. His future wife would have to endure a great deal that he never would have wished to put upon any woman, but Miss Bennet seemed equal to the task.

But that was not why he had agreed to marry her. There was something else there—a temper that matched his own, and a spark of wit and stubbornness that would serve her well.

She could have walked out. Or she could have ignored his barbs with a smile and vowed to have his fortune no matter how contemptible the husband proved to be. But she had done neither of these. She had been willing to walk away on principle, but reasonable enough to consider again the claims upon them both.

What a glorious challenge this prickly siren would be to sort out. At least she might provide some distraction from his tedium.

Chapter Nine

"Lizzy, are you positive? Sacrificing your future like this is utter madness, no matter how guilty you feel over that scoundrel Wickham's mischief with Lydia!"

"Please, Papa, be easy." Jane glanced nervously between Elizabeth and their father. "I confess, such permanent ties to an invalid also give me pause... yet Lizzy's instincts rarely steer her wrong."

"It is not Lizzy's instincts but her tender heart I mistrust in this!" Mr Bennet rounded on Elizabeth beseechingly. "Am I truly to stand idle while my liveliest daughter chains herself as nursemaid and nothing more to that dour man? You deserve a proper husband. One who can be worthy of your trust and respect."

Elizabeth studied her beloved Papa's creased brow and sunken eyes, reading the weight of guilt and love that drove his desperate arguments. "I comprehend your objections perfectly, Papa, and my ears are open wide to them. But given the choices before me, I do believe this is the right one."

Jane reached for Elizabeth's hand. "Lizzy, no one would fault you for withdrawing now before you are legally bound. Are you certain? Perhaps some excuse may be made for Mr Darcy's temper because of present circumstances, but what if he never returns to the character Colonel Fitzwilliam knows?"

She turned to face Jane's tender worry as well while marshalling her own tumultuous thoughts. "Yet there are dual sides to every scale. If Mr Darcy seems a harsh man to you, well... I glimpsed his truer colours and intellect when I spoke with him alone, and I believe much good yet thrives beneath it all." Heart quickening, she admitted quietly, "A man who was so eager to defend his sister's honour would not wish to do less for his wife... would he?"

"And if in time you come to rue this sacrifice, finding only a shrivelled soul in that wreckage and yourself bound to him forever? Lizzy! It is not pity or even quick ardour that can form the foundation of a lasting union. You have often declared you wished to settle for nothing less than love, and how are you to find... *anything* with that wretch?"

She swallowed. "I... I do not know, Papa. But I see few alternatives before me."

"And what becomes of your own character? I know you, Lizzy. If you cannot esteem your husband..." He stopped and gulped back a shuddering sigh. "Jane could bear it better. She would remain peaceable and content, but you? You are too given to sharpness, to quick judgments and eventually, to bitterness. I fear for your heart, my child—less that you will be cheated out of a true marriage, and more that you will look in the mirror one day and not know yourself."

Elizabeth's shoulders slumped, and her eyes dropped to the floor. "I can think of few things more abhorrent."

"Precisely why you must reconsider before the knot is tied!" he pressed, his posture rigid with conviction such as she had never seen in him. "Respect—perhaps he will give. But a wife, particularly one as young and lively as you, merits care, laughter, and joy of living! Children of your own... my heavens. His very injury itself may breed bitterness in time that poisons any hope of a bond with his wife before it is ever formed."

"Papa, he is not a wicked man, nor is he a stupid one."

His lined brow creased heavier. "Neither are you. Think, Lizzy. What true marriage can there be when he cannot even... be fully husband to you? What if you are tempted into ruin yourself? Do not laugh, my child—until you have ached for the lack of it, you cannot know its power."

Was that... was there something there, hinting at her parents' ill-suitedness? Elizabeth swallowed and grappled for what remained of her fraying composure. "I am not the only one I think of. Mr Darcy has suffered a profound loss. There was a moment there, however, when I saw a bit of levity... even humour. But he has precious little to laugh about now, does he? I believe the reason Colonel Fitzwilliam asked for *me* was because I can be precisely what that poor man needs."

"You are too generous with your humour, then!" Mr Bennet threw up frustrated hands. "You think of *him*, a stranger? But I say you must think first of yourself in this!

When all is iron bars and resentful longings in the dead of night... how soon before your heart grows hardened or indifferent?"

That bleak prophecy pierced Elizabeth's defences with icy dread... Could she herself grow so jaded? Yet surely, a mind and spirit well-matched could sustain them, even should deeper desires remain unfulfilled?

"We cannot read the future," she reasoned gently. "This... none of this is what I would have asked for. But I cannot have that now, can I? All I can say is that today, for a moment, at least, I glimpsed a man capable of deep devotion, whose needs and prospects fit neatly with my own."

"I am sorry, Lizzy," her father sighed, easing back into the chair opposite her. "It does seem nearly Providential—such a man needing a wife just when all hope of a respectable future for you girls seemed a distant memory—but this...?" He shook his head.

She glanced up to face him squarely, blinking back tears as she kept her tone steady. "You speak of bitterness—the sort of person I might become if I learn to resent this choice. But when you say that, I think not of myself, but of that man down the hall. He..."

She broke off and bit back a frustrated huff. When she spoke again, her voice trembled. "He has lost everything, Papa. Everything! And now his only hope is to trust a stranger—with his own life and with his sister's, and his entire family's honour. Can you not think with some measure of understanding for his circumstances? Is it so unreasonable that he would wish to put us off the moment we met him?"

Mr Bennet scowled and shook his head. It was Jane who took up the argument, leaning forward and biting her lip in discomfort. "Lizzy, I think what Papa is saying is that it does not need to fall to you to 'rescue' this man. Or to rescue your sisters, for that matter. We may not marry gentlemen of wealth, but I would far rather... goodness, I would marry old Mr Hastings and become an innkeeper's wife before I let you waste yourself here, on a man who despises you."

Elizabeth's mouth twitched. "I do not think he despises me that much."

"You say that now, before the vows are spoken" her father interrupted. "He may even think it himself, with this new, shiny prospect before him. But when days stretch into months, and then to years—"

"Am I forbidden, then, to accept him, Papa?"

He covered her small hand with his wrinkled one. Meeting her clear gaze at long last, he exhaled raggedly, then pulled her close, tears glinting silver in his tired eyes. He rallied his argument one final time. "I forfeited my right to guide your future, Lizzy. Yet I beg you—do not sacrifice all for transient debts and passing remorse! Promise me you will reconsider before the sun rises."

D AWN'S LIGHT CREPT RELUCTANTLY over Elizabeth's face, illuminating forgotten details anew—from the lavish bed coverings and ornate dressing table to the gilt-framed portrait hanging opposite her bed, featuring some powdered lady who glared down at her in disdain. And indeed, she had felt every measure of it as she tossed awake fretting half the night. Was it truly her fate to join their imperious ranks and hold sway over so many dependents?

She lay there a few moments, drumming her fingers on the silken coverlet until there was a gentle knock on the door. A maid soon slipped inside, bobbing a nervous curtsy. "Oh, you're already awake, Miss. I'm sorry to disturb you."

"You do not disturb me. Come in, please."

The girl let the door close and glided toward her window. "Excuse me. I've only come to stoke the fire and draw the drapes."

Elizabeth pushed herself upright. "No need for the fire. I expect I will not..." There was a tremble in her chest, but she forced a smile and refused to let her thoughts wander... *there*. "That is, I do not think I will be in the room this morning long enough to enjoy it."

"Shall we attend to your toilette, Miss? And your breakfast tray will be arriving shortly, but there is no need to hurry."

There certainly seemed no point in remaining abed. Elizabeth twisted and touched her feet to the floor. "Yes, thank you." She paused, studying the girl's face. "Beth, was it not? It was you who rode to Longbourn with my sister, Lydia."

Beth flushed and averted her gaze as she brought a dressing gown to drape over Elizabeth's shoulders. "Yes, Miss Bennet."

Elizabeth tucked her arms through the sleeves of the pretty, new-looking gown—now where had *that* come from? It was not one of the garments from her own trunk. She turned back to the maid and smiled. "It is a relief to see a familiar face this morning. Thank you."

Beth hesitantly met her eyes. "I were the lucky one."

Elizabeth chuckled. "How is that?"

"All the girls were wanting to get a look at you. But Mrs Hodges said the master wanted I should attend you."

"I must be quite the object of curiosity." She clenched her hand to stop its trembling. "What is being said about me?"

"More questions than anything." Beth gave a shy smile. "The colonel spoke to us all and said we weren't to trouble you overmuch. He said we'd all get plenty of time to know you after... Excuse me, Miss."

Beth broke off and went to the door to open it for a maid bearing a breakfast tray. Elizabeth could not help but notice the curious way the younger maid peeked around the door at her before Beth closed it in her face. The maid then carried the tray to a side table and invited Elizabeth to seat herself.

Elizabeth sank onto the delicate chair, eyeing the generous spread of scones, jam, and tea that she had little desire to touch. "I suppose I must resemble my poor mama this morning, twittering about like a frightened bird!" She attempted a light laugh. "If ever I lacked compassion for her nerves before, I have it in abundance today."

Beth smiled politely, but surely, she had not forgotten that scene in Longbourn's entry hall, where her mother and Lydia threw over all propriety and embarrassed them all before strangers.

Elizabeth lifted the teacup, hoping the hot liquid might settle her roiling stomach. But after a few feeble sips that tasted of nothing, she set it down again. Seeking distraction, she nodded towards the efficient girl tidying the room. "Beth, how long have you worked for the Darcys?"

"Nearly three years now, Miss. But my aunt is Mrs Reynolds, the housekeeper at Pemberley, so I've known the family all my life."

"Pemberley." Elizabeth rolled the name around on her tongue—the name of the place that would become her home, if she went through with this. "Is the house as fine as Colonel Fitzwilliam tells me it is?"

Beth's eyes flashed up. "I fancy there's no finer house in England, Miss. Of course, I haven't seen many, but..."

"But Pemberley hardly leaves one wanting?" Elizabeth guessed. "Yes, that is how the colonel described it. And are you content in your post there?"

"The master runs a fine house, and Mistress Darcy is always kind to us servants. I couldn't ask for better." Beth gave a wistful smile. "My aunt put a word in for me with the master, and he said he would see me trained as a lady's maid for Miss Darcy. That's why I came to London, you see."

"To learn under someone?" There did not appear to be another lady in the house requiring the services of such a maid, so who was to train the girl?

"Yes, I was to go to Lady Matlock's maid, but... well, then the master's accident, and then..." Beth shrugged and smiled.

"And you got overlooked in all the confusion," Elizabeth supplied softly.

"Oh, I'm not overlooked. The master never forgets, and he never breaks his word, even to a servant. I know I'll be sent when it suits." Beth glanced at Elizabeth's hair regretfully. "I only wish I knew better how to dress you, Miss. It being your wedding day and all."

Elizabeth sighed and set her cup aside. "Well, as to that, I was not brought here for my sense of fashion or my beauty. I think even if I stayed in my dressing gown with my hair in night braids, Colonel Fitzwilliam would still set the clergyman after me. So, let us get on with the task, shall we?"

Elizabeth rose from her chair as Beth went to draw out Elizabeth's best morning gown from the wardrobe. "Is this the one you want, Miss?"

Elizabeth bit her lip and considered. It was a far cry from what she had always expected when she imagined her wedding gown. But it was decent, and made over only this autumn, so it would do. "Yes, thank you."

She stood passively while Beth helped her dress, thoughts drifting unbidden to the mysterious man awaiting her down the hall. What sights had those intense eyes beheld? What thoughts and dreams filled his restless mind? And was there any hope that he could recover any of his faculties?

After Beth had fastened her gown, Elizabeth went to the dressing table and studied her pale features in the mirror as Beth styled her hair. Did Mr Darcy once imagine his future bride differently? She was hardly the fashionable heiress he had no doubt meant to marry. The lady would probably have been blonde and tall... a willowy Grecian beauty, secure in all the fashionable circles and trained from her infancy to grace the arm of a powerful man.

It wasn't supposed to be like this... for either of them. Elizabeth swallowed and tried to regulate the staggering of her breathing. If the solemn maid noted her mistress's hollow eyes and trembling hands, she made no comment, instead gently working fragrant cream into Elizabeth's palms with her head bowed.

Only after styling Elizabeth's still disorderly curls in silence some moments more did she venture hesitantly, "Are... are you quite well today, Miss Elizabeth? Should I call for Miss Bennet to keep you company?"

Elizabeth shook her head. "Hopefully, Jane is still sleeping. Let us not wake her."

"Is it your stomach, Miss? You look fearfully pale."

Elizabeth sucked in a breath. "Beth... you have known the Darcy family for long before all this." A sudden reckless impulse pushed her next whispered words out. "Tell me honestly—did you ever observe Mr Darcy behave dishonourably? Any evidence that he was ever less than a gentleman?"

The little maid's eyes blew wide and round. Before Beth could possibly formulate a politic reply, Elizabeth waved off her question, cheeks flaming.

"No, forgive me. I should not have asked you to compromise your position! Only... my own footing feels so uncertain still."

Haltingly at first, then with increasing conviction, Beth covered Elizabeth's restless hands with her own. "Miss Elizabeth, never was there a kinder or more honourable master than Mr Darcy, nor will you find one now!" Chin lifting, she declared staunchly, "Why, my aunt Mrs Reynolds praises his character above all gentlemen she ever knew, and Hodges here in London says the same."

Elizabeth allowed a slow smile. "She told me that. Forgive me. It is only that the man I just met yesterday showed me many facets of his character, and I have not the time to determine which features the most prominently."

Beth tucked the last of Elizabeth's curls into a pin and lowered her face behind Elizabeth's shoulder to smile at her in the mirror. "I don't have a young man myself, Miss, but I should think Mr Darcy will be kind to his lady. And everyone downstairs thinks you're highly favoured—no one else being good enough for him, you see."

Elizabeth released a shaky sigh. "If nothing else, Beth, your loyalty to the family is most touching. Well? I suppose there is nothing else for it. I am to marry him today, so I might as well learn to like him as well as the rest of his household does."

Chapter Ten

"REALLY, RICHARD, MUST YOU continue fussing so?" Darcy griped as his cousin fluffed pillows yet again. "I hardly think Miss Elizabeth will flee the premises if the creases in my bedding lack military precision."

Colonel Fitzwilliam arched an eyebrow. "Given your gracious hospitality yesterday, it is no small miracle the lady did not flee regardless. I tell you, Darcy, her father nearly refused to permit the match after that spectacular display of boorishness."

Darcy scowled, but regret stained his cheeks at the truth of that charge. "Well, she did not flee, so you might as well leave off."

Richard persisted in his ministrations, straightening the hair over Darcy's brow and checking a spot that he swore Giles missed when he had shaved him. "Only because Miss Elizabeth's particular stubbornness swayed him, so mind your manners today."

With a grumble, Darcy twisted his chin from his cousin's reach. "Damn it, enough! I am nervous as a bridegroom, not an invalid."

"Could have fooled me." Richard stepped back, eying his handiwork, and shook his head. "It seems stubbornness shall be a signature trait in this union. At least you shall be evenly matched there," he muttered.

Darcy cut him a glare. "I heard that."

Richard smothered a smirk. "I am certain you shall hear a great deal more in your marriage. The lady appears delightfully impertinent." His amusement faded at Darcy's stony silence. "Come now, old boy. I know this is not the wedding day you envisioned—"

"Rather an understatement," Darcy bit out. In truth, visions of his disastrous first meeting with Elizabeth still plagued him. What must she think of her bridegroom—this shattered wreck of a man? He should have stood before his future wife whole and healthy, not confined to a blasted invalid's bed! At least he had avoided leg irons for the ceremony, though at some cost to his dignity.

No doubt sensing his thoughts, Richard laid a bracing hand on his shoulder. "Miss Elizabeth did not flinch from the reality of your situation. I daresay she expects no Grecian Apollo."

Darcy tried to flex his useless legs—of course, there was no response. "But no woman deserves... this. I shall ever be a disappointment."

"Nonsense, you are made of stern enough stuff! Why, with a pretty young wife beside you each night, I wager your condition shall improve rapidly."

Darcy glanced sharply at his cousin's indelicate reference. "I cannot... Do you think to torment me into recovering the use of my body? That is not the nature of it!"

"Come, Darcy, I did not mean it that way. It is your spirit, not your body, for which I believe Miss Elizabeth may prove a cure. But that last surgeon did say it was not impossible—"

"Stop trying to ply me with false hope. Any thought of *that* must be forgotten."

"But you must confess, she is not... well, what I mean to say is that no matter the future, I doubt you will find yourself... disappointed with her."

Darcy swallowed and locked his eyes on the door across the room—the door through which she would walk at any moment. Despite himself, tentative flickers of hope warmed the cold dread in his chest. True, Elizabeth Bennet had shown courage in facing his dark humours so far... and she *was* lovely in her own unconventional way. Certainly, he had not detested speaking with her.

"The lady is... satisfactory," he conceded gruffly. "At least we managed civility when alone together."

"High praise, indeed!" Richard laughed. "Admit it, Darcy—were circumstances different, you might even anticipate this marriage."

Whatever Darcy might have admitted was forestalled as the door opened. The clergyman entered, followed by a pale Jane Bennet clinging to her father's arm. Mr Bennet moved haltingly as one stunned, shooting Darcy a poisonous glare.

Behind them, Elizabeth hovered anxiously on the threshold in her simple gown. Her freckled cheeks were bloodless, but she lifted her chin and stepped inside to meet Darcy's gaze.

"Good morning, Mr Darcy." To his surprise, her voice held steady. "I trust you are well?"

Darcy's pulse leapt erratically. "As well as I may be. And you... Miss Elizabeth?" Strange, how that name felt more familiar already.

The clergyman peered between them near-sightedly. "Shall we proceed? Are the parties willing?"

Her dark eyes locked with his, speaking wordless volumes in an instant. Then Darcy and Elizabeth drew fortifying breaths and answered as one.

"Yes. We are ready."

D ARCY STARED BROODINGLY AT his useless legs as Elizabeth bustled about, clearing away the remnants of their pitiful wedding breakfast. Their "witnesses" had all left the room moments before—Fitzwilliam to see the clergyman out and the remaining Bennets to change before their journey—but his wife had stayed with him.

Mortification roiled his gut as he watched her. His bride should not have to stoop so, playing both nursemaid and housemaid both before the heavy gold of her wedding ring had even warmed to her hand.

"I eagerly anticipate the doctor's leave to sit up in a chair, at least," he grumbled, if only to break the cloying silence. "Rather than remain always flat on my back."

"That would be good. Surely, being able to look about the room as you please will be more comfortable." Elizabeth offered a subdued smile, though her reddened eyes betrayed the threat of tears.

Darcy studied her, shame and sympathy warring within. "Does it pain you so very much to see your family depart?"

She blinked rapidly and looked aside. "Papa... and Jane... I was always closest to them, out of anyone. Yes, I shall miss them."

"Would your father not consent to stay longer? To aid your transition?"

Her smile faded. "Colonel Fitzwilliam arranged their immediate return home. Before any announcement reaches local circles."

The announcement. No doubt the earl had already seen to that detail, and his marriage would be public by tomorrow morning, with all manner of flattering phrases tactfully published about their swift "romance." Darcy's jaw tightened. Concealing his situation and Elizabeth's origins was merely politic... yet the deception irked. Still more so, inflicting further hardship upon Elizabeth by wresting her prematurely from all she knew.

"And does your family approve of this union?" He already suspected otherwise. Her father's bloodless rage throughout the ceremony spoke volumes.

Fresh tears slipped down Elizabeth's cheeks as she shook her head. "Even Jane, who could find it in her to hope for the very devil's own redemption—even she expresses her doubts. As for Mama and my younger sisters... they remain ignorant, believing me gone to my aunt and uncle's." She lifted her shoulders and attempted a laugh. "Mama thinks Uncle employs a promising clerk or two who might take one of us off her hands. We did not feel it right to tell her... everything. Not just yet."

An awkward lump rose in Darcy's throat. On impulse, he reached for her hand, so small and cold within his own. "Might I send you to visit your relations tomorrow? If you wish? You said they lived in Cheapside if I am not mistaken."

She searched his face through shimmering tears. "You are kind to offer, sir, but Colonel Fitzwilliam says your aunt, the countess, comes to formally receive me tomorrow."

Of course she would. Darcy closed his eyes, cursing his cousin's manoeuvrings. This entire situation felt like a farce rapidly careening out of control. Still, perhaps the countess's support might ease Elizabeth's way as mistress here. Certainly, once that announcement was printed on the morrow, the drawing room below would be flooded by curious Londoners, come to have a look at this new Mrs Darcy.

All too soon, Richard entered to relay the Bennets' imminent departure. As Elizabeth quit the room, Darcy gazed after her sombrely, praying he had not just condemned a bright soul to slow ruin chained to his worthless carcass.

"Richard?" He listened as the door closed, then shifted his eyes up to his cousin. "I should like to be able to look my wife in the eye."

Richard's face warmed into something like a hopeful smile. "You will, Darcy. A little more time, and—"

"Now. Today. Call that worthless doctor and see if he will permit me to at least sit up in my bed."

"I BELIEVE WE CAN cautiously try propping a pillow or two behind you, Mr Darcy," Dr James advised. "Just slightly at first, and only with ample support."

Richard perked up from his tense vigil by the window. "What of a Bath chair, or perhaps—"

"Not yet," the doctor cautioned. "But propping him on pillows should cause no harm. We shall proceed slowly, guided only by Mr Darcy's comfort."

Richard snorted. "As if he would admit to discomfort if it meant rising from his bed."

"Indeed. Colonel, will you help me to position Mr Darcy so I may examine his injury? Carefully, now... roll as one."

As Dr James prodded his spine and tested his lifeless legs, Darcy had to clench his jaw to hold back the burning tears... or at least to smear them on the pillow before they rolled him to his back again. And then he stared resolutely up at the ceiling as the doctor moved a pin up and down his feet, his calves, the inside of his knees—but there was not so much as a bloody flicker of sensation remaining below his waist.

Darcy's breath grew short and panicked as Dr James continued his examination, masking his own doubt and concern behind practical platitudes. He advised things like regularly moving Darcy to prevent bedsores, resuming more normal foods as tolerated, and shielding him vigilantly from any draughts that might enter from the window.

But Darcy heard the hesitancy beneath the confident recommendations, saw the pitying sorrow in the doctor's eyes each time he hopefully said, "We shall see how the nerves progress with time," or "The swelling may yet subside."

Then came the ultimate humiliation—Dr James delicately suggesting Darcy must not attempt marital relations in his current state. Mortification and impotent fury choked him. How dare this man casually throw his pitiful helplessness in his face, and now dictate limits on intimacy with his own wife!

"Get out!" Darcy erupted, uncaring that his voice broke on a wretched sob. He wanted to throw something, to violently expel the useless legs that betrayed him, but he could only fall back, quaking, into his mountain of pillows.

Richard rushed over, gripping Darcy's shoulders as he weakly tried pushing everyone away. "Peace, Cousin! The doctor meant no offence. Come, let us discuss something more productive."

But Darcy had turned his face away, refusing to be soothed. His outrage boiled over as angry tears tracked down his temples at last. God in heaven, would this humiliation never cease?

Richard gave him one last squeeze on the shoulder and turned back to Dr James. "How long ere we can move him from London without risk?"

The doctor sputtered in alarm. "Move him from London! He must not be moved from his *bed* for two months at the very least!"

"There must be a safe way to at least move him to the country." Richard paced the carpet in agitation as the doctor repacked his bag with maddening unhurriedness. "Remaining in London cannot be best. Certainly not best for his privacy."

Dr James looked up placatingly. "I understand your frustration, Colonel, but Mr Darcy suffered severe spinal trauma. We must allow time for the inflammation and swelling to run its course, to say nothing of any bones that remain to mend as well as they can."

"How much time?" Richard pressed. "Surely in another month—"

"Two months, minimum," Dr James insisted. "Any jostling now risks irreparable damage."

Richard raked an agitated hand through his hair. "But it has been nearly one month already!"

The doctor frowned and opened his case to begin putting his instruments away. "Then six more weeks. At least."

"Ridiculous. Such a protracted confinement itself threatens his recovery! Cannot we fashion some sort of litter? I would hire an entire team of men to carry it!"

But Dr James refused to be swayed, detailing again the critical fragility of Darcy's spine and nerves. Meanwhile, Darcy stared hollowly at the far wall as their debate washed over him. Crushing helplessness threatened to drag him into fathomless despair. Would he be trapped in this useless body and sickroom forever? Doomed to stare at the same walls each dreary day, dependent on others for his most basic needs, while life went on without him?

"Enough!" he suddenly snarled with as much venom as he could muster. "I'll hear no more foolish talk of moving what cannot be mended! Now get out, both of you!"

"But Darcy—" Richard began gently.

Darcy only turned his face away. Their hovering pity gnawed at the ragged edges of his composure. "Leave me be, damn it all."

At least the doctor withdrew, but Richard had no such decency. He paced by the hearth, heaving a sigh now and again. Finally, he stopped to toy with the wick of the lantern on the mantel. "Father means to call on you tomorrow."

Darcy closed his eyes wearily. "I am hardly fit for the earl's scrutiny."

"He comes only to help. More for appearance' sake than anything. As shall Mother, when she calls here publicly tomorrow to meet your new wife."

Wife. The word jolted Darcy from his self-pity. "Will Mrs Darcy manage that performance? She seemed... unwell earlier. I fear we have asked a great deal of her."

Richard nodded grimly and moved toward the door. "Marriage to you, even under the best circumstances, would challenge the staunchest constitution. Perhaps we might suggest she dine privately here with you? Better to prepare her for the coming ordeal."

Darcy grasped at this lifeline as his cousin withdrew. Somehow, he must offer what meagre comfort he could to his vulnerable young wife this night.

D
ARCY SHIFTED IMPATIENTLY AGAINST his pile of pillows, wondering what could be keeping his new bride. He knew a maid had been sent to inform Mrs Darcy of her husband's dinner invitation, yet the ornate clock on the mantel showed the hour already a quarter past eight. Elizabeth was now fifteen minutes late to their first meal alone together.

He glanced over the intimate table set beside his bed. In an effort to make the occasion special, he had ordered Cook to prepare a mouthwatering meal of Negus, mackerel, roasted capon, a variety of pickled vegetables, and sweet apple tarts—a menu far richer than his convalescent diet thus far. The savoury aromas made Darcy's empty stomach rumble and churn. Well, at least some part of his blasted body still functioned properly. Small consolation.

Where was she, though? Surely, even a woman grieving the loss of her family and freedom could not be so distracted as to forget her own wedding dinner. Was his bride having second thoughts already? He stared at the door that led out to the hall, willing it to open. Minutes dragged by.

He briefly considered ringing for his valet and inquiring after Mrs Darcy's whereabouts, but embarrassment stayed his hand. It would not do to seem so pathetically eager for a woman's company—even if she was now his wife. Perhaps she meant to be fashionably late to assert her independence. If so, he refused to indulge such childish antics by chasing after her.

Just as irritation hardened into resolve to begin the meal alone, the inner door creaked softly. Darcy's glance flew upward, haughty reproach on his tongue dying at the sight that met his eyes. Elizabeth—his wife, he must continually remind himself—stood hovering just over the threshold of his bedchamber. To his astonishment, she was peeking tentatively through the very door meant for private passage between man and wife. Sudden understanding pierced Darcy even as her startled gaze met his.

Of course—that discreet entrance was intended to permit private, midnight rovings between the passionate newly wedded lady and lord of the house. Activities that Darcy could only dream of now with mournful futility. Fresh shame scalded through him at the unintended mockery, until Elizabeth dropped her eyes and stepped hurriedly into the room with flaming cheeks.

"Forgive my tardiness, Mr Darcy." She twisted her hands before herself, clearly mortified. "I... I must have lost track of the hour."

Darcy tamped down the resentment churning his gut through sheer force of will. None of this awkward situation was her doing. He must make her comfortable, though the effort cost his pride.

"Please, have a seat, Mrs Darcy." He gestured to the chair arranged precisely within his limited sightline. As she perched anxiously on its edge, Darcy scrutinised her features more closely. Lingering evidence of recent tears marked her delicate complexion, along with tension in every line of her slight frame. Apparently, the full reality of her new confined existence was settling upon his young bride most painfully tonight.

"You must be famished after your lengthy toilette." Darcy strove to keep any sharpness from his tone, gesturing instead to the untouched dishes. "Let us eat before the fare grows cold."

Elizabeth hesitantly served herself small portions, though her eyes lingered almost longingly on the generous spread. As she picked daintily at the capon, Darcy could see that she forcefully restrained already impeccable table manners, lest she betray unladylike hunger. Just how long had she isolated herself weeping before deigning to join him? His stomach crawled with remorse at the thought.

"I regret if my invitation distressed you." He watched her closely between bites of capon, willing himself to patience. "Being so new to my household and habits, you should know that you have leave to dine privately whenever you wish. Simply inform me in the future."

Silent tears glittered at the corners of her eyes, though she kept them averted. When she trusted her voice enough not to shake, Elizabeth answered softly, "You are most considerate, sir, but I shall grow accustomed to... my new situation soon enough."

Darcy's chest tightened at her brave front, masking obvious homesickness. Acting on impulse, he extended his hand to cover her clenched fingers. "I know everything is painfully strange and new, with little chance to even miss what you left behind." He hesitated. "If there is anything I might do to ease your transition here, you have only to name it."

That coaxed a watery half-smile from her even as she dabbed surreptitiously at her eyes with a handkerchief. "You are too generous, sir. I shall be perfectly well on the morrow, once the initial shock wears off. Please pay me no mind."

Privately, Darcy doubted the veracity of that claim, but he merely squeezed her hand lightly before releasing it. "Let us speak of more pleasant subjects, then." Casting about, he asked curiously, "Have you discovered the library here yet? I possess a fair collection of tomes I think you would enjoy."

Her mouth turned up shyly. "Not yet, but you made mention of it yesterday. And again, earlier this morning. I begin to think you were using it as bait."

"Of course I was."

She ducked her face in a quiet chuckle as she examined her plate with her fork. "So, it is not only your cousin who knows how to work a situation for his own benefit."

Darcy sipped from his wine glass and set it aside carefully before responding. "Richard does what he thinks he must. Never be afraid to refuse, if he should ask something of you that you cannot render cheerfully. He will respect that, much as he may sputter and fume. But as for myself, I abhor all manner of disguise and manipulation. This... situation... has grated on me more than you can know."

She shifted in her chair, tipping her face to regard him openly. "You are protecting your sister. I believe a man can be forgiven a great deal—even open deceit—if his intentions are just."

"You do? So, you think the ends justify the means?"

Her brow furrowed and she looked at her lap in thought. "No... not precisely. I mean that the spirit of honesty is, at its heart, intended to help and not harm others. What good is it to be fully honest, for instance, when my Aunt Philips asks if she is looking a little too plump for her walking dress? Should I tell her something that will hurt her?"

"Perhaps if the truth motivates her to improve the situation..."

"But it will not. Therefore, all I can achieve by telling her the bald truth is to make her cry. So, I turn the truth a bit, by telling her I think she looks in the bloom of health."

Darcy shook his head. "A kindly meant mistruth about your aunt's figure is nothing to what we have proposed to do. Conceal the fact that my sister let herself be led astray, that that brute savaged her and left her with child? Pass that child off as my own... *our* own... just to keep the estate in the Darcy name?"

Elizabeth studied him as she sipped a little of her own wine. "You must have a great many people who depend on you."

"More than I can number."

"And what would become of them if the estate did fall to the next in line? Is he noble and honourable? Would he treat his tenants fairly, manage those who work at Pemberley and your London house well?"

Darcy's face closed down as his stomach roiled. "No. He... I would rather not speak of him."

"Then, Mr Darcy, if your intent is to shield those under your protection from an unjust man, I see no alternative for you apart from turning the truth to reveal its more... flattering side."

"But it is still a lie."

"Is it? Will we treat the child any differently than we would if he were our natural son?"

"Of course not. But if you erase the hard truths set in stone, inconvenient though they may be, all you are left with is an uncertain sketch in the sand—one that blows with the wind and changes whenever the light hits it differently."

She thinned her lips. "I cannot disagree with that. But perhaps the ultimate test of rightness or wrongness is your intent—your resolve not to bring harm to the innocent."

"And you trust me to know enough of the future to determine where I can safely stretch the truth and where it must be left unmolested?"

Her teeth flashed in a genuine smile. "Honestly? I do not know yet whether I can trust you at all... but I am hopeful. You have yet to harm me."

Darcy could not help but smile some in return. "Only because I am incapable of doing so."

Elizabeth's eyebrow arched, a touch of playfulness emerging in her look. "Oh, I doubt that very much, sir. Are you aware of how very dashing you look when you are not scowling at a lady?"

"Flattery already, Mrs Darcy? What do you want?"

She dabbed her mouth lightly with her napkin and set it aside, then leaned toward him. "Happiness. For both of us. Do you think that possible, Mr Darcy?"

He considered her face for a moment. By heaven, it just might be. At least she was interesting, and not unintelligent. He extended his hand to her and nodded as she rested her fingers on top of his. "Let us hope, Mrs Darcy."

"Good. Now, let us do justice to your cook's excellent dessert. May I?" She bit into one of the apple tarts with a fork, skewered it, and cupped her hand under it to offer it to him.

Well? Why not? He was already sick to death of Giles helping him eat, but this was different. If he had not been a cripple... if this was a romantic first dinner with his new bride under auspicious circumstances, and she had made such a gesture, he would have accepted, and gladly. He would even reciprocate. Darcy leaned forward as much as he was able and let her slide the bite of tart into his mouth. And delighted in the way her entire face lit up in response to his acceptance.

By the time the apple tarts had been reduced to crumbs, he knew what her laugh sounded like. And before the maid had come to clear away the tray, she had drawn her chair closer to his bed to listen to him describe the ten-mile park around Pemberley. And he had discovered a new appreciation for a pair of fine eyes in the face of a pretty woman.

Sometime after the clock struck eleven, and the aching weariness of his body, combined with the effects of too much wine had begun to overpower him, Elizabeth rose from the chair and gathered her skirts around her. "Thank you for your thoughtfulness this evening, Mr Darcy. I find I am glad to become better acquainted."

Unexpected warmth kindled in Darcy's chest at her words. "The sentiment is mutual, Mrs Darcy."

Chapter Eleven

E LIZABETH SMOOTHED HER GOWN for the tenth time, anxious energy and dread churning her stomach. She would rather face a roomful of ladies weighing her every fault than endure this torture a moment longer.

"Courage, Mrs Darcy." Colonel Fitzwilliam smiled bracingly, though tension pinched his eyes. "As chief patroness of Almack's, my mother's approval carries enormous influence."

Elizabeth managed a brittle laugh. "Then I am rightly doomed, for never have I curried favour from those who deemed themselves my betters." At his startled look, she amended, "Forgive me, I speak from nerves. Ordinarily, I welcome every acquaintance equitably."

"There is no need to be someone you are not, for my mother's sake. Simply be your natural self, and she shall adore your lively charm and ready wit."

She doubted that very much. Elizabeth pressed her lips together and said no more. How could she explain that her 'natural self' had never bothered cultivating London's rigid social expectations? That she possessed not a clue how to gracefully ingratiate herself with a society matron who likely scorned all things provincial, let alone one whose endorsement was critical to maintaining this sham marriage's fragile credibility?

Utterly out of her depth, Elizabeth peered through the window's edge as an opulent town coach bearing the Matlock crest pulled up outside. This was it. Sink or swim alone. She straightened her shoulders as the butler admitted His Lordship and Lady Matlock.

Lord Matlock charged in, barrel-chested and ruddy-faced beneath his fashionable hat. After a cursory handshake with his son and a polite greeting to her, he declared bluntly,

"Well, Richard, let us go up. I am eager to see Darcy's progress since you summoned me post-haste from Cumberland."

With a sympathetic grimace at Elizabeth, Richard followed his father upstairs. Alone now with Lady Matlock, Elizabeth dropped into a deep curtsy under the piercing scrutiny of that lady's shrewd hazel eyes. Keen intelligence and steely resolve marked the countess's ageing but still lovely features, framed by expertly-coiffed golden hair now streaked becomingly with grey.

"So, you are the creature my son claims will restore health and cheer to poor Fitzwilliam's sick room." Her Ladyship eyed Elizabeth's gown and figure critically before sighing. "Well, we have our work cut out, I daresay."

She gestured impatiently for a trunk borne in by footmen. "Come girl, help me unpack these. We must hurry to prepare you before callers arrive."

Feeling utterly stupid, Elizabeth stared bewilderedly into the trunk bursting with rich fabrics and fripperies. When she did not immediately move to assist, Lady Matlock fixed her with an impatient stare.

"Come, come, girl! We haven't much time to transform this provincial frock into something fashionable before all the world arrives at our door!"

Elizabeth jolted to life, gingerly lifting out a cut silk evening gown. "But was not the purpose for callers today merely to substantiate my background as Mrs Darcy?" She avoided the lady's suddenly narrowed gaze. "I... I confess I am unsure how to go about that as I've never moved in society."

Lady Matlock stilled, scrutinising Elizabeth intently. "No matter. We shall teach you." Some indefinable emotion crossed her face before she lifted a strand of Elizabeth's hair almost tenderly. "I confess you are not what I pictured for Fitzwilliam Darcy's wife, but my son claims you have sterling qualities of your own. You must be something rather remarkable if he managed to talk Darcy into having you." She tilted Elizabeth's chin. "Keep your courage up, and you may just manage splendidly. Now, about this gown..."

Elizabeth eyed her reflection with growing dismay as Lady Matlock's maid, Brigitte, yanked a brush ruthlessly through her unruly curls once more. This was the third attempt at taming them into smooth submission, despite Elizabeth subtly suggesting her hair would likely rebel against such harsh treatment.

"Oh!" She barely swallowed back the instinctive yelp as the brush snagged a sizable knot, her eyes watering.

Lady Matlock glanced up with a critical frown from where she was supervising Beth, pinning the hem of an elaborate morning gown. "Come Brigitte, we haven't all day to style Mrs Darcy's hair. Guests will arrive within the hour."

"But my lady, these wild locks resist capture." Brigitte gave another sharp tug, twisting Elizabeth's scalp relentlessly. "I cannot seem to make them comply as I would wish. Shall I fetch more rosewater?"

Even Beth winced in sympathy from her hovering spot nearby as Elizabeth bit her tongue. This torture seemed never-ending! Finally, she could stand the misery no more.

"Please, might I try arranging my own hair?" At Lady Matlock's astonished look, she rushed on, "I beg pardon, only I know from experience, erm... a simpler style best suits my curls."

Lady Matlock raised one eloquent brow. "Simpler, yes, if one intends to appear in the village, perhaps! But we must make a statement befitting your new status, and today is only the beginning."

Elizabeth's courage faltered. Of course, Lady Matlock had orchestrated countless society events and overseen probably a dozen debutantes; who was she to suggest alternate coifs?

As Brigitte prepared another round of hair cream, Lady Matlock studied Elizabeth, then turned sharply to Beth. "Here girl, you attended Mrs Darcy this morning, and her hair was... well, nothing notable, but neither did it resemble a frayed bird's nest as it does now. How did you dress her hair differently than Brigitte here without rendering it smooth?"

Beth flushed, curtsying awkwardly. "Begging your pardon, my lady, I... I did little but twist up some strands. I haven't much experience with formal styling." She shot Elizabeth an apologetic glance in the mirror.

Comprehension lit Lady Matlock's eyes. "I see. Perhaps we needn't wrestle quite so forcefully with what resists taming." Catching Elizabeth's hopeful look, she grudgingly allowed, "Very well, Mrs Darcy, show us what you consider 'simple and suitable' for your wild tresses."

Collective relief eased the room's strained atmosphere as Elizabeth upended her head to scrunch her curls back to their normal shape. Then she quickly pinned her hair up in a softly becoming, if relatively unfussy, style. She bit back a satisfied smile at Lady Matlock's approving hum. Sometimes, yielding produced far greater victories than outright war. And in this, at least, she could honour her true self while upholding expectations.

The delicate illusion shattered moments later as Brigitte and Beth swarmed Elizabeth to sew her into the elegant gown that required substantial last-minute alterations. But the ordeal's end drew inexorably closer, heralded by the breathless maid delivering the anticipated news of Elizabeth's first callers waiting below.

"Their names?" Lady Matlock asked.

"Lady Brockhurst and her daughter, Lady Amelia, and Mrs Spencer with her daughter, Miss Emmeline Spencer."

Lady Matlock permitted herself a little smile of triumph. "The cats come to mark their territory."

Elizabeth could not conceal the scandalised look she shot Lady Matlock. Even uncouth boys were not permitted such callous speech in front of ladies!

Her Ladyship dismissed the maid, then turned to Elizabeth. "You will have to forgive me, my dear. I have long waited for the day when Darcy takes a bride, and it is not one of their daughters, simply to see them lose their feathers. You will find me rather unrepentant at their loss, I daresay."

"Precisely..." Elizabeth narrowed her eyes and tilted her head. "How many young ladies had their hopes set on Mr Darcy?"

Lady Matlock's look turned smug. "All of them. Well! At least every unmarried lady who will march through your drawing room today, Mrs Darcy."

Elizabeth sucked in a breath and brushed a hand down the front of her gown. "I see. I hope I can do the gentleman credit."

The lady surveyed her critically and then nodded once. "You shall suit perfectly well, Mrs Darcy. Chin up and remember—so long as you hold your courage, no one can claim victory over you."

Elizabeth smoothed her skirts, rallying her nerves with a wavering smile. "Courage is rarely my failing. Minding my tongue in polite company may prove the greater challenge."

D ARCY SHIFTED RESTLESSLY, STEELING himself as the bedchamber door opened to admit his uncle, the earl, and his cousin. Any conversation centred around his wretched condition and unknown future hardly qualified as cheerful discourse. Yet there was no point in putting it off, and their boisterous company was preferable to brooding alone.

Lord Matlock charged in, bristling. "Well, boy? Report! How fare you since Richard sent that urgent summons? What does the doctor say? And what absurd scheme has my son concocted now?"

Before Darcy could voice a biting retort, his uncle rounded furiously on Richard. "I pray you possess some fragment of a sensible design for restoring order, or must I intervene with damage control?"

Curbing his irritation, Darcy interjected sardonically, "I fare much the same, sir. My back remains fractured, and my legs useless meat, but I am making progress in mastering my temper. And despite low expectations, my new bride proves less objectionable company than anticipated."

He repressed a spurt of defensive anger at his uncle's audible harrumph. "Well, at least you haven't frightened off this wife of yours yet. Seems a pretty enough girl, I suppose." Lord Matlock eyed Darcy critically. "But how the devil is she to manage you and an entire household on looks alone?"

Heat crawled up Darcy's neck. "I'll remind you, Mrs Darcy is not some decorative broodmare installed for fashion's sake. Your own son suggested her based on her other merits. Whatever burdens we all bear henceforth, she chose this marriage with eyes wide to the stark realities and expectations. I'll not tolerate hearing her doubted or disparaged."

Chastened, Lord Matlock held up conciliatory hands. "Peace, Nephew, that was unfair. We hold Mrs Darcy in the highest esteem already, have no fear. But difficult decisions must be weighed now concerning your family's immediate future."

Darcy's restless hands knotted in the bed sheets. "Then speak of something marginally productive. I am descending into madness staring at these same walls interminably each accursed day."

"Quite right." Lord Matlock stroked his chin pensively. "Georgiana must be moved to Lady Matlock's estate in Scotland without delay. Call it what you will—a pleasure tour, whatever is necessary to satisfy any curiosity. Lady Matlock has already interviewed a few potential candidates for a companion—it must be someone of the highest discretion. Of a certainty, we cannot leave the girl at Pemberley while her condition advances. You producing an heir born 'prematurely' can be swept under the rug. But I will not suffer my niece's reputation to be destroyed forever by her own servants, even at Pemberley."

Darcy lay his head back on the pillow and closed his eyes. Move Georgiana even further from all that was familiar to her with yet another strange companion? Farther from him and Richard and any comfort she might have left? Insupportable.

But the earl had not yet done. "While this initial crisis stabilises, I suggest keeping Mrs Darcy in London some months, where she can be taught and aided by Lady Matlock and where the best surgeons in the country may assist your recovery."

Panic constricted Darcy's chest. "I've no intention of lingering anywhere near Town. Hang the doctors. They can do nothing for me, anyway. I wish to make for Pemberley, to be amongst familiar comforts and see my sister before you send her off."

"See here, Cousin." Richard threw up exasperated hands. "Be reasonable! I want you out of London as badly as you wish to be away, but jostling over rough roads could badly exacerbate your injuries before the worst swelling subsides. And exposing your... precarious condition... to Georgiana might well undo the girl completely right now!"

Indignation rising, Darcy bit out through clenched teeth. "Blast it, it is not as if I would be shunted about like some damned parcel! I have the most comfortable carriages made, and I stand as the best judge of my household's welfare." Unexpected grief momentarily choked his bitter passion. "Georgiana needs steadying family support. She has only me left... And her new sister."

The ringing silence hanging after this naked admission slowly recalled Darcy to himself. Chagrined by such loss of rigid self-command, he averted his face, struggling to harness tumultuous emotions again. "I will not deprive her of what comfort I may offer."

Gentler than before, Lord Matlock cleared his throat. "There lies the rub, indeed. Georgiana does need you. But she must be secured away from gossip, while your wife's reputation must be formally secured in Town first so that Society will accept her. She will be your wife for a very long time, beyond the needs of the moment. Would you damage your family's future by harming Mrs Darcy's prospects now? Let her be known and seen."

Humourless laughter rasped Darcy's throat. "You mean let her be trotted out on display to be gawked at? Even now, the harpies circle, hungering to shred her dignity simply for daring to accept me." Outrage kindled, cracking his formidable willpower. "I'll not see my wife subjected to petty malice merely to gild appearances."

Richard got up and began to pace, as he always did. "Be sensible, though! If you two flee London pell-mell, it will only breed more salacious gossip."

Granite determination infused Darcy's stern gaze as it locked challengingly on his cousin and then his uncle in turn. "I care not a whit. Arrange whatever is needed, but I wish to depart this foetid city as soon as possible, making for Pemberley."

When they still stared dumbfounded by his effrontery, he bit out sharply, "Test me further in this, and I shall endeavour to drag myself hence by very force of will if need be. But hear me plain—wild horses could not induce me to linger one day more than absolutely necessary as a curiosity for those covetous vipers to disparage my family and pick apart our privacy. My wife deserves far better consideration from me."

The ensuing stunned silence stretched taut until Lord Matlock loosed a grunt of surrender. "Well, I can see you will not be moved. So be it. We shall contrive solutions as we may... and pray Heaven assists us all." Shooting one brooding glance heavenward as if enacting said prayers already, he took his leave, with Richard trailing after him, still voicing muted protests.

E LIZABETH FOLDED HER HANDS before her, girding herself as the drawing room doors opened to admit the first callers. Lady Brockhurst entered, feathered turban towering ominously atop iron-grey curls. Her daughter, Lady Amelia, stalked behind, sharp features pinched in disdainful scrutiny.

"Lady Matlock, such a delight as always!" Lady Brockhurst exclaimed with venomous sweetness, ignoring Elizabeth completely. "We hurried to congratulate dear Mr Darcy on his nuptials directly we heard."

"Though it was never hinted at when last we dined together," Lady Amelia noted archly. "Sudden matches inevitably provoke... curiosity."

Elizabeth bristled, but Lady Matlock waved them lazily toward seats before turning to her with smiling nonchalance. "May I present my nephew's new bride, Mrs Elizabeth Darcy? My dear, these are Lady Brockhurst and Lady Amelia, and Mrs Spencer and Miss Spencer."

Their assessing eyes raked Elizabeth's hastily refashioned gown with transparent scepticism before Lady Brockhurst inclined her head by increments. "Charmed... although I confess, my dear, I find it rather unrefined when nuptials are conducted in such unseemly dispatch. Such a shame none were permitted to share in your joy yesterday."

Before Elizabeth could unleash a scalding retort, Lady Matlock interjected smoothly, "We must blame the impetuosity of youth and attraction. Is it not delicious seeing our Fitzwilliam Darcy so thoroughly enchanted? He is just the sort to surprise us all!"

Lady Amelia's thin lip curled faintly. "Come now, not a month past, he never danced attendance at any society event. One wonders how you secured his admiration so swiftly."

"Why, the splendid charms of the countryside can kindle the most ardent romance," Elizabeth replied lightly. "Who knows what small joys drew dear Mr Darcy so often to Hertfordshire's scenic delights?"

Mrs Spencer gave an indelicate snort. "Mr Darcy has hardly stirred from the city in an age, it seems. However did you ensnare his attentions from the country, Mrs Darcy?"

Elizabeth tilted her head thoughtfully. "Indeed? You must keep very close watch upon the gentleman's travels. I assure you, he has been known to slip his lead now and again when it suits."

She fancied she glimpsed Lady Matlock hastily smothering a smile before schooling her features. Clearing her throat, the countess interjected fondly, "Oh, it was clear from the first that my nephew was utterly enchanted by this young lady's charms."

"Such daring self-expression you showcase with the styling of your hair, Mrs Darcy. So very... quaint. However do you dream up such delights?"

Elizabeth smiled wickedly. "I am afraid yesterday passed in such a wondrous whirlwind that the duty of receiving callers the very morning after my wedding nearly slipped my mind. My poor abigail made of my coiffure what she could with such notice. In hindsight, I ought to have adorned my head with a turban for fashion's sake, or perhaps feathers, but they always cause me to sneeze."

Lady Brockhurst scarcely prevented her jaw from dropping open at Elizabeth's audacity. Well and good. Let these pretentious ladies think Elizabeth had been reclining abed at an indecent hour with her new husband. So much the better. From the corner of her eye, she was sure of it this time—Lady Matlock was hardly able to contain her internal laughter.

Mrs Spencer cleared her throat delicately, her cheeks scarlet as her daughter could hardly lift her eyes from embarrassment. "Ah, indeed, my dear. I daresay, country life must agree with you extremely well. No doubt the fresh air nurtures such... rosy... complexions as yours."

Lady Matlock sipped her tea daintily and glanced away. "My dear Mrs Spencer, surely you do not confuse that new bride's blush with the flush of country air. The one would have faded as soon as she arrived in London, but the other? I believe it is there to stay."

Lady Brockhurst had recovered her wits somewhat, and she addressed Elizabeth with a challenging stare. "You *must* enlighten us as to your connexions, my dear. Wherever did you pass last Season?"

"My connexions? Why, I am sure you would not be intimately acquainted with the finer families of Hertfordshire."

"Then, have you yet to enjoy a London season?" Lady Brockhurst pressed, her hawk-like focus returning. "Have you never been presented at court or danced at Almack's, perhaps?"

"Heavens, can one even claim to have lived properly without such essential experiences?" Elizabeth placed one hand over her heart in theatrical dismay. "What a woefully deprived upbringing I must confess to, but my dear Mr Darcy was my first introduction to London society. I dearly hope I may depend on your charity in introducing me to the right people?"

She smothered a smile as ladies gasped, no doubt interpreting her words as a confession of scandal or outrageous behaviour that had somehow secured the elusive Mr Darcy's sudden proposal to a country nobody. A seduction of sorts was the only explanation they would be likely to accept. Well, if it was scandal they wanted, Elizabeth was happy to oblige their imaginations by letting them form their own notions, entirely without her input.

Before more loaded queries followed, two more ladies were admitted to the drawing room. As each successive caller passed through, thinly veiled remarks and backhanded compliments dominated the conversation. Elizabeth quickly lost track of their names, but the questions repeated themselves again and again, always with the same taint to the words.

On it wore as Elizabeth fielded presumptive comments and arch inquiries behind a politic veneer. Though these ladies eyed her as some odd provincial specimen undeserving of notice, she possessed weapons of her own. She would demonstrate that a gentleman's daughter met unkindness with grace.

At long last, the taxing ordeal ended as the final parasitic guest took her leave. Alone now but for Lady Matlock, Elizabeth permitted her rigid smile to transform into a grimace of distaste. She sank onto a silk damask sofa, feeling rather scorched.

"Well! You acquitted yourself admirably," Lady Matlock mused. "I confess, I harboured doubts."

Elizabeth massaged her throbbing temples wearily. "Pray tell, are thinly veiled slights and sly digs customary for society matrons greeting unknown brides?"

Lady Matlock's tinkling laughter filled the air. "Why, if you thought those were *subtle* slights, I have taught you nothing, my dear! But take heart." Her keen gaze warmed several degrees. "You have fine mettle indeed to have endured so stoically. Yes, I do believe you may just manage after all."

Somehow coaxed from fatigue by this first small victory, Elizabeth managed a genuine chuckle. "I certainly hope so! Matching wits works up a fierce appetite."

Lady Matlock patted her hand. "Then come, let us investigate the nuncheon menu. I confess I am famished myself after supervising those battles of propriety and jealousy so adeptly disguised as courtesy. To the dining room!"

Chapter Twelve

ELIZABETH HURRIED TO MATCH Lady Matlock's brisk pace as they swept through the servants' corridors towards the housekeeper's small office adjoining the kitchens. Mrs Hodges rose swiftly from her desk, her chatelaine of household keys jangling ominously as her eyes assessed Elizabeth with warmth. Lady Matlock provided brief introductions.

"I understand you have already met the housekeeper, Mrs Darcy? Mrs Hodges, your mistress shall rely on your experience managing affairs here, and I daresay, this house has long needed a mistress. I trust you will provide ample guidance coordinating the staff?"

"Of course, my lady." Mrs Hodges softened her formal mien, offering Elizabeth an encouraging smile. "All remains in hand awaitin' your direction, Ma'am." Before Elizabeth could mask her surprise, the housekeeper pressed a heavy ring bearing numerous keys into her numb hand.

Elizabeth scanned the formidable chatelaine, each brass key representing some unknown domain she must now oversee. Would she ever distinguish wine cellar from linen closet? Clearly, these women expected her to seamlessly assume oversight of unfamiliar duties. "You are too kind. Perhaps we might start with a brief tour of the... of the kitchens? And I should like to meet my maids and footmen." She cringed internally, hearing her voice shake on the presumptuous word 'my.' This grand residence felt no more her own than Buckingham Palace!

But the housekeeper's expression warmed further, sensing her acute discomfiture. "An excellent notion! The servants be anxious to meet their new mistress."

"They are?"

Misinterpreting her wide eyes, Lady Matlock waved one elegant hand. "Fear not, Mrs Darcy. Everyone employed in this house will show you the proper respect. This is only a formality—we shall establish routines soon enough. Naturally, no lavish entertainments will occur presently; however, certain proprieties must be observed."

Proprieties? Elizabeth's knees wobbled. Sketching a weak curtsy to the still-hovering housekeeper, she managed faintly, "Indeed, I rely utterly on your guidance to keep me from ludicrous mistakes, my lady. And you as well, Mrs Hodges."

Mrs Hodges smiled reassuringly. "All will be well, Ma'am." With an encouraging nod from Lady Matlock, she withdrew to assemble the servants. Moments later, Elizabeth found herself walking down a line of starched aprons and crisp white caps, each bobbing deferentially as she repeated their names and tried to catalogue their stations in the house. If Mr Darcy's London house, which she had been told was small in comparison to his estate, boasted this many servants, how was she to keep them all straight when she at last reached Pemberley? Finally, the introductions were over, and she drew a shaky breath.

Alone now with her formidable mentor, Elizabeth felt herself under thorough scrutiny again. "Well, Mrs Darcy, though diversions are few at present, you shall hold a formal caller day twice weekly. And, of course, accompany me calling elsewhere to establish your presence." Lady Matlock pursed her lips critically. "Additionally, the menus and household accounts will require your personal approval moving forward."

"Naturally." Elizabeth's answering smile felt fixed as panic compressed her chest. Wine lists and societal appearances were nowhere in her scant repertoire! Sensing imminent flight, Lady Matlock took her arm firmly.

"Come, let me show you to Darcy's study. More affairs await your management there." She led her down the hall and stopped before a pair of formidable oak doors, then looked pointedly at Elizabeth's crowded key ring.

Elizabeth blanched. "You cannot mean that I should..."

"I mean precisely that. Surely, you have the key."

Elizabeth regarded the heavy ring. Some were clearly door keys. Others looked like they might unlock cabinets or desks. She swallowed and tested one that looked like it fitted into a door lock, but it did not turn.

Her courage faltered. "But surely, Colonel Fitzwilliam..."

Lady Matlock snorted. "My son is many things, but deft with a pen is not one of them. No, my dear, this requires a mistress's touch. Go on, then, try another key."

After six more attempts, Elizabeth stumbled upon one that turned with a satisfying clunk. The door swung open at her touch, but Elizabeth hesitated on the threshold, wetting her lips. "Are you certain I ought to intrude on my husband's private sanctum without welcome? My father never permitted…"

"You are Mrs Darcy now, not a country squire's dowdy wife. Forgive my harshness, but so it is. Mr Darcy's social concerns are yours now, too." Lady Matlock ushered her inside the handsome masculine space. "See here? Richard left all correspondence sadly mouldering these three weeks. You must help my nephew answer party invitations and such. Too long without a reply tends to breed gossip, my dear. A wedding might be excuse enough for the delays thus far, but that must end now."

Mutely, Elizabeth gathered the intimidating stack on the desk, profoundly out of her depth. Before she could fashion a coherent reply, hurried footsteps preceded an anxious knock.

"Mother? Ah, and Mrs Darcy too, excellent." Colonel Fitzwilliam flashed a taut smile. "Darcy's particular friend Charles Bingley has arrived, requesting an audience to congratulate him on his marriage. I have refused all other callers, telling them that Darcy is discussing important business with Father today. But Bingley is a modest chap, and he is not calling merely out of politeness's sake. I think he would only return on the morrow if Darcy does not receive him."

Elizabeth squinted. "What are you saying, Colonel? You want to invite him up to see Mr Darcy? Or you want to find some other way of sending him off?"

"I believe Bingley could be trusted not to spread tales." He searched Elizabeth's face beseechingly. "Might Darcy be disposed to receive him briefly?"

Both pairs of eyes turned expectantly to her. Elizabeth's tongue clove uselessly to her palate. "How should I know?" she blurted.

"Because it is your place to know," Lady Matlock inserted, not unkindly. "Is Mr Darcy at home to Mr Bingley, or is he not?"

"I suppose… if… if Mr Darcy agrees, perhaps his friend might raise his spirits?" Impossibly, she felt herself gaining the door. "I shall inquire directly."

Safely in the hall, she pressed one hand over her lurching stomach. How was she to determine anything when she hardly knew her own mind? Perhaps the impossible would not always remain so. On quaking limbs, she mounted the stairs.

D ARCY GLANCED UP FROM his book as the door opened, irked by the interruption until Elizabeth's light figure entered. Quick pleasure warmed him when she sent an assessing look over his condition before bestowing a radiant smile.

"Well met, Mrs Darcy. To what do I owe the honour?"

Her gaze fell on his volume, brows rising delightedly. "Why, I see you have taken up Don Quixote! Preparing for another debate you shall surely lose?"

Darcy allowed himself a small smile, admiring her good humour—a refreshing contrast to the parade of sympathetic dullards who had attended him so far. "A bored man will read anything. I merely wished to better comprehend this knight you so admire."

"Knight, indeed! More like a deluded fool."

"My point exactly." His eyes lingered teasingly over her indignant flush. "You look quite fetching when passionately disputing lost causes, you know."

Colour heightened further in her cheeks before she recovered her poise. "You, sir, resemble Don Quixote more than you realise. But I came on another errand. A Mr Bingley has called, and asks leave to congratulate your nuptials personally. Colonel Fitzwilliam was not as quick to send him away as he has been with others, saying that perhaps you might wish to receive him. Shall I send him up?"

Darcy stiffened. "Bingley? Good lord... Are his sisters with him?"

"I was not told of any ladies, merely Mr Bingley himself."

Dread trickled down his spine at the thought of his genial friend pitying his wretched condition. Elizabeth searched his features questioningly as he loosed a resigned exhale. "Very well. But have Richard prepare him first for... my altered state. And if you would be so good... let him believe that there is hope for my recovery."

He expected immediate acquiescence, but she lingered thoughtfully. "You believe your friend so fragile? Or are you perhaps ashamed for him to witness your confinement?"

Darcy blinked, caught unexpectedly by her perception. "The latter, though I confess Bingley's solicitous pity may swiftly grow cloying during an extended visit. Might I prevail upon you to... interrupt after some quarter hour has passed? So he feels less obliged to linger."

Comprehension lit her eyes. "Easily done, sir."

With a rustle of skirts, she turned for the door before Darcy's softened voice halted her again. "And Mrs Darcy? Thank you."

As she withdrew, Darcy nervously smoothed the bedclothes, steeling himself. But the radiance of her answering smile warmed him long after she had gone.

A TENTATIVE KNOCK HERALDED Bingley hovering at the door, features creased in dismay. "Darcy! My dear fellow, I came the instant I heard about your marriage. Then this is... well... dash it all!"

Darcy managed a wan smile, though bitterness coated his tongue. "Please, Bingley, spare me the tragic lamentations. Sit, if you can bear remaining."

"Forgive me, forgive me!" Bingley perched anxiously on the chair edge as if fearing his friend might shatter. "I confess, it is a dreadful shock to see you thus confined. But have courage! Surely the doctors predict a full recovery soon?" His hopeful gaze strayed too frequently to Darcy's inert legs.

Squelching irritation, Darcy relaxed his rigid jaw with effort. "Time will tell. I am content enough for now."

"Well, I daresay *I* should go mad imprisoned so! Imagine being unable to stand up with your bride at your own wedding?" Bingley chuckled self-consciously at Darcy's thin answering smile. "But you always were more pragmatic than I. Truly, I hope all rights itself swiftly. You deserve to... er... enjoy marital felicity to the utmost."

Burning silence followed this well-meaning speech. "Your, ah... your sisters. Are they well?" As Bingley began to babble about all his family's doings, Darcy watched the clock, already praying for Elizabeth's timely rescue.

"Louisa married Mr Hurst recently in Scarborough. He has a fine establishment there, but they have been more often at his London townhouse. And Caroline is terribly eager to meet your new wife, once you are receiving guests, of course! I confess we were quite shocked reading your nuptial announcement in the papers. My sister was perfectly speechless for full ten minutes. Oh, Caroline had expected to call on Miss Darcy this visit, but we did not know she was not in Town with you. And then, I suppose, her reasons for calling..." Belatedly realising his insensitive assumption, Bingley trailed off, shamefaced.

Darcy could not help a satisfied grunt. At least he had not found himself saddled with Caroline Bingley. It was too obvious by Bingley's reddened cheeks what Caroline's intentions had been. Bingley claimed he had never encouraged her, but such a woman did not require encouragement. Permission and an inflated sense of her own importance were enough. Darcy glanced at the clock. Only ten minutes had passed.

"Bingley, I trust Fitzwilliam relayed to you my wishes about keeping this matter hushed up for now?" Darcy asked.

"Oh, indeed, indeed. I know you are a private fellow, and well-meaning though they may be, the storm of visitors you would incur would surely try your patience. I say, *have* you been seen by a doctor?"

"Yes," Darcy answered shortly. "He says all will be well soon."

"Oh, that is capital. I say I had dearly hoped to ask your advice on—"

Before he could say more, Elizabeth's knock shattered the uncomfortable moment. Scarcely breathing his profound relief, Darcy beckoned hoarsely, "Enter!"

Elizabeth peered around the door, locking eyes with him and lifting a silver tray stacked high with letters. Oh, blast. She was going to make him do that? Lady Matlock's doing, no doubt.

Bingley shot upright, colour rising. "Mrs Darcy! Forgive me, I ought to take my leave. So kind of you to permit me to intrude when you have scarcely had Darcy to yourself." His smile faltered briefly. "I do hope you shall both be blissfully happy."

"Mr Bingley, you are always welcome." Elizabeth's eyes softened sympathetically on her husband. "But I confess, I must steal Mr Darcy presently on some urgent household matter."

"Oh! Yes, of course." Bingley backed hastily away, though his natural geniality swiftly reasserted itself. "Before I leave, I was about to ask your advice. I understand my timing..."

"What is it?"

"Well, I have given some thought to what you were saying last spring about taking some sort of establishment for myself. There is a house I am considering leasing—a small estate in Hertfordshire, not far from some little town called Meryton."

Elizabeth startled, casting Darcy an arrested glance he could not interpret before schooling her features smoothly. "Meryton, you say? Is the estate called Netherfield, by chance?"

Bingley's smile widened. "Indeed, it is! I say, have you some familiarity with the place, Mrs Darcy?"

"I know it well, sir! I grew up not three miles from there."

Bingley's sunny countenance lit further. "You know it, then! Pray, what think you of the property?"

Elizabeth stroked her throat self-consciously. "Quite comfortable with ample acreage for sheep and crops both. My father deemed it a worthy prospect..." She faltered, glancing uncertainly at Darcy before lifting her chin. "I am Elizabeth Bennet of Longbourn, you see. Or I was."

"Bennet? Of Longbourn, you say? Why, your family would be my neighbours!" At her hesitant nod, his gaze sharpened. "I had planned to call upon the neighbourhood's principal households. Might I mention my introduction to you?"

Elizabeth clasped her hands beseechingly. "If you possess courage for independence. What I mean is that I hope you do not abandon us to local slanders, sir."

He tilted his head. "I do not understand."

Elizabeth's composure momentarily slipped. "In truth, sir, my sisters have suffered much through no fault of their own, and are presently the subject of scorn. I would entreat you to pay such malicious gossip little heed. In particular I beg, do not shun my elder sister Jane if local circles would influence you thus. A kinder soul never breathed."

Bingley's open features creased in solicitous concern. "Any sister of Mrs Darcy's shall have my utmost consideration, dear lady." Buttoning his jacket, he bowed to them both. "I thank you for the excellent advice and wish you happy. Oh…" He paused, a frown pinching his features. "Perhaps I ought to put Caroline and Louisa off calling on Mrs Darcy at present?"

Elizabeth's mouth opened hesitantly, but Darcy cut off the polite reply she was obviously trying to formulate. "Indeed. Tell them Mrs Darcy is too preoccupied for social calls at present."

As Bingley departed, Elizabeth turned to him with an odd smirk. "Prevaricating already to your friend, Mr Darcy? How quickly yesterday's lecturing on honesty fades."

Darcy shifted under her playfully arched brow. "When you meet Miss Bingley, such evasion shall seem the soul of wisdom." He reached impatiently for the substantial correspondence Elizabeth bore. "But come, if that tray you brought in is any indication, we have neglected matters requiring attention."

"'*We*,' sir? Surely, as your wife in name alone, these affairs outstrip my limited purview."

"I am afraid they fall very much within your purview. Best learn now what is to be made of what." He gestured her closer, reaching for the tray. "If you please, allow me to separate invitations requiring responses."

Riffling through, he swiftly sorted several engraved cards into one pile. "Those shall all receive polite refusals. And for these business letters, I shall reply to them myself."

She cast an eloquent eye over his posture. "While reclining like that? Can you write thus?"

"I think you will find my writing hand is not crippled, Mrs Darcy."

"It is not that. You have no solid surface, no rest for your arm. Even a breakfast tray would prove inadequate, and your writing would suffer."

"Very well," he sighed. "You will sit at the desk, and I will dictate the salient points so that you can craft suitable replies."

She furrowed her brow as if she had been hoping for a different outcome but nodded. "I hope my frivolous feminine penmanship is up to the task of answering such serious letters."

"It will have to do."

As Elizabeth made to gather the correspondence, Darcy stayed her hand. "Reply to the invitations, and we shall look over these regarding my investments, but there is no purpose in answering anything from my steward now. We quit London shortly en route for Pemberley."

"Leave London?" Elizabeth sank slowly onto the chair, staring at him in dismay. "But I have only just arrived here from Hertfordshire."

"I regret the haste, but it is necessary. We will go to Pemberley at once and collect Georgiana before we go on to Scotland... or perhaps we will have her travel on ahead, so the household does not know of my..." He shook his head. "No, that will not matter. All the servants here in London know of my accident. It cannot be kept from Mrs Reynolds, but we shall keep the doctor's prognosis quiet until—"

"Scotland!" Elizabeth interrupted.

He stared at her, baffled. "But of course. Why, you do not think we can carry on here, do you? With all of London staring at the house as if the walls were made of glass? We are already anticipating a 'premature' babe, and all too soon, Georgiana's condition will become apparent to the entire household at Pemberley. That cannot be permitted. Our only choice is to leave the country and go where we are not known."

"But... but my family..."

"Did you not swear them off yesterday?" he asked testily.

Her gaze hardened. "Taking your name does not mean I turned my back on my own."

He shook his head and waved a hand. "Forgive me, that was nought but my own impatience speaking. I told Fitzwilliam that I mean for us to be away as soon as a carriage can be fitted."

"To Pemberley, or to Scotland, as you just claimed?" Elizabeth prodded. "How do you propose travelling in your state without doing yourself further injury?"

Nettled at her sceptical tone, Darcy retorted, "I am no fragile invalid! My own welfare remains my affair."

"The welfare of your broken body wed to my care suggests otherwise." Elizabeth arched both brows. "Or would you have me stand helpless while you risk yourself needlessly from misplaced pride?"

"Needlessly? Have you no grasp of what is at stake?" Darcy erupted. How dare she question his judgement regarding Georgiana!

"I grasp that no fortune or honour on earth merits you killing yourself through stubborn recklessness to obtain it!" Elizabeth shot back. "Think, sir. You told me your sister is less than two months pregnant. It will be at least another two months before her figure changes. You could rest some weeks longer, recover your strength somewhat..."

"You cannot be so naïve as that. Know you nothing of a woman's sickness when she is with child? The maids will take note. Some things cannot be kept silent forever. We can take no chances. No, the household would expect me to arrive with my bride as soon as may be, and a wedding tour, welcoming my sister as my wife's companion on the journey, would be nothing unusual. I hope to depart within three days."

"Three days is not sufficient time for any improvement!" she cried in alarm. "What does Colonel Fitzwilliam say to this?"

"Colonel Fitzwilliam is not my master. I am, and I shall thank you to remember that."

She narrowed her eyes. "You cannot even sit up fully now without causing yourself immense pain, and you want to ride over a week in a bouncing carriage over rough roads?"

"It cannot be helped." He gritted his teeth, already dreading precisely what she described.

"You are bloody mad," she growled. "And I'll take no part in it. You may kill yourself if you wish, but I pray the colonel is able to talk some sense into you before you manage it." She was on her feet now, gathering the pile of invitations in trembling hands. "I shall respond to these alone, as you cannot be reasoned with presently. Perhaps once greater wisdom prevails, we might converse again."

She flung open the door between her chamber and his and marched through as Darcy stared after her. Why must she argue everything, blast it all? Well, he had something to say on that score. How dare she simply quit the room without letting him say his piece?

Cursing under his breath, he tossed aside the bedclothes. He would settle affairs his own damned way, without any wilful, impertinent—

A sharp gasp froze him, even as he reached the limits of what his body would perform as if he had just smacked into a window. Elizabeth had returned to the doorway and now stood, staring in renewed horror at his useless legs as comprehension crashed over her expressive features.

"F-forgive me," she stammered, her eyes still fixed on the sight of his bared legs. "I only meant to retrieve the rest of the invitations..."

Mortification raged as he yanked at the bedcovers. "Damnation, I never intended for you to see this humiliation!"

But she moved closer, all frustration fled from her softened countenance. "Please, sir, be at ease. After all, I have never seen a gentleman without his trousers or breeches." Her lips quirked impishly. "Tell me, do all gentlemen possess such abundantly hairy limbs? Or are you singularly blessed?"

Darcy blinked, tension slowly receding. "I fear leg fur is quite standard issue for the average English gentleman." He assayed a weak smile. "My valet keeps threatening to shear me like a spring lamb."

Elizabeth laid a staying hand on his blankets. "Please, do not hide on my account." She searched his features intently. "What manner of marriage are we to have, sir?"

Darcy sobered, throat constricting as his mouth ran dry. "I was plain before—I cannot be your husband in full. My desire far outstrips my current ability."

"Oh, I did not mean..." Colour stole up her neck as she gently drew the covers down once more. Darcy's heart kicked, and a surge of unbidden longing coursed through his veins as one of her hands rested on his arm.

"Surely, there are other types of intimacy between a husband and a wife. Things that may not belong to the marriage bed, but are, nonetheless, improper in any other relationship."

"I..." He gulped. "I do not take your meaning, madam."

She lifted uncertain eyes to his. "I mean... I was always dismayed when observing my parents. They merely tolerated one another's company, never seeking each other out for conversation. But three years ago, Papa took a fever. I shall never forget how Mama nursed him at his bedside! Day and night, she tended him—there was nothing she would not do. Of course, back then, I supposed it was only because she was afraid he would die and we would all be cast into the hedgerows. She certainly said it often enough. But it is proper, is it not, that she should have done that?"

He tried to swallow but found that his breathing was galloping along at such a pace as to make it impossible. "I... I suppose so. But what has that to do with me? I have no fever." Not... *that* sort of fever, anyway.

She gestured to his legs. "I was just thinking of a farm horse Papa used to have. He had injured his stifle and could only drag his toe. Papa was advised to put him out of his misery at once, but Jane and I pleaded with him to let us try to mend him. We were young and silly, I suppose, but we tended the damaged leg daily, to maintain what circulation and life remained by rubbing it with a good liniment and wrapping it with a poultice. In a month or so, he had recovered enough control over his leg that he could walk normally, and in six months, he was able to again pull the plough."

"I am hardly an injured farm horse, Mrs Darcy. If you think to restore sensation to my legs by rubbing them, why..."

"Not that, but to keep the blood moving. Your legs are still part of your body, are they not? You would still bleed if cut? Why not try to keep the flesh as healthy as possible?"

"Because it is foolishness, that is why. What matter if the skin beneath my leg fur is rosy and healthy?"

"What matters is that your heart is working to keep your limbs alive, whether you like it or not. I say we help it somewhat."

Darcy's traitorous heart quickened, though he mastered himself enough to shake his head. "I'll not have you demean yourself so. There is no restoring what is lost."

But Elizabeth smiled and pressed him gently back against his mountain of pillows. "It is no debasement, sir, but comfort freely given between partners. And I confess myself stubborn enough to try, with or without your blessing."

Chapter Thirteen

E LIZABETH PEERED OVER THE pages spread before her, scrutinising the kitchen
  ledger with growing comprehension. Across the desk, Mrs Hodges indicated various columns of figures with satisfaction.

"You're managing splendidly, Ma'am. Why, you'll soon run this household
ship-shape."

"All thanks to your patient guidance." Elizabeth smiled. The keys at her waist felt less
intimidating by the day, and she had learned her way about the house well enough that
she almost never got lost anymore. She dipped her pen to add notes on the week's menu.
At least ensuring the larder was properly supplied was well within her capabilities, even if
London's ornate rituals remained a mystery.

It had been a week since she had managed to talk her husband out of mounting a fast
coach for Scotland. She suspected it was only because he could not honestly fathom how
he was to make the journey, but he let her think it was her doing. That had won her a larger
share of the earl's favour, as well as spared her the necessity of leaving Town without even
once seeing Aunt and Uncle Gardiner. They were to come this afternoon to take tea with
her for a second time... but unfortunately, Mr Darcy had declined to meet with them.
Not that she did not understand his reasons, but she would have liked for them to at least
know him.

However, her aunt's approbation, when Elizabeth had first invited her to Darcy House
as its mistress, had buoyed her hopes beyond measure. It had not occurred to her that
Mrs Gardiner would be familiar with Mr Darcy's name, nor that she would have some
knowledge of the family's reputation in Derbyshire. But when Mrs Gardiner had entered

the Darcy townhouse for the first time, looking for all the world like she was beholding the home of royalty and blessing Elizbeth's good fortune, some of her fears eased. Perhaps her papa's dire predictions and Jane's doubts were all for nothing.

Elizabeth turned at the maid's entrance. "Beg pardon, Ma'am. The countess has arrived in the green salon and is requesting your company."

Marking their place, Elizabeth gave a last instruction for the day's menu to Mrs Hodges and rose. There were certainly no dull moments in her days... yet. Squaring her shoulders, she quit the cosy kitchen to join her guest.

Lady Matlock inclined her head as Elizabeth was shown into the blue salon. "Come sit, Mrs Darcy. There is something I must impart about the 'hospitality' before your journey north, as I understand my nephew's impatience grows by the day. I doubt that even you shall be able to delay him much longer."

Settling on the divan, Elizabeth smoothed her skirts. "You refer to the Scottish property loaned for our... extended wedding tour?"

"The very same." Lady Matlock regarded her shrewdly. "I trust you hold no illusions about lavish accommodations?"

Elizabeth summoned courage under that piercing stare. "Having toured Longbourn's crumbling dower house myself as a girl, I expect no royal luxuries. Vermin roaming the corridors and rain dripping inside seem likely."

Lady Matlock's eyes glinted approval though her mouth pinched. "I see you grasp the amenities to be had. Or lack thereof. But fear not—"

"Oh, I hardly fear discomfort." Elizabeth waved airily. "Merely tell me which wing the servants occupy, so I may have a fleet of maids deployed to scrub the mildew from my bedchamber."

That surprised a sharp laugh from her ladyship. "Servant's wing! You are most... refreshing, Mrs Darcy. Very well, I shall not trouble over preparing you. Doubtless, you will attack all inconveniences head-on." Sobering, she withdrew her list. "Now, before your escape north, we must continue to cement your status by introducing you to key prominent ladies who—"

"Must we?" Elizabeth interrupted, dismayed. "Forgive my impertinence, but I hardly relish being paraded before every supercilious gaze in succession!"

Lady Matlock tapped her list authoritatively. "You are Mrs Darcy now, not some country Miss who can hide from scrutiny. And as the husband cannot make appearances presently, the wife must shine all the brighter."

Seeing Elizabeth's discomfort, her expression softened marginally. "There, now, 'tis not so dire a duty I propose! I have meticulously selected only the most advantageous connexions to showcase you, whether highly esteemed ladies or ridiculous flatterers."

"Flatterers, my lady?"

"But of course! We shall make certain parties wildly jealous if they do not share such 'intimate' acquaintance with the new Mrs Darcy. Thereby, we make the most of your limited time in London, and also stoke the fires of jealousy for when you return. I warrant you will have a veritable bower of calling cards next Season." Lady Matlock offered a conspiratorial wink. "Now, tell me your thoughts on musicales? Lady Jersey hosts the superior one, but Lady Wilmont's is often fraught with more opportunities to be seen. And, of course, we cannot overlook driving in the Park…"

"Perhaps we ought to leave that particular activity for when I can be seen in the company of Mr Darcy. Surely, he could sit in a carriage soon enough, with no one the wiser. That might allay any gossip that I have spirited the man away and lodged myself in his house without his knowledge."

Lady Matlock shook a finger in the air. "You are very clever, my dear. And you are quite right—the longer you remain in Town without any appearances by his side, the more the whispers will grow."

Elizabeth sighed. "Much as I hate to confess it, it seems we do need to leave. As soon as possible."

"I could not agree more, but how do you propose to convey your fragile husband all the way to Scotland without jarring his broken back all the more?" Lady Matlock challenged. "Some sort of stretcher strapped between horses, perhaps? That *would* draw attention."

Elizabeth's eyes traced the salon's oriental carpet thoughtfully, recalling her earlier investigations. "The coachman showed me an exceptionally large and well-sprung carriage amongst the town vehicles. I believe one might angle a swinging hammock inside diagonally to cradle the, er… passenger safely over rough terrain."

Lady Matlock blinked in surprise, then threw back her head with a delighted cackle that rather suited a general on the brink of victory. "Well, now! It seems you possess a dash of strategy to you along with all that impertinence, my dear! What a perfectly workable solution. Of course, you must still convince my obstinate nephew to attempt such transport. I daresay persuading that wilful man against his preferences will require all your feminine charms."

"Well, there you have it. He declared the first day I met him that all my feminine charms were insufficient to sway any feeling of his. It seems that particular scheme, at least, will be doomed to failure."

Lady Matlock pursed her lips. "I doubt he is entirely immune to you, my dear."

Elizabeth shook her head. "Well, it does not matter, does it? I am useful to him, and he to me, and there ends it. I must see that he makes the journey as safely as possible, but Heaven help me to persuade him to anything he does not wish to do on his own. Perhaps the colonel may convince him."

Lady Matlock made an indelicate noise and waved her hand. "I leave such strategising to you, Mrs Darcy. Now, let us discuss with whom we shall take tea on the morrow..."

D ARCY BLINKED BACK TO the present as Giles mercifully concluded attending to his grooming. Before full awareness returned, a tentative knock heralded the maid entering with an ornately domed food tray.

"Beg pardon, Mr Darcy. Cook thought you might enjoy—"

"Is Mrs Darcy unwell, that she does not join me herself?" Darcy interrupted sharply. She always preceded the maid's arrival... at least, she had every day so far. Their fledgling routine of taking tea together each afternoon had become a highlight of his monotonous days abed... mostly owing to Elizabeth's lively presence, though Darcy refused a deeper examination of why.

Giles cleared his throat delicately. "I believe Madam is taking nuncheon with her visiting relations today, sir."

"Of course. The aunt and uncle from Cheapside." Darcy averted his face, lest his irrational pique show. What right had he to resent Elizabeth's scarce opportunities to see her loved ones under their bizarre marriage? She ought to make the most of the opportunities now, before they left London. Yet resentment festered nonetheless, as he stared at the untouched tray with sudden disinterest.

"Shall I assist you to eat, Mr Darcy? Or perhaps a book to pass the time until—"

"No. Leave me be." Darcy winced at his own curt tone but could not seem to temper foul humour. He had no true appetite, only... discontent that his lively dinner companion was diverted elsewhere today. Their debates... sometimes even fights... were his sole stimulation beyond endless brooding.

Giles reluctantly obeyed, though not before pouring Darcy a cup of unwanted tea. Scowling as the door closed, Darcy stared darkly into the piping cup's aromatic depths. What spell had Elizabeth cast that he so sharply missed her company already? Such a foolish fixation benefited no one, least of all him, for she had not married him for affection.

In a restless pique, he shoved the tea tray away harder than intended, sending the half-filled cup sloshing over to soak the linen cloth and his sheets. Darcy stared at the widening stain, obtusely satisfied by the chaos. If only all his mounting troubles could be so easily dispatched.

Mere minutes later, boots thudded from the hallway outside before Richard burst through the door, looking uncharacteristically harried. He paused only to take in the spilled tea with momentary bewilderment before taking a chair to grin at Darcy.

"Afternoon! I come bearing the latest on-dits if you fancy a diversion." Without waiting for a reply, Richard helped himself to an untouched pastry from the abandoned nuncheon tray.

Darcy eyed his cousin keenly. Richard was rarely so insouciant without a deeper purpose. "To what do I owe this dubious pleasure?"

"What? Can I not simply share idle pleasantries?" Richard bit into the pastry, still grinning enough to seem forced. "Father bemoans endless political outrages at the club while Mother is vastly entertained, driving the countess set into shrilly jealous snits over your new wife..." He tilted his head. "Where is the charming Mrs Darcy today, anyway?"

Stifling irritation, Darcy replied coolly, "Apparently, my bride entertains her relations this afternoon. Was there a purpose to your visit beyond prattle?"

Richard's smile collapsed as he set his plate down with a ringing clatter. "Very well, straight to it, then. I thought you should know Wickham comes before the Assizes tomorrow morning."

Darcy fought the dead stiffness in his back to rise higher on the pillow, outrage lending strength. "And you did not see fit to tell me sooner?"

Richard arched a brow as he finished his pastry. "And have you work yourself into a lather over something you cannot control? I have it in hand, as much as possible."

"Tell me precisely what you know."

"Little enough." Richard slumped wearily. "Naturally, I shall stand witness against the snake, detailing events as I discovered them. But without you there in person bringing accusations..."

He trailed off leadingly until Darcy barked sharply, "Well? What chance of seeing justice properly done?"

"Were the full breadth of his sins known, Wickham would likely swing or face Australian exile."

"And let it be known what he did to Georgiana? Or..." Darcy passed a hand over his legs.

Richard spread his hands. "As matters stand, the outcome remains uncertain if he pleads innocent before the judge. It was, after all, you who attacked him first."

Darcy stared furiously into space as his cousin voiced quiet warnings, the words barely penetrating fury's red haze. All his bitter helplessness converged to rancid hatred that the villain yet drew free air after destroying innocent lives. Georgiana... and now himself. Where was righteous justice?

"So..." Richard inspected the tea tray again, this time settling on a biscuit. "What will you do if Wickham goes free tomorrow?"

With effort, Darcy found some measure of ragged temperance once more. "It matters not. Whether he is condemned or freed, there remains but one place for me." He met Richard's troubled gaze squarely. "I shall join my sister as soon as arrangements allow. But I am not afraid of him."

His cousin nodded solemnly then rose to take leave. "Then we shall redouble our best efforts on your behalf. Perhaps Providence may smile upon us." He stood and buttoned his jacket. "I am for the Old Bailey tomorrow morning. I expect I will be seeing you directly afterwards to inform you of the outcome."

E LIZABETH GLANCED UP AS her Aunt Gardiner studied the large portrait over the mantel. "Very handsome, but then, I should have expected no less. Is this a true likeness of Mr Darcy?"

Following her gaze, Elizabeth nodded slowly. The vigorous young gentleman with windswept hair astride a massive grey stallion seemed to taunt Darcy's present grim reality.

"So, I am told. The late George Darcy commissioned it just before his passing, and the housekeeper tells me it was his favourite likeness of his son." Her eyes traced the painted features softened by youth.

"I can certainly understand why. That portrait conveys more than simple appearance. It seems to copy a bit of the gentleman's personality about the eyes and the posture."

Elizabeth turned to swallow a bit of her tea. Heaven help her if she had ever encountered Mr Darcy looking like *that*. She would have had a dreadful time mastering her heart, even at the very first glance. "I confess I find my husband's countenance even more striking in genuine intimacy."

"Indeed? I always heard the young Darcy cut a rather imposing figure. His father was known to be a very good man. Is the son the same?"

Elizabeth hesitated. "I believe so. Yes, yes, I think he is a very good man. If somewhat disappointed by present circumstances."

"I should think! A fall from his horse—how very tragic. But it is his good fortune that you were already on the brink of marriage and could come to help him through his recuperation." Aunt Gardiner sighed. "I am only sorry it could not be a proper church ceremony, where we might have tendered our well wishes. But with Lydia's recent... misfortunes, I suppose that is for the best. I must say, you have been very sly with us, Lizzy! You never did satisfy me as to how you and Mr Darcy first met. It must have been last spring, when the regiment all came to Meryton? That cousin of his is a colonel, is he not?"

She smiled thinly and made a noise in her throat that was not precisely an agreement, but neither was it a denial.

Aunt Gardiner eyed Elizabeth keenly. "Does marriage agree with you then, Lizzy?"

Elizabeth smiled wistfully. "I am content, Aunt."

"I should think the wife of Fitzwilliam Darcy ought to be able to say she is far more than simply 'content.'"

"Oh!" Elizabeth shook her head and forced a wider smile. "Truly, I am. Mr Darcy and I are not of similar temperaments, you know, but he can be most animated when we debate favourite volumes in the library. He has a... a very pleasing smile. Though, often..." She hesitated, seeing again Darcy's shuttered gaze when she tended his legs each night. "Often of late, the troubles he carries prevail over his spirits, despite my efforts at lightening them."

Uncle Gardiner patted her hand comfortingly. "Understandable, of course. He is probably a serious young man, as was said of his father. And certainly, his injury causes him much pain. But take heart! Mr Darcy shall be hale and active again soon, I've no doubt."

"Soon, yes." Elizabeth managed a watery smile at their cheer, longing to unburden her oppressed spirit. Yet she could not shatter their optimism with harsh truths. Darcy would likely never stand proudly astride a stallion again.

"Are you certain there is nothing we can do to help you settle in, Lizzy?" Aunt Gardiner pressed gently. "You do seem somewhat... subdued. We only wish for your happiness, my dear, but it was all so very sudden, you know."

"Of course." Elizabeth blinked rapidly to dispel a rush of tears. "Mr Darcy is unfailingly considerate. Truly, I could not ask for better. Oh! Have you heard from Jane of late?"

Mrs Gardiner almost immediately forgot her questions about Elizabeth. "I had a letter only yesterday. She says that Lydia is... well enough. As are Mary and Kitty. Your father is even more often in his library than before—I suppose because he misses you, Lizzy—and your mother is in high spirits owing to your marriage."

Elizabeth rolled her eyes briefly. "I am sure she is. I had a letter only this morning from Jane, in which she mentioned rumours of a new neighbour intending to lease Netherfield. Did she write to you of that?"

"Yes..." Aunt Gardiner furrowed her brow. "A Mr... Binglay, was it not?"

"Bingley, yes. I have met the gentleman, for he is a friend of Mr Darcy's."

"Is he, indeed! Well, that is fortuitous. Surely, he will be friendly to your relations. Well!" Aunt smiled widely. "Perhaps with such happy circumstances, all is not lost for your sisters at Longbourn, despite Lydia's unhappy incident."

Elizabeth sighed. "I can only hope."

Chapter Fourteen

D ARCY GLOWERED AT THE far wall, tension coiling ever tighter as he awaited word of Wickham's fate. The session should be well underway now, and soon justice would be meted out at long last... if the damned useless lump his body had become did not sabotage matters completely. What he would sacrifice to stand in person, hurling accusations 'til they stuck and saw the villain properly punished!

"Your tea, Mr Darcy." Giles hesitantly interrupted his dark musings.

"Confound it, man, set it anywhere and leave me be!" Darcy immediately regretted biting out at his faithful manservant and softened his tone with effort. "Forgive me, Giles. My temper frays this morning."

"Yes, sir... of course, sir..." Giles retreated hastily, leaving Darcy to stew in silence—impatience with waiting on the outcome of the trial now combined with regret at how he had erupted at poor Giles.

Some minutes later, a feminine throat cleared from the doorway as Elizabeth entered, one winged brow arched eloquently. "I passed a rather harried valet below stairs and thought to discover the cause." She levelled Darcy a reproving gaze. "I hope you do not customarily abuse servants so before you even break your fast, sir."

Darcy could not help a lopsided grin, even as he scrambled to defend himself. "What abuse? I merely corrected some minor negligence."

At her indelicate snort, he protested, "I spoke in haste, distracted by affairs beyond my control."

"And do you consider that the conduct of a gentleman, sir?"

Despite himself, the tight knot in Darcy's chest eased somewhat, beholding her. Few others dared reprove him so, and yet instead of affront, he felt his rigid mouth curving mutinously.

"Indeed not. Only irascibility from being long abed makes me sharp." He held up placating hands. "What punishment do you decree for such misconduct?"

"Hmm. Two sonnets extolling the virtues of patience and equanimity immediately." Eyes alight with suppressed mirth, Elizabeth tapped her slippered toe expectantly.

What the...? She could not be serious. Such frivolity on a day like today? But...

Well, what else did he have to amuse him? Darcy cleared his throat and pressed one hand theatrically to his breast. "What cruelty, to demand poetry without the gift! 'Twould surely drive the sanest man to vexation." He slanted a sly look. "Might I pay you coin instead to end this persecution?"

"Certainly not! Your fine words are the price." Elizabeth wagged one dainty finger. "Best begin redeeming yourself, sir, lest I oblige you to write a quarto's worth!"

"Vexation! Dost demand me spout flowery rhymes while all sense flees under duress... Oh, hang it all, I have lost track of my lines. If you want me to spout poetry, you shall have to fetch me a quill and paper."

"I will remember that next time." Still alight with playful laughter, Elizabeth leaned in closer to his bedside. "Shall I adjust your pillows somewhat, Mr Darcy? We cannot have you less than perfectly comfortable."

Darcy hesitated, suddenly aware of his pounding heart. Truthfully, he needed no cosseting just now. Yet the prospect of her soft hands so near, of silken curls grazing his cheek, of stealing her sweet floral perfume was painfully tantalising. When else might he know his wife's tender touch? For certainly, he had felt nothing at all when she ministered to his lifeless legs, though his eyes had followed every stroke of her fingers with hungry fascination.

"I... yes, if you would. These blasted pillows will not flatten properly." He schooled his features to impassivity, cursing the threadbare deception. But longing eclipsed dignity as she nodded graciously.

Perching beside him, Elizabeth carefully slid one hand beneath his shoulders, emanating comforting warmth even through linen and goose down. With the other, she gently fluffed and smoothed each pillow just so, brows knit in concentration. Ensnared by her nearness, Darcy ceased breathing altogether, overwhelmed by dizzying awareness of smooth skin and moist pink lips barely a handspan away.

As if sensing his burning focus, at last, Elizabeth glanced up. Time fractured as her eyes locked—naked comprehension flashing in their coffee depths. Eyes widening, she took a sharp breath that lifted her bosom alluringly... then time crashed remorselessly back, and she looked abruptly away. Cheeks colouring, her hands withdrew, leaving a hollow absence.

Bleak self-recrimination flooded Darcy's gut. To encourage such dangerous attraction was unconscionable, however innocently she offered her companionship. A gentleman controlled base impulses, yet Darcy feared his starved senses might grasp at any feminine comfort she unwittingly provided. How long before stolen moments like these destroyed him utterly?

Silence hung suspended until Elizabeth smoothly changed tones, taking the chair beside him and pouring herself tea as if nothing remarkable had just transpired between them. "Well! On more practical matters, I have been consulting your coachman about safe travel options for your comfort."

Darcy blinked back from turbulent emotions, his voice emerging gruff. "No need. Richard has arranged everything."

"Oh? Do tell what ingenious solutions your officious cousin has implemented."

"Some sort of low pallet across the coach seats for me to recline upon."

"I see." Elizabeth set her cup down, lips pursed sceptically. "And do you believe jolting along uneven roads in such a manner will prove... restful?"

"Richard deemed it sufficient, and options are limited." Irritation pricked Darcy anew at her polite doubt.

"Well, naturally, Colonel Fitzwilliam knows best, being infantry, not cavalry," Elizabeth murmured. Was that a hint of sarcasm? "Still, I wonder if a gently swaying hammock within might not absorb more—?"

"Preposterous coddling." Darcy cut her off impatiently. "I've no patience to indulge every absurd feminine notion for the journey."

Something glittered in her eyes—that stubborn temper of hers making an appearance, but she mastered it with a clearing of her throat and a cool look as she resumed her tea. Belated guilt prompted Darcy to an awkward explanation. "Forgive my tone, Madam. Discussing this humiliation pains me."

"Of course." Quiet empathy resonated through Elizabeth's hushed words. "I only seek to ease the burden as I may. But we need not speak on it now." After a fraught pause, she ventured gently, "I understand Mr Wickham faces justice for his crimes today?"

Darcy whipped his head up, startled. "However did you—?"

One corner of her mouth lifted. "Servants gossip. And I know your ways a little by now. You have been out of temper all day." Her small hand covered his. "I pray he gets what he deserves."

Mute with sudden relief in having a confidante who shared his wishes, Darcy turned his palm up to clasp her fingers. If this be the sole gesture of tenderness his affliction permitted, he would cling to it desperately. For now, vengeance and vindication must suffice.

ELIZABETH TRIED VALIANTLY TO lose herself in the open book as Darcy took his turn reading aloud. But tension thrummed too strongly in them both, fracturing any illusion of diversion as they awaited the fateful word. Sensing Darcy's restless anxiety mirroring her own, Elizabeth longed to ease his discomfort somehow. Yet, with constraints between them, even casual intimacy seemed barred.

When the door opened abruptly, admitting Colonel Fitzwilliam, dread crystallised instantly in Elizabeth's mind. One look at Richard's grim visage and Darcy barked out sharply, "Well? What news?"

Richard opened his mouth only to close it helplessly, shamefaced sorrow meeting Darcy's fervid stare. "There were... irregularities in witness accounts. Enough to introduce reasonable doubts of pure villainy. And without you there in person to present evidence..."

"Damnation!" Darcy's fist pounded the mattress. "Do not tell me that snake has slithered free on a technicality?"

"It was hardly a technicality. They said you barged into the rooming house with violent intent and attacked him first."

Darcy growled. "I should have just called him out."

"A courtesy reserved for a gentleman. Wickham is no such thing."

"Did you mention his debts? The reports of other ladies he has ruined?"

"Unfortunately, neither of those are hanging offences. Moreover, as none of his other accusers stood in the dock today, such testimony was worthless."

"Outrageous. Was there no one else to bear witness?"

"Oh, yes." The colonel folded his hands. "Someone mentioned that pistol you had in your pocket."

"Every gentleman walking that part of town at night carries a pistol! It is not as if I meant to use it in cold blood."

"And it was observed that an announcement of your recent marriage was printed in the papers. Someone said that you must not have suffered too grievously, as you are now a happily married man and no doubt too occupied with your new bride to make an appearance in the dock."

Elizabeth watched the fury boiling beneath Darcy's taut jaw and coiled arm muscles. She tried to signal the colonel that perhaps he ought to cease with his explanations of the trial for now, but he spoke on, heedless.

"I am afraid the magistrate felt confined to upholding narrow letter of the law regarding—"

"Devil take narrow interpretation! Where lies justice?" Darcy erupted. "Does no punishment await that rogue?"

Colonel Fitzwilliam sighed heavily, raking one hand through dishevelled hair. "By rights, he should have faced a court martial for desertion before any other charges were brought. That would be my doing, I am afraid. I pulled strings with his colonel, thinking attempted murder of a gentleman was the more grievous charge. However, he did not go free today but was remanded to the custody of his regiment. Justice has slipped our grasp this time, I fear, but perhaps the militia may have their way with him."

Quiet outrage emanated from Elizabeth as cold reality sunk in. So, the man who had irrevocably ruined both Darcy's life and her own would escape all reckoning? Somehow, a charge of desertion, harsh as the sentence might be, was nothing to what she felt the man deserved. Bile rose in her throat.

Sensing her distress, Darcy reached for Elizabeth's hand, offering what bracing comfort he could. To Richard, he muttered grimly, "Then we quit this damned city posthaste. Events play into our hands after all—charged with military justice rather than civil, none shall connect us with that libertine's path by the time we reach Scotland."

Finality weighted Colonel Fitzwilliam's solemn nod. "Just so. I shall make preparations for your immediate departure."

D ARCY ENDURED THE AWKWARD process of being manoeuvred onto the makeshift pallet spanning the space between the carriage seats with grated patience. Dawn was still an hour off, and the coachman would have to rely on the horses' eyes to avoid rough parts of the road until better light, but they were departing now, nonetheless. Necessary evils, he reminded himself, to secure freedom from London's whispered speculation and reach Georgiana at long last. Though the undignified conveyance irked profoundly when Richard leaned through the door to bid Darcy farewell.

"Safe journey to you both." False cheer in Richard's tone belied the pitying look he attempted to conceal. "I shall join you within a fortnight or so, once affairs are tidily wrapped up here."

Darcy only nodded tersely until the door shut, sealing him alone in the darkened space. Or nearly alone... Elizabeth's skirts grazed his shoulder, given scant space to situate herself with his pallet consuming nearly the whole of the interior. Uncomfortable silence reigned as the coach lurched into motion over uneven streets. Neither dared acknowledge the awkward intimacy as they unavoidably jostled together with each rut and hole. Darcy clenched his fists and focused on ignoring the pain in his upper back. Surely, he could withstand a bit of discomfort if it won them a swifter escape.

As the coach picked up speed, he relinquished any attempts at dignity, clutching the padded sides as each rut in the road rattled his spine mercilessly. "Here, sir, take some laudanum for the pain." Elizabeth uncorked a vial, her face etched with concern.

Darcy turned his head away, refusing to escape through mental fog. "I will endure." He would retain mastery over his own senses at least.

Eventually, he slipped into fitful dozing, though peace eluded his restless mind. When at last daylight permeated behind the curtains, Elizabeth drew them aside so they could look out on the rain-soaked countryside rolling by. Darcy craned desperately to see out the window, but his flat prison permitted only shifting glimpses of nondescript tree branches and sky mocking his thwarted mobility.

"We shall stop in Meryton this afternoon to change horses," Elizabeth ventured after a while. He felt her assessing look, knowing she guessed his frantic yearning for fresh sights. "Perhaps we should take rooms there, rather than pressing on for this first day."

Darcy's restless hands knotted against renewed shame. "And have all your friends discover the truth of your bizarre circumstances, mere days after leaving them? You cannot think that once you are sighted in Meryton, a dozen of your neighbours would not race to greet you or gossip about you."

She swallowed and leaned against the squab, her profile tight and anxious. "Naturally, they would."

"And knowledge of my... No, not until after... We press on. Better that we should be remarked on as little as possible." He ground his teeth as the carriage jounced over a hole, pain blazing sharply.

"Well, we ought not to travel too far today. I agree with the doctors—as many reasons as we had for fleeing London, it was not best for your recovery."

"Recovery? As if there is anything to recover."

Her jaw hardened. "Your comfort, then."

He shook his head. "I would rather suffer more myself if it means getting to Georgiana all the sooner."

She thinned her lips and fell to silent staring out the carriage window. And just before they rolled into the streets of Meryton some while later, she drew the drapes. But there would be no concealing that ornate crest on the carriage door. He should have had Richard cover it, but as it was, they would just have to pray to luck.

The stop in Meryton lasted mere moments before they were back on the road. And no one had run to offer felicitations to the new Mrs Darcy, so perhaps they had made good their escape. Darcy sighed in relief as they gained country roads again, and Elizabeth pulled the drapes aside.

But that was when the sun caught the gleam of a tear in her eye. He watched her steadily for some minutes, but she refused to either dash it away or acknowledge his gaze. She just stared out at the wandering countryside they passed, her throat tight, and her breathing fiercely shortened. And there was nothing whatsoever that he could do about her homesickness. He closed his eyes, so he did not have to see it any longer.

Yet relief remained elusive, even when he surrendered to fitful dozing. Agonised dreams held Darcy trapped immobile while nameless visions in scarlet swirled just out of reach, punctuated by merciless jolts from the carriage rattling his tender back brutally. He resurfaced with a wounded groan past gritted teeth.

"Enough."

He opened his eyes when Elizabeth rapped on the carriage roof and called to the driver. "Simmons? We will stop for the night at the next inn, no matter what its accommodations be."

She sat back and shot him a look that dared him to challenge her. He sighed and tried to loose a breath. "Are you defying my express wishes, Mrs Darcy?"

She crossed her arms. "I am. I suggest you accustom yourself to it, Mr Darcy."

E LIZABETH SURVEYED THEIR CRAMPED rented room dubiously. Apparently, this remote inn seldom saw refined gentle patronage, boasting only one chamber on the ground floor that was even close to suitable. Which left little alternative for their sleeping arrangements tonight.

It was not as if she had not tried. They had arrived at scarcely three in the afternoon, taking a light, early meal, and considering what options were available—even sending the coachman on ahead to inquire at the next posting inn near Barnett. The simple fact was that fine gentlemen travelling north from London usually did not stop their travels for the day in this hamlet but pressed on toward St Albans. But that was not an option on this journey.

Glancing at her stiffly silent husband, throat constricting, Elizabeth hesitated before the obvious practical solution. "The hour grows late to keep Simmons waiting... shall I take a shared room on the next floor, then?"

Darcy frowned. "Staying alone amongst strange travellers hardly seems proper for a new bride. And there is your safety to consider."

"Sharing this room with you appears to be my sole option besides the common parlour, then." She eyed the lone bed pointedly. Seeing colour rise on Darcy's sharp cheekbones, Elizabeth rushed to suggest, "I shall rest in that chair tonight, of course."

Before Darcy could muster a reply, Giles entered on swift heels to assist preparing his master for slumber. With an awkward throat-clearing, Elizabeth escaped to pace the courtyard rather than witness that humiliation layered upon her husband.

Cool night air did little to relieve her churning thoughts. The rhythmic creak of signage over the door echoed her roiling disquiet. This marriage was beginning to demand things of her she had not had time to prepare herself for. Tonight especially, confined in strange quarters with the man... What further compromises lay in store? And what would the morrow bring?

Squaring her shoulders against the chill, Elizabeth turned back indoors. What else was there to do? She had sworn herself to this union, and even now, when she asked herself if she had leapt too hastily, she could not reasonably say that she would have had any other options. For Jane and her younger sisters, this was... well, it was better than the hedgerows. Mr Darcy had not told her of it, and neither had her father, but Jane wrote a few days ago that Mr Darcy had provided a modest dowry for each of the Bennet girls—with Jane's being the largest share. That was... well, that was very good of him, and entirely unasked for.

And Mr Darcy seemed like a man she might have liked rather well, had life gone differently for him. Whatever came next must be weathered together now.

She entered to find him struggling vainly to shift higher against bolstered pillows. At her appearance, his head fell back, face shuttering instantly, though pained frustration lingered. "You returned. Nothing remotely comfortable about this situation, yet I suppose concessions are required for now." He stared at the bed coverings morosely.

Ignoring his provoking tone, Elizabeth dredged a thin horsehair chair from the corner. "Nothing proper about a lawfully wedded man and wife sharing a room at a crowded coaching inn?"

His gaze almost smouldered when he looked up at her. "Ours is not a traditional sort of union, Mrs Darcy. Do not tease me so."

She sighed, softening somewhat. "It is only my way when I am frustrated, myself. And as I said earlier, this chair suits nicely for me." She retrieved a spare quilt and wrapped it around her shoulders before settling awkwardly into cramped angles that guaranteed stiff joints come morning. Through slitted eyes, she watched the emotions playing over Darcy's taut profile.

"I should sleep on the floor, then. You cannot possibly fold yourself up in that chair all night. You ought rightly to take the bed, but even straw on the floor for one or the other of us is more fitting than imposing my invalid's habits on you."

"Nonsense, sir. This horsehair perch shall suit perfectly. Even army barracks could boast no more character to recommend them!" She fanned out a blanket and hid herself beneath it before he could articulate any further objection.

"You mean to sleep in your travelling gown?" he asked sharply.

"Until you go to sleep, and I can change. Yes."

Unyielding silence reigned until Darcy reluctantly conceded her determined roosting. "Still," he muttered after a moment, "at least you should have something more. I insist you take my thicker blanket against this dank chill." Straining painfully up, he held out the fine woollen bed covering before she could refuse, adding gruffly, "I shall not have it said that Fitzwilliam Darcy was so stingy that his wife had to conjure an ague just to keep warm in her chair at night."

Elizabeth hesitated, but his arm was not dropping. Softly, she eased out of her chair and gently retrieved the proffered blanket, careful not to jostle his precarious balance. "My thanks, sir. Only if you promise to wake me if you should become chilled yourself."

He harrumphed something vaguely affirmative, then closed his eyes. Silence resumed, marked solely by their tandem breathing in counterpoint. As her husband sank towards a fitful doze, Elizabeth watched him for signs that he was, indeed, soundly asleep. Once she heard the first rattle in his throat, she put aside her blankets, crept to the darkest corner of the room, and slipped into her nightgown.

She was startled once, as she fastened the last few buttons—Darcy's breathing shifted and deepened, punctuated by sharp groans and muted whimpers of pain. She leaned to get a better look at him around the bedpost, surveying his face as the low firelight illuminated the creases on his brow. It would seem that there was a deal that he yet masked when he was alert, but now, with his defences entirely evaporated, all was laid bare.

And she was the one who had to see it.

A few seconds later, she was tucked back into her chair once more, but she did not keep that woollen blanket. Better it should cover him, when his body was already battling so hard. Besides, she used to sleep with her window open all the time. What was a little autumn chill? She shivered down inside her blanket and closed her eyes.

And thereafter followed no further nocturnal disturbances but fire's dying pops and lodgers' muffled snores permeating the timbers.

Chapter Fifteen

D ARCY WATCHED THE HUSHED dawn creep over rolling hills as Giles and the other footman carried him to the carriage. Today should finally see their party reach Pemberley after five gruelling days rattling on these infernal roads.

He shifted uncomfortably, everything below his waist mercifully numb, but his tender back protesting sharply against even slight movements nowadays. At least soon, he might sleep in his own bed, unmolested by jostling wheels striking each rut and hole. And it was not only his back that was made to suffer now—his stomach roiled queasily again at the thought of yet another day bouncing along in a supine position, playing hostage to the questionable fare upon which he'd been forced to sustain himself and the coil of the coach springs.

If only he had thought to order that contraption Elizabeth suggested before they departed Town! But that opportunity was lost to pride and despair. As if summoned by his thoughts, Elizabeth herself peeked through the carriage door, face etched with concern though she summoned a smile. "Well, sir? Shall we press on toward our destination?"

He nodded tightly; jaw clenched against fresh throbs. Her searching look pierced through his bravado, though, and she ventured gently, "Might we try suspending you in a hammock across the coach just for today? I did have a broadcloth and some rope brought for that purpose."

He lifted his head. "You did?"

"If the discomfort increases, we shall, of course, stop, but you may find it eases the—"

"And swing about like a hooked trout all the way?" Darcy scoffed, not liking how easily she was able to read him. "I foresee only amplified nausea befalling me instead."

Elizabeth folded her arms defiantly. "Truly? Worse than currently ails you?" One eloquent brow lifted in challenge until Darcy glanced away, conceding her point. Blast it all, he never could deny her suggestions outright when she spoke reason. Especially when such beguiling determination lit her fine eyes to a crackling fire.

Much as Darcy despised admitting weakness, refusing Elizabeth's earnest care came equally hard these days. For four of the five nights they had spent on the road, she had taken a corner chair in whatever room they had been able to find for him. The necessity of seeking smaller inns that were unlikely to be frequented by anyone he knew, combined with the requirement of a ground-floor room for him, had made it almost impossible to secure anything resembling respectable—let alone comfortable—for her.

But she had yet to complain. Rather, he awoke every morning with the warm blanket he had desired for her to take tucked carefully around his body, instead. And when Giles came in to attend to him, she would ramble about somewhere in the yard or the common rooms, and never failed to bring back some interesting little curio or observation to light his morning.

Her selfless patience through awkward nights and tedious miles had stirred an unwanted tenderness in his breast... one he hardly dared dwell on. Surely, no obligation bound her except their strange marriage vows. But she had been gentle... and far kinder than he deserved. One only wondered how long it would last before she tired of playing nursemaid.

With a bone-weary sigh, Darcy nodded curtly. If aught could purchase some brief respite from ceaseless agony and perhaps even permit him some genuine rest, he must make the attempt or be utterly useless on arriving home.

"Oh, very well, though I insist we stop after half a mile, should this experiment fail."

"That is agreeable." Working cleverly, Elizabeth supervised as Giles and Simmons contrived a makeshift hammock slung securely across the coach interior without sway. Gingerly, they transferred Darcy onto the taut canvas. To his grudging surprise, with his weight evenly suspended, the rocking of the carriage as they settled him already felt less jarring.

Elizabeth poked her head around the corner, surveying him.

"Well, sir? Is it as fearsome as you expected?"

"Somewhat less so," he confessed.

"Excellent! I see, however, that I have miscalculated one small detail. With the canvas strung from all four corners, there is nowhere left for me to sit. Perhaps I might ride in the other carriage with Giles and Beth."

"And have the new mistress of Pemberley arrive for the first time in the servants' coach?"

"Well, it is either that or I..." She gestured to the canvas beside him.

Darcy swallowed. Hang the worry that she might jostle him, or that he might inadvertently crush her with his greater weight once they began moving. He had fully intended never to permit anything that resembled temptation with her—and he was already slipping vastly beyond even his wildest fears. Why did she have to be so blasted... competent? Few things stoked his admiration as strongly as that quality.

"I do not see any other option," he confessed after a moment.

"But what if I bounce into you?" She tipped her head and winced as she surveyed the arrangements, no doubt imagining just which parts of her would necessarily be pressed against him, with no way to support herself other than his broken body.

"Would you rather ride on the top of the carriage? If you can bear the discomfort of the necessity, it would be my preference for you to..." He cleared his throat. "No need to compound the indignity by having my wife trundle alongside the baggage and servants." The prospect irked ridiculously.

Elizabeth's lower lip disappeared between her teeth. She glanced over her shoulder once, and a few seconds later, Darcy caught a glimpse of Giles' arm as he handed her in. She eased her way toward him, fumbling once when the canvas dipped, and she had to catch herself with her hands. She shot him a nervous look before she clambered up on her knees once more, then, rather clumsily, flopped to her side, then rolled to her back and tried to sit up.

"Have a care," he groused. "I do still have sensation in my rib cage."

"Oh! I am so sorry." Elizabeth braced her hands under her rear and tried to slide backwards for some semblance of sitting upright by his head, but the canvas only rocked and toppled her back down. And just then, the carriage lurched into motion.

"Oh, dear," Elizabeth grumbled as she tried to pull herself upright again. "I am afraid this is even less dignified than I had hoped."

"There is nothing else for it. You will only kick me in the shins if you keep trying to sit up," Darcy hissed through gritted teeth.

She paused, studying his face, and an impish twitch curled her mouth. "Well... at least it wouldn't hurt."

Darcy's face went slack. Did she just...? His eyes narrowed, and then it happened.

He laughed.

For the first time in nearly two months, he laughed, though it cost him a painful twinge through his mid spine as his ribs expanded. It was worth every shock of pain and then some, just to exhaust that heaviness that blew out of his lungs.

Elizabeth's grin widened, equal parts mirth and relief, as her reckless giggles joined his. "Oh, I am sorry! I could not resist. I know it was cruel, but it just slipped out, and..."

"Never mind that. Here. Lie back." He anchored his elbow between them and lifted his hand for her to steady herself as she shifted to recline beside him. It cost some bumping about, but she was mercifully quick. And a few seconds later, Darcy was lying beside his wife.

He gulped and stared at the carriage roof, all traces of his amusement vanished. He had never thought... well, hang what he had thought. Perhaps he had not been "thinking" at all, and now it was time to pay the piper.

Once, he would have sensed his awareness of her through every nerve and sinew of his body. Her presence would have burned his flesh and set fire to his blood. But now, the scorching was on an even more intimate level, for he could hear her heartbeat. Feel, even as if it was his very own veins, the hammering and surging of her pulse and stumbling breath as she jockeyed to settle near him, but not *too* near him. And the throbbing in his chest swelled to excruciating as he slammed his eyes shut against the sting.

"Well, sir?" Elizabeth's voice murmured in his ear—soft and low, and dipping into tones that ought to be reserved for... other things. Not this. "Does this meet with your approval?"

He swallowed and opened his eyes. She had propped one elbow up, just above his shoulder on the canvas, while her cheek rested on her hand as her eyes slipped over his torso.

He squirmed as far as he was capable, meaning to shift away from her, but he found he could not. Nor... did he precisely want to.

"Oddly enough," he confessed, "I find your... weight... gives me something to brace against." He glanced up at her apologetically. "I trust you are not terribly uncomfortable?"

She drank in a sigh and lowered herself still more along his side until her head nestled on the canvas beside his shoulder. "I am exhausted, that is what I am. It seems that passing

several nights in hard chairs is not the most practical way to sleep." She stifled a
yawn. "How long until we reach Pemberley?"

He smiled and felt his torso melt a little further into the gently rocking canvas of
her makeshift sling. "About three hours."

She sniffed, and he felt her face burrowing a little deeper beside him. "Good. Be
a gentleman and let a lady sleep."

Darcy smiled and allowed his eyes to drift closed as well. That was a capital
idea. Lulled by the gentle sway of the hammock and Elizabeth's soothing feminine
nearness, Darcy slipped into an exhausted slumber. If this be dangerous weakness,
he wanted not strength ever again.

"I BEG YOUR PARDON, Mr Darcy... Mrs Darcy. We're a mile from Pemberley.
I thought you should know."

Elizabeth started and sucked in a breath as she surfaced from a deep slumber,
in which she had felt warm and strangely content. Brief disorientation faded as
consciousness identified the manly shoulder her cheek rested upon... and the gentle
hand cradling her head. With a startled gasp, Elizabeth jerked up, cheeks flaming as
Darcy's impassive dark eyes studied her.

"Forgive me. I did not mean to make you my pillow!" she stammered. His stoic
features proved unreadable, though surely such familiarity must discomfit him.
Struggling upright proved predictably futile as the carriage hit a rut when it rocked
into motion again, spilling her awkwardly across Darcy's chest.

"You are determined to do me in, Mrs Darcy," he grunted. "Might I suggest you
wait at least until our... eh... heir is born?" He winced as she scrambled off him.

Face aflame, Elizabeth babbled some profuse apology and would have levered off
him instantly had his gruff voice not detained her. "Mrs Darcy, your hair is quite
askew. If you would allow me..."

To her astonishment, his long fingers deftly smoothed several errant curls behind her
ear, knuckles barely skimming her burning cheek. Such casual intimacy left Elizabeth
momentarily speechless under that heavy-lidded gaze. Before she could rally coherent

thought, Darcy withdrew his hand casually and cast his eyes up to the carriage roof once more.

She placed a hand on her cheek and found it hot to the touch. "Thank you. I... I'm afraid I do not know where my reticule is with my little glass, but... Oh! Did we really sleep these last three hours?"

"I imagine we slumbered through two changes of horses, as well. Given what Giles reported, you should be able to glimpse the lake out that window soon."

Elizabeth's eyes widened, and she clambered forward on hands and knees to peer through the drapes. No lake was in sight, but a flaming bower of red and gold trees rimmed her vision. A distant squawk overhead drew her eyes upward, to a spear of geese fanning over the tree line. She sighed.

Right about now, Sir William and her uncle Philips and perhaps even her father would be taking to the fields with their muskets for an afternoon of slopping through the marshes in hopes of a goose for the table. They usually brought home more mud than fowl, and one afternoon each year usually sufficed for their seasonal amusement, but the sound of their laughter as they would approach Longbourn in the evening was one of her fondest girlhood memories.

Would they go this year? Or would Lydia's folly have ended even that innocent amusement? Elizabeth tipped forward to try to look out the window a little more, but with another rut in the road, she lost her balance and had to grasp the hand loops. And her husband made a noise in his throat that sounded suspiciously like a chuckle.

"I suggest you cease wriggling henceforth. The canvas will only tip you over regardless." Was that faint amusement lurking in his tone? "And despite feminine curiosity, the sight of Pemberley's grandeur remains beyond your reach from this undignified vantage point. I daresay you will have time enough to see it later."

"But I wish to glimpse—" Elizabeth broke off as his eyes fixed knowingly upon her.

"You will only crease your gown more. And..." His gaze traced her features almost softly. "You sport imprints of my coat buttons across one cheek already. I should hate for you to add a bruise to the other cheek."

Face flaming brighter, Elizabeth scrubbed at her complexion with one glove, though the damage likely remained. With as much grace as possible, she settled back, hands folded stiffly atop her stomach and eyes trained safely heavenward. If only her pulse would steady so easily!

Biting her lip, Elizabeth ventured cautiously, "I have not yet mustered the courage to ask... does your sister know aught of your accident, sir?"

His jaw worked angrily. "No. Richard merely informed her by post that I suffered minor injuries from a fall in Hyde Park. Nothing of consequence. I only require some weeks of further recovery, necessitating absolute rest." He snorted. "She still thinks I am her strong older brother, as always."

Elizabeth scowled. "Thus, the falsehoods and concealments multiply. Layer upon layer of them, it seems."

"And do you think it does not trouble me?" he snapped. "I despise it! Dishonesty has never been my custom." He blew a sharp breath, bitterness saturating each word. "Yet here I am, utterly reliant for basic dignity upon servants and devices. Forced to mislead my own sister regarding the future now denied all of us!" His face contorted, revealing depths of anguish before the stoic mask slammed down once more.

Chastened, Elizabeth covered his clenched fist gently. "I know how such deception wounds you. But consider, there may be wisdom in protecting Miss Darcy until she is ready to hear the full truth."

"You think so, do you?" Darcy snatched his gaze away. "By rights, she deserves to know her ruin is nearly complete! But Richard deemed ignorance safer for now..." His voice roughened. "God forgive me, I shall tell her everything once we arrive."

Alarmed, Elizabeth squeezed his hand. "Sir, have a care! Such overwhelming revelations could undo one so young!" At his doubtful scowl, she pressed earnestly, "Miss Darcy has already endured much, from what you told me. And I am not proposing that you do not tell her the truth. You said it yourself—false comforts cannot be sustained. But why lay more burdens than she can bear all at once?"

At Darcy's sceptical grunt, she pressed further: "Did you not willingly sacrifice your own comfort and desires on the altar of her well-being? Then extend patience regarding difficult realities as a selfless loving sacrifice."

Darcy touched his cheek and blinked. "She will have only heard about you a day or two ago, from my last letter. I doubt not she is filled with all manner of questions, not the least of them being what is to become of her."

Elizabeth rolled up on her elbow to look him in the eye as the rocking of their canvas mattress slowed to a halt. "In that, then, she must know the truth from the first moment you enter the house. Her brother has done, and will continue to do, everything in his power to see her secure."

His jaw clenched, and his mouth worked faintly. "Much good that will do her."

A lurching halt a few seconds later heralded their arrival. With the motion of the carriage ceased, Elizabeth smiled one last time at Mr Darcy, then pushed herself upright and slid toward the door as a footman opened it. And she peeked out the door and beheld her new home for the first time.

Her breath arrested on a soft "oh!" of wonder as Elizabeth beheld soaring stonework and towering windows outshining every possible fancy. But it was not just the house—pristine lawns, natural clusters of trees, and a gentle wilderness garden just edging into her view captured the simple grandeur of the home. This truly was kin to heaven on earth. Impulsively, she turned to share the moment's awe with her new husband.

Darcy had lifted his head as far as he was able, a keen light in his eyes that had not been there a moment ago. He seemed to be waiting for something; that strange look he often got when he looked at her hooding all expression and feeling.

But then, when she smiled in wonder, his mouth turned up in satisfaction.

"Welcome to Pemberley, Mrs Darcy."

Chapter Sixteen

A GONIZED HEAT FLOODED Darcy's face as two footmen manoeuvred the
stretcher bearing his rigid frame into Pemberley's imposing entrance hall.
Returning home thus, crippled and wholly reliant upon servants who had formerly
known him as hale and commanding, felt unendurable.

Especially when his dear sister must shortly behold this pitiful specimen once
deemed by all to be a pillar of strength. Would anguished disbelief fill Georgiana's
trusting blue eyes? Or worse still, dawning disgust at the shattered cripple her
brother had become? Darcy swallowed hard against rising bile. Either reaction might
break him irrevocably.

"Where... is Miss Darcy... presently?" Darcy's strained query emerged hoarse,
dreading her first glimpse of this pathetic wreck.

The housekeeper, Mrs Reynolds, fluttered close, dismay clouding her normally
cheerful mien despite obvious, valiant efforts at summoning a smile. "I believe she
is taking her afternoon tea in her room this afternoon. That has been her custom
since returning from Ramsgate, sir. Shall I have word sent of your arrival?"

Darcy clenched his jaw against scalding emotion. "Nay. Allow me time to... collect
myself privately first."

"Very good, sir. I shall have a cold collation sent to your room as well."

By sheer force of will, he wrenched attention leftwards towards Elizabeth hovering wide-eyed, one small, gloved hand drifting to touch a soaring Doric column. Even
awestruck distraction could not disguise her escalating discomfort. Anxious sympathy
squeezed Darcy's chest tighter still, if that was possible. All this was profoundly unnatural

and new; of course, his unfamiliar bride must feel overwhelmed by the yawning grandeur meant to intimidate.

But how was he to present her? For years, he had planned this moment—long before he ever gave thought to who would wear the title of Mrs Darcy, he had worked out the precise wording, the manner in which he would present his home with its new mistress. It fell to him to usher in a new life, bring a new mistress to his home who would become the heart of the estate, so long left hollow after his mother's death. She would be of Society's finest circles, adept at hosting lavish balls and knowledgeable at all the affairs of the estate to which she would have to turn her hand. And she would be beautiful and demure, stately and graceful... He would carry her over the threshold—no stiff formality ought to rob him of that family tradition—and, setting her on her feet, he would proudly present her to each curious person arrayed before her.

But now, none of that would come to pass. Elizabeth probably knew how to take baskets to tenants, but could she plan a Twelfth Night Masque? Host everyone for miles around for a May party people would talk about for years? And while she was endearingly fetching... comical at times, and occasionally even high-handed, he could not say that she was the poised, graceful beauty he had once envisioned on his arm. She was not tall and willowy, not smooth as cream in new circumstances. Her eyes were wide, and her nostrils fluttered in nervousness, even now.

There would never be any thought of carrying her through the door, ensuring her first introduction to his home was in his possessive embrace, showing to all that she was *his*, and that she belonged there. And, probably because of the housekeeper's manoeuvring, only a handful of the servants were even arrayed to greet them. Under present circumstances, it was probably for the best, but it stung in a fresh new way. One more disappointment... one more hope shattered.

Yet he could provide Elizabeth with some fragile sense of belonging. He gestured with his hand as formally as he was able. "Mrs Reynolds, may I present my new bride, Mrs Elizabeth Darcy of Hertfordshire." Uttering those words whilst flat on his back seemed almost farcical. In proud imaginings of this pivotal moment, Darcy had stood smiling beside his radiant new mistress, certain of a joyous welcome by all. Instead, his worthless carcass sprawled mute and limp.

Elizabeth blinked, rallying her courage, and executed a graceful curtsy towards the handful of assembled staff despite visible nerves. "I look forward to knowing you all."

Mrs Reynolds dipped low in return, unconcealed delight shining past dismay. "The pleasure will be ours indeed, Ma'am!" In an undertone to Darcy, she added reassuringly, "Worry not, sir, I shall escort our new Mistress to suitable rooms directly."

Mute with relief on Elizabeth's behalf, Darcy suffered renewed shame borne aloft on his stretcher through endless hallways towards his isolated chambers. Perhaps they should not have come to Pemberley first, but had Georgiana escorted directly to them in Scotland. This was all... more than he could countenance.

INTIMIDATION AND CURIOSITY FLOODED Elizabeth as she followed the stately Mrs Reynolds into the majestic chambers reserved for Pemberley's mistress. Sheepishly, it occurred to her that these rooms were now her domain to oversee and maintain—an astonishing notion for a humble gentleman's daughter more at home in visiting tenants than hosting soirées!

"I shall leave you to get settled, Ma'am," Mrs Reynolds said after pointing out the bell pull and assuring Elizabeth that tea was on its way. "Will there be anything else?"

Elizabeth turned and stammered, "No! I thank you, Mrs Reynolds."

Unsure where to cast her gaze first, Elizabeth drifted towards sunlight streaming through imposing windows perfectly framing idyllic autumn grounds under nature's russet canopy. The panes overlooked sloping hills and a distant lake, nearly stealing her breath with unspoiled beauty. Timidly, she peered downward, half expecting to glimpse wealthy ladies taking afternoon constitutionals along meticulously tended paths. But no fashionable promenaders in sight—only a gardener tugging a cart and two stable lads exercising spirited horses across the meadows.

Tearing her eyes away from tranquil vistas, her awed inventory shifted indoors across furnishings that likely overshadowed Longbourn's total yearly revenue. Thick, expensive Turkish carpets muffled her nervous footsteps as she roamed between polished museum-worthy bureaus and lavish framed artwork. She trailed one gloved fingertip down intricately carved bed posts swathed in sumptuous silk damask, then perched cautiously atop embroidered coverlets worth a thousand times her meagre pin money. Surely, such indulgent grandeur was utterly wasted upon plain Elizabeth Bennet.

"I hope everything be to your satisfaction, Ma'am." Elizabeth whirled at the unexpected voice. Beth hovered just within the dressing chamber's doorway, clearly uncertain whether she ought to enter. She kept her gaze properly downcast. "Please inform me if there's anything you should need. My aunt can send for a proper maid for you."

Elizabeth managed a tremulous smile, though nerves still gripped her stomach. She reminded herself that appearing confident and comfortable with command came part and parcel of overseeing this household now.

"I am sure I shall require your guidance familiarising myself with the house, Beth. For now, kindly ask Mrs Reynolds to supply me a tour of these rooms when she has the opportunity. It can wait until after tea."

"Straight away, Ma'am." Beth curtsied and began to turn away, but Elizabeth stopped her.

"Beth? I shall speak to Mr Darcy and Mrs Reynolds about continuing your education as a lady's maid. And, perhaps if you are so inclined, you might work with me? Unless you prefer Miss Darcy, of course."

Beth's face went awash with a relieved smile. "I'd be right proud to work with you, Ma'am."

Elizabeth dipped her head. "I am sure we will have much adjusting to do, no matter the result. Thank you, Beth."

The maid bobbed a quick curtsy. "Very good, Ma'am! Shall I assist in changing you into fresh attire?"

Elizabeth readily agreed, and within a quarter of an hour, she was clean and fresh, and Beth was closing the door to go speak with her aunt.

Alone again amidst splendour that still felt alien, Elizabeth drew a bracing breath. Doubtless, most ladies of her new station would sail into this role without a second thought. She must simply rise to the challenge before her as situations dictated, rather than yield to uncertainty. Hopefully the capable Mrs Reynolds would appear soon and prove as capable and considerate as Mrs Hodges in London.

Where did one even begin to familiarise herself with her surroundings in a room boasting enough artwork to furnish the British Museum? Inevitably, her gaze drifted out the windows once more, where it seemed the whole world spread out at her feet. And this was the view she had missed from the carriage! Never had she seen a landscape where man's taste had done so little to disrupt nature's beauty.

Shortly after Beth departed, a light rap sounded at the door. She opened it to admit the housekeeper herself, and just behind her was a maid bearing a tea tray. The maid set the refreshments on the small table and curtsied before proceeding to pour steaming aromatic comfort into delicate China cups. Mrs Reynolds watched every move as if assuring herself that the maid did nothing to displease the new mistress. Once the tea was poured, the maid bobbed another curtsey and left.

"Mrs Darcy, please do tell me if there is anything I can do to make you more comfortable. I shall have your trunk unpacked directly, and shall I order anything particular for the evening meal?"

Elizabeth's eyes were still straying about the room, but she readjusted them to the woman's face. "Oh! Nothing particular for my tastes. I am still learning Mr Darcy's preferences, so for tonight, at least, I shall trust in your judgment."

Mrs Reynolds smiled in satisfaction, pride evident in her face. "Of course, Ma'am. I hope to assure you that I will personally see that the household meets with your satisfaction."

Elizabeth offered a nervous yet genuine smile. "The pleasure is mine, Mrs Reynolds. I appreciate your warm welcome, as I confess these unfamiliar surroundings are rather overwhelming just now." She accepted the proffered teacup and saucer. "Have you been with the family long, then?"

"Since the last master, Mr George Darcy, married Lady Anne, Ma'am. I came with her from Matlock as a young maid myself. I confess, I am terribly fond of the master and the young Miss, and I hope I may help you to feel quite at home soon."

"I appreciate it, Mrs Reynolds. Would you begin by showing me my way around? At present, I am frightened that I may sleepwalk and get entirely lost in the night!"

Mrs Reynolds smothered a smile and extended a hand. "Let us start with your wardrobe, Ma'am."

She had only begun orienting Elizabeth around the most immediate chambers when another maid entered discreetly after tapping at the door. "Begging pardon, Ma'am, but the Master requests you join him to meet Miss Darcy."

Elizabeth caught her breath and smiled tightly to the housekeeper. "Thank you. Tell him I will be there in a moment."

D ARCY BRACED HIMSELF AS a maid ushered his sister into the bedchamber. Georgiana hovered just past the doorway, wide blue eyes already shimmering with tears above hollowed cheeks that wrenched his heart. Though pale and wan from her recent trauma, to him, she would ever remain the toddling angel who bestowed messy kisses on his cheek and claimed he was her hero.

"There you are, sweetling... come here." Darcy grappled to inject warmth into his tone despite his awkward posture.

With a choked cry, Georgiana flew across the room to embrace him fiercely. "Oh, William! I was so frightened when we heard you were injured!" Drawing back anxiously, she searched his face. "Does it pain you terribly? How long did the doctor say until you can move about?"

Darcy managed a taut smile, cursing inner reserves constantly tested since this nightmare began. "I shall mend well enough soon, have no fear." When her lip trembled, he added gently, "We need only avoid any jostling during the days ahead."

Georgiana wrung her hands, blinking back tears to fix him earnestly. "I shall read to you for hours, anything to help the time pass until you are back on your feet again!"

Bile rose in Darcy's throat at her naive assumption of inevitable recovery. How could he crush such innocent faith? Eyes squeezing shut briefly, he rasped, "Georg ie..."

A hesitant knock forestalled the dreaded revelation a moment more. Gratefully, Darcy called for the person outside to enter, pulse leaping as his new bride's arched brows and inquisitive eyes met his gaze when the door opened. Sudden relief coursed through him. Surely, Elizabeth's easier manners in conversation could help smooth the impending revelations for Georgiana.

Clearing his throat softly, Darcy found his voice. "Mrs Darcy, may I present my sister, Miss Georgiana Darcy." Though his smile felt fragile as glass, no trace of turmoil rippled his polite words. "Georgiana, dear, I wish you to meet my wife, Elizabeth Darcy."

Georgiana turned from him and managed a shaky curtsy, eyes fixed upon the floor. "Mrs Darcy. I... I bid you welcome to Pemberley." Despite her strained efforts, her tentative words poorly masked her dismay that she was now forced to share her brother's attentions and affections.

"Georgiana, I believe you will find Mrs Darcy to be a friend," he supplied, hoping it would ease some of the fears he could see stiffening his sister's spine.

Anxiously, his sister flicked the briefest of glances upwards before dropping eyes once more to study her knotted hands. Dash it all, he should be the one embracing her himself, finding some way to comfort her without further disturbing her fragile equilibrium.

Meanwhile, Elizabeth sank into an answering curtsy, compassion radiating from her warm smile as she greeted the girl. "I do hope we may become dear friends, Miss Darcy."

Georgiana's complexion remained alarmingly wan, and she was twisting her fingers in agitated silence. Was his normally gentle sister actually so overcome as to forget all polite niceties?

"Georgiana?" Darcy prodded anxiously when she still failed to adequately reply. "Come now, have you nothing further to say?"

As Georgiana remained frozen in distressed silence, Darcy felt his frustration inexorably rise. How dare his sweet sister greet Elizabeth with anything less than warmth after all his new wife sacrificed on their behalf! Leaving her family, trundling across the country with his miserable frame, coming here to be a mother to a child that had no connexion to her, and all for Georgiana's benefit!

Temper firing his tongue before reason could intervene, he snapped, "I taught you better manners than such sullenness toward my wife!"

Even as the harsh words fell between them, Darcy bitterly regretted his loss of patience. Yet the damage was done—Georgiana visibly recoiled as if physically struck, crystal tears welling over to trickle down ashen cheeks.

"I cannot... you should not have..." His sister's broken weeping undid Darcy's rising anger instantly. Would his thoughtless temper now crush her spirit completely?

But before he could form any softening words for Georgiana, she whirled with a choked sob of distress towards the door. As it crashed violently behind her, the ensuing silence reverberated with accusations against his failures.

Darcy risked a glance toward Elizabeth, shame scalding his neck at her raised brows and compressed lips. "Forgive my sister's rash temper, Mrs Darcy. It seems I handled that rather ill."

"Rather ill?" Elizabeth repeated in astonishment, casting her eyes to the ceiling. "Sir, your sister is overwrought with everything she has endured! I hardly think your impatient censure improves matters." Shaking her head, she moved briskly towards the door. "If you will excuse me, I shall see what comfort I can offer."

As the door shut decisively on Elizabeth's retreating form, Darcy sank back against his mound of pillows. Heaven almighty... between his shattered body and cratered relationships, would anything of worth remain unscathed?

H URRIED FOOTSTEPS ECHOED DOWN Pemberley's upper corridor as Elizabeth sought some glimpse of Miss Darcy's fleeing form. The poor girl was clearly distressed and overwhelmed—small wonder, given recent traumas now compounded by her guardian's thoughtless temper. Yet door after door stood firmly closed, their silent grandeur offering no clues where Georgiana hid herself.

Halting near the passage's end, Elizabeth at last detected muffled sounds hinting at another person's presence within the last bedchamber. Pressing gently nearer, she could distinguish the unmistakable weeping of a broken-hearted young lady emanating through the oaken panels.

Throat constricting in sympathy, Elizabeth raised her hand to knock before hesitation checked the impulse. What possible comfort could she offer this tender stranger so wary of her intrusion? Any confidence must be hard-won, given the fragility of her spirits and fortune lately. Still, she could at least attempt the olive branch their awkward relations desperately needed.

Lightly tapping at the door, she queried softly, "Miss Darcy? May I enter?"

No reply issued for several strained seconds until a wavering voice choked out, "If... if you wish."

Cautiously turning the handle, Elizabeth peeked inside the dim interior. There, seated huddled upon an embroidered window seat was Georgiana Darcy, golden curls in tumbled disarray about her slight figure shaken by quiet sobs. At Elizabeth's hesitant approach, she jerked her tear-stained face away to stare fixedly out the mullioned panes.

Anxiously perching opposite on a padded bench, Elizabeth searched for possible openers to diffuse the crackling tension. But words crumbled uselessly under that weight of hurt and mistrust separating them.

Finally, Georgiana muttered almost to herself, "I assume you have heard about... about me?"

Elizabeth's lips thinned. Silently, she dipped her head.

Georgiana dashed fresh tears away, bitterness overtaking soft features. "Well, go on. Pronounce me a vile seducer, or a foolish innocent ripe for ruin. I care not anymore."

"Surely you cannot believe yourself culpable for another's crime against you!" Elizabeth leaned forward, willing the girl to meet her earnest gaze. When Georgiana shrugged miserably without replying, she insisted more firmly, "The fault lies solely with the gentleman who betrayed your trust so cruelly, Miss Darcy."

At this, Georgiana whirled on her, features contorted by anguished remorse. "Is it not seduction when the fool believes poisonous lies, abandoning all propriety and virtue? When she... tries to abscond with him, caring nothing for consequences?" Her voice broke on a wretched sob. "I am forever despoiled! No one respectable shall ever..."

She buried her face in hands as slender shoulders shook with renewed weeping. Slowly, the bitter sobs dwindled to occasional hiccups allowing measured words again. After long moments, Georgiana rasped hoarsely, "Forgive me. You must think me pathetic, indeed, carrying on so before strangers."

"Sometimes our nearest confidantes make the harshest judges." Elizabeth hesitated before adding quietly, "If it lends any comfort, you may find me less a stranger than most in one sense." She waited until one reddened blue eye peered at her over sheltering fingers before continuing gently.

"I was introduced to your brother after he discovered my youngest sister Lydia had fallen into a similar ruin." Elizabeth looked down, throat tightening. "With the same man. Foolish, she was indeed. Yet it does not eclipse my love for her, nor erase the villainy of the man responsible."

Timidly, Georgiana fully emerged from behind her hands, a painfully vulnerable sheen coating her cheeks. "Truly?" At Elizabeth's nod, she whispered, "Then you do not despise me for bringing shame onto everyone associated with me through my own blind stupidity?"

"Never that!" Elizabeth declared staunchly. Impetuously, she moved to sit beside the cringing girl, extending her handkerchief into her lap. When Georgiana slowly covered Elizabeth's hand with her own trembling fingers, an impulse prompted sudden daring.

Drawing Georgiana gently against her shoulder, she embraced this wounded stranger who, by chance, bore the dual mantle of sister. "The past cannot be altered, but the future remains unwritten for us all. Have courage, Miss Darcy."

Georgiana's eyes closed, and her body began to shake. "Courage... I never had such a thing."

Elizabeth sighed, her gaze wandering to the window as the girl wept against her shoulder. "Then you must discover it, and quickly. I expect you will have need of it."

I MPATIENCE GNAWED AT DARCY'S composure as silence lingered after Elizabeth followed his sister out. Surely, assessing Georgiana's state and providing whatever feminine comforts she required need not consume endless minutes? Yet each anxious glance towards the still-closed door proved fruitless.

When, at long last, definite footsteps echoed in the corridor, Darcy bolstered his flagging spirits with monumental effort. No matter the unseemly frustrations or sharp words born of weariness, he must smooth Elizabeth's reception on Georgiana's behalf now. Surely, between two intelligent women, when so much of their fates was entwined one with the other, matters stood hopeful of patching up again.

As Elizabeth entered, carrying the dignity only distressed gentlewomen can achieve, his irritation dissipated entirely before her arched brow. "I apologise for Georgiana's outburst, Mrs Darcy. Pray, was she very distraught?"

Elizabeth moved to the chair opposite his bed. "More bewildered, I think, by overwhelming events than truly distraught. We reached some degree of... understanding together." At his hopeful look she elaborated bluntly, "I confessed an intimate acquaintance already with thoughtless sisters and predatory gentlemen. That forged the needed affinity rather swiftly."

Despite himself, Darcy winced under the accuracy of that bald assessment. "Did you at least acquaint her fully with my own... situation? She persists in labouring under the misconception of my inevitable recovery."

"And crush every shred of hope so soon after restoring her courage? Let her cling to comforting fictions a while longer. Too much harsh truth at once might break even the staunchest spirit."

Her words held an unmistakable warning. Chastened, Darcy looked away. "Time is not infinite. I must tell her about our plans for the babe before we depart. And she must be made to understand the reason for them. Were I healthy..." He shook his head. "She knows me too well. No doubt, she thinks I will send the child to be raised by a gentle farmer, and that will be the end of it. I cannot imagine how it will torture her to see the child brought up under this very roof."

Elizabeth eased into the chair beside him. "Or perhaps that might comfort her."

"Comfort her! How? When the child's very existence serves as a daily reminder of what that beast did to her?"

"I expect it will be *you* who has the harder time forgetting that detail. You underestimate the love a mother can have for her child, no matter its origins."

He studied her—the wistful look in her eye, the way her cheeks pinked softly as she turned her face away and swallowed. That was a feeling she would never know, would she? "Perhaps," he conceded slowly. "While I do not agree, I pray you are correct... for her sake. But we have little choice, do we? I..." He cast a hand over the blankets. "Well. You know the rest."

Elizabeth thinned her lips and drank in a sigh as her gaze returned to him. "I think the time to speak to her of that must be soon, but not today. And perhaps not tomorrow, either. Let her first accustom herself to me, that she may learn I do not mean to usurp her place in your heart and that she might discover that she can trust me. If you tell her everything before she understands those two things, it may break her."

He sighed and nodded. "Very well. But we must act soon. Before we leave for Scotland."

"And when do you plan for us to go?"

Darcy shifted against his pillows. "Within a week at most. My intent is to spend tomorrow securing travel arrangements without exciting undue speculation. A wedding tour, of course. I never comprehended the practice of inviting a female companion on a honeymoon, for in my mind, escaping other people's company is the very reason for taking such a trip. But I suppose in this case..."

"It will be thought quite the norm," Elizabeth supplied. "But we must be away for so long... surely, that alone will spark some talk."

"Not if I can help it. Richard has agreed to drop hints that we have gone from a brief tour in Scotland, then on to Portugal for the winter."

"More lies?" Her brow edged upward.

"Would you give the matrons of London our direction so they can call on us for Twelfth Night? No, this is the only way."

"And am I permitted to tell my family where I really am?"

Darcy's gaze had wandered from her face to his blanketed toes, but at the painful twinge in her voice, he looked back up. "No. I do not think that is wise. You can send letters through Richard in London, and he can forward them on—we claim his army connexions make for faster post through the Continent. Perhaps no one will think twice."

At her incredulous stare, he added defensively, "Come, you do not think it will be remarked upon if the family of the new Mrs Darcy starts sending letters to Scotland when she is rumoured to be out of the country for the winter? Our departure must appear utterly commonplace, else tongues wag!"

Her jaw was clenched, but she closed her eyes and appeared to be counting off the temperamental outburst before she unleashed it. "I begin to comprehend theatricality is a Darcy hallmark. Very well, I assume we are to bring Giles for you. Miss Darcy and I have few needs, but I would like to bring Beth on the journey."

"Out of the question. Giles, I trust, and his presence is necessary. But we shall hire some local girl to attend you and Georgiana, as well as a hired coachman. I do not intend for anyone else from Pemberley to know..."

"I trust Beth." Elizabeth crossed her arms and stared at him, her expression impassive.

If that was her way of forcing him to her will, she would find him rather immovable on the subject. Darcy ground his teeth and prepared to wait her out, but then she did something that left him completely undone. That one eyebrow of hers slowly curved upward. Now, no longer did she look like a sullen woman, denied her will, but a worthy opponent, who knew she had him precisely where she wanted him.

He cleared his throat. "Very well. But I trust you will exhort her to supreme secrecy before we depart? Without disclosing the full reason until after we are away?"

Elizabeth smiled sweetly. "But of course. I do possess some tact, Mr Darcy. One of us must, after all."

He narrowed his eyes. "Indeed."

Elizabeth pressed her hands on her thighs and rose. "Make your preparations, then. I shall have to make a pretence of accumulating a suitable wardrobe for a winter in Portugal. Do you suppose fur is in fashion? I fancy Scotland will be much colder..."

"Where are you going? Surely, we have more to discuss of Georgiana—"

Elizabeth paused, one hand resting upon the door frame as she glanced back. "Mrs Reynolds awaits to finish the tour you interrupted earlier, recall? We shall speak more later."

And with that, she was gone, leaving Darcy oddly bereft by her absence. Blasted inconvenient that Elizabeth's good opinion somehow emerged paramount in his thoughts lately. Hopefully, Scotland's isolation must surely cool this irrational craving for her lively company and comely form. Although a deep, uneasy suspicion warned him it might be quite the opposite...

Chapter Seventeen

CRISP AUTUMN AIR FILLED Elizabeth's lungs as she wandered slowly along the gravelled path edging Pemberley's woods. In mere days, the estate had sunk into her soul with a sense of belonging she never anticipated. Yet undercurrents of sadness tugged the tranquil vista out of focus, hinting all here might yet be an ephemeral illusion.

The crackle of falling leaves soon recaptured her gaze upwards. Against an iron-grey sky, the vibrant red foliage formed nature's glorious cathedral to frame her solemn thoughts. How sharply life had shifted course, landing simple Elizabeth Bennet as mistress of all this! But she could not quite content herself with all the trappings of this new life she had chosen. Once one of five lively sisters; now solitary days stretched before her, with scarcely any prospect of laughter or even hope of future joys. The usual consolations of an arranged marriage such as hers—children of her own—were to be denied her. So, what was there but a grand house and depressing relations?

Her unlikely marriage had gained security for herself and hopefully her sisters... but at a steep cost, indeed.

Yet melancholy swiftly gave way before gathering resolve. Were not life's richest fruits cultivated despite—or perhaps even because of—imperfections and gnarled places along branches one climbed? And Mr Darcy was, at least, a man she could respect. Certainly, a companion of agile wit was far better than merely comely form in lasting unions.

Her brisk pace slowed as her thoughts strayed to Pemberley's isolated master. How swiftly her initial disdain towards the embittered cynic had transformed! Behind his protective armour, a quiet humour and ready compassion shone, freely given to innocents like Georgiana. And goodness knew, her own pertness and quick tongue had met with receptive debate rather than an offended temper. The more she witnessed her enigmatic husband's tender solicitude towards nearly everyone around him, despite his own feelings of disappointment and bitterness, the more confidently she could invest her future here.

Without a conscious decision, Elizabeth found her footsteps turning back towards the manor. Perhaps a part of her melancholy was a dread of all the looming uncertainties before them this winter. Settling that and being able to start planning with some sense of confidence, would surely ease all their spirits.

She really must seek out Miss Darcy soon regarding the imminent journey to Scotland. It would be better if the news came from her instead of Mr Darcy, because with it would necessarily be attached rather heavy tidings about her brother's true prognosis. And there was also the rather daunting prospect of a winter's exile in the north. If Elizabeth was homesick in this beautiful place, how much worse would it be for Georgiana—emotionally fragile and used to the comforts of Pemberley—when they carried her off to Scotland?

Sweetgrass and decaying leaves perfumed each bracing lungful of fresh air as Elizabeth traced a meandering path back to the house along Pemberley's gently sloping woods. How refreshing to finally stretch her legs away from London's foetid city streets! At least that was one pleasure that always cheered her and focused her thoughts.

Upon returning to her room, Elizabeth was walking towards her dressing room when something caught her eye on the writing desk. A single letter lay centred atop the polished rosewood surface, with her uncle's seal on top. Her stomach clenched reflexively—surely no new calamity had befallen her family again so soon! *Please* let it be good news... She broke the plain wax seal with trembling hands and scanned the few brief lines within.

My Dearest Niece,

I cannot express the joy your letter brought! Your accounts of the countryside make me quite jealous. I hope to receive another letter when the weather permits, telling all about exploring those lovely Peak District fells. And despite your evasiveness, I am certain that fine husband of yours proves attentive company on long rainy evenings. With your ready wit to spark his and such a pleasing countenance besides, I am confident in your mutual felicity. I daresay we shall soon hear happy news of a little one blessing Pemberley's halls before long! Forgive my indelicacy, but you know I cannot resist hoping for the earliest possible word. I wish you all happiness and await further news as you settle into your new home. Your uncle has promised that we shall come to Lambton to visit my family late next summer, and...

The letter went on, framing such delightful fancies that Elizabeth let herself sag against the furniture. All need not be lost... her family was still quite her own. A few terrible months lay ahead, but after that, all could begin to right itself. Spirits suddenly lighter, Elizabeth asked a passing maid where she might find Miss Darcy. It was time to face the inevitable.

"She's in the music room, Ma'am," the maid supplied.

Elizabeth thanked her and tucked Aunt Gardiner's letter in her pocket. Then she turned about for a few seconds, trying to remember which way the music room was. She could have asked the maid, perhaps, but she had lived in this house a full three days now. The mistress ought to know her way around.

A right and then a left, she thought... and then toward the arched corridor with the wide double doors. Elizabeth pushed a door open and glimpsed their quarry's golden head bent industriously over some task at the pianoforte. It looked as though she was turning pages, trying to decide what to play next. Perhaps the girl was in a peaceful, meditative mood. Elizabeth hated interrupting that promising prospect, but it was better than springing this news upon Georgiana while she was weeping. Thus emboldened, Elizabeth crept forward.

But the anticipated soothing melody of Mozart or Bach never sounded. Instead, a halting, discordant series of notes plunked randomly from the majestic instrument. Elizabeth's small advance faltered—clearly, Georgiana's distress today was not much diminished since their arrival.

As the erratic tempo subsided, Elizabeth cautiously approached behind the slumped girl's shoulders. A weighty sigh briefly preceded Georgiana, raising her face towards the blurry painted cherubs gambolling across the distant ceiling. Elizabeth tentatively cleared her throat.

"Excuse me, Miss Darcy, I had no wish to intrude." At the lacklustre glance her way, Elizabeth hastened on. "I merely hoped to speak with you. But another time perhaps—"

"No indeed, Mrs Darcy, you do not disturb me." Georgiana pivoted woodenly on the polished bench. "I was somewhat at loose ends and merely hoped for some diversion." Her tight smile held no mirth. "Do you like Beethoven?"

"Very much." Elizabeth glanced over the girl's shoulder at the piece she had resting on the piano. "*Funeral March for the Death of a Hero*?" She puckered her lips. "My sister Mary played that piece quite often, just before I left Longbourn."

Georgiana flicked a sullen glance at the music. "It seems fitting. Did you need something?"

Elizabeth shook her head, settling beside this sad young stranger she had somehow acquired as a sister. "Truly, I only wished for company, if it would not trouble you. My presence need not disrupt your practice in the slightest." She gestured aimlessly at the intriguing sheets of musical notations before them. "Would you like me to turn the pages for you?"

A long beat of silence stretched between them before Georgiana answered tonelessly. "There is little here to admire, I fear, for I own no true desire for playing just now." Her small white hands lay forlornly on her lap. "Still, I could hardly remain in my room another day—yet nothing captures my interest, either. Useless, it seems, without William to talk to. I wish he would just come down here and rest on the sofa while I played. Surely, that would not be too much for him."

At this stark vulnerability laid bare, Elizabeth swiftly changed course. She had intruded too hastily, clearly—sharing now would serve little purpose until better trust built confidence between them. Gently, she closed slender fingers around Georgiana's icy ones.

"Then we shall sit quietly here awhile until inspiration strikes one of us. Perhaps peace waits simply on stillness to make itself known?" A comforting lie, that, yet it coaxed from Georgiana the ghost of a less haunted smile. After long minutes ticked by, Elizabeth tried again in neutral tones. "I always preferred Bach for melancholy hours. Do you have any here that—"

Abruptly, Georgiana twisted to face Elizabeth directly with unguarded desperation etched starkly in her young features. "Elizabeth, I know William has talked to you about it. I must know what is planned for me." At Elizabeth's open dismay, she rushed on pleadingly, "Surely you comprehend? If William means to send me away somewhere in disgrace, better to have it all out now!"

Shocked understanding rose even as Elizabeth grasped those frantic hands firmly between her own now. Of course—Georgiana assumed the worst banishment rather than stay under her brother's fastidious roof. "First, calm yourself, dear girl. Your brother would never do such a thing. It... well, it will certainly be hard, but you are not to be banished."

As Georgiana marginally slackened from taut misery into limp dejection, Elizabeth forged on before her courage deserted her utterly. "In truth, your brother and Colonel Fitzwilliam think it wise that we remove you to Scotland... temporarily. Some months in quiet seclusion from judging eyes appears to be the most prudent solution before your... condition becomes obvious."

Oddly, it was Elizabeth now blinking back burning tears, watching the youngest Darcy absorb the news. Timidly, Georgiana whispered at last, "And do you and William mean to stay with me there until... you know... or does he plan only to install me somewhere far from polite society all alone?"

"Your brother would never see you abandoned to strangers! Nay, we shall make the long journey all three together. He insists most firmly on it."

"But what future awaits my child?" Her voice emerged with a cracked, tortured whisper. "Surely you see this pretence solves nothing! There will still be a... a..." She sniffed and wiped the back of her hand across her face. "What does he mean to do with my baby?"

Gathering tattered courage, Elizabeth ventured delicately, "Why do you suppose your brother was so swiftly married if he did not aim to protect your child within the family?"

The crease between her fine brows deepened as Georgiana slowly pieced the bewildering fragments together. When appalled understanding dawned at last, she clapped one hand over her mouth in pure horror.

"He... he cannot mean to claim my illegitimate baby as his own?" A horrified sob escaped her white lips. "With himself posed as the father and you... It cannot be!" Georgiana clutched her midsection as if physically pained. "I beg you, tell me I misapprehend!"

But Elizabeth could only bow her head, tears slipping free at such innocence violated by harsh realities. "Come, you know in your heart he acts only from deep love and honour—both for you and Pemberley's legacy."

"Love!" Georgiana spat bitterly. "Love never saw the light of day when he chooses my humiliation over death or the mendicant's life! 'Twould be far kinder to take the Spence and be done!" She wrung tormented hands through tangled golden waves. "What 'love' lets William forever see my ill-gotten by-blow under his roof? How is this endurable, either for him or for you? And what about me? Did he think to ask what *I* wanted?"

Elizabeth winced as fury turned inward, the anguished girl's pain becoming a self-scourge striking cruel blows. "Dear heart, nobody thinks to torture you! What say you dry these tears now, and we try—"

"He hates Wickham! I know he does! I never knew until... but I have seen it, and I cannot imagine why he would ever take the child." Wild sobs punctuated her cry. "Why would William endure constantly seeing such a bitter reminder of my ruin?"

"I understand it was Colonel Fitzwilliam's suggestion after... after your brother's accident." She halted there, throat constricting.

Instantly suspicious, Georgiana stiffened. "William would never agree to anything like that merely upon Richard's say." Sudden premonition blanched her young features as she grasped Elizabeth's hands fiercely. "I can see you know some secret. Tell me! What about his accident?"

Elizabeth closed her eyes. There was nought but honesty left, however painful. "The physician said... said your brother may never fully recover. That he may never... I am so sorry."

"No!" Georgiana recoiled wildly as guttural sobs shook her slight frame. "He is strong—this cannot be true!" She stared beseechingly at Elizabeth through watery blue eyes. "Why, I recall how swiftly William was back in the saddle after breaking his ribs in a riding accident! He will ride again... he must!"

Elizabeth was shaking her head, her eyes downcast. "It grieves him terribly. You must know that he endures much pain in his back still, but he has no feeling below the waist. He... he means to act to ensure that not only is your child safe, but the Darcy legacy will live on."

"No!" Georgiana was waving her hands blindly. "You are lying! I am going to him right now, you will see! You don't know my brother, he—"

"Miss Darcy, please. Stop a moment and listen before you rush to him. Think what he suffers, and you will see that you both need—"

But her compassion met only angered rejection as Georgiana leapt up, toppling over the sheet music bench with a resounding crash. "It is well enough for you to prate meaningless comfort with two living parents and a houseful of sisters besides!" she sobbed wildly. "But he's my only brother. He *has* to be well!"

Elizabeth bit her lip against a helpless groan, casting desperately about for any lifeline that might hold purchase in such churning agony. But Georgiana was already gone, the door slamming so that the room reverberated with a mocking echo. Elizabeth sank onto the piano bench once more, cradling her forehead with both hands. "Well..." she mumbled to herself. "That went well."

It seemed her husband was not the only one in this family who could muck up important conversations.

"*B*EING IN A SHIP *is being in a jail, with the chance of being drowned.*" Darcy grunted derisively, flipping pages in the leather-bound tome upon his coverlet in disgust. "'*And cheer and joyfulness in misfortunes, far beyond the little his wit or words are able to express.*'Hmph! Clearly, Master Boswell never endured shattered limbs and petticoat overcrowding beneath his own roof for long, miserable months!"

He dropped the book to his lap, too apathetic to consider throwing it, as he would have a fortnight ago, but too impatient to continue reading. He frowned down at his feet, thinking ruefully that at least his uselessness confined him far from any ships, real or rhetorical. If only his frayed temper might likewise find a sanctuary so distant from distressed gentlewomen and well-meaning colonels.

A sudden commotion at his bedchamber door dispelled further musings. But any irritated call for order died upon his tongue as the culprit burst inside ahead of anxious servants. *Georgiana!* And clearly, something or someone had dealt fresh anguish, judging by her wild, dishevelled appearance as his distraught sister flew heedlessly across the room.

Darcy's heart quickened with alarm as hysterical sobs wracked her slender shoulders. What could possibly have unsettled her so?

"Georgie! Pray, calm yourself, sweetling, and tell me what or who has you so distressed." Darcy held out beseeching hands as Georgiana flung herself face-down across his bedding, her incoherent weeping muffled in the coverlets. Dismayed, he glanced helplessly over her bowed head towards the open doorway where Elizabeth hovered, her brow pinched and pained as she met his questioning gaze. She turned to tell the servants to leave them alone, then looked back at him with a deep breath and a shake of her head. Darcy managed a nearly imperceptible shrug in baffled response.

At length, Georgiana's heaving sobs diminished enough to gulp air, enabling partial intelligibility as she twisted sideways with her scarlet-stained face still pressed into his lap. "I cannot believe what Mrs Darcy just said! It cannot be true!" Georgiana collapsed in bitter weeping across his bed covers.

Ah. So, Elizabeth had finally revealed the harsh extent of his impairment. Well... it had to come.

"Dearest, you must listen..."

"It cannot be true!" She searched his stricken features pleadingly. "But why else would you bind yourself to my ruin and child if any other hope yet remained? Nothing makes any sense."

At her anguished deduction, Darcy lifted his free hand to her sodden cheek, thumb brushing away fresh torrents in vain. Egad, would every attempt to spare his sister's feelings only compound her heartbreak further? "I am sorry, Georgie, but there is very little hope."

Georgiana frantically mopped her cheeks, still shaking with grief. "But William, you must rally quickly and be whole! Say this is not permanent!"

At her stricken pleas, Darcy's mouth seemed to turn to ash, and he could hardly find a word to say. Gently, he suggested, "My limitations currently appear dire, but in time perhaps—"

"No!" Georgiana cried, staring beseechingly. "Stop speaking in vagaries! I must hear plainly there remains legitimate hope of your recovering fully as before!" Her frantic grip tightened. "Surely, there is some doctor who can mend you!"

"I…" He sighed and rubbed his eyes. "I wish there were."

The stark, vulnerable trust in her reddened eyes lanced Darcy straight through. "But perhaps in Paris! I have heard of surgeons there who study the body in ways that are not lawful here, but they can—"

Mutely shaking his head, he forced leaden words forth in an emotion-roughened voice. "No, sweetheart. What Mrs Darcy told you was the truth. I shall never stand or walk unassisted again."

His admission broke open the floodgates as Georgiana crumpled with hitched, keening sobs across their clasped hands. There was nothing for him to do but to rest a hand on her heaving shoulders, and to glance up at Elizabeth once more. She had hidden her face from him—only her cheek visible, but she was listening. She had probably come more for his sake than Georgiana's, and just knowing she was there… well, that was some strength for him, after a fashion.

"Georgiana, all will be well in time, only have faith…" Even as false comforts spilt from his lips, Darcy knew she read the tragic truth beneath. Nothing could restore what fate had forever stolen.

Instead of replying, Georgiana only renewed her passionate weeping over his shattered legs as the horrendous future awaiting them crashed violently over her in waves. When, at last, she mastered her grief enough to rasp hoarsely again, a new sort of bitterness laced her cry, wrenching Darcy's heart anew.

"I cannot ask or endure such unnatural sacrifice! Please rescind this madness, I beg of you!"

"And what madness do you speak of?" he asked gently.

She gulped back a sob, her body quaking even harder now. "How c-can you endure p-pretending to take my ruined reputation as yours? It shall utterly despoil your own name!"

"Georgiana, whatever nonsense is this? You cannot think that I consider protecting my only sister 'ruination'! On the contrary—"

But Georgiana persisted. "Only think what permanent sacrifice you embrace, agreeing to raise my child! Can you truly forgive *that*, William? Oh, what I have cost you!"

Darcy's eyes squeezed shut, his tangled doubts nearly choking him, even as he tried to sound certain for her sake. How could he make her understand fully without crushing every hope? "My accident is none of your doing, but I shall safeguard your future no matter the burdens now mine to bear, little sister."

At this Georgiana stilled, horrified suspicion dawning on her face. "My doing... yes, it was! Tell me the truth, William. This is no mere riding accident like Richard said—do not lie! My folly has brought disaster far exceeding simple disgrace." She grasped Darcy's hands frantically. "I know my blame now, William! It was Mr Wickham, was it not? You challenged him to a duel, and he finally found a way to strike you through me!"

Darcy flinched from the unintended blow, throat constricting uselessly. That was the last thing he had wanted her to learn... but it was too late, for he could read her anguish in every line of her features. Swallowing hard, he finally grated out, "I... did seek out the blackguard for revenge. I fear that rage blinded me to reckless risks... and grave consequences none foresaw." He broke off as realisation made her face crumple in wretched sobbing once more. Desperately he reached out, but Georgiana recoiled from his comforting touch, wrapping both arms fiercely about herself.

"This is because of my stupidity!" She scrubbed both hands over her streaming cheeks, eyes wild with self-loathing fury. "Yet still you shackle yourself to the architect of your downfall, assuming guardianship for her bastard child though it shall publicly shame you!"

"It will not, for no one shall be the wiser. The child shall be my heir."

"But what if it is a girl? You cannot control that. Have you no consideration beyond Pemberley's reputation or fortune?"

Darcy's heart splintered anew under her guttural self-reproach, her torment now fully exposed, chilling his very marrow. "Peace, Georgie! You misconstrue my motives entirely."

Concern sharpened Darcy's tone despite his resolve for gentleness. "I assure you, guarding your future welfare and honour outweighs any other—"

"Honour?" Georgiana gave a scornful cry. "Where lies such when our deception must eventually emerge? Even if no one else ever learns of it, I shall never forget. Your wife shall never forget. No lifelong joy shall ever attend your marriage bed due to my sin! How can you live with that?"

"You speak in madness born of distress! Nothing occurs here without free consent. Mrs Darcy and I chose this path willingly." Frustration put an acerbic bite in Darcy's retort as his pounding heart mourned the frightened innocent before him. "This solution aims to secure your rightful place, untarnished by one scoundrel's violations. Any sacrifice on my part is trivial payment by comparison."

At this, Georgiana only buried her ravaged face into clutching hands with a miserable groan. Blindly, she rocked there at the bed's edge, like a grieving penitent awaiting sentencing by an unsympathetic judge. When Elizabeth hurried close behind, murmuring comfort, however, Georgiana violently shrugged away proffered solace without lifting her head.

"Mrs Darcy cannot comprehend, either!" Georgiana flung accusingly towards the silent woman now hovering helplessly. "Who is she, anyway? Someone so desperate to become Mistress of Pemberley that she would—"

"Georgiana Anne! By God, you shall show proper respect to both myself and my wife, whom you so undeservedly maligned! Attempting the restoration of your prospects deserves utmost gratitude, not accusation. I'll hear no more, do you mark me?"

At his unwonted harshness, Georgiana recoiled as though physically struck. Frozen there, blinking owlishly for a long minute, her gaze brimmed slowly once more until tears spilt unheeded down waxen cheeks. When finally, she broke the stony silence again, all fury had drained, leaving only a broken whisper.

"My child destroys your peace. Surely, ruin shared cannot be worth such cost, dear brother? Just send me away!"

Her small frame drooped forward to rest lethargically against his chest then. Gently, he smoothed her tangled curls, bitterness melting before this poignant evidence of her shattered innocence. Still such a child...

"Georgie, love, hiding away serves no one's good ultimately." He kissed the sweet brow upturned to him beseechingly. "Some battles raging inside cannot be fought in isolation.

Do you not yet see that walking together binds up all wounds far better than solitary misery?"

When her sniffles gradually faded into exhausted, irregular breathing, Darcy risked a cautious glance overhead. There lingered Elizabeth still, heartbreak and compassion naked on her lovely features. In that suspended moment, complete accord aligned their minds clearer than ever before. He would need her more fiercely than ever he had realised, if this odd little family of theirs was to stand any chance of eventual healing.

Chapter Eighteen

THE CREAKING CARRIAGE SWAYED gently as it rumbled further into Scotland's stark, windswept terrain. Elizabeth peered between thinning stands of hardy evergreens and rugged crags dusted white with the year's first snowfall. Such desolate beauty whispered of isolation that penetrated clear through to the bone. Certainly, more majestic vistas abounded than their current outlook. Yet something about the graceful austerity spoke to Elizabeth's soul.

And she seemed not to be the only one. Beth had ridden with them from Pemberley, and were it not for the occasional gasp of awe at the terrain or cheerful smile Elizabeth had coaxed from her, it would have been a gloomy carriage, indeed.

A sigh softly escaped the carriage's other occupant nestled under fur throws and blankets in the seat opposite. Elizabeth studied Georgiana's pale features, leaning listlessly against the velvet cushions as the mournful countryside unfurled past icy windows. The poor girl had hardly spoken three sentences together since departing Pemberley six days ago, drifting wraithlike in a cocoon of wounded misery through changing inns and tedious days of bone-rattling travel. Though equally fretting for Georgiana's fragile state and that of the gentlemen riding ahead in the larger conveyance, Elizabeth redoubled her efforts at buoying the girl's flagging spirits.

"If we are fortunate, perhaps once we arrive this evening, we can enjoy some mulled cider to ward off this penetrating chill." She rubbed her gloved hands briskly, awaiting a response. "I daresay, our gentlemen would also welcome warming draughts after such a long, cold day."

"Mmm." Lacklustre acknowledgement emerged, muffled through woollen layers that swaddled Georgiana nearly to the eyes.

Undaunted, Elizabeth persisted, "Do you suppose we will arrive soon?" She tried unsuccessfully yet again, peering past the heavy velvet drapes obscuring the carriage window. "Your aunt once mentioned Cairngorm's striking vista with a fairytale castle spanning the next valley."

At this, Georgiana roused marginally from gloomy reverie. "Cairngorm is no enchanted palace but a draughty old fortress from the mediaeval age." She grimaced faintly. "Neglected as most secondary estates are, once some distant ancestor departed for grander prospects."

That was not a promising prospect. Seven months they would have to... no, more like eight, by the time Georgiana and the child were strong enough to travel. And they must live in some dilapidated ruin? She dared not contemplate what essential comforts they must now forfeit. Fixing a smile firmly on her face, Elizabeth instead tried for optimistic tones.

"Why, how delightful! We shall play valiant chatelaines defending beloved people from savage foe." Seeing that her weak jest elicited no answering spark, she reached to squeeze Georgiana's listless hand. "Courage, dear girl. A few months' quiet restoration, then we journey home to happier prospects."

"Home?" Bleak bitterness twisted that single choked word. "No sanctuary remains to me. My reputation lies in ruins... nothing left but disgrace." Georgiana's shattered whisper spiralled into hitched weeping once more.

"You are missing the point," Elizabeth replied, some of the patience fading from her voice. "The entire reason we are here is to *protect* your reputation. Here now, that is enough gloom. Can you not think with some optimism and faith in your brother and your cousin's efforts to protect you?"

Georgiana flicked her gaze toward Elizabeth, and there was a faint concession there—a sniffle, a broken look, and then she buried her face in layers of wool.

On they jostled miserably, as the eternal hours further unravelled any lingering optimism. They should have stopped at the last inn. Elizabeth tugged the curtain aside impatiently, looking with some dismay at the fading light of the day. Her husband must be suffering terribly by now, but the ostler at the last stop had assured them they were almost to their destination. "Almost..." she mused. "Such an imprecise word."

Half an hour later, the gloaming's slate light illuminated a battered wooden signpost reading 'Cairngorm' in faded lettering near a gap in a towering forest. Elizabeth bolted upright, attempting to glimpse more through the icy panes. This had to signal the journey's end at long last!

The carriages emerged from woods' shadow onto a snowy ridge with crumbling twin towers distantly visible across frozen moors. Elizabeth felt the prickle of unease travelling her spine that had nothing to do with frigid temperature. Was that truly to become their refuge this bitter winter?

The wheeling carriages circled towards a weed-choked central courtyard containing nought but a dry, cracked well and decaying horse trough. Apprehension gnawed at Elizabeth's composure, noting the state of disrepair surrounding them. Georgiana only gazed numbly out at the cracked flagstones and weather-worn parapets before turning mournfully aside once more.

Elizabeth unbent her taut frame, feigning cheeriness she hardly felt. "See here, we shall ask Lady Matlock's steward to institute some much-needed updates on the morrow! Tonight at least brings respite from ceaseless jouncing." At Georgiana's mute shrug, she rallied gamely on. "Let us find which chamber boasts the fewest drafts and plan rejuvenations come daylight."

"I just want to lie down," Georgiana sighed.

Elizabeth spared her another glance as the coachman got down and came to the door. "I cannot argue with that."

T HE CEASELESS BITTER CHILL leaked through every gap in the ancient stones, stealing away what little warmth Darcy's meagre fire provided. He stared broodingly across the barren room—this place of supposed refuge felt less like a shelter and more like condemnation borne of desperation and subterfuge. Little wonder Lady Matlock had not bothered returning to look after her property if these were the best accommodations on offer!

At least several days of enforced rest upon arriving had eased the relentless agony in his back following that hellish coach journey. Now, slight shifts of position beneath the mound of linens caused but the occasional grimace, rather than stifled groans.

The sharp rap of knuckles against his chamber door heralded Giles entering. "Good morning, Mr Darcy. Shall I sit you up a bit today?"

Darcy nodded curt assent despite inward flinching. Necessary manoeuvres still ignited twinges through his spine. Yet he persisted doggedly, small victories each day towards regaining some measure of precious self-sufficiency.

Propped finally upon numerous pillows, Darcy scanned the barren landscape visible through the dingy cracked glass. Outside, Georgiana wandered forlornly across iron-hued moors wrapped in woollen layers, a melancholy wraith drifting untethered about as the gloomy winter sun sank fast. His useless fists knotted in the bedsheets—if only his own crumbling body did not make protection of her wounded soul impossible!

"Giles, please invite Mrs Darcy here," he barked abruptly into the gloom. Rare sparks of lightness permeated these dreary confines only when in Elizabeth's company. His manservant nodded in compliance before departing. Oh, how Darcy resented being relegated to merely requesting another's presence rather than staging command as once his right.

Yet impatient vexation eased moments later when Elizabeth entered, her vibrant, concerned gaze warming his surly mood, somewhat akin to emerging sunshine glowing through persistent Scottish mists. "What might I do for you, sir?"

"You can stop calling me 'sir,' for one. It is ridiculous. We are married, are we not?"

A twitch edged the corner of her mouth upward. "Then, what am I to call you? 'Fitzwilliam' reminds me too much of that obnoxious cousin of yours, and 'Willy' seems a bit..."

"Just call me William," he grumbled.

"So long as you stop calling me 'Mrs Darcy' all the time. I rather detest it."

He sat up straighter. "Detest it? What is wrong with it? The Darcy name is a proud one."

"Oh, it is not the name itself to which I object, but the fact that I am no longer 'Elizabeth' when I wear it."

Darcy blinked and relaxed somewhat against his cushions. Blast if she did not have a point. It was not as if she had taken his name out of affection. And she was far too wilful to readily submit like a proper wife... perhaps that was what he liked most about her. She looked him right in the eye and did precisely the opposite of what he asked unless it suited her to do otherwise. And he admired her all the more for it. How was it this woman alone provoked in him contradicting urges to both snarling rejection and blasted giddy yearning simultaneously of late?

"Very well, then. Elizabeth it is."

She smiled serenely. "Thank you. Now, what crisis made you call me away from dusting the sitting room with Beth?"

Darcy nodded towards the barren winter vista framed in the window's icy panes. "If weather permits, might you walk with my sister on occasion? She sorely needs companionship lest the melancholy consume her completely."

As Elizabeth moved closer, Darcy studied her dark eyes—the ones that made his insides quiver when they looked at him. When she leaned over his shoulder to look out the window, a wave of rosewater fragrance washed over him, and unwelcome longing threatened his composure again.

"Of course, if she will permit me. To be quite honest, I do not know how much good I can do at present."

"Probably none," he replied—in a voice that sounded a good deal more choked than he liked. "But she ought to know..."

Elizabeth leaned back and studied him. "She ought to know what?"

He shook his head. "Nothing."

"It is never 'nothing' with you, so what did you mean to say?"

He released a breath, letting his eyes graze over her cheeks... the soft curve of her neck and the loose tendril of hair wisping against her chest. "Only that I find your company... well, rather vexing, to be honest, but vastly preferable to solitude."

"Oh!" She laughed. "I say, William, you have taken care to study your compliments well. Do such pleasing phrases arise on the spur of the moment, or do you meditate on them when I am not around?"

"I *meant* it as a compliment," he retorted, his fist knotting the blanket over his legs. "Sometimes all one can bear is solitude, but you... well, you are better than being alone."

Something between her eyes softened, and her smile mellowed. "Then, if that is the truth—"

"I would not have said it if it were not."

"If that is true," she repeated, leaning into him with a stern look, "those may be the loveliest words anyone has ever said to me."

He let her hold his gaze willingly. She had a way of looking at him that made him feel as if she had captured something inside… as if she could sway even his heart with just a glance, and she seemed perfectly innocent of the power she held.

"Well," he said at last. "I daresay you had better remember them, because I will doubtless say something in the next day or two to make you think me a brute again."

Her smiled widened. "No doubt. Yes, I shall go to Georgiana now. Perhaps sunshine and brisk exercise may lift our spirits all around."

Following her departure, Darcy slumped against the bolstered pillows, his thoughts stewing. Soon, mental confinement would pose the greater trial as endless empty hours yawned before this useless lump of flesh now barely capable of lifting a book. Surely, some worthwhile occupation might yet present itself during this forced exile? Scant opportunities within these mouldering walls though, blast and confound it all!

No sooner had the notion crossed his mind than excited voices echoed up from below, indicating unexpected arrivals beyond their small circle of outcasts. Visitors of some sort. And he not even able to look them in the eye to determine if they be friend or foe!

Darcy strained fruitlessly, attempting to discern the rapidly approaching commotion, vexed that his formerly unquestioned authority now relied upon others deigning to keep him apprised. Perhaps Elizabeth would consent to relay him the details if he managed a polite request for information rather than an imperious summons. That chance evaporated as the lady herself darted back in, cheeks endearingly flushed.

"Curiouser and curiouser! Apparently, our first intrepid visitor braved rocky roads and the threat of more snow specifically to meet Castle Cairn's mysterious new occupants. Giles received the man—a Doctor Ewan Douglas awaits below, self-proclaimed as not only our nearest neighbour but the preeminent physician for miles around. I have not yet spoken with him. Ought we welcome him up, or send the kind doctor packing back across the moor?"

Darcy scowled, instinctively mistrusting meddlesome do-gooders. But a refusal would only have the perverse effect of strengthening local gossip. Not that he had looked to make himself amenable to the locals, but… well, Georgiana and Elizabeth might benefit from some assistance nearby, in case of anything unforeseen. Forging his composure, he arched one brow sardonically. "We might permit the man a brief audience since he exerted such effort. But impress strict confidence regarding private affairs!"

"Naturally, I shall convey the necessary discretion. Will half an hour suffice before I invent some pressing household matter as a pretext for cutting discussion short?"

Despite himself, answering warmth kindled along Darcy's spine, quite independent of crackling fire or extra blankets. Elizabeth's sly insights and sparkling humour alone penetrated the pervasive gloom surrounding him. Surely, even this inhospitable isolation must bear some redeeming qualities if she remained close at hand? Buoyed by that fragile possibility, he waved her off to handle their intrepid guest.

E LIZABETH HURRIED DOWN THE winding stairs toward the modest entrance hall. Though bare-walled and threadbare compared to the splendour she left behind, cheer blazed in the hearth. Already a flurry of activity emanated from the small wing housing the kitchen as Beth bustled to assemble refreshments without benefit of extensive staff.

Elizabeth tucked a stray lock behind her ear and straightened her gown before stepping into the parlour. Their visitor half-rose from his chair in automatic courtesy despite mud-spattered boots and a greatcoat that no one had remembered to take from him. One Doctor Douglas by his earlier introduction.

"Mrs Darcy, welcome indeed!" His jovial, weathered features creased around grey eyes that missed little, softened by ready humour. "Apologies, milady, if such an early call caused disruption. I've my rounds to make, but I could not overlook greeting a neighbour." His lilting accent was thick with his Scottish origins despite the precise cadence of a gentleman's education.

"No, indeed, we are honoured by your visit, sir." Smoothing her skirts demurely, Elizabeth settled opposite her ruddy-faced guest. "And I trust you shall not stand upon ceremony here, nor judge our rustic accommodations too harshly."

His warm chuckle eased the lingering awkward formality at once. "A simple repast suits me, lass. I've passed many a winter eve dining sparely off the land whilst tending crofters in isolated steadings across the glens." His throaty burr strengthened, recounting such exploits.

Some minutes later, when Beth shortly arrived bearing the tea tray and a loaf Giles had procured from the market that morning, Doctor Douglas exclaimed in delight, slapping his knee. "Far more generous than I'd looked for, m'dear! Indeed, we have much in common if you've knowledge in coping without Town's luxuries."

Elizabeth found herself at once in charity with the gentleman's unaffected nature. As she poured two cups from the mismatched set with a steady hand, she confessed with only slight hesitation, "In fact, solitude was what my husband desired most during his recovery. I trust your medical discretion regarding private matters...?"

Doctor Douglas waved a large hand benignly. "Recovery, you say? No doubt the gentleman suffered some grievous injury to chase him across the border away from London's best sawbones. Likely, they are leeches all! Why, training as a surgeon with the Black Watch gave me skill in mending every manner of battlefield wounds. I'd be honoured to offer my services if it pleases you."

His eyes gleamed with such earnest willingness that an immense surge of relief swept through Elizabeth. Perhaps Providence had delivered help precisely when it was needed most! Setting down her teacup, Elizabeth rose to grasp Doctor Douglas's calloused hand in gratitude.

"I cannot express what a godsend your generous offer proves, dear Doctor! In fact, Mr Darcy did consent to an examination by you. If I may be so bold, permit me to bring you up directly."

Chapter Nineteen

E LIZABETH ASCENDED THE STAIRS slowly before the affable Doctor Douglas, her instincts torn between relief at his offer of assistance and trepidation over what such an examination might reveal. Giles, who had been waiting in the hall, caught Elizabeth's glance and followed them. His assistance would most likely be necessary.

At Darcy's chamber, she tapped lightly before cracking open the door. "The doctor, Mr Darcy, as you permitted. Shall I have Beth bring up tea while you confer privately?" Though his solemn nod granted leave to withdraw, something unspoken in Darcy's shuttered gaze bid her linger. Hesitating, Elizabeth inquired gently, "Or ought I remain nearby during your discussion, in case I am needed?"

Darcy cleared his throat gruffly, a familiar signal of his discomposure. "I should welcome your impressions later regarding the fellow's advice." He avoided meeting her searching eyes. "That is, if you have no objection."

"None whatsoever." Well, that was not entirely true. She had never been present during any such exam. She did not even sit in the room when Giles came in to shave Mr Darcy... William... but there was something in her husband's eyes that begged her not to go. So, she stayed, settling on a chair in the corner where she could discreetly look away if necessary.

"Well then, sir! Let us explore what ails you presently and how we might effect improvements." Doctor Douglas rubbed his great hands briskly, every inch the man of science, while Darcy eyed him warily.

"As I understand it from Mistress Darcy, you suffered a terrible mishap resulting in...that is to say, your condition...?" He trailed off delicately as if uncertain how to politely phrase the delicate issue.

Darcy's jaw tightened, but he replied succinctly. "A fall. From a staircase. Some weeks ago. No sensation remains below the waist."

"I see, I see..." Doctor Douglas murmured, brows lowering pensively as he tugged his whiskers. "A grievous injury, indeed, and tragedy to be so confined. Well, let us have a look, then..."

He shifted forward, but Darcy tensed, knuckles white, clenching the bed linens. "I'll spare you needless prodding only to declare me hopeless, as London's pack of vultures have already done." Frustration simmered below his terse tone. "What possible good comes from repeating the farce?"

"Indulge an old country sawbones in satisfying his scientific curiosity, eh, lad?" Kindly eyes crinkled with his sympathetic smile. "If only to assure that travelling worsened nought, nor rule out what relief may yet be coaxed by diligent care."

Grudgingly, Darcy nodded permission. As Doctor Douglas peeled back the linen bedclothes to reveal inert legs beneath, Elizabeth noted the quivering of her husband's throat and the way he would clench his eyes, only to open them seconds later in distrust.

Methodically, Doctor Douglas tested responses up and down Darcy's legs, hope slowly seeping from his creased brow. Finally, he leaned back, stroking his grizzled chin absently. "Sensation fails completely, you say? That does not preclude attempts at restoring circulation. Mayhap a little simple rubbing—"

"My wife attends the task nightly without discernible results." Darcy bit off tersely. "Now, may we conclude this farce? I would rest before supper."

"Of course, of course!" Their visitor waved a conciliatory hand. "But if I may, I would like to examine a little more deeply, to see if aught may be done for your comfort and health."

Darcy sent a quick glance to Elizabeth. Then his jaw clenched, and he gave a short nod. "Very well."

As the doctor's thick fingers reached to fold back bed linens concealing Darcy's legs, he shot Elizabeth a deferential glance. "Forgive me, Madam, perhaps whilst I examine sensitive regions...?"

Darcy cut off the suggestion with uncustomary heat, piercing Elizabeth with a silent yet unmistakable plea. "Mrs Darcy may remain as she sees fit. Proceed, Doctor."

Settling back warily, Elizabeth watched Doctor Douglas commence a methodical inspection along Darcy's thighs and calves, testing reactions through firm pressure and probing. To his credit, Darcy tolerated the manipulations stoically, jaw clenched against any untoward discomfort as minutes wore on.

Eventually satisfied with his analysis, Douglas peered closer at Darcy's taut features. "Relax, sir, I shall be most cautious. But further investigation requires you to be rolled onto your stomach, I fear." Between his burly grip and Giles' steady assistance, they gingerly shifted Darcy's face down atop the linens.

Biting her lip, Elizabeth turned aside discreetly until the physician's ongoing commentary indicated the appropriate time for observing again. She looked up hesitantly as Doctor Douglas traced fingers down Darcy's naked spine, evaluating vertebrae one by one from between his shoulder blades to his... *well*. Elizabeth closed her eyes and prayed for it to be over soon. This was more than she had bargained for.

"Here, I surmise original trauma occurred, am I right, Lad?"

At Darcy's muttered assent, the doctor carefully probed the region, brow lowered pensively. "Significant bruising and inflammation long since faded, though a deal of swelling persists. Tell me, sir, in the earliest days, did agonising pain plague this area constantly?" He pointed to an area just above the injury.

Darcy remained mulishly silent until Elizabeth softly interjected, "My husband endured substantial discomfort that eased somewhat after concluding our travels here, I understand. I was greatly concerned that our travels may have injured him more, but..."

"Mmm..." Doctor Douglas tugged fingertips through iron-grey whiskers. "And where, precisely, does the sensation fail?"

Haltingly, Darcy provided the details until the examination finished. Only after he was carefully repositioned amidst pillows and attended by Giles did their visitor sigh heavily into the laden silence. Elizabeth tensed apprehensively—surely, if a positive prognosis existed, Douglas would voice it straight away? If he even knew his business, which, unfortunately, they had no way of knowing.

Instead of discussing his observations, Douglas inquired gravely after the London surgeon's findings regarding the spinal cord trauma. At Darcy's blunt summation of permanent paralysis and life of confinement, he weighed his words before responding delicately.

"Whilst I cannot gainsay learned physicians with the advantage of their fine instruments, have a care in presuming a definitive prognosis this soon." He held up placating hands to their excited questions. "Time may bring about some gradual healing or adaptability, supporting greater mobility than currently believed possible. I should say Mr Darcy is well on his way to being able to move about in a Bath chair, for example."

Doubtless reading the desperate hope in Elizabeth's expression, he added kindly, "At the very least, take comfort that prolonged bedrest and travel has caused no further damage."

Scant comfort, yet Elizabeth clung to it even as Darcy bit out caustic dismissal. "Of what value is vague optimism now? Why pretend any sort of reprieve awaits my wretched carcass?" He slashed one hand savagely, as if to banish their meaningless platitudes.

"As you say, then." Their visitor's easy composure smoothed the ruffled atmosphere instantly. With a deferential bow to his difficult patient, he allowed Elizabeth to show him downstairs.

In the main hall, Doctor Douglas caught her sleeve urgently. "I ken well why the poor gentleman clings to bitterness. He is not the first man I have seen facing this fate."

Elizabeth lowered her eyes. "Doctor, is there anything I can do to help him? You saw it yourself—my husband is a good man, but the anger, and the frustration... Surely, even the best of men may crack under the circumstances. I do not know what to do."

"Time, Mrs Darcy. Your husband has the look of a man who was active and strong before this. He must be given a chance to adjust to his new circumstances. Still, despair may yet defeat where the injury failed. Keep his spirits tended as diligently as any wound."

"And how am I to do that? Every pleasure is now denied him."

The doctor looked as if he had meant to turn away, but he paused and offered a slow smile. "You are a clever woman, Mrs Darcy. I daresay if anyone can find a way, you may be she. Your husband is a lucky man."

"I doubt he would agree with that," she sighed.

"He will. One day, madam, he will. Now, before I take my leave, is there anything else I can do? The village market goes on Tuesdays, usually, but occasionally you will find it more frequent. There is a peddler who comes through once a fortnight, but I am afraid you have just missed him. I am well supplied with any necessities you may require for your housekeeping, and my kitchen girl is clever and resourceful."

Elizabeth smiled and shook her head. "We are well enough, but..." She bit her lip and glanced out the window, where she could see Georgiana sitting under a tree with her head down. "I wonder if you might know of a midwife in the area."

The doctor's eyes kindled with a new kind of warmth. "Ah, Mrs Darcy. You ask how to give joy to your husband? I believe you already have your answer."

Elizabeth fought back the look of shock that no doubt registered on her face and forced a smile, instead. "Indeed."

Doctor Douglas nodded, chuckling. "Yes, I know one. My wife. I shall have her call on you tomorrow, will that suit?"

Elizabeth let go of a heavy breath. "Thank you, sir."

T HE LINGERING GOLDEN RAYS of the setting sun did little to penetrate the perpetual gloom pervading Darcy's bedchamber. He stared across the barren room as Giles helped ready him for the tedious night ahead. At least with ample pillows propping his useless frame slightly upright, Darcy could briefly pretend some tenuous connexion yet remained, binding him to the vigorous man of former days.

"Shall I stoke the fire higher tonight, sir?" Giles inquired. "These old castle walls admit every draught despite Mistress' best efforts stopping all gaps and cracks."

Darcy suppressed a resigned sigh. Even should the flames rage hot enough to ignite ancient floorboards beneath, he would still be chilled to the bone. The place might well blaze to the ground, and he would be the proverbial helpless babe dependent on others wrestling his dead weight to safety. "Very well."

He averted his face as Giles professionally tended to his nightly ablutions. Darcy stared grimly overhead, mastering cold fury as his manservant gently adjusted his lifeless legs beneath the blankets. Relegating Giles solely to valet-cum-nurse had been one of the greatest indignities of this entire ordeal. The man had such talents that he ought to be dressing London's finest gentlemen, with others constantly trying to woo him away with higher wages. That was why Darcy had brought him on five years earlier—because he was the best. And now, what had become of them both?

At long last, Giles concluded his preparations. "Will there be anything else tonight, Mr Darcy?"

"No. You may retire directly." Darcy's curt words emerged sharper than he intended. As the door clicked decisively shut on the servant's departing footsteps, Darcy loosed a guttural groan into the empty bedchamber. Stagnant hours of tedium awaited before even the illusion of rest would present itself to his wrecked frame.

The quiet knock some minutes later sparked instinctive irritation, instantly tempered by anticipation—Elizabeth. Even her tentative entry washed his bleak existence with beauty's glow and lively wit. Unconsciously, Darcy's rigid posture relaxed as she approached the bedside. Strange how this woman alone eased his bitterness without empty platitudes.

"Are you quite settled for the evening, William? Might I adjust your pillows at all?"

"Giles has already attended to that." Blast surgeons and colonels for imposing his invalid's existence upon a vibrant woman! Yet his life seemed... somehow more bearable with Elizabeth near. Still, he must discourage her tender heart from overextending on his behalf.

"I am adequately situated. You needn't attend to me further." He schooled his patrician features to impassivity under her searching gaze. "I shall not keep you from more pleasurable pursuits."

An indelicate snort met his shoddy evasion attempt as Elizabeth collected a jar of scented cream from the nightstand. "What endeavours, precisely, do you imagine fill my days as I am snowbound in this crumbling fortress? Knitting booties for the babe, perhaps? Nay, tolerating your irascible moods is my chief entertainment."

Despite himself, Darcy's traitorous lips twitched towards a grin even as he rejoined sardonically, "You need not be so blunt about it."

Elizabeth merely chuckled softly and pressed him back firmly against the mound of pillows. Before he could voice further objections, she had taken a seat at the end of the bed, facing away from him, as her small capable hands commenced massaging the fragrant lotion gently along his legs and feet as she had every evening. Never straying past his knees, her movements remained strictly utilitarian, and Darcy had inevitably surrendered all attempts at dodging her ministrations after that first awful night.

When he closed his eyes, he could almost imagine that he *could* feel her hands. Surely, it was no more than his imagination, for nothing else had registered such a response from him. But every night, the same sensation awoke in him at her touch. Perhaps some mystical energy truly did flow from her slender fingers to penetrate his unresponsive nerves and tissues.

More likely, primal yearning to know her tender touch was illusion enough. Even the objective, curative motions along his inert frame stirred traitorous reactions no gentleman voiced openly where a lady might hear. And yet... this beguiling siren who was somehow his wife by law, if not in actuality, was perhaps the one thing that bound him to a body that no longer worked as it ought. Did Elizabeth even realise how thoroughly she undid his vows of self-containment? Surely not, judging by her detached concentration whilst kneading lotion into his skin.

Desperate for distraction, Darcy ventured gruffly, "I understand the local midwife called today, per your request."

"Yes, indeed. She thought *I* was her patient at first, but she required little enough explanation when I corrected her."

"You are certain she will be discreet?"

"What I am certain of is that Georgiana is hardly the first unmarried English girl to find herself under Mrs Douglas's care." Elizabeth's soothing fingers methodically worked lotion down his left calf without glancing up. "But I told her we were here to inspect the property at the behest of Lady Matlock, and that we had brought Georgiana because her husband was away on the Continent."

Darcy snorted softly. "Clever, but no one would be such a fool as to believe that an invalid and his newlywed wife would travel all this way with a pregnant girl just to survey some long-neglected Scottish estate."

Elizabeth's shoulders lifted, but she did not look up. "Probably not, but Doctor Douglas assured me his wife was most capable and could even reside here when Miss Darcy's time draws nigh."

"And how did Georgiana receive this Mrs Douglas?" Unable to resist, Darcy watched the graceful movements of Elizabeth's capable hands along his leg, the arch of her slender wrist disappearing into lace-edged sleeves. Strange yearning swelled his chest, painfully aware that no real sensation transmitted beyond sight alone to betray her touch. Would he ever experience those delicate hands entwined through his curls or trailing teasingly lower along his torso instead of merely this therapeutic ministering? Even to kiss her knuckles in fervent gratitude seemed forever denied now.

Oblivious to his tortured longing, Elizabeth answered absently. "I believe your sister answered the midwife's questions readily enough before retreating upstairs. Whether she permits an actual examination remains uncertain."

"Well, I shall speak to Georgiana about cooperating fully with this Mrs Douglas." Darcy sighed wearily. "At least we must determine precisely when the babe may arrive, though I suppose female matters rarely conform neatly to physicians' predictions." Wry exasperation briefly lifted his mood despite nagging fears. "I only pray it shall be a boy. That would make this whole sham at least worthwhile."

At this fervent utterance, Elizabeth twisted to meet his eyes, her talented hands stilling against his shin. "Surely, we must prepare for either eventuality regarding the child. As my mother loved to remind us, her every scheme produced five daughters, despite cocksure certainty that several of us would be strapping lads." She grinned impishly, though swift sobriety followed. "Truly, William, if Providence grants us a girl, are we doomed beyond reprieve? Is Pemberley's next heir truly so horrid?"

He gazed back at her for an unbroken moment, his throat tight. "I would not trust the man with a dog, to say nothing for the hundreds of people who would fall under his power. Including you and Georgiana, if I were to..."

She paled. "And there is nothing else to be done? No way of breaking the entail—No! Do not answer that." She sniffed and chuckled. "Did I not hear my mother lamenting that very thing for years?"

He shook his head. "My great-uncle nearly bankrupted the estate. Selling off land Pemberley depended on for its solvency, gambling it away, and mercifully dying of his excesses and passing the property to his younger brother before he had ruined his family and plundered the property completely. My grandfather spent a lifetime repairing the damage—buying it back acre by acre, tending to the farmlands that had either been over-harvested or neglected altogether, and he wanted to be sure such a thing could never happen again."

Her features had softened. "I suppose that makes sense." Then, she seemed to catch herself and resumed her ministrations. "Still, it is dashed inconvenient. Bloody nuisance, actually."

He smiled. Sometimes, she sounded like a man... or at least not like the gently bred lady she was, and he rather liked it. And somehow, she was working her way through all his defences. He had sworn none could further violate their last sanctuary, and yet Elizabeth was slowly, patiently dismantling the stone walls he had erected.

"And is it certain, absolutely certain, that this man you do not trust *is* the nearest male relative? There are no other possibilities?"

Possibilities... his mind instantly leapt from the true subject of her question and onward to his own prospects. Were there any... possibilities? But what was the use? There were simply no acceptable answers to any question he could ask. "Let us speak no more on it tonight." He feigned an offhand yawn, looking deliberately aside. "Has there been no further word about the estate's steward coming soon? Pray remind me when we expect the fellow."

If Elizabeth noted his abrupt conversational swerve, no indication touched her serene features. "I believe Lady Matlock's letter mentioned Mr MacTavish was to have arrived by yesterday. I wonder what can have kept him?"

Darcy frowned. "I wonder what manner of 'steward' he actually is, given what you have told me about the condition of the house and property."

She tilted her head thoughtfully. "According to your aunt's letter, he tells her that rents have declined since tenants began struggling even before this latest blight."

"Yes." His eyes lingered on Elizabeth's shoulders as a tendril of hair, worked loose from its pins, coiled around her ear and dangled against the nape of her neck. He swallowed. "That... that would create a difficulty."

Elizabeth hummed softly as she got off the end of his bed and moved to the other side. He could feel the sinking of the mattress... he *should* be able to feel the heat of her hip against his thigh. Darcy closed his eyes and gasped for air. "I should think some minimal restoration is required, despite present finances, even if I have to fund it myself. I'll not have you or Georgiana sleeping in a draught if..." He faltered, words turning to bitter ashes in his mouth.

Hang it all, he could not even remember what had got them on the subject or what he was planning to say next. All he could think of was the deftness of her fingers, and what they might feel like sunk into his hair.

But Elizabeth only nodded calmly, one hand drifting featherlight down his instep. "Large expenses would probably not endear us to the tenants."

"Elizabeth?"

She looked back, a fine line pinching between her brows. "What?"

"Do you..." He fumbled for words, but there seemed no way he could phrase what he wanted to know without sounding inane or insecure... perhaps he had become both of those things.

"William?"

He let go of his breath. "Nothing."

One of her brows climbed her forehead. "When are you going to learn that assuring me it is 'nothing' is the surest way to convince me that it really is 'something?'"

Darcy wetted his lips. "I was... merely wondering... how many times have you been tempted to just... get in the carriage and leave? Go back to Pemberley or even Hertfordshire and leave all this behind?"

She twisted a little more to look at him better. "What do you mean by that?"

"I mean Georgiana and I... we have no choices anymore. But you..."

"I gave up my choices the day you put your ring on my finger."

"But not really. You could leave all this behind if you really wanted to."

Elizabeth turned away again, studiously avoiding his gaze. "And bring open scorn upon myself and my family, so soon after... everything? You overestimate my sense of daring and recklessness, William."

Somehow, her flustered vulnerability only enhanced her appeal, loosening his tongue once more. "Or you underestimate your quality... Elizabeth."

She stiffened and turned back to him, her eyes wide. Her throat trembled with an indrawn breath, and she looked hastily away again. "I am but a desperate daughter of a ruined family. One of hundreds, no doubt, who just happened to catch your cousin's notice at an opportune moment. We all do as we must."

His words emerged rough and gravelly. "I... Indeed." He swallowed tightly, cursing the lost opportunity. Willing hands and generous heart deserved frank openness rather than his inveterate evasions. Yet Darcy's protective instincts ran too deep, making him hesitate to admit vulnerability where Elizabeth might feel obligated to further sacrifice herself just to ease his guilt. Far wiser to leave unspoken any tender yearnings that might accidentally take advantage of her kind heart. "Perhaps I... perhaps you will find one day that all was not sacrificed. That... there may be some pleasantness to look forward to."

She paused once more as a deeper blush stained her cheeks. But the vulnerable instant passed as Elizabeth hastily stoppered the bottle of lotion and rose. The loss of the moment pierced him sharply until she ventured, almost shyly. "I suppose we both contribute as we may, then. Perhaps even the most devastating trials reveal their graces in time."

Something twisted within Darcy's chest at the quiet meaning infusing her words. Swiftly, he turned aside, throat constricting painfully against a sudden sting in his eyes. Tomorrow, perhaps, he might find the courage to say more. But for now, just knowing she was next door as he slept...

Well, at least it was no longer the *lowest* level of Hell that bound him.

Chapter Twenty

S UNLIGHT GLINTED OFF GLAZED windowpanes, sparkling brightly enough to belie the frigid winter air as Elizabeth strode briskly across the barren moor. She savoured greedy lungfuls that seared only pleasantly now after weeks of braving Scotland's unforgiving winter climate. Frosty clarity perfectly suited Elizabeth's restless mood this morning.

These invigorating daily constitutionals provided her sole opportunity to escape the cloying confines of the draughty old ruin that was now her home. Not that tending necessary tasks indoors proved terribly onerous alongside cheerful Beth. They had established a domestic rhythm this past fortnight, preparing the decrepit old "castle" against the bitter months ahead. Securing provisions, banking fires against the perpetual chill, filling gaps that admitted icy blasts through crumbling masonry—all such duties filled her waking hours. She had a purpose, at least... but these last few days, she was more restless and unsettled than usual.

True, she had never been required to personally lay up stores for winter or help kindle cook fires in the morning, but it was not the endless rounds of sweeping, stitching and scrubbing that so oppressed her spirit of late. Rather, loneliness borne of isolation from her loved ones gnawed at her as the dreary winter days bled together.

Were Mama and her sisters well? Did Papa take comfort in his library's faded volumes when he missed Elizabeth most? And what had become of her family's honour? Had they recovered at least a shred of their dignity thanks to her marriage? She clung desperately to the promise of travelling near Longbourn next spring, as well as her aunt's last letter relaying hopes of a summer reunion.

Meanwhile, solitude remained Elizabeth's sole balm, when yearning for connexions beyond this tiny household overwhelmed her aching heart. Beth was kind and sweet, but she had not the sort of personality or way of thinking that permitted her to jest or speak casually with her mistress. Georgiana tried to be friendly... or it seemed like she was *beginning* to try. Elizabeth had to wonder what Georgiana had been like *before*. Perhaps one day, after so much of the upheaval of the present was safely behind them all, she would have a chance to know. But for now, just being with Georgiana drained Elizabeth of every last gasp of her emotional fortitude.

None save William himself provided the sort of company she longed for. His mind was even nimbler than hers, and that wry darkness in his humour reminded her so much of Papa that she felt at home in speaking to him right from the beginning. Indeed, he seemed to feel things as deeply as she did, and he had an expressive turn of thinking that challenged her to match wits with him as few had ever done.

But... well, to be truthful, he just needed so much from her that, at times, she would have sold her soul just to have someone to talk to who demanded nothing of her. He could not help it, and she knew what she was signing up for when she entered this marriage. But some days, a breath of fresh air was all that stood between her and an apoplexy.

Pausing atop a barren knoll, Elizabeth turned her face fully into winter's caressing breath. Trees stretched leafless fingers into the pearly heavens, echoing the soaring reach within her own soul on this crisp, glorious morn. If she closed her eyes against the icy landscape, she could almost fancy Jane's gentle laughter or hear Papa calling her into his book room for a rousing debate. The bittersweet reminder usually soothed rather than stoked further pangs of homesickness. But this morning, phantom voices stirred only resentment that every small freedom seemed granted solely at William's pleasure. And he would probably need her again soon.

Scowling fiercely against threatening tears, Elizabeth crammed her sodden gloves into her pocket and scrubbed one chilled hand over her face. This brooding gloom was unlike her; she must regulate these unsettled emotions before bitterness took a deeper root. Had not Papa cautioned her against that very thing—that one day, she might become so warped and bitter that she would not know herself? With an effort, she forced the traitorous fears back and turned resolutely over frosted fields towards the distant tumbledown walls she could just glimpse.

Strange that this isolated fortress both sheltered tender shoots of belonging between her unlikely new family and also severed their small circle utterly from the wider realm.

Were it not for Doctor Douglas's periodic visits, she might well imagine only this little clutch of refugees from Pemberley inhabited all creation! A tempting fancy, perhaps, to embrace Romantic ideals of rapturous isolation with beloved kindred spirits, but hard reality rudely banished girlish fancies. Neither William nor Georgiana welcomed her deeper intimacy, nor she theirs, in truth.

So, Elizabeth clung desperately to their awkward domesticity as a slender bulwark against darker emotions lurking traitorously in the wee hours. Best to hasten back from restless fancy's snares and resume her placid calm before that brooding chasm swallowed her completely. Thus fortifying her wavering composure, she crested the next rise full in view of the castle's cracked ramparts.

A lone smudge of colour upon the otherwise empty landscape gave her pause—the unmistakable figure of Beth waving a kerchief to hail her. Anxiety roiled instantly to life as Elizabeth pelted headlong downslope without further thought. Surely, some new crisis? Had Georgiana fallen, or had William...? Breathless, she reached Beth within minutes, though her fearful query was met with only a shaking head and placid reassurance.

"Beg pardon, Ma'am, no cause for fright! The master merely wishes to see you straightaway, that's all."

Dismay rapidly displaced alarm as Elizabeth read the unspoken urgency in Beth's timid features. Likely just another tedious estate matter William judged important enough to disrupt her rare freedom! Did the man not comprehend that even thirty minutes without his clamouring demands was her only sanity some days? If this so-called urgent summons proved a mundane query easily addressed later over supper, she swore she would give Fitzwilliam Darcy a sharpish piece of her mind!

Seething resentment fuelled each angry stride toward the bedchamber, where awaited Pemberley's demanding lord and master. Not two days past, William had confessed that aching loneliness haunted him through tedious, uneventful days of involuntary confinement. *Hah!* As if he were the only one who felt lonely and bored! What could she *possibly* know of it?

But Elizabeth choked back that thought as soon as it crossed her mind. Her lot was certainly not the worst, and giving in to self-pity or resentment benefitted no one. With a sigh, she removed her bonnet and smoothed a few wayward curls, then opened the door.

Darcy looked up from a ledger with an expectant expression as she entered. "Ah, there you are, Elizabeth. I was just starting to wonder if—"

"Yes? You wished to speak with me?" Elizabeth interrupted brusquely before he had quite finished his sentence.

Displeasure etched his saturnine features at her curt interruption. "Indeed, though clearly at some inconvenience. No doubt I am distracting you from more agreeable diversions?"

Striving for at least outward courtesy, despite her simmering impatience, Elizabeth removed her pelisse and gloves. Best to conclude this vexing interlude swiftly and retreat where her restive mood disturbed none. With a strained smile pasted firmly in place, she took the chair opposite him by the bed.

"Of course not. I was just taking the air, which cannot be terribly important. The moors provide unparalleled views that I wished to admire, but of course, that can wait."

She spoke lightly, even as resentment tightened her throat. Had she not toiled tirelessly to ease his isolation, being the ever-attentive companion for a man unable to stir beyond this bed? Did he think of that whilst casually pulling her from too few beloved moments outdoors, away from his ceaseless demands? Unable to resist a sly gibe, Elizabeth continued airily. "Naturally, if you expect to need me during my outings, please advise me before I set out, so I shall remain close enough to be recalled in case of an emergency."

At that pert challenge, Darcy arched one imperious brow as his disapproving frown deepened. "I hardly think there will be any crisis during your morning walk that merits calling you back. It was you who decided to break off your enjoyment, not I who forced it upon you."

"That was not the way it was conveyed to me, when Beth said 'straightaway.' Your word, I presume?"

His look darkened. "I can hardly go to you when I desire to speak with you. I must depend upon your leisure, it seems."

Elizabeth thinned her lips, making one last attempt at cooling her temper, but the words that popped out of her mouth were anything but cool and tempered. "Well? What was the matter?"

Stiff silence at this jab finally broke under its own awkward weight as Darcy frowned severely. "Forgive such a gross imposition upon your precious hours of freedom, Madam. I sought your assistance in inventorying larder provisions ahead of the coming storm tonight. Giles tells me we may be under snow for a week or more. But by all means, do not let mundane domestic affairs distract you overlong from more delightful amusements outside."

Was that barbed emphasis on her wifely duties intentional, to shame Elizabeth for irresponsible neglect? Outrage flared as she clenched white-knuckled hands under the edges of her skirts, summoning her tattered patience. "Not at all! I am more than willing to address whatever concerns arise for the household. Though I admit to some confusion as to why Beth portrayed the matter so urgently. I have hardly neglected my duties, and surely such routine tasks can pose no dire crisis requiring my immediate presence?"

"I hardly think it unreasonable to request your input to ensure our survival through the winter months." Darcy's testy words emerged as he shuffled papers unnecessarily to avoid her searching eyes. "However, if providing sustenance and shelter for us all fails your exacting standards for noteworthy tasks, by all means, feel free to ignore such trifles henceforth!"

Anger sparked dangerously within Elizabeth at his condescending tone, shattering her already strained composure. They glared at each other, mutual pique rapidly escalating towards recklessness. Why must even reasonable discourse degrade to bickering lately? But words were already spilling forth unchecked, as desperate frustration multiplied anger threefold.

"For heaven's sake, William, remember that I never requested this cloistered existence, stripped of all my familial connexions! I gave them all up for you and Miss Darcy! Do not dare impugn my dedication simply because my temporary exhaustion over constraints beyond my control demands an occasional respite!"

His angular features hardened instantly under her unexpected show of temper. "My goal was hardly to pass summary judgement on any dereliction of duty, but rather to see that my own concerns warrant some place in your priorities in the future!"

Elizabeth surged up in outraged fury, pacing before the hearth to avoid slapping him silly. "Priority over my last vestiges of liberty beyond endless household accounts or awkward conversations? Always, I must hover within ready summons even during these brief escapes. Tell me plainly—am I a wife or a servant, existing solely for your beck and call?"

"Servant! I—" Darcy clenched a fist before his face as if catching the words he had meant to pelt her with. He sucked air between his teeth and closed his eyes before he spoke again, his voice low and cold. "I call only when necessity dictates, Mrs Darcy, with care not to overburden you. And you think this is me treating you like a servant?" He laughed sarcastically. "What would you prefer? That I send an embossed invitation?"

She rolled her eyes. "Yesterday morning, it was a question about finding material for Miss Darcy's clothing needs—a matter I had already attended to. Fifteen minutes later, it was a request for a different book to read. Ten minutes after that, it was a summons to remind Giles to ask after purchasing a cow in milk when he goes to the market—but he had already gone, which you recalled when I reminded you—and half an hour later, it was—"

"You have said quite enough, Madam! I fully comprehend your feelings. Perhaps I shall take care to create a list of all the day's conversations to be attended to in a single meeting for your convenience?"

Elizabeth gritted her teeth. "I am not your steward, Mr Darcy!"

"No. You are my wife, and a dashed hideous fate it must be for you."

She clenched her fists, readying a scathing retort as dangerous sparks in William's eyes warned against pressing him further. But a brisk knock broke in, cutting off the hot-tempered words sizzling on her tongue... which was probably a mercy. At Darcy's impatient bellow to enter, it was none other than Colonel Fitzwilliam who strode inside, wearing an insouciant grin.

"What-ho, Cousin! I bring tittle-tattle from Town. News of your marriage and whirlwind honeymoon trip has shaken the very foundations of London society, so here I stand, come to bask in marital felici—." His cheery hail broke off abruptly, surveying their twin furious expressions. "Good God, your faces suggest I interrupted preparations for mortal combat!"

"Rather just a bracing civil debate between spouses. Now, for what purpose do you come, Fitzwilliam?" Darcy's scowl deepened, gaze shooting icy daggers towards his befuddled cousin.

"Am I intruding? Clearly, the happy couple desires more privacy than I anticipated. Perhaps I shall hie me back to London and—" Colonel Fitzwilliam's knowing smirk shifted rapidly into bewilderment as Elizabeth stormed wordlessly past him into the hallway, allowing that accursed bedchamber door to slam deafeningly loud in her wake. Childish outbursts shamed her further, but another instant breathing stifling air with William's obstinate temper threatened her precarious composure completely.

Elizabeth seethed down twisting staircases as anger slowly surrendered to bitter remorse and exhaustion in equal measure. However strained their tentative accord grew under lengthy confinement, surely open breaches of courtesy only magnified the misery further?

She was never the most patient of women—that honour would go to Jane, or perhaps Charlotte—and her patience had long since exceeded its limits. Dashing sudden tears aside, she tugged the hood of her pelisse higher over streaming eyes and stumbled out into bracing winter air once more. Better solitude than murdering her vexing new husband with one of his ornamental fire irons!

Chapter Twenty-One

D ARCY WATCHED THE DOOR slam behind Elizabeth's retreating form, shock and remorse piercing him sharply. Blast, what demon had possessed him to snap at her so when she had done nothing to deserve his temper?

"Well!" Richard whistled. "Should I, er... call her back?"

"Believe me," Darcy grumbled, "that is the *last* thing you should do right now."

"Ah. Unfortunate timing on my part, then, for I had dearly looked forward to seeing at least one smiling face after such tedious travels, and Mrs Darcy seemed my best bet."

At Darcy's answering scowl, his cousin cleared his throat awkwardly and dragged the chair nearer the bed with feigned nonchalance. "Well, I come bearing news on other fronts, at least, if you've no wish to discuss personal matters. Wickham's court martial pronounced him guilty of desertion, along with drunkenness whilst on duty. Apparently, several other less savoury accusations were raised against Wickham's character but struck from the official record. He ought to be safely on his way to Australia by now."

Darcy snorted bitterly. "Transportation is too good for that devil. He deserves to be hanged, not exiled to the Antipodes to thrive like blasted Robinson Crusoe."

Richard waved a hand airily. "Let all memory of that accursed bounder fade into obscurity now. Mayhap the terror of wild oceans and foreign cannibals will accomplish what more civilised justice regretfully cannot."

Brooding silence lingered until Darcy loosed a sceptical grunt. "Save two ruined gentlewomen under this very roof whose peace he stole forever!"

"Two? I only count one. You think Mrs Darcy still suffers as well?"

"More than anyone, I warrant." Darcy sighed. "But go on, what other cheery updates do you bring?"

His cousin shifted uncomfortably before forcing brighter tones. "Oh, I brought the post from London for you, including several letters for Mrs Darcy. I am certain she must be craving word from her family by now."

Darcy eyed the letters but shook his head dismissively, his emotions still raw from the argument. "Best wait to approach her until she is good and ready to greet you herself. I'll not have her accusing me of more rudeness when her temper remains unsettled."

"Come now, old chap! Surely, letters from her family are just the balm the poor woman needs right now. Cooped up with your glowering self in this gloomy old house, no one else to talk to for miles around. It is a wonder you have not already strangled each other... or at least that *she* has not strangled *you*."

Darcy shot his cousin a glare. "I do not remember you being so callous before."

Richard scoffed and got out of his chair a little to shift it closer. "I was not referring to your physical condition, but to which of you is surely the most difficult to live with. You would have been a tricky sort of husband for a woman to manage long before any of this."

"And precisely what is that supposed to mean?"

Richard settled again in his chair with a sigh, stretching his back after what had, no doubt, been over a week of nonstop bouncing in a carriage. "I mean, you are so damned exacting and demanding of yourself, and you always refused to take any sort of wife where you could not hold the same expectations of her. And while I believe Mrs Darcy is probably precisely the sort of woman you ought to have been seeking all along, now that you were both forced into a situation that was, I confess, less than ideal, well... I should think it might take a bit of adjustment of your expectations. And hers, no doubt." Richard folded his hands and studied Darcy with a pensive look. "Surely, homesickness is not least among her present trials."

Grudgingly acknowledging the truth in this, Darcy huffed. "Oh, very well! But exercise care, presenting those letters to her. She has the teeth of a viper when she chooses, and you probably want to keep that hand."

Richard chuckled. "Now there, I know you are exaggerating. You never could fool me, Darcy, whether at cards or anything else. Your cheek twitches when you are trying to bluff, did you know that?"

Darcy crossed his arms and looked out the opposite window. "I do not know why you value the ability to prevaricate. No gentleman ought to master the art."

"Well, perhaps not, but it is at least a useful skill to be able to spot a liar." Richard paused, waiting for Darcy to look back at him. "Truly, how is Mrs Darcy? She did not strike me as one who was formed for ill humour. Tell me today was an anomaly."

Darcy nodded slowly, refusing to hold Richard's gaze. "She is..." He swallowed. "I... I truly cannot say."

Richard leaned forward, bracing his elbows on his knees. "Hmm. Well, we must see to that. I think Mrs Darcy's present happiness ought to be our first priority."

Darcy blinked and focused his gaze back on his cousin. "Elizabeth? Why her? Georgiana is the reason we are here, after all."

"And neither you nor Georgiana have a prayer of being right in the head without her as your anchor. Egad, Darcy, are you so thick that you still do not know why I brought Elizabeth Bennet to you almost as soon as I saw her? If she is well and happy, then I can have some hope for you and Georgiana." He stiffened back in his chair, grinning as he reached for the bag of letters he had brought in. "It was either that, or I would have to play governess myself. But Mrs Darcy is prettier than I am."

"Fortunately for her."

Richard grunted and got up. "Indeed. Let me beard the lioness in her den and see if I might soften her somewhat with my offering. If I should fail to return by sundown, send a note to my mother, will you? Tell her I perished in noble combat."

Darcy snorted as his cousin went out. As if Elizabeth was some she-devil, waiting to strike! But she *had* been out of sorts these several days, and that ready smile of hers had been curiously more and more absent from her face. His fault, he knew. What sort of husband was he who, instead of giving happiness to his wife, only distressed her?

But Richard's bold proclamation that his own happiness hinged on Elizabeth's, well... That was a curious notion. He would have thought it to be the reverse—that it was *his* duty to be content and central to all the household so that his wife might know peace. But that was now no longer possible in the conventional way, was it?

Stewing on this thought, Darcy wrung his fist in the coverings on his bed in leaden silence while he waited for Richard's return. He ought to have reacted with more understanding toward Elizabeth's frayed temper, rather than defensive pique. She was not the woman to be cowed by a husband's will, and so much the better, for such a woman would have long since cracked under these circumstances. Elizabeth might give him a solid tongue-lashing. She might even declare that she despised him and wished she had never seen his face.

But she was too stubborn to break.

And he would be lost without her. Whatever else Richard had hoped to accomplish by urging them to marry, the one thing Elizabeth had brought into his life was hope. But that hope, it seemed, was his alone. Truly, he had ruined her prospects and condemned her spirit to slow strangulation. The knowledge ate at him bitterly.

When Richard returned some time later empty-handed, he took the chair with a satisfied sigh.

"Did the letters please her?" Darcy asked, more sharply than he meant.

"They must have. She gasped, kissed me on the cheek, and ran upstairs with them clutched to her chest."

Darcy frowned at his feet. Elizabeth had never kissed *him* on the cheek. And why would she be so informal with Richard, whom she had met less than a dozen times? He cleared his throat. "That is... that is well."

"Speaking of 'well,' I've not yet asked about Georgiana. Where is she today? Mrs Darcy said Georgiana keeps to her room more often than not."

"I believe she does. Surely someone has told her you are here, though."

"Yes, Mrs Darcy sent the maid to her. I take that to mean my dear cousin has not yet warmed to your wife?"

Darcy grimaced. "In truth, my sister is still elusive, retreating behind a wall of courteous silence I cannot seem to breach. Elizabeth stands a better chance of coaxing Georgiana from her melancholy when they stitch together in the afternoons. Elizabeth had to insist upon it, to much protestation on Georgiana's part, I understand, but they have managed to make it something of a daily routine now, I believe. But as for signs of any sort of trust or rapport developing between them... I cannot say."

"Well, that is hardly surprising. Look what happened the last time Georgie trusted someone. And she is too much like you, you know."

Darcy narrowed his eyes. "By which you mean?"

"She would rather suffer loneliness than let herself be wounded again." Richard twisted in his chair, setting his elbow to rest on the winged back as he surveyed Darcy's expression. "Which leads me to ask... how are you, Darcy?"

"How do you think I am?" Darcy erupted. "I must have my needs tended like an infant, I cannot stir from this bed, my wife is weary of the sight of my face, and my sister weeps in misery every time she thinks of me! *And you ask how I am?*"

"Darcy..."

"Leave off with the platitudes, Richard. You cannot know what it is to never..." He closed his eyes and gulped against the knot in his throat. "Do you know what it is like? All the things I am, everything I ever had or wanted, gone in an instant! Instead of the leader my father raised me to be, I am now an invalid, dependent upon everyone else for my very survival! And without even the comforts of home, but this... this hell-hole in the wild of Scotland with the dead of winter approaching, no friends to aid my wife against hardship, no joyful anticipation waiting for my sister as she suffers the maladies of her confinement... nothing!"

Richard sank more deeply into the chair with a soft groan. "This enforced pretence was my suggestion, though never did I foresee how painfully solitary the reality would become for you all." He searched Darcy's shuttered features intently. "Come now, Cousin, take heart! At least your new wife causes you some small happiness still, despite all?"

To Colonel Fitzwilliam's evident dismay, Darcy only released a cynical huff of laughter. "How can you be so blind?" He turned brooding eyes to the empty hearth, bitterness choking his tone. "The truth is I have ruined Elizabeth Darcy as profoundly as myself. Marrying me has smothered the very qualities that I cherish in her."

He glanced back at his cousin's stricken face. "Oh, do not pretend to be shocked! My accursed temper drives her from me frequently of late. Small wonder she flees to the lonely moors, given the choice between my wretched company and winter's solitude!" Darcy looked deliberately away again. "No matter the outcome now, I have destroyed Elizabeth's spirit beyond hope of redemption."

Colonel Fitzwilliam ran an agitated hand through his dishevelled hair before exploding heatedly. "Confound it all, Darcy, you think too lowly of yourself and too meanly of other souls' resilience! What evidence suggests Mrs Darcy's spirit is anywhere near breaking?"

He surged forward to grip Darcy's arm insistently. "Did I not witness with my own eyes how she faced down obstacles that would send most ladies swooning? Bah! She swims determinedly through deep waters beside you when she had every right to refuse this marriage."

"Not for me. And not even for herself, but for her family—a family she is denied now, because of me!"

"Come now, Darcy. These times will be behind you soon enough. Trust me as once you did—Elizabeth possesses the temperament and fortitude to weather far worse than the current troubles with you. Have faith in the woman as well as yourself!"

His fervent optimism sparked a faint inner warmth thawing Darcy's bleak despair. Might Elizabeth forgive his thoughtless temper in time, if he redoubled his efforts in keeping bitterness at bay? Darcy mulled this new delicate hope silently as the mantel clock marked relentless seconds.

Eventually, he muttered grudging agreement to appease his cousin's hovering fretfulness. "Oh, very well. Perhaps the lady's formidable character bears little permanent damage from my black moods. Your meddling has served *some* purpose, at least."

"Bloody right. I've not charged cannon and musket with the faithful, nor collared a turncoat without learning a thing or two about reading what is in a man's heart. Or a woman's, for that matter. Mrs Darcy may have a ferocious bark when she pleases, but it is far worse than her bite. And woe to the man who brings home a guard dog that cannot bark at all."

Darcy closed his eyes and shook his head. "I'll try to overlook you comparing my wife to a dog. Look, is there something else we can speak of?"

"Ah, yes. I had meant to get round to the other reason I came. I have brought you a Bath chair, all the way from London."

Darcy tried to sit up a little straighter. "You have?"

"I believe the surgeons all said you ought to be able to try it some little by now. I don't suppose there is anyone local to whom you have applied for advice?"

"There is. Some wild-haired Scot who speaks with a brogue and smiles too much. Says he studied medicine while with the Black Watch."

"A soldier! I like him already. Well, I daresay he can tell you if you are at further risk of injury if you wheel about the house. It might do something to lighten your moods, at least, if you can leave this bloody chamber."

Darcy let go a heavy sigh. "Yes. It would make a difference. I appreciate the consideration."

Richard offered a pinched scowl. "It was not you I was trying to consider, but Giles and your wife. But mayhap I was mistaken. You will not make their lives more difficult now, will you, chasing round flagstone on three wheels?"

Darcy's mouth twisted into a sardonic half-smile. "God only knows."

E LIZABETH HURRIED TO HER chamber, clutching the packet of letters tightly. Her name scrawled in Jane's beloved hand stirred a swell of homesickness and relief. At last, word from her family!

Beth called an anxious query from below as Elizabeth rushed upstairs, but she merely waved the post briefly in answer without slowing pace. Right now, communion with Jane and Papa far outweighed any casual discourse or bother with household affairs! Upon entering her bedchamber and bolting the door, Elizabeth sank in breathless anticipation onto the coverlet's edge. Five letters addressed by Jane lay in her lap like long-delayed manna in the wilderness of her strange, lonely existence as Mrs Darcy.

With trembling care, she split each missive's seal to reveal varied pages covered in familiar scripts she had despaired of glimpsing again so soon. Joyful tears misted Elizabeth's vision as she arranged the dated pages by order of when each was penned. Eagerly, she raised the first precious sheet up close, imagining beloved faces as she read. The first pages began with her Papa's shaky pen.

Dearest Lizzy,

I hope Pemberley's library measures up to a certain bookworm daughter's elevated standards! With all those venerable old masters keeping sentinel, I daresay you shall have your hands full, preventing the dust from accumulating too terribly. Do remind the hapless Mr Darcy that reading in the afternoon sun often leads to fatigue and nodding off. I advise checking his pillow placement to ensure his comfort should Shakespeare prove soporific. I trust the man does rouse himself to decent conversation after a fashion?

Elizabeth rolled her eyes and shook her head. Papa had no generous thoughts for her husband. But at least that was proof enough, if she ever needed it, that this marriage had been *her* intent, not some whim pressured upon her by her family. She read on.

My own dear library feels much diminished without your lively presence to vex and challenge my limited patience. Jane tries to condole with me in your absence, but as beautiful as your elder sister is, she is a hopeless case at chess, to say nothing for Sophocles. Pray, write often before I become incurably dull!

Elizabeth smothered a watery chuckle. Poor Jane, trying to keep their father distracted! It must be miserable for both of them.

Next, she lifted Mary's earnest scrawl, almost hearing the sanctimonious tones lecturing thus:

Sister Elizabeth,

Rumours swirl over your abrupt elopement with some wealthy man! I hope it was an honourable exchange, and not done out of any disrepute. Whilst I refrain from indelicate curiosity over particulars, common decency requires your new husband to address Papa most seriously...

Good gracious, even at a distance, Mary's censure stung! Elizabeth frowned, flipping the page over to seek kinder lines than Mary's sermonising. Ah, here shone her better nature, cautiously extending an olive branch:

However, I understand Miss Darcy to be a skilled musician near my age. Pray, when you write soon, inquire whether she might share certain new sheet music to copy for my improving repertoire? Any duets to loan during your forthcoming visit will be kindly received.

Paper rasped faintly as Elizabeth shuffled pages to uncover Mama's elaborate script next:

Oh, my dearest Lizzy!

Such delicious news reading your nuptials announced in the papers! But you are a cruel girl, denying your Mama the honoured privilege of witnessing your splendid match to Pemberley's esteemed master! What excuse has your Aunt Phillips now for whispering behind our backs about poor darling Lydia? And Lady Lucas, now there is a fair gossip if there ever was one, but she was quite upstaged when I showed her the rags from London that were all astir about 'the new Mrs D being seen in the salon of Lady M!' They are all quite put out, my dear, for apparently your hairstyle has made them positively green with envy. My clever Lizzy, simply everyone in Meryton has read about it by now!

I simply do not understand why it was all so hushed up when you wed, though. I blame your father, for he simply would tell me nothing of it until it was all done. He claims it was

Mr Darcy's wish, on account of Lydia's little adventures, but I say that is a bit of nonsense. As if Mr Darcy's high standing does not eclipse any thought of scandal or disgrace!

I declare, now that it is quite known whom you have married—as I said, it has been in all the papers—we must remedy your sisters' exclusion from invitation lists immediately when you return from abroad! Even one glimpse of your opulent circumstances is a snub to the nose of those spiteful Lucases and Longs! Soon, all Meryton will fawn at my skirts as mother of the new Mrs Darcy, mark it!

Have you many carriages, my dear? And did your husband provide you ample pin money to have a proper winter wardrobe made up, as befits your station? I have never had time to teach you where all the best warehouses are, but I declare you need not be frugal in this. Do write at once with every detail affirming your consequence as I brace myself for preparing the finest spread to showcase long-awaited felicities!

Your loving Mama

"Oh, Mama!" Elizabeth despaired briefly, but swiftly tamped the familiar annoyance down. At least her family's restored consequence permitted renewed socialising, even if their mother focused solely on smug self-importance. Although Papa must endure Mama's pleas to take her to visit Elizabeth in London or Derbyshire considerably longer, since she remained ignorant of certain key details.

Faint rustling at the window announced winter, unleashing icy claws as darkness descended outside. Elizabeth tugged the counterpane around herself more securely, her spirits much heartened as she prepared to peruse the letter's closing lines penned by Lydia:

Lizzy, why must you run off and marry so slyly? Kitty and I wanted to come to the wedding and throw flowers. You recall that I saw him first, but I did not think so very much of him then. But Papa says he is rich, so I think I would have come to like him better, after a fashion, had I been introduced to him properly. So, has this rich husband of yours any officers amongst his acquaintance? You must introduce a few at Pemberley when we visit, for I declare myself utterly deprived of dancing these ages past!

Lydia

P.S. Kitty says despite being horrid vexed by your secrecy, she expects lavish gifts as your favourite sister now!

A wistful smile lingered as Elizabeth dashed sudden tears away and reached eagerly for the next epistle from Jane:

Dearest Lizzy,

My spirit yearns to be sure that you have found marital felicity. How I miss my closest confidante! My only consolation lies in hoping Mr Darcy brings you happiness, despite everything else, and with the prayer that you may be the sort of sister Miss Darcy needs most, even as you have ever been to me. Write and describe your lovely new home and relations soon...

Thus, Jane's sweet missive flowed onto a second page with the sisterly encouragement and assurance she stood ready to join Elizabeth in Derbyshire or London, whenever circumstances permitted. Oh, how delicious that offer sounded! If only Jane could come now... Elizabeth flipped through the pages of all the letters, singling Jane's notes out from among all the others to piece them together into one cohesive sequence of events since she had left them all.

We have a new neighbour at Netherfield! Mr Bingley proves an amiable gentleman, and his tenants all claim him to be an obliging landlord thus far. In truth, he shows particular solicitude to Papa and to me. He says he met you in London, and that he has been friends with Mr Darcy for many years! Such news, naturally, spread like wildfire through Meryton, and I daresay it has done its own mischief, because now simply everyone wishes to learn what fortune befell you...

...Mr Bingley has called on Papa twice now. We were not invited to the Assembly that Mr Bingley attended when he first arrived, but there is talk of another public ball in a few weeks, to which we are all invited. I have to think that the change in our circumstances is thanks to you, Lizzy, though I still hate to think of you sacrificing yourself for us. Pray, tell me you are happy...

...I apologise for taking so long in writing again, though I expect you have not yet received even the first letter I sent, as Colonel Fitzwilliam has promised to forward all these on as soon as he is able to go to you in Scotland... Oh, dear, I ought not to have written that, as only Papa knows where you have really gone. We told Mama you had gone to Portugal for a honeymoon, but she insists on saying you are in Spain.

I was invited to dine with Mr Bingley's sisters last week. It was meant to be a simple outing, but Mama insisted I go on horseback in a terrible downpour, and I caught a fearful cold. I was too ill to return home, and so my friends insisted that I stay with them. What I would have given to have my sweet Lizzy there to cool my forehead with a cloth! But I expect your husband needs your kind attentions more, so I made do with Miss Bingley. She is kind, though not a warm woman. Her sister, Mrs Hurst, pays me every solicitude, but Lizzy, they seemed most eager to have me out of their house this morning when I was well enough for Papa to finally send the carriage for me. I am sure I must have been a terrible burden, but Mr Bingley was all sweetness when he handed me inside and assured me he was eager to hear of my full recovery...

...Mr Bingley is to host a ball at Netherfield! Miss Bingley brought our invitation only this morning. Lizzy, we are all invited, even Lydia! I cannot think on it without shuddering somewhat, for I know she has been little forgiven in the neighbourhood, but with Mr Bingley's staunch approval of our family in public, there is none who dare to speak against us. Particularly not after Mr Bingley asked for my hand for the supper set. Oh, Lizzy, I wonder if he fancies me? Charlotte Lucas says it appears to be a very promising inclination, but what does Charlotte know? I fear she has not received a single offer to dance, which pains me. I dearly hope she is not destined to permanent spinsterhood. She jested to me the other day that she ought to have discovered whether your Mr Darcy has any cousins lying about. I did not wish her to think too long and hard about Mr Darcy's family, so I said the only cousin I knew of was our own cousin, Mr Collins, who has sworn off any of the society from Longbourn, so it was not likely we were to see him this winter. But I cannot think any of us would find him agreeable company anyway. Besides, he cannot possibly have eyes as blue as Mr Bingley's. I wonder if he will like the new shoe roses I mean to order for the ball?

"Bless you, Jane!" Elizabeth clasped the last letter to her heart, elation soaring at this first glimmer of her family's restored connexions and the redemption for which she had sacrificed her own marital hopes. Papa could hold his head high again, Mama could now boast to her friends, Mary, Kitty and Lydia were not entirely shunned. Perhaps Jane might even discover happiness with that sweet Mr Bingley!

Such tender reflections nudged lingering guilt that Elizabeth had cruelly flung her petty grievances into William's lap. His burdens by far dwarfed her meagre trials, and she could not have had a few moments of patience for him? His good name had bought her family's honour. The very least she could do was to swallow her pride and apologise to him for letting her spitefulness get the better of her.

Sighing heavily, Elizabeth set aside the scattered pages to stretch hands grown stiff from clutching them. She rose to stand, arms outstretched as if she could embrace her family as she had those letters. Oh, how she ached to hear their dear voices! For however trying their quirks, these personalities comprised home's comforting patchwork quilt, wrapping snugly around her solitary heart now.

And of quirks... well, she knew plenty. William was as mercurial and idiosyncratic as any of her family, and she did not dislike him for it. Rather, it made him interesting. Relatable. And she had blasted him for being... well, *him*. Remorse quickened Elizabeth's steps back down the twisting passageways towards his chambers. Best make amends before any grudges could be formed. But as she approached his door, she heard a bark of laughter on the other side from Colonel Fitzwilliam, and an answering low rumble from William that sounded more amused than surly.

Perhaps later. Elizabeth quietly backed away without disturbing them. Whatever regrettable words her impatience had flung earlier, she could let him enjoy a few minutes with his cousin before interrupting to force her apologies on him. She would speak to him later, when she went in for that evening ritual of tending to his nerveless limbs.

Why had she decided to take that duty on? Giles could have done it, and probably with less embarrassment. He could have done more, actually. But if the traditional intimacies of marriage were to be denied them, Elizabeth felt this was one thing she could do to connect with this man she had married. To do him some small service, and in the process, pass a few quiet moments each evening getting to know each other better, in the only way they could—by talking. Low voices, with the candles partially snuffed, and the thoughts and worries of the day behind them for a few hours.

He was more at ease in those few minutes than any other time of the day. No longer training his mind on business, often less restless, and willing to simply sit in quiet companionship with her. It was the only time she felt like someone actually understood her, and truth be told, she looked forward to that feeling. Words were not always necessary.

But the way he would look at her sometimes in the evenings... well, she had to wonder just what faculties he did have. Was there... anything he *could* feel? Or was it strictly a utilitarian ritual for him, a mere submission to the necessity of keeping his circulation as healthy as it could possibly be?

She paused to swallow, laying a trembling hand upon her own door latch. It did seem wicked, sometimes, the way she came alive when she arched her palms around those thick, hairy legs of his. Such wanton thoughts had no place in this marriage.

But friendship... well, that was certainly possible, and she would do all she could to try to rebuild that tenuous thread she had probably almost snapped earlier today. Just as soon as she had him to herself.

With a lighter heart, Elizabeth returned to her room and took up a quill.

Dearest Jane...

Chapter Twenty-Two

RICHARD STAYED JUST ABOVE a fortnight with them, and Darcy had never been more grateful to have his cousin's meddlesome presence. A winter storm had chased Richard in on the afternoon of his arrival, and the residents of that old Scottish castle were obliged to shelter as best they could, for coming and going was impossible.

Fortunately, Elizabeth, Beth and Giles had seen well to their provisions, so much so that they wanted for nothing but a bit of water that did not freeze between the kettle and the cup. Darcy had never been so cold in his life—even accounting for that time he and Richard had got "lost" in a Derbyshire blizzard the winter he turned ten. That had been only half an hour's worth of misery until Father had found them both. This was unending torment, with blasts of frigid air driving them all into the central rooms of the house, sheltering around a roaring fire that consumed far too much wood for the heat it delivered.

But the days were not without their mercies. Chief among them, for Darcy at least, was that three-wheeled contraption with the velvet, pin-tucked cushions and the leather strap for his waist that kept him securely in place. It was humiliating to be strapped in his seat and wheeled about like an infant in a pram whenever he wished to move from room to room, but humiliation had become an old friend by now, and at least he *could* move from room to room again.

The first thing he had done was to have his bed removed to the ground floor in what had previously served as a study of sorts. The windows were far too draughty, and the room was not appointed for a wardrobe or any of the other niceties that made for a proper bedroom, but he no longer had to be carried down the stairs if he wished to move about in his chair.

He could be among people when he chose and hear the day-to-day conversations that once he might have ignored as meaningless. Now, they were bread and milk to him, as he listened hungrily for commonplace phrases like Elizabeth asking Georgiana to pass her the sewing basket or Giles and Richard taking turns hauling in wood for the fire and snow to be melted for fresh water.

Perhaps it was his imagination, but it did seem that Georgiana had warmed by degrees. It might have been Richard's arrival, or perhaps it was the effect of time, wearing smooth the rough edges of fortune's mischances. Possibly it was Georgiana's growing dependency upon Elizabeth's company, for even Darcy could see, now that he was in the room to see it, that it was Elizabeth who continually steered the rudder of his sister's raw emotions toward calmer waters.

Or it might have simply been the advancing of her pregnancy. According to what the midwife had told Elizabeth, his sister had passed that trying first term and was now settling into more comfortable months. Her emotions would be less in turmoil, the morning sickness had passed, and the reality of the thing was making itself known to all by now as Georgiana's figure began to change.

This, he feared, was as easy as it would be for the foreseeable future—a quiet moment in the eye of the storm.

Sixteen days after he arrived, there was a sufficient break in the weather for Richard to make his escape back to London. He left one Tuesday morning, with the icy winter sun barely risen over the frozen heaths, promising to post all their letters and send on whatever word might be had of news from London, Longbourn and Pemberley.

And so, it was a quiet, morose gathering all the rest of that day as winter's gloom seemed to tighten its grip on those who remained behind. Darcy poked at the fire some, then, when he had heard Georgiana sigh for at least the fifteenth time, he had Giles wheel him into the makeshift secondary study to pore over ledgers and accounts of the estate. He must give Lady Matlock a reckoning, after all. It was not only for his own benefit that she had offered the use of her property, but out of concern that it had been too long left without oversight.

Darcy scowled at the latest tenants' reports awaiting review, scattered across his desk. Sorting through the old steward MacTavish's disaster of incomplete maintenance logs and vague property surveys made muddling through estate affairs a discouraging task, even on his most lucid days. Which today decidedly was not.

Bracing both clenched fists against the wooden chair arms, Darcy strained forward, attempting to slide a particular tenant petition closer without toppling ingloriously face-first atop the desk. After two weeks of adjusting to wheeled mobility, he still struggled with the contraption's perpetual imbalance, as what remained of his muscles' memory continually sought to adjust his seated posture. Which, of course, resulted in nought but tipping dangerously whilst scrambling to prevent a humiliating collapse. Surely, he ought to manage simple paperwork without requiring rescue like a blasted porcelain doll!

The door opened just as Darcy's tenuous balance wavered. Instant mortification stung harshly, even as gratitude surged in equal measure when Elizabeth swiftly grasped his chair's backrest to sweep it back under him, restoring his stability. Galling to require his wife to play nursemaid, but it was better than earning himself a bloody nose by smacking it on the desk. Again.

"My thanks," Darcy muttered once the room stopped its dizzy spinning. Suppressing irritation at his hunched posture, he slowly straightened against the confining support strap intended to keep him from toppling sideways during just such undignified moments.

"For what?" she asked blithely. "I only came in to ask if you were in the mood for *Poularde à la Montmorency* for the evening meal. Or perhaps you would prefer *Caneton aux Pêches?*"

A slow grin overtook Darcy's face. "Where did you find a French chef in these parts?"

Her mouth curved smugly. "I did not say I had, nor did I promise I could deliver. I merely asked which of the two options you preferred."

He laced his fingers across his lap. "Neither. I am sick to death of chicken, and I never cared much for duck. See if you can conjure *Filet de Bœuf.*"

"I will see what I can do." Her lips pressed into a friendlier smile, and she came closer. "Gracious, William, when was the last time you let Giles trim this mane of yours?" Her hands smoothed the dishevelled hair from his brow with a casual intimacy that never failed to ignite unwise cravings for more tender caresses. As the heated energy thrummed invisibly between them, he finally forced himself to pull his head away.

"The scissors required sharpening. Dratted things pulled more hair than they cut last time, but Giles has been too busy with other matters to take a stone to them. I should have hired a man of all work from the village long before this, but..."

"But you didn't trust anyone." Elizabeth stepped back, framing her hands behind her back at the dip of her waist, and gave him a knowing look. "Did you? Admit it."

His cheeks warmed. "In this strange place, with three women under my care and myself unable even to stand up in your defence... but perhaps the doctor can give us a reference, and now that the weather has taken a better turn for a few days..."

She lifted her chin in a definitive agreement. But then her chest rose and fell in a sigh, and she touched the edge of his chair.

"You, ah... were not in the process of injuring yourself when I walked in a moment ago, I hope?"

"Not on purpose." He grimaced. "This time."

"My timing was fortunate, then?"

"Indeed, since my clumsy contortions nearly capsized this blasted contraption altogether,"

She crossed her arms. "That single wheel sticking out in front makes it difficult to push up to the desk properly. There must be something else we can do to make this chair work better for you."

"There is. Find a miracle worker, so I no longer need it."

She made him a pinched scowl but smoothed it away with a grin. "Richard told me someone he heard of had one that could be steered. It had some sort of handle that came up in the front, but he did not know where to find one like that—and he thought Giles and I would not thank him for it, if he did find one."

He arched a sardonic brow. "Funny. 'Richard,' now, is it?"

"Well, you cannot very well expect me to use the formal address when I am swearing at someone, can you? 'Richard' is easier to shout."

Darcy chuckled. "He got under your skin, did he?"

"Like a leech. Did I ever tell you how he got me to go upstairs and talk to you a second time?"

Darcy leaned forward and pulled a ledger closer because he was afraid he would not be able to keep a straight face if he held her gaze. "I would imagine he dared you. And you cannot resist a dare."

She snorted. "I very well can. But he more than implied that I was being a coward for not telling you off as you deserved."

"Like I said..."

She swatted at his shoulder, then reached across the desk to pull the stack of papers closer to his reach, without even being asked. Darcy's hand closed on them, and he looked up, letting his gaze linger on her soft cheek... those thick, black lashes...

He cleared his throat. "Thank you."

Elizabeth lifted a shoulder. "We cannot have the master of Pemberley kicking his chair over and sprawling across the floor with a bruised knob on his head, can we? Why, imagine the dire scandal. All the cats of the *ton* will believe your nobody of a wife did it to you!"

Despite himself, answering laughter spilt from Darcy's lips, though laced with bitterness. "Dire scandal already exists, simply through my inability to prevent the need for this cursed chair. It is just that no one of any consequence knows about it yet, but rest assured, they will." Ashamed by this evasive harshness, he risked a glance upward, expecting to glimpse hurt or pity darkening her sparkling eyes.

Instead, Elizabeth studied him solemnly. "Scandal is far too weighty a word for circumstances beyond your control," she murmured. "No shame exists in merely requiring additional assistance sometimes." Slim fingers gently traced the rigid line of Darcy's jaw as she whispered. "You are still the same man, Fitzwilliam Darcy."

Words choked in his throat, holding her earnest gaze as warmth radiated outward along strained nerves from everywhere her featherlight touch grazed his taut skin. Before the unwise cravings sparked fully to life, Elizabeth stepped back, almost as if she, too, required a moment to remember the reality of things. How instinctive was the intimacy that lit between them these days. It both panicked and thrilled him in equal measure.

Desperately shifting his mental footing, Darcy cleared his throat gruffly. "Well, I apologise for dragging your attention away from more important affairs."

"What more important affairs? Georgiana just went upstairs for a lie-down, and Giles and Beth have matters well in hand. To own the truth, I am bored to death and craving *something* to do. So, I thought I would come in here and annoy you."

"Hardly an annoyance." Darcy gestured across the desk's disorganised surface. "You could try making sense of this disaster. My blasted clumsy fingers make a proper mess, shuffling papers one-handed while using the other to keep from toppling sideways."

Elizabeth leaned over his shoulder, surveying the muddled paperwork as tantalising curls grazed his cheek. A wisp of floral perfume—rosewater? No, there were faint undertones of lavender blended in, as the aroma surrounded him in a delicate haze. She hummed thoughtfully, sorting through various tenants' complaints and ledgers. Darcy's lingering dizziness owed little now to the unbalanced chair.

"Well, well, perhaps there was a reason for Mr MacTavish's sheepishness during your blistering interrogation yesterday," Elizabeth observed lightly, though steel laced the sly words. "Drunken negligence nearly burnt his crofter's cottage to the ground two winters past? No wonder icy draughts plague your study if similar lackadaisical oversight riddles all the properties under his care!"

Darcy snorted. He, too, had noted vague supply records and undocumented maintenance gaps, hinting at long neglect across all of Lady Matlock's Scottish holdings. "Incompetent wastrel! Small wonder rents continually decline and tenants grumble, if this constitutes acceptable management of estates."

He smacked the stack of annual financial reports sharply. "A steward at least ought to provide fundamental upkeep on properties, ensuring the tenants remain securely housed against Scotland's harsh winters. Was the man too sotted to realise he was inviting disaster, ignoring obvious disrepair?"

"Likely, the poor fellow only wishes to keep his head down and to be left in peace," Elizabeth mused gently. "Some men simply lack the ambition to rise beyond base comforts, which can be attainable through modest effort. But come, even inept help proves scarce this far north." One slim shoulder lifted fatalistically. "If old MacTavish stumbles occasionally in his duties, well, we must kindly redirect his fumbling rather than issue more scathing reproofs."

Darcy's frustrated grunt acknowledged her compassionate wisdom, but he could not forgive past negligence as easily as she. And what would Lady Matlock have to say on the affair? Bring her husband into the matter, that was what she would do, and poor old MacTavish would be worse than out of a job.

But any thought of Matlocks and MacTavishes evaporated within seconds, for Elizabeth had crossed round to the opposite side of the desk to peer at the haphazard stack. And when she leaned forward to gather the papers into neat piles, she unwittingly offered him a view that... well, if *anything* could make him feel *something* again, that would probably have done it.

"THERE. ORGANISED AND READY for you to make sense of it... if you can." Elizabeth's brow furrowed as she shook her head. "Most of it isn't even legible."

Darcy pinched the bridge of his nose and cast aside his quill. "Would that there was a decent library in this cave. I have had quite enough of staring at chicken scrawl, and I cannot tell you what a relief it would be to read something printed in proper English."

Elizabeth straightened and cocked him a saucy grin. "I have just the thing! It may not be a book, but it is almost as good. If you do not mind my company a little longer."

Darcy coughed. "I suppose I will survive if yours is the only company to be had."

"My feelings exactly. You are tolerable, I suppose," she crooned sweetly.

He rolled his eyes. "I knew you were going to fling that in my face one day."

"Oh, I assure you, it will be more than once. Now, close your eyes while I conjure something much more pleasurable than ledgers and letters of business."

He arched one brow curiously, despite himself. "Pleasurable, you say? That is a word that can have many meanings."

"And you will never find out what it means this time until you close your eyes. No cheating, William."

"Very well." He closed his eyes and felt a puff of air as she fanned her hand over his face. Then, footsteps racing out of the room... and back in. The fluttering of the stacked papers as she cleared the things from the desk, a clatter of his inkpot, and thumping. Quite a lot of thumping. "What *are* you doing?" he asked at last.

"Open your eyes and see." Impish triumph flashed in her eyes as Elizabeth swept a hand over the desk's surface, displaying an old wooden chess set. "Behold my wondrous discovery earlier when I was scavenging above stairs with Beth! Likely an antique, by the game's elaborate craftsmanship, yet all the pieces are present. Fancy a round or two, William?"

Unaccountable delight bubbled up in Darcy's chest, chasing gloomy shadows back momentarily. He had not indulged in that favourite pastime since before taking the reins of Pemberley, and he had scarcely ever met a woman who enjoyed the game. "You know how to play?" he asked dubiously.

"My dear husband, do you not think that chess is one of every proper young lady's usual accomplishments?"

"No."

"And neither did my father. Which is why he taught us to play... well, Jane and Mary and me. But Mama said it was a waste of our time, so Kitty and Lydia never bothered." She sighed.

"And remind me again, which one of your sisters went astray?"

Elizabeth quirked a brow at him. "Touché. Shall we?"

He reached forward and claimed the black pieces to begin setting them up. "By all means, Fair Lady. Lay out your armies upon the battlefield! Never let it be said I avoided meeting any foe boldly."

"Careful, sir, for my innocuous façade hides a ruthless warrior's instincts, once roused." Laughing eyes gave lie to Elizabeth's feigned hauteur as she set intricate figurines precisely across the worn chessboard. "Consider yourself forewarned and gird for war."

Darcy warmed with anticipation as he watched his petite wife circling the game table with military precision, lush hairpins askew, creamy throat clenched in mock ferocity. Elizabeth Darcy proved far lovelier than any classical muse, bringing this wintry barren existence momentarily to life again. Impulsively, he smiled, engaging her fiery glance.

"Then your deadly forces stand arrayed, Madam General," Darcy invited with a courtly flourish, wrenching his mind from the intoxicating imagery. "Might we sound the opening cannonades?"

Elizabeth's fingers closed on her first pawn, eyes alight with competitive thrill. "The honour of first foray is mine, good sir! But make your answering move cautiously, lest your ranks suffer a trouncing."

The merry campaign launched in earnest, punctuated by strategic feints and jabbing wordplay woven seamlessly through each player's manoeuvres. "Ha! My spear throwers would skewer your knights at forty paces," Elizabeth taunted. "Far wiser to retreat behind your ramparts before my archers shred you."

She crowed loud victory minutes later, capturing three key cavalry pieces, forcing Darcy's king into indefensible terrain. "Well, sir, what think you of my martial prowess now that the field lies wide open for final assault?" Elizabeth purred, a halo of victory wreathing her laughing face.

Something fierce and tender surged within Darcy's breast, staring mesmerised by his wife's radiant savagery. How life's bleakest domains bloomed vibrant wherever she passed, untouched by darkness. Surely, fate had conspired to bring some good to him through their unlikely union.

Unaware of his arresting study, Elizabeth prompted expectantly, "Do you concede the battle as mine, then? For your beleaguered monarch cannot withstand many—"

"Never!" Darcy interjected staunchly. "Ignominious surrender earns nought but bitter scorn. Nay, Madam, we fight on, devising a brilliant counterattack!"

He adored the sound of her affronted gasp as he captured her queen with a lowly pawn, checking the king viciously. "What now, Madam Tactician? My troops stand ready to meet all sallies."

"The devil take your eyes! Full unfair, dazzling me with masculine wiles rather than attending honest play," Elizabeth huffed indignantly.

"Masculine wiles, indeed. No one ever accused me of any sort of sleight of hand."

"Only because they do not know any better. Stop smiling, William, for it is entirely unfair. I had best finish trouncing you swiftly, lest I fall prey. Particularly if any of us want to eat anything besides melted snow for dinner—I promised Beth I would help her."

Vexation stung briefly that their pleasant pastime must conclude so soon. But he could not very well occupy his wife's every moment, particularly since she was almost single-handedly managing their comforts after Fitzwilliam had left them rusticating away for the remainder of the long, bitter months ahead. When peace and stability hopefully resumed come spring, he vowed to share plentiful diversions with Elizabeth. For now, he could simply imagine a "someday" that did not involve isolation and secrets, and when Elizabeth might take her ease more by his side.

Only a few minutes later, Elizabeth had successfully checkmated Darcy's king between her encroaching bishop and last triumphant knight, smug satisfaction making her face glow like the sunrise.

"I declare the campaign yours, Madam General," Darcy conceded. "But tomorrow, I demand a rematch. Your lucky streak cannot hold indefinitely."

Elizabeth leaned over the desk and boldly set her hand on his cheek as she brought her forehead within inches of his. "Mr Darcy, I am counting on it."

And then she was gone, leaving Darcy's head spinning over more than the chessboard.

Chapter Twenty-Three

N EARLY A MONTH HAD passed since Colonel Fitzwilliam bade them all farewell, setting off to rejoin London society's elaborate holiday celebrations. Far removed in their isolated Scottish estate, Elizabeth busied herself preparing for a much simpler Yuletide as Pemberley's newest mistress... except this was not Pemberley, and they were not expecting any guests with whom to make merry.

But reviewing the modest trove of handmade gifts she had collected to give to her new family tomorrow gave her a warm, satisfied little thrill. Her first Christmas as the lady of the house, and it did not seem as though she had entirely made a cake of it. Though each token was humble, having been crafted out of whatever Giles had been able to procure for her when he went to the village market, she fancied they would still be prized and laughed over.

Humming softly, Elizabeth smiled down at the small pile of completed presents tucked nearby. Despite simple meals and meagre seasonal adornments here at Castle Cairn, a sense of contentment had blossomed over the past weeks. While nothing could replace the family she had left behind, the small little band of temporary outcasts she had joined were... well, they were family now, too, after a fashion. Particularly William.

Glancing up from embroidering a bookmark—a final little gift for her husband—Elizabeth watched as Georgiana bent intently over her needlework nearby. A glimmer of winter sunlight through the frosted pane haloed the sweet girl's golden curls, reminding Elizabeth of their first awkward meeting when she had still feared Georgiana might never accept another woman usurping Darcy's affections. How much had changed since then! The timid smiles and playful humour Georgiana had begun to reveal more freely in recent days were more like the sister Elizabeth had first hoped to find. Perhaps there was still hope for the girl's happiness, after all.

"How fares your project, Georgiana? I am nearly finished stitching this bookmark for your brother." Elizabeth held it up at arm's length and tilted her head. Careful stitches secured the bright crimson thread trailing along fine lawn edges. If one did not look too closely, they might actually assume she was skilled at embroidery, with the lucky way some of the stitches had fallen.

"It is just a handkerchief." Georgiana worried her needle through the small linen square. "I make him one every year, and every year, I think I will find something different to give him, but then I end up just stitching his initials in yet another scrap of white linen."

"Oh, come now. He uses those handkerchiefs every day, and occasionally, one is spoiled or lost. He must need a replacement by now."

"William never loses anything. He has a drawer full of them back at Pemberley. I know, because I sneaked into his room once when I was twelve."

"Well, if he keeps them all, he must have a use for them," Elizabeth returned stubbornly as she got up to survey Georgiana's handiwork.

"Yes, perhaps he will use them to stop up the gaps in the eastern window."

Elizabeth giggled. "Or maybe he fears he will get a terrible case of the sniffles!"

Georgiana's features went still, and it almost appeared as if she had stopped breathing.

"Georgiana?" Elizabeth leaned down to peer into the girl's face. "What is it?"

Luminous blue eyes blinked up at her. "He might, you know," she whispered.

"Might what? Get a cold? Heavens, in this draughty old place, it is a wonder we do not all have pneumonia."

"I asked Richard about it," Georgiana continued as if she had not heard. "About what happens to men who are bound to their beds."

Elizabeth sank into the closest seat. "And what did he say?"

"You don't want to know."

"I assure you, I do."

Georgiana stared back at her, her nostrils fluttering and her eyes filling with tears as she closed her mouth sullenly. Just when Elizabeth had begun to think Georgiana would say nothing, she blurted out, "They die. All of them."

"Well, that is original. We all die."

"No, I mean young. They get a cold or something trifling that would not do much harm to them otherwise, but they are no longer strong enough to fight it off."

Elizabeth's mouth opened, then closed again on a wordless retort. Well, of all the... that could not be true! She blinked vaguely as her eyes drifted upward in thought. No, it could not be true, because how many old invalids had she heard of who had not left their bed in an age? William was growing more vigorous and active again every day, and never once had he shown signs of illness.

"Why would your cousin say such a thing to you?" Elizabeth huffed at last. "Oh, I shall box his ears, the old troublemaker!"

"Because it's true," Georgiana sniffed. "He said that their limbs stagnate, and their lungs fill, and they cannot digest their food as they used to, and—"

"Georgiana." Elizabeth grasped the girl's shoulders and rocked her until she looked up. "Stop it. Your cousin Richard is many very vexing things, but one to cause worry when it is undue is not one of them. Now, tell me plainly. Did you force him to tell you the worst-case scenario?"

Georgiana swallowed and shook her head, trying to look away. "I had to know."

"And why would you torture yourself like that? Is William not well? Is he not regaining some of his strength all the time?"

"I had to know because it is all my fault!"

"Georgiana..." Elizabeth wetted her lips, trying to moderate her voice. "We have been over this. It is not your—"

"It is, because I lied to him!"

Elizabeth stared, her cheek twitching as she tried to grasp what the girl was saying. "You... you lied? About what?"

Fraught silence swelled tighter by the second until Georgiana gripped Elizabeth's hand fiercely within her own. "It was because of what I told him that William went back to London. It is my fault he got hurt!" Her eyes filled with anguished tears. "And for too long, you have all pitied me and believed the unforgivable falsehood upon which William traded everything to salvage my honour!"

"What... Georgiana, what are you trying to say? That you..."

"He did not force me." She sniffed and stared flatly at Elizabeth as the tears began to spill out of her eyes, but she refused to dash them away. "Mr Wickham. I went away with him willingly. I went to his bed willingly. For three days, we travelled north together, and I..." She sniffed again as the trail of tears became a steady streak down to her chin, but she refused to break her stare. "He did not force me."

Shock jolted through Elizabeth as fragmented puzzle pieces shifted, revealing uglier truths concealed below the surface layers. Lies and sins and disgrace... did Georgiana actually mean to confess wilful complicity rather than innocent naïveté in that horrific summer scandal? Elizabeth could not decide whether empathy or outrage clamoured loudest in her head, for even if Georgiana had behaved wantonly and wilfully, the burden of sin did not fall solely upon her tender shoulders.

"Georgiana, you were only fifteen..."

"Sixteen. I turned sixteen the day before William found me."

Elizabeth sighed. "You were betrayed. You had a companion who was meant to shepherd you, and she broke your trust by permitting a single man access to you."

"Because I welcomed his company!"

"A wise guardian would still have found a way to preserve your reputation and safety in the process," Elizabeth sallied, her voice rising. "And I cannot credit this tale of you being entirely complicit, because your brother told me your face was bruised and you were weeping when he found you. Your false sense of guilt has made you imagine worse—"

"I am not imagining it, Elizabeth," Georgiana interrupted. "I went entirely of my own accord, and I was quite content until we reached London."

Elizabeth narrowed her eyes. "What happened in London?"

"He..." Her throat convulsed, and she finally closed her eyes to squeeze out the tears. "He said we... we were going to stay there s-some weeks. Until he... he got his money."

"I would have expected no less, from what I have been told of the man."

Georgiana's voice was shaking more and more now, and the words were starting to garble over each other. "I t-told him we should j-just go to my brother, an-and he would give us my dowry so we could be m-married in the church. B-but he-he s-said we-we were going t-to Scotland to be m-married ov-over the anvil, b-bec-cause W-William w-would t-take me aw-away otherwise."

Elizabeth knew not what to say. Georgiana was heaving sobs now, her fingers curling around her face as more broken phrases poured from her about what a fool she had been, how she had let that man deceive her into thinking he loved her... but then came worse tidings.

"I s-started getting angry with h-him b-because he w-wouldn't listen," she gasped. "I knew going to Sc-Scotland was sure d-disgrace and I s-said I would not g-go!" She clasped her hands over her face and crumbled into pitiful wails of remorse.

Elizabeth took a deep breath and smoothed a hand over Georgiana's shoulder. "So, he struck you?" she guessed softly. "To make you stop questioning him?"

After a few seconds, the girl nodded, but it was another full minute before she recovered her voice enough to speak. She dragged in a deep breath, wadding that new handkerchief she had been embroidering for her brother between knotted hands. She took several more breaths, letting Elizabeth whisper words of comfort as she collected herself.

"He knocked me down," she whispered. "And when I protested, he hit me again, until my cheek was bruised, and my lip was bleeding. He..." She closed her eyes and squeezed more tears out. "He said I would... would learn my place. And that once he had my dowry, he would teach me not to talk back to him by doing whatever he pleased with me—he even said he would leave me in that place to amuse other men!"

Elizabeth was boiling in rage by now, but she fought to keep her tones steady. "And then what happened?"

Georgiana shook her head. "I... I do not know. He went downstairs. Or maybe he left the boarding house altogether."

"Why did you not seek help? Did he lock you in?"

The girl released a bitter laugh. "Where was I supposed to go? I was ruined. I knew it. No one would receive me after that. Even William would have cast me out." She gulped back a sob and then shrugged. "Or so I thought. But sometime later that evening, after I had cried myself to sleep, my brother burst the door open and... Well, you know the rest," she finished in a whisper. "I let him believe what he had to believe. He was so furious, Elizabeth! He could never countenance that I had... you know."

"So, you lied about being..." Elizabeth's brow creased. "Being forced."

"I thought William would never speak to me again! It was bad enough that I went with Wickham!"

Elizabeth closed her eyes and squeezed the girl's shoulder. "It does not change the fact that the man deceived and used you, then became violent when you defied him."

"But William might not have gone back to serve justice if I had not let him think—"

"Stop!" Elizabeth cupped Georgiana's face and forced her to stare into her eyes. "Just stop. Do you honestly think it would have changed your brother's outrage one whit? I say you *were* coerced, but in a manner that was just as heinous as if that fiend had outright violated you. He fooled you, tampered with your feelings, and tricked you into giving what you would otherwise not have. You were—*are* a child, Georgiana! You have no business consenting to a grown man, especially one who meant only to use and discard you."

The girl hung her head numbly, and if she heard Elizabeth's words, she gave no indication.

"Georgiana, you must believe me. It would have changed nothing, save this additional burden of guilt you have been carrying around. Is this why you have been so inconsolable?"

Georgiana huffed a little and shook her head. "One of a hundred reasons, I suppose."

"You have to tell your brother."

Horrified blue eyes met Elizabeth's. "No! I cannot—if William hears the truth, that I deceived him and then... and then that happened to him because of my lie... What if he does die, Elizabeth? What if—"

"Then you will have this guilt over your head forever," Elizabeth bit out. Then she sighed. "Come, now, it will not be as you fear. He may very well be angry, and not unjustly. But he will also forgive you, because the sum of the affair, Georgiana Darcy, is that you are his sister, and he is a good man. You were used badly by someone you trusted. You were foolish, yes. Deceitful, indeed. Of course, you knew better, but it is time to stop bludgeoning yourself with this. There is a child on the way, and your brother loves you enough to give up everything to see you both safe."

Georgiana had nearly stopped breathing, and she reached for Elizabeth's hands to grip them like a vise. "I deserve it, I know... but do you think worse of me now, Elizabeth?"

Elizabeth drew a breath—such an earnest plea deserved an honest answer. "I am dismayed that you would let your brother believe the lie. He who loves you so much that he... that he would consent to marry a stranger just to protect you and come to this god-forsaken place to suffer with you. But..."

She returned the squeeze of Georgiana's hands. "I do not think badly of you. You have suffered much already, and your response was that of a girl not yet grown to maturity. But this?" Elizabeth let go of one of Georgiana's hands to tuck a sodden curl behind her ear. "This is the beginning of growth, and I am proud of you for facing the truth at last."

Georgiana's forehead creased, then crumpled altogether as she dove into Elizabeth's arms, quaking with tears. "Will you come in with me when I tell him, Elizabeth?"

Elizabeth embraced the girl, trying to offer what strength she could. "Yes. Yes, I will come."

"COME IN, COME IN! Please make yourselves at home." Elizabeth smiled brightly, welcoming Doctor Douglas and his wife across the draughty threshold. "We were so glad you could join us for our quiet little Twelfth Night supper. I apologise that it is not a formal masque or an elaborate do."

Mrs Douglas laughed merrily, handing over a bottle of amber spirits. "Feast or famine, it's the company one wants, not the trappings."

Elizabeth accepted the bottle gratefully and ushered them towards the modest dining room where a crackling fire beckoned. "Indeed, the pleasure is all ours. You will see I truly am uncultured, because the table is already set, and I have neither place cards nor a butler to summon us in to dine. No, no, Giles and Beth, we shall not stand on ceremony tonight." She gently motioned for them all to sit comfortably together around the humble sideboard as friends.

What their informal Christmastide board lacked in fashionable French cuisine, it made up for tenfold with familiar smiling faces breaking bread together. No hired entertainment or elaborate costumes tonight—just this small circle of neighbours toasting the hopeful year ahead beneath the great house's ancient rafters.

It was not long before their modest feast was complete, and comfortable silence reigned as everyone savoured the warming spices lingering on their tongues after sharing traditional wassail toasts. Despite necessary economies this Yuletide season, far from the lavish Christmastide balls Elizabeth once vaguely imagined would fill her days as Mistress of such a venerable estate as Pemberley was, this intimate communion in their little Scottish refuge with loved ones glowing in firelight seemed richer by far.

Particularly when observing formerly aloof William, relaxed and engaged with their guests rather than brooding alone. Twinkling candles reflected answering sparks in his dark eyes as Dr Douglas enthusiastically held forth, explaining some astonishing new surgical technique from the Continent. Who could have foreseen that Pemberley's esteemed master might entertain a humble country surgeon and midwife as favoured intimates? But then, nothing in the past year had unfolded precisely as any of them expected.

Unbidden, an affectionate smile blossomed as she watched her husband now bantering easily, with hardly any trace remaining of the embittered invalid who sullenly watched the world pass by those awful early days. Deeper happiness yet warmed her, noting Georgiana's golden head also bent eagerly toward animated conversation with Beth. Less than a fortnight earlier, Georgiana had still been watchful and ready to despise the world, but since baring her soul to her brother, exposing the untruths she had tried desperately to keep buried, it was as if a great anchor had been lifted from around her neck.

Indeed, William had been angry when Georgiana told him the truth. He had gritted his teeth, and his countenance had changed shades at least three times. But before a furious word could pass his lips, he had reached for his sister's hand and then embraced her with shaking absolution that, Elizabeth could see, had cost him a great deal of his pride. But in the end, it had purchased for him a measure of peace, and that was well worth any price.

How dramatically both Darcys were transformed lately! Watching William's restless hands no longer fidgeting listlessly, but instead gesturing in lively discourse, filled Elizabeth's heart to brimming. Was not this growing tranquillity the sweetest fruit harvested this past autumn?

Across from Elizabeth, Beth bit into a crumbling slice of Twelfth Night Cake, giggling alongside Giles over their mismatched dessert plates without care for propriety. Georgiana beamed at Elizabeth when her slice of cake yielded the hidden bean, and Doctor Douglas offered another toast.

Glancing up, her eyes caught William's from across the room. The candlelight softened his rugged features as he smiled warmly back at her. For a long moment, they gazed at one another, the sounds of merry conversation fading around them. The corner of his mouth turned up, and he mouthed something... "*Well done,*" it looked like.

That warmed her from the tips of her toes to the roots of her hair. It might not be much, but she had navigated her first "festive dinner party," humble though it was—complete with shattered protocols and broken societal boundaries, but everyone seemed content.

But that... that was not why he was congratulating her. He flicked his gaze to Georgiana, as she laughed at something Mrs Douglas had just said, and then his shoulders lifted in a deep sigh as he gave a slight nod. *That* was what he meant. Whatever else might come, somehow, they three had found one another this winter. And that was certainly worth toasting.

Heat flooded Elizabeth's cheeks as she glanced to the side and realised Mrs Douglas was observing their lingering stare. Quickly she looked away, chagrined to be caught openly mooning over her husband. But the wise woman merely smiled knowingly and turned to smile at her own husband.

Reassured, Elizabeth met William's tender eyes again as joy swelled her heart. No need to hide their growing bond—not from this kindly company who knew too much that the rest of the world must never find out.

Some while later, they had all retired to the sitting room to gather around the most robust hearth in the house. Giles positioned William's chair to take best advantage of the heat, and Elizabeth, though she would have liked to sit beside the fire with him, decided to play the proper hostess and take a seat between Doctor and Mrs Douglas on the sofa.

The conversation shifted into predictions of another snowstorm rolling in that night, and whether it would be followed by a harsh wind or rain that cut through the marrow and froze one's heart out. Doctor and Mrs Douglas determined they would stay for but a half hour longer, relishing the last of their drinks, before lighting out for home. But something in the doctor's countenance drew Elizabeth's attention as the whiskey in his glass reached lower and lower levels. She touched the doctor's arm, eyes narrowed. "Is something amiss?"

Doctor Douglas started, then grimaced. "No, nothing. Forgive an old man his scattered wits tonight."

"Come now, something is clearly troubling you." She glanced discreetly toward William, anxiety fluttering. "You keep staring at Mr Darcy."

The doctor gestured to her to tip her head aside as he spoke into her ear, voice lowered. "You've cared devotedly for your husband these three or four months since his injury. Tell me, do you notice any... changes recently?"

Elizabeth's gaze flew to William, realisation dawning. Though still as immobile as before, had he not regained some of his vigour most days? He was not implying what Georgiana feared... that William's condition was deteriorating... was he? "I have seen nothing to alarm," she murmured.

"That... er... belt round his waist. The one that keeps him in the chair. He wears it constantly, does he not?"

"Not without complaint. But yes, Colonel Fitzwilliam and Giles fashioned it for him because the first time he tried his chair, he slipped to the floor the instant they stopped pushing him forward."

"Yes, I recall. He leaned on it rather constantly at first. But have you noticed that tonight, it drapes slack across his lap? He no longer requires it."

Elizabeth followed his indication, and her jaw dropped. "I had not... but now that you mention it, you are quite right. But... what does that mean?"

"Oh! Perhaps nothing. Or perhaps... no, I am sure it is nothing."

She leaned closer and whispered incredulously, "Do you say that he is recovering somewhat? I was told the London surgeons declared it hopeless!"

"I only note promising indications—straighter posture, easier mobility. See how he is able to shift his weight from side to side now? It could be something as simple as improved strength in his torso, permitting him to compensate somewhat for the lack of ability to balance elsewhere."

Elizabeth felt crestfallen. Yes, surely that was all it was. But that, too, must be some mercy, must it not? "You examined him again only last week, and you said nothing of any of this."

"Because I cannot be sure, Mrs Darcy. He says there is no recovery of sensation. But I will say that the oedema I noted upon my first examination has entirely vanished, and I am as sure as I can be that the bones and ligaments remain stable, though probably terribly strained."

"But what does that mean?"

"As I say, Mrs Darcy, it is much too soon to speculate. Even if the vertebrae are still intact, the nerves themselves might have been damaged or severed by some internal force. But I am encouraged. Yes, rightly encouraged. We shall see what another six months brings, aye?"

"Six months?"

"Or a little longer," he grunted under his breath. "A year of recovery, and you should know the limit to which you can expect improvement. I wish I was a clever enough surgeon to be able to open up a man's back and suture together whatever might be snapped in twain, Mrs Darcy, but there is only one Healer capable of that. And it seems, perhaps, your Mr Darcy might not entirely have exhausted his supply of miracles."

Elizabeth's gaze refocused on William as he closed his eyes briefly, basking in the warmth of the fire as his features relaxed for a moment, and her heart squeezed for this man... the man she had grown to love. What the doctor was saying... could it be true?

These were dangerous fantasies. Oh, she could not let her mind wander there, stoking hope where it had no right to flourish! But if it could be true... if there *did* remain some kind of healing for him...

"What can I do?" she hissed. "Please tell me. Is there anything I can do?"

"Precisely as you have done, Mrs Darcy. No more, and no less."

Elizabeth swallowed and subsided. Yes. Precisely as she had done… which amounted to nothing, did it? But then, William drank in a sigh and roused slightly, and his eyes found her. And he smiled.

Well… perhaps it was a little more than nothing.

Doctor and Mrs Douglas lingered a while longer until a resurgence of lightly falling snowflakes hastened their farewells. After bundling warmly against frigid elements, they mounted their carriage and were gone—early, as far as Twelfth Night celebrations usually went, but it was late enough for Elizabeth, who wanted nothing more than the quiet of her room and to warm her toes by the fire. Closing the heavy oak door firmly against the biting wind left in their new friends' wake, Elizabeth turned, smiling down at William in his chair beside her.

"There, now! Our first merry holiday gathering concluded most pleasantly, I declare." Teasing joy threaded her approving words as William reached up, clasping her outstretched palm within his own to press a fervent kiss there. And the warmth cascading through Elizabeth owed nothing to the roaring fireplace nearby as he smiled tenderly. He had never done that before.

"Indeed. Your first society event as hostess was a triumph this night."

She chortled. "What, society? Let me survive a Twelfth Night dinner party in London with Lady Matlock's friends in attendance, and that will be saying something."

"Hardly. Anyone can don a masque and play a scripted part. It takes a true lady to shine like a queen in a dilapidated hall."

She let him pull her a little closer; let him slide an arm around her waist and press his cheek to her décolletage as his shoulders rose and fell in a long breath. Hesitantly, she permitted her arm to drop around those broad shoulders and leaned into his curly brow. "Joyous Epiphany," he murmured.

She feathered her fingers through his hair and closed her eyes. "Yes. It was, rather."

Chapter Twenty-Four

D ARCY SIGHED SOFTLY AS Giles wheeled him toward his downstairs bedchamber. Elizabeth would soon appear to spend those last few moments of the evening with him—the brightest part of his days. Though he could only imagine the smooth touch of her hands, simply spending those moments alone with her—listening to her talk, or just watching the way her fingers worked over his skin, how the hair fell over her brow—she brought quiet to his soul when everything else in the world made his skin crawl with futile restlessness.

Tonight, however, reluctance tempered his eager craving. Days of holiday cheer and tasks must have thoroughly exhausted her. Aye, he would part with half his soul if it meant he could retire to his room and look forward to his usual moments of intimacy with his wife—such intimacy as it was. But surely, the pleasure had to be all on his side. And tonight, he had not missed the weariness fogging her sparkling eyes, or the way her shoulders finally slumped when their guests departed.

He could wait. If she came in after Giles left him—and he knew she would, because she always did—he would take her hands in his, rather than letting her try to rub life into his legs, kiss them each in turn, and implore her to rest. After all, no one had earned it more.

As Giles rolled him into his room to prepare him for sleep, bittersweet yearning swelled within Darcy at the thought of feeling his bed shift as she settled beside him again. Before the door closed, Darcy gazed down the shadowed corridor towards the stairs that led to her chambers—chambers he had never even seen. Chambers, which, by rights, should have adjoined his own. How naïvely he'd once dreamed of being welcomed into those chambers by a blushing bride to share his ardent caresses behind that discreet adjoining door, unifying sacred passions between adoring newlyweds through long, blissful nights...

Instead, solemn reality met Darcy each morning in this marriage of convenience, with Elizabeth dutifully fulfilling a nurse's role as his awkward limitations dictated. Yet her tireless compassion bathed his paralysed days with beauty far surpassing his fantasies. Somewhere along that back-breaking journey to Scotland and the slow settling in since, she had utterly conquered his last defences.

Now, Darcy burned fiercely to truly drink of the goblet of wedded bliss. To let himself believe, even for a moment, that theirs was a union of mutual desire and longing—that she saw something in him that he could give her, and that she actually *wanted*.

Oh, she needed him. She had made that plain the day they first met, and he had been no less honest with her. And she was good to him, faithful to her promise and generous in more ways than he could number. But *want*... love, affection, unbidden and freely given... now, there was another matter entirely.

How could she truly desire a man who was... no longer a man?

Fiercely, he blinked back grief-stricken tears before they could swell his eyes or leave a crack in his throat. If Giles noted his master's trembling cheek or rapid blinking as he completed the evening ministrations, the wise valet spared him any further humiliating notice. He simply tended to the fire, stoking it to warm the room, and asked if there was anything else Darcy needed before he retired.

At Elizabeth's gentle knock a few minutes later, Darcy eagerly bade her enter. She came in with a weary, yet affectionate smile that sparked an answering glow within him. "Is Georgiana gone to bed?" he asked, mostly for lack of something else to say.

"Some while ago. She said her ankles were swollen and her hips aching and her... well, you would probably rather not hear the rest of her discomforts." Elizabeth sank with relief onto the corner of the bed and gingerly pulled back the blanket over his legs.

Darcy searched her features in the firelight. Shadowed eyes told of lingering fatigue, though she masked it well—not well enough to conceal it from him, though. He had spent too many hours studying her face not to see the slowness of her expressions, the deadened spark in her eyes. His conscience smote him sharply.

"Elizabeth, we need not keep our usual routine tonight if you are worn thin. Please, simply rest now."

Her hand rested on his leg—damn, what he would give to feel that, even for an instant!—and she blinked back at him, somewhat sluggishly. "But Doctor Douglas says this is helping. He says we ought to continue as we have—"

"And we shall, once you are rested. Surely, you have a warm fire and a... a mountain of blankets to comfort you in your own room."

Elizabeth smiled faintly and stifled a yawn. "No. I sent Beth to bed, for she was even more tired than I was. I know how to build a fire, though. I can have the room warm in no time."

"But your room faces the north, does it not?"

She tried to smother another yawn. "Yes. What of that?"

"And having been left cold all day, even the water in your wash basin is probably frozen. You cannot possibly..."

"I am used to the cold."

He narrowed his eyes and caught the involuntary tremor of her shoulders. Blast, she was freezing even now! He could not send her off to her frigid bedroom, bone-weary and shivering. What if it made her ill? Darcy reached out, asking for her hand. She gave it with a curious look on her face, and he squeezed, chafing her icy fingers. When she shivered harder, he hesitated. "Perhaps you might rest here a moment until the fire heats up? At least warm your limbs for a moment."

Elizabeth worried her lip. "I would not wish to inconvenience you."

Darcy swallowed tightly. Did she find his worthless body offensive? How could she not? He was no longer master of any of it! But aloud, he only said in a voice that sounded flat with restrained desire, "You could never be an inconvenience." He dared extend a shy invitation, hiding his aching hope. "Only let me offer you some small comfort. You are freezing, Elizabeth."

When she still wavered uncertainly, Darcy coaxed gently. "I am more than usually chilled as well. We could perhaps share our warmth? If... if it does not... does not trouble you." He used his free hand to try to pull himself awkwardly to the side, making space, and holding his breath.

She was staring at his hand still, until one more quaking chill seized her shoulders and left her clenching his hand all the tighter. "That..." Her teeth actually chattered as she passed a longing glance over the blankets and the empty space beside him. "That sounds like heaven right now."

She was not leaving? Not shuddering in revulsion and making her escape? By thunder, his heart was going to burst! Darcy held his breath as she eased closer, her brow creased with hesitation. She cautiously reached for the corner of the coverlet and underlying blankets, her eyes slipping to his as if asking this one, final permission.

He answered by tugging them away himself and offering his arm to support her, and that was all it took. Elizabeth sucked in one last gasp from the cold and slid gingerly beneath the heavy blankets. And if he could have felt anything, he would have thrilled to how her icy toes dragged along his calves as she snuggled against his chest—he could certainly see where her feet were under the blankets. That was going to have to be enough.

Darcy tensed as Elizabeth nestled closer, acutely aware of her slender curves moulding along his inert frame. Would she recoil, finding his battered body repulsive? But she only sighed softly, her head coming to rest upon his shoulder. Carefully, he circled an arm about her, desperate not to seem presumptuous.

"Have I hurt you? Ought I shift—" Anxiety laced her low whisper.

"Nay, you could never hurt me." Raw longing carved each rasping word. How must she disdain such a failure of a husband who could not even properly pleasure his wife! Yet wonder kindled, feeling Elizabeth nestle trustingly within his clumsy embrace as if she truly wished to be there beside him.

Tentatively, her palm came to rest over his drumming heart. "You are wincing. Are you feeling any pain tonight?"

Darcy sighed raggedly, the bittersweet agony of unfulfilled desire threatening to crush his fragile composure. He could not bear for her to mistake the writhing frustration churning inside him for physical torment instead.

"Only the exquisite torture of holding Heaven's glory within my arms, yet being denied..." Mortified, he broke off as heated blood scalded his cheeks. Fiercely, Darcy blinked back tears of humiliation. She deserved a passionate lover rather than this hollow ruin of manhood.

But Elizabeth tilted his chin gently back toward her. "Breathe, William."

He choked on a sarcastic laugh. *Breathe? How?* "I am trying, love."

The endearment slipped out before he could master it, though he gasped and stiffened as if he could recall the word. "Elizabeth, I did not mean..."

Her eyes had grown glassy, and her lips parted softly in shock. "Did not mean... what?" she asked in a hushed voice. When he did not answer immediately, her expression tightened, and she leaned closer. "What did you not mean, William?"

His vision was blurring again. Confound it! He never meant to lay that guilt on her—confessing these feelings that nearly blinded him and robbed him of breath every time he looked at her, only to have her unable to reciprocate. But it was too late now, for she had heard, and she was waiting to hear it again.

His breath was stumbling in short bursts as he tried to find the words, but the only ones that would form—aye, refused to be banished from his tongue!—were foolish, dangerous words. Words that could shatter this tenuous, amicable relationship they had managed to build.

But Elizabeth had no intention of letting him shelter behind his fears. She slid her hand up his jaw, feathering her thumb over his cheek and coaxing him to lean a little closer. "You can feel this," she whispered.

A jolt of agony swept over him when the puff of her breath warmed his lips. Numbly, he nodded, his eyes never leaving hers.

"And you can feel this." Elizabeth's fingers sank deeper into his scalp, sending fire through every nerve in his body—even, he fancied, the ones that had lain dead for months.

He could not help the pained whimper in his throat, any more than he could help the way his head dipped lower, and then lower still. "I think I would feel you from the grave, Elizabeth," he whispered. "God help me. I love you—more than life and limb, more than Heaven itself. I love you."

She did not answer—not in words. But an instant later, her sweet mouth was caressing his, her arm sliding over his chest, round his shoulders, warming him and making him feel whole and alive. And where did he suddenly find the strength in his body to pull her to him? He could not know, but in the next instant, he was wrapping her more fully around him until her weight rested on his chest, and his hands were smoothing down the sweet lines of her waist and back.

She was not hesitant or modest in her kisses, but her lack of experience was plain in the way she would pause now and again—the way she seemed to ask for guidance. Aye, his sixteen-year-old sister knew more about the ways of men than his wife of several months! But if Elizabeth was uncertain, he was more so. What could come of such wanton expression? What could he give her but kisses that could lead nowhere?

But that was when Elizabeth herself pulled back, bracing herself on his chest with her forearms so her hands could cup his face. "I love you, too William."

He shook his head. "You are wasted on me. You deserve—"

She cut him off with another kiss—this one deeper, more sensual and bolder than all the rest. She lingered, as if drinking him in, and even as she withdrew, she sucked his lip between hers and smiled with an almost intoxicated euphoria when she let it slip away. "This is where I want to be, William. May I stay?"

Stay? What did that mean? What about... well, there were a hundred reasons why it was unwise. Why he should send her back to her room at once... cold and alone...

But he was already nodding mutely, his body betraying his mind's protests. If Elizabeth wanted to stay, then by Heaven, who was he to stop her? "Are you sure?" he whispered.

Elizabeth drank in a sigh and slipped down his chest, fitting her body into the crook between his arm and ribcage and pillowing her head on his shoulder. "Yes, I am sure," she murmured sleepily as her arm draped over his middle. "If you do not mind."

Mind? He would be mad to object! So long as she truly understood... Hang it all, of course, she understood. She was no fool. And she wanted him, for some strange reason—wanted whatever comfort he could offer, though it seemed insufficient.

"No." His voice cracked on the word. "I do not mind. In fact, I... I do not mind."

"Good." Her ribcage swelled beside his in one more deep sigh and a yawn, and she said no more.

Wordlessly, he clasped her fast, confident no earthly darkness could dim the beacon of loving grace Elizabeth brought to his barren existence. Whatever tomorrow held—whatever explanations must be offered, new paths to search out, and new confessions to be examined in the light of day—for tonight, at least, Darcy knew paradise, for it lay nestled safely within his sheltering arms.

WARM CONTENTMENT ENVELOPED ELIZABETH as she drifted slowly back to consciousness, still caught in a blissful dream. Sunlit meadows unfurled under endless azure skies in her tranquil imagination, joyous laughter echoing from... somewhere. But dimly, she became aware of something else that broke the fragile harmony. Something discordant and muffled. Hushed voices gradually penetrated slumber's haze, bleary confusion mingled with determination to wake fully and investigate whatever required attending.

She blinked reluctantly against the golden dreamscape already fading as her alertness sharpened. It took several seconds of orienting herself before shocked mortification crashed over her, realising precisely where she was, and nestled against whom. Fiery heat scalded her entire body, feeling William's rhythmic breath gently stirring her unbound hair.

She was still wearing that same gown she had worn at dinner—rumpled probably beyond hope without a full washing. And the fire in the room was dying down. Giles would probably be in at some point in the night to either rebuild it or bank the coals. What a shock she would give the poor man! But... no, she did not want to leave. Not yet.

She arched up to see her husband's face better. That was when she had first fallen for him—that day they met, when she saw his guard lowered in sleep, the gentle sweep of his brows over his closed eyes. Eyes that she had already known snapped with intelligence and hid a multitude of feelings that he was too private to share.

But he had shared them now. *He loved her...*

What did that mean? Those were not the words of an invalid to his nurse, the person he looked to for his day-to-day needs. Those were the words of an impassioned man, locked in a frame that had betrayed him, crying out for understanding and begging her to see him for the rich soul behind those expressive dark eyes... not the limited body that refused to function as it once did.

Elizabeth traced the side of his cheek and listened as his breathing deepened. If only they had known one another before this all happened. If only she could have been held by him, just once...

Was it worse, she wondered, to spend one's life longing for what they cannot know? Or to pine for what they once had, and lost? Both were bloody unfair! How could Fortune see fit to strip such a good man of his strength, when a viper like Wickham walked about hale and whole? Elizabeth's lip trembled as she caressed William's jaw, and she lay her head again on the rising and falling of his chest.

That was when she heard it—the voices outside that had awakened her in the first place. Beth, calling for the mistress—for her—and Giles's heavier footsteps out in the hall, saying he did not know where she was, but he was going to saddle a horse.

Elizabeth lifted her head. What the devil?

The sudden creak of a heavy oak door in the hallway outside jarred her into action. Chewing her lip, Elizabeth reluctantly slid from under the blankets and went to the door.

Dread coiled around her heart as she pulled the latch and opened it. Giles whirled in shock, then offered a quick bow and a relieved, "Mistress. Thank Heaven."

Elizabeth eased into the hall, closing the door behind herself. Beth's face was ashen, and the girl was trembling. "Beth? What is the matter?"

"It's Miss Darcy, Ma'am! Please come swiftly. She took badly ill in the night, vomiting and bleeding, with terrible pains." Fat tears streamed down the maid's stricken features.

"Pains? And blood?" she repeated numbly.

"It's too early, is it not, Ma'am? Not until May, Mrs Duncan said, but there was so much blood everywhere!"

Reeling awareness slammed Elizabeth like a physical blow—these were not the typical discomforts of pregnancy, but a traumatic miscarriage, like her mother had suffered the winter when Elizabeth turned eight years old. A boy she had lost, almost fully developed. A son, who could have broken the entail and brought joy to his parents and security to his sisters, but something happened—something that almost cost her mother her life and ensured that no more Bennets would ever be born at Longbourn.

This... this sounded much the same, and it could threaten Georgiana's life itself if she did not have help now. Merciful heavens, surely they had endured enough trauma and heartbreak?

But her spine stiffened instantly, marshalling her strength against rising bile and panic's cold knife. Personal fears must submit to calm pragmatism, lest chaos claim more victims this bitter dawn. There was not a moment to lose.

"Hasten upstairs, Beth. Tell Miss Darcy I will be there in a moment, and we are sending for help. Giles, bring Doctor and Mrs Douglas urgently. No—stay! Is it snowing hard? What of the roads?"

Giles shook his head bleakly. "'Twere a good thing the doctor and his missus left when they did, Ma'am. There is no way of getting through now with a carriage, but mayhap on horseback..."

"No. I'll not have you risking getting caught in a blizzard."

"I can go, Ma'am," he assured her. "I will get through, for the young Miss—"

"Giles, it does none of us any good to have you frozen to death before you even reach the doctor!"

The young man balled his fists and stepped closer, daring to level eyes with his mistress. "I can make it, Mrs Darcy. The master will never forgive me if aught happens to his sister and I did not go."

She softened a little. "Giles, it is not your courage or your fortitude that is in doubt. If the roads are as bad as you say, how is the doctor even to come to us? In the dark, with the wind and snow blowing in his face? He would be lost before half an hour had gone."

He hesitated, his gaze lowering. "I could bring him in the morning, Ma'am—the minute the storm breaks. At least it's a chance. For Miss Darcy."

Elizabeth swallowed and deliberated for a moment. Then, she set her hand on his shoulder. "Go, then, and Godspeed. Beth?" she called upstairs, hoping the maid could hear her. Seconds later, Beth's head appeared on the stair.

"Yes, Ma'am?"

"Once you have seen to Miss Darcy, slip round to the kitchen and start boiling some linen. I will be up directly."

Dismissing them, she whirled back to the door and sucked in a fortifying breath before racing to the bed. "William? William, wake up!"

Her husband's eyes closed tighter still, then opened groggily. He squinted at her in the midnight gloom—he could probably not make out more than her silhouette in the glow of the fire grate. "Elizabeth?"

"There is something wrong with Georgiana."

He pushed his arms under himself and straightened. "What? What is it?"

"I do not..." She pushed his chest down, forcing him to lie back. "I do not know. Beth said she is having pains and bleeding. I am going to her right now, and Giles has gone for the doctor. Blast, I should not have told you..."

"Should not have told me? This is my sister! Where is Giles? Have him help me into my chair!"

"She is upstairs, William. In her room. I told you, Giles has gone for the doctor, and you can do nothing to help Georgiana anyway. Beth and I will do all we can, but I thought I should... oh, I should not have worried you! I am sorry for waking you. Try to rest, and we will—"

"Bloody hell, I cannot rest now! She needs help!" He threw the covers off his legs and lurched as upright as his body would allow—all stomach muscle, as his legs offered nothing, and he seemed to hit an invisible wall in his efforts.

"I told you, William, there is nothing you can do, but... pray for her. Yes, do that. I have to go to her!"

She started to turn away, but William's hands captured hers, arresting her. She spun back.

"Elizabeth, she is my only sister. She's a child. Do..." His voice broke, and his face crumpled as his body shook in sobs. "Oh, God, do something! I cannot lose her, too!"

Elizabeth tried to swallow the sudden knot in her throat as she leaned down to press a quick kiss to his lips. "You will not. I... I promise."

Chapter Twenty-Five

PROMISE. WHAT IN THE world had made her promise? As if the power of life and death were hers to mete out! Of all the stupid, foolish things she had ever said, that might just prove to be the most devastating.

She could only pray for a miracle, so she would not have to take her husband's hand tomorrow morning and confess that she had lied to him.

Elizabeth had bolted from William's door, heart hammering wildly against constricting ribs. She could hear Beth in the kitchen, stoking the fire in the stove and splashing water from the kettle. Good, that was good. They would need—

But then, from upstairs, an agonised scream rent the air, and Elizabeth's blood froze. "Dear heaven," she breathed. "Surely it cannot be... surely we have more time yet before..."

Near hysterical pleas for help guided Elizabeth's precipitous dash upstairs, taking the twisting steps two at a time. She burst into Georgiana's bedchamber and the coppery tang of blood turned her stomach. Terrified blue eyes awash with tears pinned her as the panting girl choked brokenly. "My baby! It's too soon! Help, Elizabeth, please!"

Instantly, the trained gentlewoman usurped girlhood's blind panic, voice emerging steady despite emotions seething beneath the composed surface. "Hush now, darling, all will be well. Giles rides this instant to fetch Doctor and Mrs Douglas. They will be back in a twinkling." Another lie... but the girl doubled over in the bed and was in no condition to hear the truth.

Georgiana only whimpered, curling around her swollen middle. Elizabeth could only stare aghast—Beth had been right. The bed linens, Georgiana's night dress, and even her bared ankles were covered in blood. Elizabeth closed her eyes and breathed a quick prayer, then clutched Georgiana's hand.

"Hold tight, sweet one," she murmured. "Only a little longer... hold fast to me." Elizabeth smoothed damp golden curls back, murmuring empty reassurances. Inside, icy dread gripped her vitals. There was no possibility of Mrs Duncan returning soon enough to do the girl any good. She was going to have to help Georgiana herself. But how? She knew nothing about delivering even a healthy baby, let alone one in this state—whatever state that was. Was there even anything she could do to relieve the pain?

Pain... William's laudanum! He never used it, because he hated the spinning helplessness it always induced. It was still on the bedside table of the upstairs room he had abandoned when Colonel Fitzwilliam brought his Bath chair. But was it wise to give to her now? Would it hurt more than it helped?

Elizabeth watched the girl's quaking and shivers, moaning for help or relief, and she mopped the sticky curls from her forehead. Right now, the pain seemed to be overwhelming her, racking her small frame with agonised convulsions until she could only beg for Elizabeth to make it stop. "Georgiana, I will be right back," she promised.

She raced down the hall and into the room nearest the stairs, and inside the dark room, she fumbled around on the table until her fingers closed on the cold amber bottle. On her way back, she met with Beth, who was just coming up with a steaming kettle and a basket of linens.

Elizabeth poured a dose of laudanum down Georgiana's throat while Beth held her up. Then they hovered helplessly over the whimpering girl, wringing out linen cloths to press over her clammy brow and using more to stanch the flow from her womb.

"Dip more cloths in warmed brandy, Beth!" Elizabeth swept a fringe of hair back from her face as she raced to keep up with the haemorrhaging. "The alcohol will clean the... oh, dash it all, I do not even know if it even matters, but we can try. Quickly—there, thank you!" She grasped the wad of linens and tried to raise Georgiana's hips. That seemed like the right thing... but no, would that only make matters worse?

"Georgiana, squeeze my hand," she ordered. "I need you to focus on my face. Tell me what you are feeling, darling. No, no, do not close your eyes yet!"

But Georgiana could only quake in agony, clenching an arm over her stomach as she crumpled to the side. It was not that she was being uncooperative—more that she was overcome by the pain and could hardly even focus on the words Elizabeth was shouting at her.

Neither Elizabeth nor poor Beth truly understood the intricacies of childbirth, yet they fruitlessly sought indications of what ought to attend the travailing mother now. Surely there must be more to aid her through this torment besides cooling her head and letting her crush their hands while pleading for relief?

Desperate instinct urged her to examine whether the babe progressed along the birthing canal—yes, there was something to that, she seemed to remember. Two years ago, she and Jane had stayed with their aunt Gardiner when she was nearing her second confinement, and they had been in the next room—had heard everything the midwife had said and done during Mrs Gardiner's labours. But she lacked the courage to explore that intimate realm, wholly unfamiliar to her, potentially causing greater harm by tampering ignorantly there.

Haltingly, she tried questioning instead, praying Georgiana might describe symptoms hinting at appropriate actions to assist the crisis. "Can you feel any advancing pressure, dear? Any urge towards, er... pushing the babe along?" Even voicing the awkward query made Elizabeth squirm internally with sympathetic pain and embarrassment.

But Georgiana only convulsed tighter, jaw locking against another guttural scream. "Make... it... stop! No more, I beg mercy!" Panting heavily, she grated as another spasm passed, "I just want this ended now. It is like knives sawing me apart!"

Agonised denial twisted Elizabeth's heart. Everything they had endured—all the hopes pinned on this babe, and Georgiana's future—the very reason she had been brought into this family in the first place! It seemed all would be gone by morning. *Please*, she prayed. *Spare the mother, at least... Spare Georgiana...*

Grimly, she pressed the laudanum vial into those white lips again, praying its numbness brought some vestige of relief whilst Georgiana still clung desperately to fading hopes. All she could offer was small comfort, keeping the girl as calm as possible while leading her gently towards the dreaded understanding that her child would be born... and lost this tragic night.

Her head snapped up a moment later when leaden thumping echoed down the passage before an agonised groan wrenched the air. She exchanged a questioning look with Beth. Could that be Giles, already returned from the doctor? Turned back due to the snow? She got up and raced to the door to see what it was... and nearly fainted from shock when she saw her husband prostrate on the floor outside.

"William!" She dropped to his side immediately. Had he dragged himself by his elbows, all that painful way from his downstairs chamber, up those winding stone stairs, and into the hall outside Georgiana's chamber?

He lifted his head, panting, his face streaked with sweat. "Is she... Georgie... Tell me she is not..."

"Fitzwilliam Darcy, what are you doing here?" She cupped his dear face and shook her head, proud tears tumbling over her cheeks. "You are the most exasperating, troublesome man..."

"My sister!" he interrupted. "I heard her cry out a moment ago, then she went silent. Tell me she is not..."

Elizabeth shook her head. "It is very bad, and I do not know how to help her. But she lives."

His frame collapsed in relief. "Help me to her."

But Elizabeth gaped back in horror, shaking her head. "No, William, you cannot. Even a husband is not permitted—"

He pushed a hand under his chest to roll halfway over, his eyes bloodshot as they bored into her. "Devil take it, Elizabeth, who is the master here? I see no husband to comfort her! There is no doctor or midwife present! Whose bloody rules are you following, anyway?"

She sucked in a breath and relented, but not without a caution. "She may not want you there."

"Then she can send me away, but she cannot send me away without knowing I came to her. That I tried... Elizabeth, please. Help me. My arms are done in."

She sighed, then nodded. "Very well. I... I do not know how to help. I am not strong enough to carry you."

"Bring a blanket," he said tersely. "I can roll onto it, and you can... Egad, that I would have to ask you to do this."

"Enough of that," she admonished. A moment later, she was back with a rug, for it was the only thing she could find loose at a moment's notice, and they had fashioned a sort of litter for him to ride on as she and Beth dragged it through the door.

Even as his eyes found his sister, Elizabeth's heart squeezed. Her poor love would shred what little composure remained to him, seeing his sister suffering so, with her life's blood possibly draining away. There was so little they could do to stop it!

Georgiana turned her head listlessly at their approach. Apparently, the laudanum was starting to have its effect, for her spasming had eased somewhat in just the last few minutes.

Had she given the girl too much? She had used the same measure for Georgiana as for William, but he was twice his sister's size. Oh, dear, what if...

"Georgie, can you hear me?" he asked, his voice low and broken.

Georgiana moaned and nodded softly, her lips trying to turn upward. "My baby... William, I cannot..."

"Shh," he soothed, reaching up to take the hand she draped off the bed for him. "Never mind that now."

"But what will happen?" Georgiana insisted, her words starting to slur a little. "Is he... Elizabeth, is my baby dead?"

All eyes fell to her—Georgiana's lanced with pain and fear, Beth's with confused panic, and William's with so much longing and urgency that it was like a knife in her chest.

"We cannot know yet." Elizabeth squeezed one of William's clenched fists gently. "Some premature travails still deliver a healthy child. My aunt experienced some troubles, and was brought to bed early, but—"

"Not this early," Georgiana whispered. A tear slipped down her cheek, and she closed her eyes, her throat convulsing in faint sobs as the drug towed her under a cloak of oblivion. Free of pain, for a little while, at least.

"Elizabeth?" William's voice rose in pitch, and he sat up straighter in alarm.

"It is only the laudanum I gave her. There is nothing else I could do for her but to try to ease her suffering until the midwife can come. Perhaps just being able to rest will help her to hang on until help arrives."

Thus, the endless minutes trickled past, drenched in tears and blood whilst Georgiana weakly fought the inevitable loss. Grim understanding carved deeper lines upon William's weary features. Elizabeth and Beth brought a wide wingback chair from the corner for him, and between them both, they got him settled into it so he could squeeze his sister's hand whenever another spasm rocked her in her sleep.

But there was no rest for Elizabeth. William kept stirring—once, the strange hallucinations of exhaustion and fear almost made her think that his knee twitched in his restlessness, but it was only her imagination. He kept shifting side to side in impatience, first twisting to look out the window as far as he could, next leaning forward to be sure Georgiana still breathed.

At last, he snapped, "Where is that blasted midwife?"

Elizabeth exchanged a look with Beth. "William, the storm. Giles went, but I was afraid he mightn't get through safely. But he insisted, said that even if the doctor and Mrs

Duncan could not come immediately in the night, he could bring them in the morning." She shook her head. "I do not know when they will arrive... or even if Giles made it in the snow."

He sagged, hissed an expletive, and then drooped altogether. "You are saying we've nought to do but pray? Damn." He propped an elbow on the wing of the chair and leaned his forehead on his hand. "All my prayers lately have gone unanswered."

"**S**HE'S STILL FIGHTING, WILLIAM."

Dawn crept over Georgiana, moaning and thrashing as Elizabeth gripped Darcy's trembling fists with her own. They had kept a gruelling vigil hour after hour with no relief while his sister bled endlessly. Where in blazes was the doctor?

As panic consumed him, Darcy grappled with fresh doubts—had Giles even made it on horseback through the blizzard? And even if he had, could anyone possibly get back in time to save Georgiana now?

He tensed as another agonised spasm tore muted screams from his young sister that shattered his soul. Yet Elizabeth continued ministering tirelessly beside the drenched sickbed, her voice remarkably steady, unlike his. However ignorant medically, she responded to each crisis decisively, never yielding space for hysteria to take root. He admired that stalwart courage deeply, as she smoothed damp golden curls back from Georgiana's tossing head, murmuring soothing nonsense through the gruelling hours.

In the gaps between spasms, Darcy noted Elizabeth subtly flexing her trembling fingers or twisting the linen strips with excess vigour—subtle cracks in the valiant façade, hinting that she second-guessed every improvised attempt at staunching his sister's deteriorating condition. Likely, Elizabeth's medical ignorance terrified her, but she refused to indulge or display her own private doubts, lest he or Georgiana notice. By God, how Darcy wished he possessed even half her stoic rigour in this catastrophe! To remain emotionally anchored required far greater endurance than lashing out frustration over enforced passivity.

As the ordeal dragged interminably into late morning, gnawing hunger gradually eroded their tenuous reserves by degrees. Elizabeth nodded wearily for Beth to bring some bread and cheese from the kitchen that might sustain them a little longer through this nightmare. But even with a crust in hand, Darcy's stomach roiled too violently to consider eating whilst barbaric whipcracks of pain flayed apart his young sister. He could only imagine how Georgiana's heartbeat must be pulsing more erratically now, and will for her to keep drawing those faltering gasps a while longer...

Muffled voices outside wrenched every fibre of Darcy's being taut as hope exploded wildly again. He craned fiercely towards the window, crying out in hoarse confirmation that riders were pushing their way through snowdrifts. Could Giles have brought the doctor, after all? Scarcely allowing himself to believe, Darcy clutched Elizabeth's wrist as they froze in wordless dread and soaring anticipation—until shouts heralded Doctor Douglas himself hastening inside at last!

Even as relief sagged Darcy's rigid frame, it felt short-lived when the door opened, and Doctor Douglas and his wife turned ashen, assessing Georgiana's condition. Their stricken glances took in the pale face on the sheets, the pile of bloodied linens by the door, and Mrs Douglas could not contain a faint gasp. But in a heartbeat, they sprang to work, with Mrs Douglas efficiently inspecting his sister's breathing and pulse—competent ministrations that were tragically long overdue to make any real difference.

"Mr Darcy," Doctor Douglas murmured gently, "Best come away with me now, sir. Giles, my man, will you—?"

But Darcy shook his head. "I will stay."

"Sir, this is women's work. What must be done... Nay, it is too shocking to be witnessed by a brother. Come, let us take you downstairs."

"No! Not downstairs!" he roared. "No farther than the next room. I will not be so far removed when she... I will not go downstairs."

The doctor thinned his lips and nodded to Giles. "Very well. Come away, then, my man." They both bent, allowing Darcy to put his arms around their necks, and they shared his weight as they bore him into the next chamber. Through the fresh hell of being forcibly banished outside his sister's sick room, Darcy distantly understood Elizabeth going ahead of them, saying, "I will get the door. You can place him on my bed."

Her bed. Somehow, in this calamity, he had finally breached the alluring doorway of Elizabeth's private quarters. But even that intimate revelation held only bitter irony, for she was already rushing out, with little more than a tender squeeze of his hand as she went.

Darcy lay back on her pillows, still thick with that rosy lavender scent that was all Elizabeth's. There was nought but shock and dismay left as even Giles withdrew to tend the tired horses that had carried them all here. Darcy was now quite alone and hollow, staring at Elizabeth's cold bedchamber hearth. No welcoming fire or joy awaited him here like a proper newlywed, only the bleak confirmation their family would soon be further gutted.

He had seen it in Mrs Douglas's eyes—she'd believed the babe lost, even before she had made her examination. Was he going to lose Georgiana, too? Had not the fates already demanded enough without taking a gentle girl who had endured too much already in her short life? Howling anguish and seething fury consumed him by turns as endless horrific minutes bled past, hearing muted weeping and cries of pain beyond that closed door.

He did not even register falling into a fitful doze until some interminable time later when Elizabeth slipped inside. Her hand slipped under his cheek, gently placing a pillow beneath his throbbing head before collapsing beside him, overwrought and exhausted.

He lifted his head. "Georgie?" he pleaded.

Elizabeth nodded wearily. "She lives. She has lost a lot of blood, William, but... Doctor Douglas is hopeful."

"And the babe?"

She closed her eyes and turned into his chest, her voice broken on a sob. "It was a girl," she whispered.

He sighed and tightened his arms around Elizabeth's waist as she buried herself deeper into the cave of his embrace. Shattered man he might be, but this one thing, he could manage. He could hold his wife when she wept.

Chapter Twenty-Six

A WEEK HAD PASSED since Georgiana's miscarriage. Elizabeth entered the room quietly, carrying a cup of tea that Beth had just poured for Mrs Douglas. The midwife was sitting with Georgiana, who was finally sleeping soundly. She was still pale and recovering from the blood loss and pains over that traumatic night. Mrs Douglas had stayed to care for her, preparing healing teas and broths and ministering to the girl as she now faced the aftereffects of all she had endured.

"How is she today?"

Mrs Douglas made a thoughtful face as she sipped her tea. Then she set the saucer aside and stood, motioning Elizabeth into the hall so they could speak without disturbing Georgiana. "Her colour is returning, and she has shown no dangerous fever or sickness. These are good signs." The midwife hesitated. "Provided sufficient rest in the coming weeks, I expect a full recovery."

Elizabeth sighed in relief. "When I sat with her last night, she woke herself weeping. The poor child! She was inconsolable." She shook her head. "She did not even want this child."

"Och, the poor lass." Mrs Douglas clicked her tongue. "Often the way of it. There be no explaining the curious mysteries of a mother's love for her own."

Elizabeth tried to smile. "I know. In truth, I... I am broken for her, but I know not what to say, or how to help her."

"Fear not, Mrs Darcy. Her heart will mend in time."

"And what of her body? Will she..." Elizabeth hesitated, thoughts of her own mother's traumatic loss still haunting her. "I know it may be years, if ever, before she thinks of this again, but will she ever be able to conceive a child safely, after all this?" she whispered. "I am sorry for pressing now, but there may never be anyone else I can ask without... Well. Would it be safer for her if she never..."

The older woman chose her words carefully. "There is damage, I'll not deceive ye. But I have seen women bear healthy children even after much trauma, so it is not beyond hope."

Elizabeth squeezed her eyes shut, kneading them, and sighed fervently, "If only she had been spared this! After everything else she has endured—losing her parents, having her heart broken, and then William... It is as if Fortune has decreed she is never to enjoy a life of peace."

Mrs Douglas patted her hand gently. "You mustn't give way to such thoughts. The young lass has been luckier in her family's support than many girls in such straits."

Elizabeth faltered, unsure how much to say. At last, she ventured, "I suppose you have, perhaps, already guessed. It was no 'officer husband stationed on the continent' who fathered the babe."

"'Tis not my concern who the father is or was. All I see is a girl what needs tender care, and she has it." She smiled and shook her head, gesturing to the next door down the hall. "Miss Darcy has the finest of brothers in Mr Darcy."

Elizabeth glanced over her shoulder. "Yes, my husband's devotion to his sister's well-being quite carried me away."

"You've a perfect right to be smitten by the gentleman. I have seen many a lass turned out by her family in her state. Left to fend for themselves as best they can, which is a fearful fate. But his care for her—and for you, Mrs Darcy—puts my heart at rest. He is a remarkable brother."

Elizabeth smiled through the sudden tears in her eyes. "He is a most remarkable *man*."

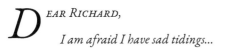

*D**EAR RICHARD,*
I am afraid I have sad tidings...

Darcy sat propped amongst the pillows in Elizabeth's bedchamber, quill poised over a half-finished letter to Richard detailing Georgiana's horrible brush with death. Losing his niece was monstrous enough—however much the circumstances of the child's conception had grieved him, the horrid way her life had been snuffed out before it ever began smote him even more piercingly.

But nearly losing Georgiana completely in the aftermath had shattered him anew. By God's grace the greatest danger was past, his sister slowly recovering down the hall under Elizabeth's and Mrs Douglas's tireless care. She would live. Whatever else that meant, he had not lost her utterly, but it had been a near thing.

Winter's icy shroud had finally lifted this morning. Doctor Douglas had located a trusted rider willing to discreetly bear the tragic missive to Richard, once the roads became passable again. Darcy rubbed his reddened eyes, struggling to order the tumultuous emotions into coherent sentences for his cousin. How to adequately describe the harrowing hours crouching helplessly at his sister's bedside, Georgiana's lifeblood slowly draining away before them all? Only Elizabeth's stalwart compassion through that horrific night had anchored Darcy's sanity amidst the chaos. He dipped his quill and continued.

You may be assured that she is as comfortable as we may make her, and every day sees some little improvement in her colour, if not her spirits. I am advised that we must not attempt to move her for at least another fortnight, perhaps longer. As soon as she feels strong enough to travel, we intend to return to Pemberley—long before June, as we had initially planned.

While the sudden loss of the babe has, perhaps, eliminated one source of my concerns for the future, it has raised the ugly head of another. What becomes of the entail? For even if the child had survived, it was a girl child, and all hope of saving Pemberley through that means was lost before it began.

Be so good as to consult with legal counsel. My solicitor will be able to direct you to all the pertinent documents, and I include instructions for him to cooperate fully with your investigation. Unless I am mistaken, the recent disposition of the presumptive heir will preclude him from claiming the inheritance, should I pass before he does. Which, I fear, is not an altogether unrealistic possibility.

I know the limits this injury has placed on my expectations. You and I are no fools—I am one insidious illness away from the grave in my condition. Which is why I urge not only haste, but supreme discretion. I would not have Elizabeth know...

His throat constricted, quill halting over the page. During those dark, endless hours, admiration for Elizabeth's courage and quick wits had transformed his already passionate feelings for her into ardent devotion bordering on worship in his breast. Never once did she yield to hysterics despite lacking any medical experience. Instead, Elizabeth battled fiercely for Georgiana's fading life with fierce pragmatism. And after the doctor and mid-wife had done all possible, she kept on—comforting them both while her own exhaustion wore her to a pale shadow of herself.

A husband could search several lifetimes and never uncover Elizabeth's equal. As Darcy gazed at her empty pillow beside him, fervent longing swelled within. If only he could be the man she deserved... one who could truly cherish her as a husband ought.

There was one mercy in all this—one thing that sustained him and made him hope he could offer her some fraction of what she had already given him. And that was that each night this long and harrowing week, she had collapsed into bed beside him—when she did sleep. His own bed was still downstairs, where he could easily shift into his Bath chair. But the only place for him now was as near his sister as he could possibly be, whether that meant the chair beside her sickbed, or Elizabeth's room next door.

At first, he had felt badly that he had taken over his wife's sole refuge in this house, leaving her no possibility of retreat or seclusion when she became overwrought. But one thing he had discovered in these waning hours between death and life: Elizabeth thrived in a crisis. That was not to say that she craved it or would be the sort to create drama and anxiety when it did not present itself of its own accord, simply to satisfy her thirst for intrigue. But a certain iron would enter her spirit when it was needed most, and she became somehow the strongest version of herself.

But after the critical moments had passed... when her soul needed a respite and her patience was worn paper-thin... why, those were the moments when she had begun to turn to him. There was so little he could do for her, but he could dry her tears. Tease a smile back onto her face. Offer her what precious little warmth his body had to offer when she collapsed for her brief periods of sleep.

For now, it was enough. But what would happen when, one day, it was not his sister who was the main cause of her stress and anxiety, but himself? To whom would she turn then?

It was something he did not like thinking about, and rarely permitted himself. He simply had no answers against the inevitable. Darcy swallowed and dipped his pen once more to finish the note for Richard.

E XHAUSTION BORE DOWN ON Elizabeth's shoulders as she sat vigil in the bedside chair. It was that drowsy, bleary time of afternoon, when the house was too quiet save for the ticking of the clock on the mantel, and Elizabeth's eyelids were growing heavier by the moment. Weak afternoon light filtered across Georgiana's sleeping face—peaceful at last, despite the trauma that still haunted her gaunt features.

Elizabeth rubbed gritty eyes, yearning to grant the slumbering patient a few undisturbed hours before necessity demanded more vile-smelling herbal draughts were poured down that tender throat. She must not sleep now, lest Georgiana rouse bewildered and afraid. But bone-deep weariness still dragged Elizabeth's eyelids inexorably downward...

Abruptly her chin jerked up from her chest—she had not even realised she nodded off! Muddled disorientation cleared swiftly though as she met her charge's sombre blue eyes studying her intently across the crumpled linens.

"Georgiana! Forgive me, I did not mean to doze." Elizabeth smoothed back tangled hair, rallying her wits. "How are you feeling just now? Are you in need of anything?"

The girl shook her head mutely, listless gaze drifting over rumpled bedclothes still bearing faint russet stains despite Beth's best efforts at laundering them.

When Georgiana still did not speak again, Elizabeth leaned forward, searching her averted face. "Do you have any pain? Perhaps I might mix another drought..."

"There is no need." Georgiana's hoarse near-whisper rasped louder in the stark room's heavy silence. "I... I feel nothing now. No pain in my body, that is. But..." She clenched her eyes, and a tear squeezed out.

Elizabeth reached for one limp hand lying atop tangled blankets. "Dearest, it will be well. Grief always ebbs in the fullness of time."

Georgiana flinched subtly at her tender touch but did not pull away. "Even... even when one grieves over something wicked?" The ragged whisper emerged nearly inaudible as she squeezed shut burning eyes against scalding tears.

"Wicked?" Elizabeth's bemused query trailed off as dreadful comprehension sank like icy claws. "You cannot think you are being punished for something."

"And why should I not be? How many times did I wish that baby away? And then when it happened, I cried because I had lost it! I am a fickle, horrible person, and God is punishing me!"

Gently brushing tangled golden curls back, Elizabeth whispered, "Georgiana, that is not how it works. You are not being punished, and Heaven does not take away a child just because your feelings were conflicted about it."

Georgiana trembled harder, still refusing to meet her earnest gaze. "Yet I wished this child gone almost every day since I learned of it! How could it not be that my bitter prayers willed it so?" Choking back wrenching sobs, she burst out, "Am I not wicked, wanting freedom from what I brought upon myself? And even wickeder still when it was taken away, and I wanted to keep it? What right had I to wish that?"

"Nay, never wicked!" Elizabeth squeezed her quavering shoulders firmly as fresh tears coursed down Georgiana's hollow cheeks unheeded. "Of course, you felt conflicted. Confused... who would not be? But this is not your fault, and no one expects you to make sense of your feelings now. Why, it is not as if you actually did the child wilful harm!"

"N-no..." A violent headshake punctuated denial as tangled emotions warred across Georgiana's distressed features before she whispered faintly, "Believe me, Elizabeth. I know I l-lied before, but I never did anything like that. Th-there were moments I dreamed of cradling the babe tenderly...b-but whenever I started thinking about... you know, how it would really be, that it would not be mine, I would cry all over again!" She dashed away scalding moisture, gasping harshly around the painful lump choking speech, "S-so you see, 'tis my fault entirely it perished! Will-William must surely despise me now!"

"Your brother could never despise you." Elizabeth blinked back her own sympathetic tears. "He knows well how fiercely you loved the child despite everything—we could all see how stricken you were. That goodness outweighs any human failing."

When Georgiana could only rock weakly back and forth, anguished eyes squeezed shut, Elizabeth sighed, rubbing the trembling shoulders bracingly. "Darling, such torment serves no purpose! We cannot comprehend precisely why these things befall us, yet you must trust in divine mercy making all things eventually right."

Her bleak nod acknowledged the well-meant comfort, but misery still tightened pain-etched features. After long minutes, Georgiana rasped miserably once more, "I wish I could believe that... truly I do! Only now, William shall know nought but endless grief on my account." Her haunted eyes finally lifted, overflowing anew with anguished tears. "With my b-baby lost, what hope remains to save Pemberley from that monster when William cannot sire an heir himself?"

Elizabeth winced inwardly. Yes... there was that. "Hush now, fretting over distant 'what ifs' serves little good! Rather, save your strength. Let us look to your health first." She squeezed Georgiana's icy hand within her own. "Do not trouble yourself unduly over Pemberley's fate or your brother's prospects. Divine providence has provided thus far."

"Always you counsel faith!" Something kindled in Georgiana's defeated posture—bitter challenge, perhaps? "Do you not comprehend that William is now condemned to lifelong invalidism? And even if, by some miracle, he does not die too young from some disease, how are you and he to have a son?"

Elizabeth flinched. "I... I do not know, Georgiana. We have not spoken of it, but surely there is some way..."

Georgiana's frantic grip tightened, her eyes brimming with fresh tears. "He married you hoping somehow my son might pass for his own to secure Pemberley's legacy! And now I destroyed his one hope."

Elizabeth sighed heavily, struggling to order tangled truths and platitudes into coherent reassurances. But before she formulated any response, Georgiana lurched upright, panting harshly. "I cannot stay abed another moment!"

"Careful!" Elizabeth leapt up, bracing the swaying girl as another spasm contorted her pallid face. "Here, allow me to assist you."

Ignoring Georgiana's protests, Elizabeth slipped a supportive arm around her, gently guiding the girl's faltering steps behind the privacy screen shielding the chamber pot. Lingering until necessity concluded, she then hovered watchfully as the girl slowly crossed back, clutching the bedpost for support.

"That's progress! Can you manage a chair for awhile perhaps? Best not push too swiftly lest your bleeding increases again, but..."

"Not the chair, but can you help me with the pillows, like you do for William? I despise lying flat any longer!"

"Of course." Effusive relief nearly buckled Elizabeth's knees seeing her young sister-in-law moving again at all. Once Georgiana was carefully propped against the cushions, her colour already improving somewhat with the change of position, Elizabeth impulsively hugged her with quavering laughter. "You gave us quite the fright, nearly slipping away! I vow William aged a decade that horrific night..."

Something softened the wretched emptiness haunting Georgiana's expression at the mention of her devoted brother. Ducking her head almost shyly, she whispered. "You must find me a most troublesome sister foisted upon your happy union."

"Never imagine it!" Elizabeth squeezed her trembling hand fiercely. "I would not even be here, were it not for you."

Georgiana permitted a wry smile that reminded Elizabeth so much of William that it made her heart skip a beat. "And are you sorry for that?"

She leaned close with a scandalous-sounding whisper. "Not for a moment. Now, let me pamper you outrageously as befitting someone who has just defied death. Fancy a cloth for your face, perhaps? What if I read aloud to you?"

The responding ghost of a smile heartened Elizabeth considerably. But the fleeting levity extinguished abruptly at Georgiana's next earnest whisper whilst searching her face intently. "What you said before—you were right, you know. I know not why such dreadful fortunes befell us all, nor what comes next. I just worry for William."

"Yes." Elizabeth sighed as she tucked Georgiana's legs in more securely with the blankets. "So do I."

"He had one chance! It seemed so perfect, too—poetic justice, do you know?"

Elizabeth's brow furrowed as she shook her head. "Know what?"

"Why, William's means of escaping that scoundrel, though he nearly perished trying to defend my honour from him! How fitting it was to think that I could help—that even though he was nearly the means of our ruin, he was also the architect of his own."

"Georgiana, I really... what are you talking about?"

The girl sat up straighter. "Surely you have heard. William must have told you who would come to assume his place someday at Pemberley, if..."

The truth began to erupt in the chill of Elizabeth's veins like a thread of dynamite, set to claw away at her innards. "You cannot mean..." She blinked uncertainly. "Mr Wickham? Whatever connexion exists there?"

Georgiana recoiled sharply at the sound of the name. "How can you not know this? His mother was Father's cousin, making him the maternal grandson of Pemberley's former master. He is William's wretched heir now!"

Chapter Twenty-Seven

D ARCY DRIPPED WAX ACROSS the edge of the folded letter, pressing his seal firmly into the small red puddle. He waited for it to cool, then penned the direction on top for Dr Douglas's courier. And none too soon, for a knock preceded the doctor entering, palms rubbing briskly against the lingering chill.

"Good day, Mr Darcy! Did you have that letter finished?"

"Just here, Doctor." Darcy handed the missive over with a curt nod of thanks. "I appreciate you securing a reliable courier willing to carry this to Colonel Fitzwilliam in London."

"Of course, of course! No trouble at all." Dr Douglas placed the letter carefully inside his bag. "Vital family business is risky to commit to the regular post, of course. Although..." He hesitated, tugging his grizzled beard pensively. "I confess some curiosity whether you plan to relocate your household soon?"

Darcy tensed, guardedly schooling his features before replying neutrally. "What leads you to think that?"

The doctor waved one broad hand airily. "Och! Canna blame an old doctor's nosiness. With Mrs Douglas coming home today after nursing your sister this week past, I naturally wondered..."

He trailed off meaningfully as Darcy looked aside, jaw clenched. At length, Dr Douglas ventured, "Forgive my indelicacy if you still mourn the loss. But now your sister mends apace, 'tis only natural to consider the future."

Darcy glanced away, watching the crystalline flakes swirling beyond the frosty windowpane. Naturally, removing Georgiana from Scottish exile and returning to Pemberley was foremost on his mind. "I expect we shall depart soon enough. A little more time for her to recover her strength..."

"Just so, just so." Mercifully, the doctor did not press for particulars. "Well, then! Since I still have you conveniently abed, perhaps you might permit one last examination? Purely to satisfy my medical curiosity over your uncommon injury."

Darcy smothered a derisive grunt. Nothing about paralysis was fascinating beyond the catastrophic sentences it pronounced. Yet refusing risked insult when Dr Douglas only wished to be of assistance.

There was nothing to be found—of that, he was certain—but once Georgiana was well enough and they set out for Pemberley, it might be some while before he could secure the services of another doctor he did not loathe. It might do just to see that his flesh remained healthy, for it seemed his health, or what remained of it, was now the only thing he had with which to protect Elizabeth and Georgiana. Darcy nodded curtly, bracing himself for more meaningless tests and platitudes that changed nought. This necessary farce concluded, he might regain precious solitude all the more quickly.

Deft fingers prodded along Darcy's spine professionally as Dr Douglas hummed under his breath. He could feel the doctor's touches as they trailed down the middle of his back until the pressure disappeared entirely. "Remarkable stability and healing in the vertebrae, though nerves remain stubbornly unresponsive, I gather?" At Darcy's terse grunt, he asked, "And how fare other physical developments? Your inner workings, sir?"

Mortification scalded his face as Darcy stared fixedly into the pillow, refusing a response. Surely, no gentleman endured such an indelicate interrogation! But the doctor persisted, damn the man. He would be hanged before he spoke about *that*.

"Come, lad, surely matters of natural bodily function emerge more, er, predictably since the initial crisis? 'Tis only healthy as the internal trauma heals."

Oh, what was the use? It was not as if Douglas was going to run and tell Richard or the earl. He might tell Elizabeth, though... no, surely, even Douglas had better manners than that. And it meant nothing, anyway. As the doctor said, it was only... to be expected. Haltingly, Darcy confessed to resuming more regular patterns in necessities he still only discussed with Giles 'til now. Anything beyond that was not information he would ever share, not even with Elizabeth!

"Excellent progress, indeed!" Dr Douglas encouraged, missing his flaming discomfort entirely. "Now tell me, have there been any flickers of sensation in your legs of late? Any response at all to touches along here..."

He ran professional fingers firmly down Darcy's right calf, peering intently for reaction. "Reflexive twitches sometimes develop gradually. Or skin awareness returning in patches—"

"Why do you speak of it as if there is any improvement to be had?"

Douglas glanced up. "Yours is a most puzzling injury, sir. Why, I have seen others who... well, but for your lack of sensation, I can see nothing whatever wrong with your spine."

"Obviously, matters are wrong enough." Darcy jerked his head aside, throat constricting harshly against the cursed longing the doctor's tentative words sparked. How fiercely he craved embracing sweet, unfettered liberty again, instead of crawling through life's grey shadows! Yet he dared not fan fragile hopes over half-understood medical notions. It was only his imagination that fuelled fleeting fancies of increased sensitivity on certain nights... in particular locations... when Elizabeth...

"Mr Darcy?" Dr Douglas prompted gently. "You needn't fear speaking plainly to me. Any positive developments lift your prognosis, however trivial they might seem."

"There is nought to tell." Darcy snapped bitterly before mastering his tone once more into calm impassivity. "There is no return of sensation, and even if there were, what would it signify? Half my body remains lifeless as marble, regardless, and it always shall!"

"Patience yet! 'Tis early days..."

"'Early days'... Just as the doctor in London said last September. It is nearly five months, and I am dead from navel to toes."

With a heavy sigh, Dr Douglas repacked his medical satchel and donned his greatcoat. "Well, sir, I can only repeat my earnest wish that your fortunes turn for the better swiftly. Your charming wife and sister, too! Fine ladies, the both of them." He smiled benevolently through his bushy whiskers. "I shall leave you the name of a colleague in London if ever a second opinion is desired. Fare thee well, Mr Darcy."

Alone again, Darcy blinked hard against burning moisture, battling increasing self-reproach on top of simmering fury. All his useless carcass achieved lately was offending well-meaning people or lashing out unjustly in bitter despair! How would Elizabeth react, knowing her husband's wretched secrets and outbursts?

Impatient rapping interrupted his escalating frustration. Probably Giles, come to tend to him as he always did in the late afternoon. "Come!" he bellowed.

But instead of Giles, the fine-eyed woman who presently owned his thoughts stood, regarding him from the doorway. Lightness surged through Darcy at the welcome sight. If any earthly balm existed to salve his battered soul just now, Elizabeth's soothing presence was it.

But the look on her face when she stalked to his bed was anything but soothing.

"Why did you never inform me that George Wickham was your heir?" She pushed the lap tray from before him, almost spilling the ink from the well on his makeshift writing desk.

"Have a care, Elizabeth! You will ruin—"

"Hang what I will ruin. Why did you never tell me? Your own sister fully expected that I was privy to the knowledge!"

Darcy winced beneath her searing glare. Blast, he should have known she would find out eventually. "Georgiana shared more than was advisable," he began cautiously. "I wished to spare you any undue anxiety until absolutely necessary..."

"I'd call this necessary!" Elizabeth flung back. "We are shackled in wedlock, bound to blunder ahead together regardless of what happens, yet you omitted the little detail that one day Pemberley could fall into George Wickham's depraved hands? Were you not going to prepare me at all?"

Darcy opened his mouth, but it was a moment before any words came. "I... I set aside a portion for you—your father, who did not even approve of me, found it more than generous. The dower house would not be safe for you, but there is enough for a fine apartment in London or a country cottage somewhere—"

"And who controls Georgiana's future? Tell me she would not fall victim to that man again!"

"No! No, she—she would become Richard's ward until she married or came of age. And Wickham could not touch her dowry."

"Then..." She shook her head. "Why did you say you would worry for us? Certainly no one wants to see him ruin the estate or mistreat the tenants. Bad enough, that, but you specifically said you feared for *us*. What power would he have?"

"None but what you give him. That is just the problem. He... egad, I can hardly even speak of it."

"He would throw her into the hedgerows, as Mama always said," Elizabeth retorted, her voice thick with sarcasm. "I do not think Miss Darcy hardly has to worry about that, with a dowry of thirty thousand pounds."

"It is not that! He would blackmail her. Threaten to tell the world what he had done to her—I would not put it past him to bully her into marrying him, just to prove he could."

Elizabeth stepped closer. "But you said Richard would protect her. He would be dead before he let that happen."

Darcy sucked in a sigh, and his fist squeezed a knot in the bedding. "Exactly."

"You do not think... No, he is not a murderer! Is he?"

He clenched his jaw. "He... Wickham and I grew up together as boys. I always noted his avarice. Rarely was it tempered by good sense or any notion of fairness. He would do or say anything to get what he wanted. My father also remarked on it, and I implored him to speak to Wickham's father on the matter when we were still young. But my father had too much respect for old Mr Wickham as a gentleman, and never..."

"No one ever corrected him?" Elizabeth guessed.

Darcy sighed. "George Wickham used to lock up the maids until they were missed in their duties. He would wait until they went into the still room or somewhere else he could secretly bar, and then he would only let them out if they granted him certain favours. If they refused, he would report that he had caught them dallying with the footmen, and they would be punished. And if they yielded, he only did it again... until one day, I caught him."

Her eyebrows rose. "And?"

"And I called him out behind the stables. We were both bruised and bloodied when we came back, but I felt justice had been done, and my honour was satisfied. That is, until Richard heard of it the next day when he rode over from Matlock to take his leave before he purchased his commission." Darcy shook his head. "Richard gave him the same thrashing as I had, but he was four years older than we were. When Richard walked back, he had no bruises. And George Wickham could hardly see through his right eye for a fortnight."

"So, Wickham hates the colonel even more than he envies you?"

"Wickham knew what he was doing, going after Georgiana. He had planned it—even down to sending Mrs Younge to interview for the position of Georgiana's companion. He knew that through Georgiana, he could target both Richard and me. I simply found her sooner than he could expect, and that merely by luck. So... while I cannot say Wickham would be capable of doing harm to Richard just to get to Georgiana, he certainly has an axe to grind. It is not a thing I wish to leave to chance."

"And you did not think I should know about this?" Agonised betrayal bled starkly across Elizabeth's fine eyes, her rapid breaths lifting the creamy fichu edging her heaving bosom. Never had Darcy beheld anything more captivating than his wife's magnificent passion at this moment. If she would but pour it out upon his willing flesh next! Heat seared his cheeks at the mere thought of her unleashed ardour... But the fantasy vanished swiftly. Even if now were the time—which it was not—there was no use.

"I did not tell you about Wickham because there is some hope of breaking the entail," he said at last.

That rendered her momentarily speechless. Darcy seized the opening, desperately capturing her clenched fists within his own shaking grip. Gradually, her ragged breaths calmed until she sank mutely onto the mattress edge. Pressing a fervent kiss across her icy knuckles, Darcy then whispered hoarsely.

"You are right to reproach me, Elizabeth. I owed you the truth, but instead, I said nothing." Remorse roughened his tone. "Old habits bred reluctance speaking that fiend's name, lest I acknowledge his power somehow... but no more excuses. You deserve only honesty."

"What is this you were saying... about breaking the entail?"

"I do not yet know if it is possible. Wickham has been found guilty of desertion and transported. At least, that was what Richard told me. If that sentence was carried out, I do not think he is eligible to inherit. How could he? But I need it clarified in writing, so I have asked Richard to see to the particulars with my solicitor. If I am right, and no other male heir can be found, then it goes to the courts to decide what is to be done."

"But that is still... terribly uncertain." Her mouth puckered in thought. "What do you think they would decide?"

"I would press for the right to pass the estate to you or Georgiana, or, better yet, to Richard. If the entail is broken, truly and completely, I could arrange in my will for it to go to whomever I please. Richard has the power, the experience, and the connexions to protect all of you if—"

"Shh..." Elizabeth pressed a finger to his lips. "This... this is a hideous topic. Why are we so certain any of this will even become an issue? You are not ill. There is no reason to think—"

"There is no reason to think I will outlive any of you," he replied gently, pulling her hand down and cupping it into his. "Not now. And I will not leave anything concerning the ones I love to chance."

"And are you certain, absolutely certain, that Mr Wickham is the only heir?"

Darcy sighed and nodded. "Yes. The entail specifically named 'heirs male of the body of Wendell Darcy—my great grandfather. He only had two sons, and each of them only had one child. Well! Only one legitimate child, but that is all that matters, anyway. Believe me, if there were another cousin out there who could be named heir, I would step aside, and gladly. But there is not."

"So…" Her eyes fell to their hands, and she chewed her lip in thought. "The entail is uncertain… sending the matter before the courts would prove uncertain… there really is only one way to be sure." Slowly, her gaze lifted to him, and a strange light flickered in her eyes.

"No. No, Elizabeth, it is impossible. I cannot…"

"I did not mean you. But you were willing to raise Georgiana's child as your own."

"Georgiana is, at least, a Darcy. It is a stretch, but technically, if her child had been born a living son, he would have qualified as next in line after Wickham." He cleared his throat. "To say nothing of the… er… natural father's qualifications."

"But surely, there are other girls in similar predicaments. What becomes of them, if no one helps them? What becomes of their children? We could give a child a home and save Pemberley at the same time."

He gazed at her, his throat turning dry. "I… I cannot, Elizabeth. I suffered enough guilt already, planning to pass off my blood nephew as my own son. I never would have considered it if…" He shook his head. "No. Wilfully tampering with legal succession? Living a lie just to see the future twisted as I like it? It is abhorrent."

She sat back. "So… what, then? We… try to… ah…" She reddened and gestured to him.

Darcy's ears burned. "Much as that would be my preference, it is not possible now. Egad, if I had but known you a year ago!"

She tried to smile and captured his restless hand, brushing a stray curl behind one ear self-consciously. "You would not have liked me, even a little. I daresay I would have been 'not handsome enough to tempt you,' or some nonsense."

Darcy winced playfully. "I deserved that."

"Why *did* you never marry sooner, if an heir held such importance for Pemberley's future? I doubt it was because you lacked options."

Darcy smiled sadly, marvelling that he had never confided such details even to Richard. Yet with Elizabeth, the words flowed without effort. "Because I waited and hoped for a partner who could be a true companion as well as Mistress. One whose lively mind and steadfast heart drew me. Not merely a decorative heiress to grace my arm and salons." He traced one curved cheek softly. "I wished for a marriage as I saw my father share with my mother."

Anguish clenched Darcy's throat anew, imagining how profoundly he still disappointed all her rightful hopes in a husband. "Had I but met you sooner, before everything shattered, perhaps..." He broke off, cursing fate's callous whims leaving nought but bitter star-crossed thoughts between them now.

But Elizabeth cradled his jaw tenderly, coaxing his face back up. "You are a good man, Fitzwilliam Darcy. And you are a clever one. Did I also mention stubborn?"

He could not help a smirk, even through the gloom that had begun to darken his mood. "I believe it has come up."

"You will find a way—something that does lie within the bounds of decency. I know you too well to believe you will simply give up when the future of those under your protection remains unsettled."

Despite himself, answering warmth kindled in Darcy's chest, yet weary acceptance increasingly weighed his words these days. "If Providence wills the name of Darcy to end with me, I must bend obediently to that design with what grace remains, though it cost my heart's blood. But not all hope is lost." He offered her a crooked smile. "I might still outlive all of you."

Elizabeth laughed. "Including Mr Wickham."

"Especially him."

She leaned closer and cradled his jaw with sudden tender ferocity. "And that is why I chose you, Fitzwilliam Darcy."

"My rapier wit and dashing sense of humour?"

She shook her head and arched a brow. "You think of others before yourself. Even when it costs you everything."

Then her sweet full mouth sealed over his own, passionate benediction searing Darcy's very soul. Helpless to resist newly awakened cravings, he banded her slender form fully against himself, unleashing the fervent kiss's full, seductive promise. It could not last... could not render the promise her touch seemed to offer... but it was enough for now, just knowing that one person in this world saw him for who he was—before, after, and through it all.

Chapter Twenty-Eight

D ARCY SHIFTED RESTLESSLY IN his wheeled chair as he looked out from his study window across the familiar grounds of Pemberley. A month and a half had come and gone—six weeks since Georgiana had almost perished in that lonely Scottish ruin Lady Matlock called a "castle." Once she could sit up for periods together, then walk about with her usual vigour and eat a hearty meal, Darcy wasted no time in bringing her back to Pemberley, where she could recover her strength in familiar surroundings.

And familiar they were... but different now, at least to him. A knot worked into his throat as he strained to look beyond the borders of his windowpane. Here and there, the spikes of green and yellow poked through the snow from the bulbs his mother had planted—flowers that would be invisible through most of the year but pushed their heads out of the ground now, when their presence brought cheer to the late winter gloom. He yearned to hunt out all those hidden flower beds himself, to share them with Elizabeth as they watched nature's resilient renewal. It would be perfectly in tandem with his family's gradual mending process after more than three gruelling months wintering in Scotland.

But Darcy could no longer explore his beloved trails and dells as in former days. Those dizzying London specialists had insisted his paralysis would never improve. He would not move beyond this infernal contraption. How it stung, being relegated as solely a spectator to Pemberley's seasonal awakening now! Worse still was knowing Elizabeth had probably already explored each picturesque vista alone—all those late February surprises that his mother and father would enjoy together—whilst he brooded indoors. They ought to have been discovering every enchanting nook together, hand in hand...

His brooding was interrupted as the study door opened abruptly, admitting his uncle the earl without ceremony. Darcy restrained his annoyance as his uncle gave his wheeled chair a cursory acknowledgement before draping himself into the armchair beside the hearth with trademark brusqueness.

"Well nephew, I trust Georgiana is recovering apace? Up and about and her old self again, eh?"

"She continues regaining strength slowly." Darcy shifted, discomfort prickling under his uncle's assessing stare. Must they delve into painful topics so soon? Not even the customary social niceties before Lord Matlock began planning whatever he was planning?

"Just so, just so." The earl gave an awkward cough. "Glad to have you all safely out of that desolate Scottish hovel, regardless. Lady Matlock will not even hear of going there. I told Richard it was blasted lunacy to send you all there for the winter, but he would not heed my complaints."

Darcy drummed his thumbs together. "We were well enough. We had privacy, which was our chief requirement."

"And little else. Scottish exile never benefited gently nurtured ladies, whether young or old, and add to that a... well, an unfortunate, er..." He chuckled, though it held a palpably uneasy edge. "At least our Georgiana need not now fret herself over her, er, delicate condition henceforth. Back as though nothing ever happened, which I cannot say is lamentable."

Darcy tensed, clasping the armrests fiercely. How dare his uncle gloss over the calamity and anguish haunting Georgiana still? "Confound it, sir, my sister nearly perished birthing a child she grew to want desperately, despite all the scandal it would have brought!" His voice rasped raw, knuckles white. "Can you really overlook how it crushed her, losing the babe and nearly her own life?"

The earl winced, scrubbing one veined hand down his craggy features. "A grievous outcome no one disputes, Darcy. Might have spared her that sorrow, I suppose." He cautiously met his nephew's stormy glare. "Yet she bears up admirably under female troubles from what Mrs Darcy wrote to Lady Matlock. You must own the ordeal concluded more mercifully than if she had been carrying to term."

"If that is what you call 'mercy'..."

"Come now Darcy, easy!" Lord Matlock lifted both broad hands. "I meant naught unfeeling regarding the girl. But what good comes dwelling over troubles now in the past?" His penetrating gaze studied Darcy's clenched jaw intently. "Unless of course, your injury weighs heavier of late?"

"Not at all." Darcy refused to voice the scalding frustration chafing him. He arched one sardonic brow. "Indeed, I am grateful that escaping frozen Scotland allows me to resume estate affairs here personally, rather than entirely by remote decree. And this... contraption Richard secured for me is a godsend. I can accomplish significantly more from my desk than the sickbed upstairs."

"Ha! Good lad." The earl nodded approvingly before turning a professional eye over the ledgers strewn haphazardly across the mahogany surface of Darcy's desk. "Famous good to have you take the helm again. A house like this wants a proper man guiding it." Lord Matlock's tone turned grave. "Speaking of—have your solicitors begun the process of breaking that cursed entail? Let us have done with that damnable business once and for all!"

Darcy frowned and leaned forward to pluck a stack of letters forwarded from London off his desk. "I am afraid it may prove murkier than expected."

The earl settled forward intently. "How so? I thought those legal fellows believed we had good cause, with Wickham sentenced away. That was what Richard said."

With a frustrated sigh, Darcy explained, "It is early yet. I have only received two letters from the solicitors investigating the matter."

"Naturally. These things take years sometimes."

"Indeed. But there are some loose ends. They initially felt assured on grounds of Wickham's crimes and subsequent transportation, making him an ineligible heir. But questions around precedents and technicalities are muddying matters."

He tossed the stack of letters back on his desk. "My solicitors argue that we still have a valid claim against the entail. But they have yet to receive the proper paperwork to verify Wickham's disposition and absolute known location, which they must have before they can even begin to assess matters. It may drag out every detail for ages."

The earl rubbed his jaw thoughtfully. "Indeed."

Darcy scrubbed a hand over his face, tension gathering in his shoulders. "I cannot stomach leaving Pemberley's fate or my family's future hanging interminably throughout some slow legal morass."

Lord Matlock surged half-upright, face mottling. "Confound those pettifoggers! Surely, we can find some definite solution without waiting on the courts. We should take this to a higher authority. I have connexions in the House of Lords, Darcy. There are some voices—fringe voices, mind you, but they speak loudly—regarding the legalities of entails and the injustice of a good family's heritage being passed to some obscure, and probably ignorant relation just because the gentleman sired daughters and not sons. I am certain they can devise some inventive solution given time to—"

"No." Quiet resignation steadied Darcy's forceful tone, though anguish bled raw in his chest. "If you make a case of it, Pemberley shall be at the fore. I'll not bring scandal to this family fighting public legal battles without the certainty of a favourable outcome. While I would welcome any political overtures that would permit the amending of archaic entail laws altogether, for now, I shall strive to rebuild my health and strength as much as possible so I may be of some use to my family should calamity strike."

Despondent silence lingered until the earl's weathered features softened. Grasping Darcy's rigid forearm, he whispered gruffly. "You cannot play Providence single-handedly forever, lad. Let us fretting old guardians shoulder our rightful burden protecting the family legacy."

Darcy tried to chuckle. "And just what would you do? There is nothing to be done but to wait out the matter."

The earl fell quiet for several seconds, and then he grunted in impatience. "Enough of this—you are home safe. Georgiana is safe, and you have a charming wife to ease your cares. Perhaps matters are not as we would have wished. I, for one, always wanted you to wed an heiress worthy of the Darcy name, but—"

"There is no one more worthy than Mrs Darcy," he broke in. Then he squirmed faintly, and his eyes drifted out the window. "Even myself."

The earl's face fell slack for a moment, as if he were trying to decipher Darcy's meaning and would not accept it. Then he forced a smile, apparently deciding to take the quip as a jest rather than Darcy's deep-rooted sense of insufficiency.

"Well, well, you would not be a red-blooded man if the lady did not please you. She is fetching, in her way, and perhaps in the only ways that signify. Yes, I wager the lady has a number of... qualities."

"How droll you find the matter," Darcy retorted caustically. "Did you somehow overlook the fact that I had to be carried in and out of my own house, unable to budge from bed on my 'wedding tour'?"

"Well, I daresay you are mended sufficiently now!" Dry humour lit the earl's sharp features at his nephew's fulminating glare. "That clever wheeled throne means you needn't go dancing at balls, which you always hated."

"Indeed, and one of the first things I learned about Mrs Darcy is that she adores the amusement. What pleasure can I give her in that regard?"

"Not all pleasures are sought abroad. And with such a warm bed at home, I cannot see why you would bother, anyway. Surely, your pretty young wife gives you enough to look at—sufficient to... er... lift any man's spirits, eh?"

Darcy clenched rigid fists against the armrests as his uncle's crude words sparked wholly unorthodox mental images. He schooled his face to impassivity, refusing to indulge the heated cravings that tormented him already. "Your crass imagination exceeds even my patience! Pray save such ribaldry for your club fellows rather than casting vulgar aspersions on my wife!"

"Temper, temper Darcy! I meant no harm—certainly, I would not disrespect Mrs Darcy's honour. I only mean to say that perhaps with such inducements for you here at home, perhaps we need not be so concerned about legal documents and entails and such."

Understanding dawned—blast! Did his uncle really think that was how it worked? That temptation and willingness alone were sufficient to resurrect what was now dead? "Do you not think I would have already... attended to *that* if it were possible?" Darcy snarled. "I will thank you to leave my private affairs to *me*, none other!"

"Just so!" The earl offered reluctant acknowledgement, even as speculative shrewdness lingered behind his penetrating gaze. "Forgive my indelicate questions, nephew. But the only thing that is truly necessary to put a stop to all these troubles is for Mrs Darcy to bear a son."

Darcy narrowed his eyes, a hiss escaping his lips. "By heaven. You would not dare suggest such a thing."

"I cannot believe you have not already done so, Darcy. Surely, you must see how it is the simplest—"

"Not another word!" Oh, what he would give to have one of those chairs Elizabeth had told him about that he could steer himself! But then he would still need someone to push it for him... push it out of this room, so he could close the door firmly on Lord Matlock's outrageous suggestion.

"Well..." Matlock cleared his throat. "I say, Darcy, it is only the next reasonable consideration. You are not the first man who—"

Before the earl could utter whatever disreputable thought was on the tip of his tongue, a brisk knock sounded on the door of the study. "Come!" Darcy called in relief.

Elizabeth herself appeared, her lovely curves silhouetted becomingly in the late afternoon light. Conflicting impulses warred within Darcy—fierce protectiveness melding with profound tenderness—or was it possessiveness? Whatever it was, it was visceral and very real. No, he would never, *could* never ask Elizabeth to lie with another man just to give him a son he could call his own. The earl could just go hang.

Utterly oblivious, the old rogue sprang up in delight, taking Elizabeth by the hand. "Why, here is the lovely lady now! Mrs Darcy, we were just speaking of you." He pressed a smacking kiss against her fingers, drawing a startled look. "You must be happy to be back home at Pemberley after that hard winter in the north."

Elizabeth glanced at Darcy—that question in her eyes... she could read his discomfort, he was sure of it. But she pasted a smile on her face for the earl. "The comforts are certainly appreciable. A room without draughts and a fireplace that gives proper heat are among Pemberley's charms. But we were not without our enjoyments in Scotland," she answered lightly, retrieving her hand. "Do forgive my interruption, gentlemen. I merely wished to confirm our dining arrangements. Shall you join us as planned, my lord?"

Lord Matlock glanced at Darcy with a line drawn between his brows but then turned back to Elizabeth. "I think my nephew has wearied of me for the day. Forgive me for begging off, Mrs Darcy, but I believe I will call for my carriage. I hope your hospitality may be extended for another time."

Elizabeth dipped her head. "Of course. Please give Lady Matlock my regards."

"Indeed. Indeed." The earl bowed faintly to Elizabeth once more, then turned fully to Darcy. "Think on what I said, lad. You've a duty to your family, after all."

Darcy ground his teeth as the earl went out. He was still staring at the closed door, his face on fire and his fists clenched until one of Elizabeth's slim fingers worked its way into the knot of his hand. She read his moods, and probably even his mind with uncanny perception now. Small wonder, after all they had been through already. He drank in a breath and smiled up at her. "I did not know we were hosting a dinner tonight. I thought the earl only meant to call for a short conversation."

"Yes, and I got rid of him for you. I thought it was neatly done, did you not?"

"Very tidy."

"Now, what was it he said that has the veins standing out on your neck? My heavens, your eyes are even shot with blood. I should not be surprised if you broke a tooth with the way you are gnashing your jaws. Shall I guess? Something to do with Richard."

Darcy chuckled and finally released the heated breath he had been keeping back. "Richard is rather a scapegrace in your eyes, is he not?"

"No one else ever had the audacity to call me out to my face—before you, that is, but I actually like you." She came closer and cupped his cheeks, then one hand smoothed his hair fondly. "But I suppose he is a good-ish sort of rascal, for all that."

"All lies." Darcy was already grinning. How did she always manage that? He could be steaming about the most aggravating of frustrations, but the minute she smiled at him, he was no better than a puddle at her feet. "If you did not like my cousin, at least a little, you would have banished him long ago."

"Not so, for he can be quite useful. This chair, for instance. Now I get my exercise in wandering all over the house trying to find you. And he did bring me letters from my family. So, you see, I am perfectly happy to use him for the convenience he provides, just as he was satisfied to use me for his own ends."

"A rather scathing indictment of the circumstances, my love."

She lifted a shoulder. "I speak as I find. Now, I shall tell you what I actually came in here to say. I hope you have worked up an appetite fuming at Lord Matlock this afternoon."

Darcy pulled her closer, wrapping one arm around her waist as far as he could reach while her fingers started to twirl lazily in the hair at his temples. "And why is that?"

"Because I am finally able to make good on my tease from some months ago. We are to have *Filet de Bœuf* this evening, with many thanks both to your well-stocked larder here at Pemberley and that absolutely astonishingly talented cook. Wherever did you find her?"

"I did not. My father did. I confess, I do have an appetite after that business with my uncle, but I fear a slab of beef will not soothe the craving." He let her rock his head gently as she toyed more boldly with his hair, and his eyes hazed a little—besotted again by her.

She smiled and leaned close to his ear with a scandalous whisper. "And what is it you crave?"

Darcy gave a tug with his arm. "Come here, Elizabeth."

She moved almost reluctantly at first, letting him move her only as far as she could imagine moving... and then her face lit up when she comprehended his meaning. A moment later, she was reclining in his lap, somehow contriving to situate herself in the confines of his chair without topping the wretched thing over. She wrapped an arm around his neck and nuzzled his forehead until her breath tickled the nerves over his scalp and sent fire everywhere... almost everywhere.

"Is this what you meant?" she whispered.

In answer, Darcy tipped up his chin to hers and gently brushed her satiny lips, marvelling again at this rare woman who saw beyond his splintered limitations into his very essence. Whatever sacrifices or adjustments must be made, on this one thing, he was unyielding. Elizabeth Darcy was his lifeblood—his, and no one else's.

Chapter Twenty-Nine

E LIZABETH FIDGETED IMPATIENTLY AS Beth laced her into a forest green dinner gown, her fingers drifting every few seconds towards the stack of letters on the nearby table. After months without word, somehow the thick packet from Longbourn had been surreptitiously delivered while she was downstairs with William! She had not even noticed it until Beth began dressing her for dinner, and it would be rude to send the maid away, but she was not sure how much longer she could wait. This collection of missives from her family was like a delicious smidgen of normalcy this evening. Her loved ones were only ink and paper away...

"I'll try to hurry so you have time to read them before going down to dinner, Ma'am," Beth said around the hairpins between her teeth.

Elizabeth turned and chuckled. "Am I that obvious?"

"Begging pardon, Ma'am, but you smile most whenever reading Miss Bennet's letters—the ones that came last winter." She plucked up a length of Elizabeth's hair and gave it a twist, expertly letting it fall as it would without forcing it to conform to some unnatural shape. "It must be very fine to have more word from them."

Elizabeth hummed in agreement. "I wonder how Lydia is after everything... well, you know all that. And Jane—you remember Jane, do you not?"

"She was right kind to me, Ma'am." Beth met Elizabeth's eyes in the mirror. "Though not as kind as you were."

"Only because she is shy. I am too impertinent to be as kind as Jane."

Beth smothered a smile and shrugged. "I always liked someone who was a bit irreverent, although Aunt Reynolds says I am very wicked for it."

Elizabeth laughed and turned around to take Beth's hand. "You haven't a wicked bone in your body. Truly, I do not know how I would have survived the winter without you."

Beth blushed, then bit her lip and hid her eyes as she went back to work on Elizabeth's hair. "It were we who were lucky to have you, Ma'am."

Elizabeth's eyes pricked at this unexpected heartfelt loyalty. Impulsively covering Beth's industrious hands, she addressed her young attendant's bowed head earnestly. "I fervently hope to prove worthy of such warm trust. And there, you have made me look as presentable as ever I may. Why don't you take a respite yourself? I believe..." She paused and listened again for the sounds from the next room. "Yes, indeed, it sounds as if Mr Darcy has just dismissed Giles. That young man might be in the mood for some conversation."

Elizabeth smiled at Beth's immediate blush and giggle. Indeed, she had guessed correctly—something had been brewing in that winter exile in Scotland besides a change in her own feelings. She squeezed Beth's hand. "Go on, now. Should Mister Darcy inquire why I am late to dinner, say I've urgent correspondence, and I will come to him when I am right good and ready." Beth's merry laugh followed the girl out the door.

Hungrily, Elizabeth broke the Bennet crest seal on multiple letters postmarked from last November through late January, tearing into Jane's familiar elegant script first. The earliest enthusiastically described that much-anticipated Netherfield ball finally transpiring in late November—the lavish event clearly exceeded already feverish local expectations:

"Oh, Lizzy, I do wish you had been here to see it! Such magnificent decorations featuring Mr Bingley's favourite blue shades made candlelight shimmer like an enchanted lake amidst fairy mists across Netherfield's grand ballroom and dining hall. I shall not soon forget Papa beaming proudly whilst Mr Bingley himself opened the ball, soliciting my hand for the first two sets! Both were lively country reels, ensuring a happy elevation of spirits even had my partner's charms proved disagreeable. (Which, of course, they could not!)"

Elizabeth grinned at that too-familiar sly irony. How clearly Jane penned these lines before Mama whisked her away to gossip. A delighted laugh escaped, though, at her sister's pleasure. Jane was long overdue for the right sort of man to see her for the treasure she was. The missive's coy postscript hinted deliciously at blossoming romance.

"I confess anticipating Mr Bingley requesting a private audience soon. Naturally, Papa must provide formal consent, yet my intuition finds ready accord with our amiable neighbour's gentle character... Pray Mr Darcy confirms my discernment of his dear friend's affable virtues?"

"Bravo, dearest Jane!" Excitement leapt within Elizabeth. At last, her sweet sister's tender heart discovered worthy reciprocation! Mr Bingley proved a most agreeable prospect indeed... at least, William had spoken well of the man.

But why did no subsequent celebratory letter disclose the results of Mr Bingley's anticipated proposal? Instead, Jane's later December notes perplexed Elizabeth deeply. The earliest hinted at bewildering disappointment after Netherfield's dazzling ball:

"Our amiable neighbour departed rather abruptly this morning. I understand it was merely business in London that called him away, but I confess disappointment. Following such particular attentions all autumn, surely business could wait... or perhaps it is I who ought naturally to wait. Surely, he is not the man to rush coming to an understanding, particularly if any plans thereto hinge on the business for which he departed. Whilst his devoted sisters expressed unfeigned regret at their brother's sudden departure, their farewell visit yesterday reassured me matters seem not calamitous. For naturally, gentlemen's affairs respect no convenient season. Oh, Lizzy, I do miss you fiercely, for I know I could count on you to soothe my anxieties. Mama is not the most comforting counsellor at such times."

Elizabeth's brow furrowed. What possibly justified Bingley's precipitous quitting of Netherfield, once hosting such a spectacular community celebration? Anxiety skittered uncomfortably as she lifted the next letter, dated three days afterwards:

"Despite fervent prayers that Mr Bingley hastens back to claim my hand as dearly hoped, Mrs Long stopped me in Meryton and expressed her condolences. Why would she do that, Lizzy? Mama thinks she is merely being spiteful out of jealousy, for Mr Bingley seemed to prefer me to her nieces, but she did not look spiteful. Indeed, Lizzy, I know not what to think. I shall bide my time until he returns, as I know he shall."

Gradually, Jane's later letters described festive preparations for Christmastide throughout November—the joyful pastime tempering gnawing disappointment that

Bingley and his amiable party (including Miss Bingley and new Mrs Hurst) never returned nor sent excuses that she mentioned. Despite Jane's customary optimism, Elizabeth noted sharpening anxiety threading each neatly penned line. An uncharacteristic outburst edged Jane's next startling revelation on the new year's first eve:

"Miss Bingley wrote to me at last, and her letter has cut the deepest of all. Apparently, Mr Bingley finds that his leased accommodations in London prove so vastly superior to anything Hertfordshire has to offer (in which summation, I am sure she included me) that none of their party shall ever again winter 'rusticating' at cold, 'cheerless' Netherfield. And Miss Bingley claims to be all eagerness to meet with Miss Georgiana Darcy again.

Lizzy, I had begun to wonder at it, and now I am sure of it. Miss Bingley had her sights set on your husband from long ago, and she is quite at the end of herself over losing him to you. But she does not mean to lose the connexion, and so she intends to save Mr Bingley for Mr Darcy's sister, when you all return from 'Portugal' this spring. Oh, the things I did not tell her! I trust she will learn soon enough the truth of Mr Darcy's condition, but you might be on your guard for Miss Darcy. As for myself... I have not the words to express the ache in my heart. He never said as much, but I truly believed Mr Bingley cared for me..."

"The wretched man! And that viper of a sister!" Indignation boiled Elizabeth's blood, flinging scribbled paragraphs to the priceless Axminster carpet. The knave toyed deliberately with Jane's tender sensibilities for sport! And Elizabeth herself had not been at hand to comfort her. That perhaps stung the most. Thank heaven that by the next letter, Jane had prudently retreated to Aunt Gardiner's comforting bosom over Twelfth Night. At least that removed Elizabeth's temptation towards unladylike cursing.

"Aunt counselled patience, should Mr Bingley recant his decision to remove to London for the amusements of the season. Yet Papa and Uncle Gardiner both pronounced that gentlemen seldom reverse decisions once ardour inevitably cools. Perhaps this humbling winter season has served to teach me about guarding my heart most carefully, Lizzy, lest fortune's fickle winds batter where logic ought to prevail."

"Oh, Jane!" Elizabeth dashed sudden angry tears away, fury seething for the cad who crushed her sister's sweet, trusting hopes. Despite maintaining outward composure, Elizabeth's furiously pounding heart recognised bitter experience speaking through Jane's brave words. Her own romantic hopes had weathered a violent shattering... twice now.

First, upon initially glimpsing William's formidable figure those long months past—the powerful embodiment of masculine vigour and arresting intelligence, already shackled to a body that had failed him. And to that man, she had pledged herself with nothing but hope. Yet within days, it seemed, that man had blossomed beyond recognition into her devoted life partner through unimaginable adversity—his body perhaps irreparably broken, but his spirit strengthening Elizabeth far greater than the healthiest whole man ever could.

A particularly winsome miniature on Jane's discarded letter caught Elizabeth's roving glance—likely executed by their Aunt Gardiner, who had always been a talented sketch artist. Jane's Madonna-like features graced the delicate portrait framed within the arching boughs of a barren apple tree. Somehow, both poignant fragility and stubborn resilience radiated from the tiny image. Fresh determination firmed Elizabeth's quivering chin. She had survived her own bitterest disappointments. By Heaven, Jane deserved protection from this undeserved heartbreak!

There was only one thing to do. She marched straight towards William's bedroom. He would still be there, because she had not heard the doors open or anyone carrying him down to dinner yet. She could hardly work the latch, for her arms brimmed with Jane's letters like hard evidence for some courtroom trial. Without knocking, she burst inside.

"William! Why would Mr Bingley toy with my sister's heart and then abandon her without an explanation?" Her husband looked up, features softening into concern as he set his book aside. "He what?"

"It was the scandal with Lydia, I am sure of it. He acted as if it was nothing, so much so that he led Jane on to believe he was on the brink of offering for her hand, but then he simply vanished without a word of explanation. That must be it. No one could fault Jane herself. It has to be that he decided he could not suffer the gossip."

Displeasure darkened William's striking eyes as Elizabeth thrust Jane's creased letters underneath them for proof. His harsh frown deepened reading the unhappy tale before finally tossing all aside.

"This will not do! I shall write to Charles directly and have the truth out. I warrant it was Miss Bingley, rather than Charles himself, who orchestrated their removal. She is... ambitious. No doubt she wishes him to marry somewhat higher."

"Yes. Jane thinks she means for him to marry Georgiana!"

"And you know what a dim view I will take of that. She will be marrying no one anytime soon. Be easy, Elizabeth. I will have an answer from Bingley himself. It is likely that his sister's ambitions alone took him away, and sadly, he is too easily led. Perhaps the right word may send him back where he ought to be."

"Truly?" Hopeful relief sagged Elizabeth's exhausted frame into a nearby chair, swiping irritably at treacherous damp cheeks. "You believe Mr Bingley's capricious abandonment is not my family's fault?"

"No, indeed!" Darcy declared stoutly. "At least, not entirely. I warned Charles repeatedly against raising hopes where he has no intention of satisfying them, and he knew of your family's... circumstances... long before he met your sister. Never has he disappointed any lady that I am aware of. This is all gallingly out of character. He must be made aware of the folly of listening to that sister of his. She never was worth the price of the satin he paid to keep her in high fashion."

Elizabeth frowned as she took back the letters that William handed her. She was hardly acquainted with Mr Bingley beyond that one brief meeting. Might she unwittingly have swayed him towards abandoning Jane? "When last we spoke..." She faltered, voicing private fears difficult even with William who cherished her foibles and all. "Well, I worry perhaps some veiled censorious advice mentioning the local opinion of my family soured your friend's opinion towards uniting with us through Jane?"

Indignant surprise lifted William's sharp brow. "My friend's optimism often overshadows his better judgement, 'tis true. But Bingley is no cad. At least, he never was before. Either he fixed his interest wilfully upon Miss Bennet despite fickle tides of gossip, or else he possesses no depth of character worth having at all! I'll discover which swiftly."

Elizabeth slowly smiled, gratitude welling within her breast. Bless her husband for his steadfast words, shoring up her courage once more. "Thank you, William."

His tight features relaxed somewhat. "You seem surprised. Did you not think I would speak up for my sister-in-law's honour?"

She worked up a smile for him and let him weave his fingers through hers. "Of course. I just did not expect you to look as angry as I felt over it."

"Your family is my concern now, too, Elizabeth. One day, I must meet them all... what is it?"

Elizabeth cringed. "Oh... I have told you very little of Mama..."

"Be that as it may, I have met Miss Bennet, and I found her a lovely woman—or, as lovely as I was capable of finding any woman at that moment. Certainly not deserving of such infamous treatment."

She let a teasing grin tug at her cheeks. "'Lovely,' Mr Darcy? Regrets at choosing the younger sister instead of the elder?"

William laughed and tugged her into his lap, and this time, she came more readily. "Not for an instant. You were not afraid of me, and I rather liked that."

E LIZABETH SURVEYED THE LAVISH tea service arrayed across the Pemberley sitting room's polished table, satisfaction momentarily overtaking fluttering nerves. After her conference with the redoubtable Mrs Reynolds, everything stood immaculately appointed for Lord and Lady Matlock's visit this afternoon.

The costly China gleamed pristinely, complemented by steaming pots of fragrant tea nestled on intricately crocheted trivets. Delicate pastel petit fours were artfully arranged surrounding an imposing silver epergne laden with succulent hothouse fruits that would have fetched one hundred guineas at a Mayfair bazaar, she'd wager. And to think she was the mistress of such a house! This was not the duty that had stood foremost in her mind the day she had met William. And she was not altogether certain she was prepared for it—to step into the shoes of the likes of Lady Anne Darcy, whose portrait still hung in the sitting room, surveying all she did.

While Lady Matlock had been nothing but supportive so far, Elizabeth still felt somewhat in awe of her refined aunt-by-marriage. This would only be the countess's first visit to Pemberley since Elizabeth had returned to Derbyshire. She appreciated the guidance Lady Matlock offered through her letters, but hosting her eminent in-laws remained mildly daunting.

But at least Mrs Reynolds knew her business. Hopefully, this impressive array proved sufficient, even if Elizabeth still felt woefully out of her depth. And William looked satisfied when the footman brought his chair in, so that was enough for her.

As the mantel clock softly chimed four, Elizabeth twitched aside heavy velvet drapes, peering out frost-speckled windows overlooking the lawns that were gradually awakening under spring's flirtatious kisses. Somewhere near, she heard the merry shouts of young stable lads frolicking through their afternoon exercises with sleek equine charges. That reminded her of something she had been thinking of for William... but it could wait. For now, the peacefulness blanketed her roiling nerves momentarily until a brisk footman entered on quiet heels.

"Excuse me, Ma'am. The Earl and Countess of Matlock have arrived." His deferential bow preceded the two imposing figures that swept inside.

Elizabeth settled into her chair across from Lady Matlock, surreptitiously studying the countess' refined poise as Pritchard, the butler, efficiently distributed steaming cups of tea. Lady Matlock wasted little time on social pleasantries once the servants departed. Setting her tea aside, the countess eyed Elizabeth keenly. "Do tell me dear, how fares our sweet Georgiana lately? Letters make a poor substitute for conversing face to face on tender matters."

"She improves daily. I believe the spring sunlight and familiar comforts have done a great deal to raise her spirits." Elizabeth took a bracing sip of tea, avoiding the shrewd evaluation from those piercing eyes.

In truth, Georgiana remained almost wraith-like from Scotland's gruelling ordeal—seldom venturing beyond her private chambers unless Elizabeth dragged her out. But surely, confiding that much would only stoke undue concern. Better to allow William to address his sister's state appropriately.

His lordship helped himself to a biscuit, scrutinising his nephew openly. "Tell me you do not plan to lock the girl up here forever? She must get out and be seen some by those who know her, else it breeds gossip."

"And whom would you have her see, my dear?" Lady Matlock tsked. "I say 'tis better to keep her in seclusion for now, at least until certain matters can be settled appropriately. Surely, we cannot have her grieving the wrong person or saying the wrong thing."

Elizabeth flinched, wrong-footed by this abrupt talk of how to manage a girl who was still recovering from so much. Fortunately, William betrayed no reaction beyond thoughtfully swirling his teacup.

"Naturally, we consider Georgiana's best interests going forward." He met Elizabeth's anxious glance steadily. "But there is time enough before fully re-entering society's glare. My sister deserves some months peacefully recovering away from speculative eyes."

Lady Matlock hummed noncommittally at this temperate reply, sharp gaze drifting towards Elizabeth again. "And does Mrs Darcy play nursemaid still? I dearly hope our

Georgiana is not still keeping to her bed. Mrs Darcy, you cannot permit that child to consume all your energies."

Discreetly wiping clammy palms along her skirts under cover of the polished table, Elizabeth attempted a reassuring smile. "I assist where I am able. Miss Darcy has very much her own mind, and I do not undertake to change it unless necessary. I have, however, been encouraging her toward daily outings in the fresh air."

"As you should—even gentle exercise will go a long way raising the girl's spirits, and aids recovery greatly." Lady Matlock pronounced approvingly. "You are family now, and she must welcome your support. Just so! What are your feelings on Miss Darcy's gradual re-entry into society, then?" One greying brow lifted inquiringly. "The Season commences sooner than you can imagine. Shall you present yourselves together, perhaps?"

Elizabeth blanched at this gracious yet utterly impossible suggestion before Darcy smoothly intervened. "We shall follow the doctor's advice on activities best suitable for Georgiana's full restoration. And by doctor, I mean the only one she has seen—that Scottish curiosity and his wife who saved her life. They gave all directions for her care until she was well enough mended to leave, and I will not expose her to the inspection of anyone else." He offered his aunt a conciliatory smile. "Whatever comes, my sister knows we guard her welfare and her reputation against all threats."

Lady Matlock waved aside such stoic assurances. "Do think seriously upon suitable options, nephew! With salacious gossip circulating round the unverifiable origins of your bizarre elopement and extended absence, curious eyes will demand answers." Her shapely shoulders lifted elegantly. "And will do so only the more vehemently when your own condition becomes known. Some will press for gossip—true or otherwise—that could undermine the very discretion you fought to preserve."

"They would not dare!" Lord Matlock bristled indignantly before his wife's quelling stare moderated his bluster. "Well, really, my dear! Our family commands sufficient clout to silence impertinent curiosity. Why not squash any such impudence right now?"

"And how precisely do you suggest managing that, my lord?" Elizabeth asked before she recalled their stations properly. Hastily schooling her inappropriate tartness into grave deference, she amended awkwardly. "I only mean—surely every family risks some idle speculation even under the happiest fortunes?"

"Quite so, my dear," the countess rejoined. "But in this case, where one of the most sought-after bachelors of London—formerly, at least—is concerned, it will be far more than 'idle speculation.' The tittle-tattle will be swift and vicious, and it will not be confined to Darcy alone."

"Then I agree with Lord Matlock. Surely, spending one's life dodging gossip is not preferable to facing down critics directly?"

She felt Darcy's intense focus assessing her unguarded outburst and refused to meet his gaze. Foolish, slipping into her informal Bennet ways before Lord and Lady Matlock! Why could she never rein in impulsive words at critical moments?

But Lady Matlock's thoughtful silence unnerved further, her fan tapping one cheek absently until she suddenly proclaimed. "I rather admire the notion of courage facing trouble head-on, Mrs Darcy! Perhaps we might reframe the dilemma at hand?"

Shrewd eyes glinted as she turned deliberately from her nonplussed husband back toward Darcy with new vigour. "Accept that despite some rather curious behaviours on your part, society at large remains ignorant to anything amiss regarding our Georgiana." One aristocratic hand sliced the air decisively. "Therefore, to salvage your sister's reputation we must uphold certain necessary fictions."

Unease skittered warningly as Elizabeth noted her husband's wariness. "What, precisely, are you suggesting, Aunt?" he asked.

"Well, dear nephew, during my years presiding over dozens of debutantes, I saw many a girl's good name preserved through... a creative presentation of facts. Your charming wife proves quite adept already on that account, I believe." Amused approval lit her eyes towards a mortified Elizabeth.

"I, my lady?" Elizabeth laughed in disbelief. "What have I done to make it seem like I could uphold a public façade?"

Lady Matlock rolled her eyes and sighed. "My dear, your entire marriage was a bandage on a bleeding wound. Do not tell me it has not occurred to you that the same medicine would not mend the sister as salvaged the brother."

"You cannot suggest forcing Georgiana into marriage!" Outrage momentarily loosed Darcy's ironclad composure. He clamped his jaw, measuring a few breaths, and continued in a somewhat more reasonable tone. "She is sixteen. She deserves protection, not to have some counterfeit suitor foisted upon her!"

"See here, boy!" Lord Matlock interjected sternly as Lady Matlock hastened to intervene.

"Peace, Fitzwilliam! We only suggest ensuring your sister's future with a re-spectably discreet marriage rather than permitting any hazardous speculation. And you can leave off glaring, nephew—it is only good sense!"

Disbelieving fury rendered her husband speechless before Elizabeth found her voice. "Surely, matters are not so wholly desperate. Why, Georgiana is so young! What gentleman of worth would even consider marriage to a girl of such tender age?" She spread helpless hands. "Can you not permit the poor girl more time?"

"Mrs Darcy speaks with reasonable caution," Darcy bit out through clenched teeth, clearly restraining his outrage with strained effort before turning pointedly toward his aunt's composed figure across the tea service. "If you find the man willing to marry a girl of sixteen, he is not the sort of man I would trust. Perhaps you forget that my sister is hardly some inconsequential pawn in the service of the family's reputation. Her welfare remains my charge first and foremost against all threats, no matter how officious or well-meaning!"

Stunned silence met this emphatic defence until Lord Matlock snorted derisively, shaking his head. But Lady Matlock merely sighed, leaning forward to lightly touch her seething nephew's rigid forearm. "Calm yourself, Fitzwilliam! We only suggest what unsentimental good sense dictates." A rueful grimace briefly marred her usual poise. "You cannot deny the girl's prospects now depend wholly upon our manoeu-vrings, uncomfortable though that proves."

"Uncomfortable!" Elizabeth could not restrain her scalding retort, heedless of propriety now. "To casually barter away my sister's future happiness before she has even had a chance to leave girlhood behind?"

"My dear, I believe we had ample physical proof that Georgiana has, indeed, left girlhood behind."

Elizabeth's mouth dropped open. "And she has a chance now to reclaim what measure of innocence she may! Let her simply be a young lady in her brother's house for some while longer. What can be the harm in that?"

Lady Matlock blinked, clearly nonplussed by Elizabeth's unorthodox interjec-tion, before surprise softened into wry understanding. "Well, now! Evidently, you inherited our family's fiercest protective instincts along with Darcy's name." Gently patting Elizabeth's hands between her own, she continued calmly. "Let us kindly clarify matters before disaster results, hmm? Indeed, to consign any debutante into marriage against her inclination seems an abhorrent cruelty."

Soothed by this concession, Darcy slowly relaxed his confrontational posture, glancing uncertainly between the warring factions. "Then what, precisely, do you propose here, Aunt? I must know Georgiana is wholeheartedly willing and ready before I even present her with this choice."

"Just so, nephew." Lady Matlock echoed conciliatory tones. "I merely suggest investigating likely candidates for gentle introduction once she feels prepared. After recent strains upon her constitution, surely a private, gentle courtship would be the safest, avoiding a gruelling debut Season?" She shrugged eloquently. "Particularly for one no longer an innocent ingenue. She may unwittingly give away too much of her... previous experience, and *that*, Darcy, would be... unfortunate."

Elizabeth flinched inwardly, wishing they could erase the past so easily. Surely, even discreet marital prospects remained remote whilst Georgiana wrestled with profound hurts? But before she voiced that thought, Lady Matlock smoothly pressed onward.

"As her guardian, your steadfast protection is essential in guiding my niece towards someone worthy." Her piercing eyes held Elizabeth's uncertain gaze. "Particularly in shielding her tender sensibilities. Therefore, why not subtly inquire after appropriate gentleman through trusted connexions as possibilities arise?" A placating smile replaced arguments. "That seems a sensible solution reconciling family honour and Georgina's merits, does it not?"

"Perhaps..." Reluctantly Darcy weighed her proposal, clearly unwilling to fully disregard either his relations' opinions nor Georgiana's interest. Yet defiance still tightened his jaw. "Much depends upon when my sister feels ready to entertain suitors. I will not force the matter."

"Unwise to delay, given damaging gossip surely swirling through certain circles," Lord Matlock pronounced gruffly. "There are enough rumours about your sudden marriage and disappearance already. Mark me, Fitzwilliam. Better quash spiteful tongues pre-emptively through a suitable alliance for the lass." He thumped one palm decisively. "I insist we settle the business immediately and have done!"

Elizabeth flicked a staying hand to William's arm as he straightened in his chair. He was about to say something regrettable; she was sure of it, but mercifully, the footman opened the door. "Pardon me, sir. Colonel Fitzwilliam awaits in the entry. Shall I show him in for tea?"

"By all means!" Lady Matlock summoned an immediate smile. "Do send my son here directly. We are at loggerheads in here, and Richard always did have a knack for lightening the mood."

Darcy released an inaudible sigh, shifting uncomfortably as his aunt resumed. "At least consider the options ahead, nephew. For your family's sake."

Elizabeth squeezed William's arm and was rewarded with a retiring grumble rather than the sharp retort she could see forming on his tongue.

Further heated arguments were forestalled as Colonel Fitzwilliam sauntered inside, grinning brightly. "Well met, all! Not interrupting some family drama, I trust?" His laughing expression rapidly changed, assessing the lingering tension in the room until Darcy beckoned him over resignedly without a word. Obligingly, the colonel sank down beside Elizabeth, snatching a leftover biscuit from the tea tray before addressing them all.

"Now, do share the intrigues. Let me guess. Lady Catherine just learned that her favourite nephew is off the marriage mart, and she is shopping for another?" Mischievous eyes danced toward Elizabeth. "I thought we finished that business last autumn!"

"Be serious, Richard!" Lady Matlock reproved without heat, shaking her head. "We only discuss dear Georgiana's best prospects."

"Through promptly marrying the girl off willy nilly, it sounds." The colonel remarked candidly, ignoring his sputtering father's protests as Elizabeth unsuccessfully smothered a nervous laugh. "Oh, I overheard you and Father talking in the drawing room last night, so it seems a fair guess you just dropped this on Darcy. How did he take it?"

The colonel glanced up at Darcy's stormy expression and finished chewing his biscuit. "Not well, eh? I am sorry to say, Mother, that I agree with Darcy on this. Surely, the poor lass deserves some time to mend and consider her future. Why, last I spoke with her, she had scarcely begun to smile again. Now, Mother, Father..." He plucked another biscuit from the tray and consumed half of it before he continued speaking. "... Say you introduce her to some fellow, and he takes a shine to her, weds her, and then comes back in six months to tell Darcy that he barely recognises his wife as the girl he thought he married. The indignity of it, you know—finding out suddenly that your wife truly does know how to laugh, when you thought you married a quiet little mouse? Would rob a man of sleep."

Lady Matlock sighed tolerantly. "You have a fine sense of irony, Richard. We only suggest practicalities ensuring our girl's future, nothing more. And you may rest assured that your gallant cousin guards his sister's interests fiercely!" Wry approval warmed the fond maternal smile sent Darcy's way before she pronounced. "I shall say no more on the affair for now. Goodness knows I am not without sympathy. Perhaps we needn't act for a few months, at least. After all, it is... still rather soon after everything."

That was, perhaps, the best olive branch they were going to get for the moment. Elizabeth hastily grabbed hold of it. "Indeed, my lady. Perhaps we may revisit the conversation after her next birthday."

Lady Matlock offered a thin smile. "Perhaps."

Chapter Thirty

"**W**HAT DO YOU THINK of your aunt's suggestion?"

Darcy relaxed backwards on his pillow, his eyes drifting unfocused toward the ceiling as Elizabeth sat down beside him to begin her nightly ministrations. Georgiana's situation and his aunt's solution for it were the furthest things from his mind at the moment. Always, when Elizabeth came in to sit with him, talk to him... when the scent of her washed over him, and he could imagine feeling what his eyes informed him she was doing... there was only her. He sucked in a long breath and tried to refocus.

"The notion is not without merits," he confessed at length. "Although I do not sense the urgency she does. Perhaps because I still see my sister as a child."

Elizabeth bowed her head as she worked the soothing oil into his skin. Darcy watched, mesmerised. Perhaps this seemingly pointless ritual she insisted on did him some physical good—he would never know. But what it did for his heart... well, that was too much to be set down into words. Knowing that such a woman would care so tenderly for him, when he could give her nothing in return, both made him her willing slave and humiliated him for what this marriage had lowered her to.

"I think..." Elizabeth mused softly, "... I think Georgiana is perhaps more mature than your feelings would allow. Wounded now, certainly, and for that reason alone, I would counsel patience. But I believe the very reason she fell for Mr Wickham's charms was that she desired that sort of... connexion."

Darcy lifted his head to peer curiously at her. "You think my sister suffers from indecent urges?"

"No, not that." Elizabeth frowned, and then a tug pulled at her lips. "Well. Perhaps no more than is usual. But she told me something once, not long before we left Scotland, that I had not the time to reflect on until more recently."

"And?"

"Well, it was to do with family duty, and her yearnings to be mistress of a happy home of her own. She said..." She paused and looked him full in the eye. "You will not be angry?"

"That depends." He cocked a brow. "What am I promising not to be angry about?"

Elizabeth puckered her mouth and dribbled a little more oil on his foot. "She truly believed you thought well of Mr Wickham. Being a relative, and knowing your desires to preserve the family honour and lineage, she thought you would approve of her choice."

Darcy wrinkled his forehead. "That is the most foolish thing I ever heard. What I would 'approve of' is a gentleman honourable enough to approach me in person, not some cad who seduced my young sister without my knowledge."

"Well, there is that. Indeed, her feelings carried her far from logic, but at the root of them, I believe, was a desire to do as she saw you doing—to protect and preserve her family name in the best way she knew."

"Preposterous," Darcy snorted. "What she saw me doing was avoiding mercenary marital prospects and attending to practical matters. She ought to have seen an example of prudence, not impulsiveness."

Elizabeth stoppered the bottle and set it aside, then crawled on top of the counterpane to fold her arms over his chest and smile into his face. And Darcy could have wept for all the things he could not do.

"Perhaps she thought you were taking too long in coming to the point," Elizabeth whispered, hooking her finger under his chin. "She has not your patience. And, I am afraid, neither do I."

His breath caught. "What... ah... what do you mean by that?"

Elizabeth raised up and kissed him—and it was not the sweet, companionable sort of kiss she usually bestowed on him. This one was hungry. Aggressively seductive, even.

He pushed her back. "Elizabeth, what are you doing?"

She tried to catch her breath, which was now as ragged as his, and traced the edges of his lips with her fingertips. "It might not be impossible. We have never tried."

He shook his head. "If you are suggesting what I think..."

"I know you retain... Oh, I cannot think how to say it. I have felt... when I curl up beside you at night..."

His stomach lurched. She had noted... that? But how? He was not unaware that certain functions still carried on without his immediate knowledge... Egad, sometimes the phantoms of them woke him up at night, tormenting him with imaginary tinglings and pinpricks through nerves and muscles that never stirred during his waking hours. It was as if his body was living its own life without him now, and there were, indeed... well, signs, for lack of a better term. Indications that his lower extremities were finding a means of coming to a strange sense of harmony with his mind.

But... but *that?*

Elizabeth was kissing him again, dropping her caresses ever lower from his mouth to his chin, then to the hollow of his neck as her breath seemed to coax fiery agony from all his exposed flesh... which was a considerable portion of him, because she was looping her finger through the button holes on his nightshirt and exposing his chest to her caresses.

"Elizabeth..." His voice came out strangled as he panted for mercy. "Please..."

She lifted her head. "William, I overheard what your uncle said the other day. When you were in the study."

He blinked stupidly. *Heavens, no...* "Elizabeth, you were never meant to hear... I would never lay that on you, to—"

"He was right. All this—all these worries of yours, all the things that make you fearful for Georgiana, for the tenants, for me... The legal troubles you are about to take on, the fear of disgrace and scandal—all of it goes away if I have a son."

"But... *what* you are suggesting! You would take another man to your bed?" His heart was drumming so hard that he had to press a hand to his chest. Was this what a heart seizure felt like? He could never ask that...

But it was not him asking. It was her offering... and it was he who had the power to grant or deny his wife the things she probably desired above all else. Security, a child of her own, and... and even the love of a man. The sort of love he could not give her.

Even as his soul began to crumble under that realisation, Elizabeth framed his face in both of her hands and brought his eyes back up to hers. "I would not," she stated emphatically. "I made a vow to *you*, Fitzwilliam Darcy—little as I even liked you at the time."

She attempted a teasing smile, but even that did not have the power to shift the darkness from his heart. Until her next words.

"I want you, and you alone. If I cannot have you, I will have no other, but... William, will you let me try?"

His mouth felt like cotton. "But I have no sensation. No control... Egad, Elizabeth, do you even know how it works? From a woman, all that is required is submission, but a man must... By heaven, how can you even suggest it could be possible?"

"I do not know. You will have to guide me, but just let me try," she whispered as her mouth closed over his.

And he yielded. Her hands ploughed up under his nightshirt and wove through the hairs on his chest. And that, he could definitely feel. The heat of her fingers, caressing and kneading until lava pierced through his core. The way her hands swept up and down his bare chest and shoulders, inducing tickles and shivers that rocked his being... and then the way the sensation faded, then vanished altogether as her hands dropped to caress more of him.

But for the moment, he cared nothing for that. He filled his own hands with her dewy softness, and he almost cried out in rapture when she paused her seductions to cross her arms and pull her loose nightgown off, over her head.

He had never seen her before. Never like this... creamy and bold, blushing under the heat of his open-mouthed stare, yet breathing through her nervousness until her bosom trembled with her desire. He drank her in, his greedy gaze devouring every inch of her form until unbidden whimpers of ferocious agony rose in his throat.

"Elizabeth..."

She sucked in a quaking breath, then with a daring that belied the uneasy way she bit at her lip, she took his hand in hers and placed it on her body. And all he could do, as his fingers sank into her milky flesh, was to sob.

"Elizabeth, I... Why? God in heaven, *why?*" He crumpled, the tears scalding his face as he bowed his head, and the cries racked his breast. "I have paradise in my very hands, and I cannot taste it!"

"William," she whispered as she leaned forward. Cautiously, she lowered herself so that her body was pressed against his chest, wrapping her arms around his neck to bury her face in his shoulder. "It will be well. It must be..."

"What do you know of it?" His voice broke, and his hands dug mercilessly into the smooth planes of her lower back until she flinched. He released her instantly, instead crossing his arms behind her shoulders and curling into her as his helpless moans crumbled into anguish. "You cannot know, Elizabeth! You cannot possibly know what it is, to have everything dangled before you and be unable to do a damned thing about it!"

"All I am asking you to do is hope, William. Let me... For pity's sake, you *are* stronger! I can see it almost daily! Will you not let me—"

"No!" He pushed her shoulders off him, almost violently, and repented of it in the very next instant. "Elizabeth, have I hurt you?"

She shook her head. "I know it is not what you wanted, but can you not see that—"

"No! Have mercy on me, Elizabeth, and just... just stop!" He grabbed her nightgown and thrust it at her, closing his eyes against the allure of heaven. "Go, I beg of you!"

Elizabeth was wetting her lips and looking down, fumbling with the wadded-up muslin in her hands as her shoulders began to tremble. "Please, William, I did not mean to—"

"Well, you did!" He buckled forward, wrenching his hands through his hair as the heaving of his lungs nearly cracked his ribs. "If you ever meant to make me feel less of a man than I already did, that... that was the way, Elizabeth."

Elizabeth gasped... a few scattered sobs and a heart-rending little cry... and he felt her weight clearing off the bed as she eased away from him. "William, I love you. Nothing could make me want to hurt you, ever."

But he refused to look up at her, fisting the heels of his hands into his eyes to stop up the blazing humiliation that scoured his face. "Go away, Elizabeth. I do not even want to see you."

And she did.

A SHAFT OF SUNLIGHT cracked through the drapes shrouding her room. That must mean it was morning. Not that it mattered—she was not sleeping and had not slept all night.

Elizabeth pulled her knees to her chest and buried her face in the bunched-up blankets. Why, *why* had she done that? She should have known how it would shred his manhood and rip apart the fragile understanding they had built. It was not as if they had not been clear with one another from the start!

And yet she, in her arrogance, had tried to take the matter into her own hands and force what could not be forced. Quick and clever, her father used to call her. Not easily fooled... except by herself, it seemed.

Her face still felt crusty with last night's tears. What must William be waking to this morning? Did he, too, pass the night in an agony of spirit because of her reckless attempt at seduction? How cruel she was! And what more could she have ever asked of the man than he had already given her? Nothing, it seemed, was enough to satisfy her greedy heart. And it took the anguish of the very best man in the world to expose that flaw to her.

Elizabeth did not hurry with her morning preparations that day. It was well after eleven before she found her way downstairs, finally dressed and feeling like a shattered shell of her usual self. Her mind, it seemed, was in a fog this morning, and all her thoughts, listless and unresponsive when anyone tried to speak to her. There was truly only one person she could, or should speak to, but would he even let her into the study?

She knew that was where he was. Since returning to Pemberley, he had taken up what she assumed must have been something similar to his former routine, reviewing letters of business or account ledgers every morning until the noon meal. And most days, she would join him for some of that time. He always welcomed her, and sometimes even put his work aside to challenge her to a game of chess.

But she could not think why he would welcome her today. Not when her very presence eviscerated him.

Elizabeth halted at the bottom of the stairs, her gaze wandering toward the half-open study door. She should leave him be. The library, or the blue morning room... those were safer retreats.

But just as she was starting in the opposite direction of the study, Mrs Reynolds appeared in the hall. The woman curtsied, then folded her hands over her apron. "Mrs Darcy, there is a rather... interesting development I wished to speak with you about."

Elizabeth's eyebrows lifted in mild interest, which was about all she could summon. "Oh?"

Mrs Reynolds cleared her throat nervously. "Perhaps I might speak with you privately, Ma'am?"

Elizabeth gave her assent and led Mrs Reynolds to the sitting room. Once the door was closed, she invited the housekeeper to speak.

"Well, Ma'am, it is only that I happened upon information regarding my niece, Beth... and a certain young man."

Elizabeth permitted a faint smile to crack her stony countenance. "Giles?"

Mrs Reynolds dipped her head. "Just so. I thought I should bring it to your attention, being as Beth presently acts as your lady's maid, and Giles is Mr Darcy's personal attendant."

"You thought I would disapprove?" Elizabeth asked mildly.

"Not precisely, Ma'am. It is rather common, of course. Both are young and handsome... Good souls, both of them. But I only thought you may have some qualms, given that Beth is not fully qualified for her position yet, and her personal affairs may reflect on the lady of the house. 'Twould not be seemly for me to appear to show any favouritism, either."

Elizabeth shook her head wearily. "Is there anything indecent in the way they are carrying on?"

Mrs Reynolds stretched to her full height. "None, Ma'am. Beth is a good girl."

"She is, indeed. I cannot think why I would have any objections. She did mention to me once that she desired to study better for her position under Lady Matlock's maid, but I do not see why we could not secure her whatever instruction she desires, or knowledge that I might someday require of her. But I leave that to Beth—the choices are hers, after all."

Mrs Reynolds seemed to draw an easier breath. "Indeed, Ma'am. But it is more than a simple attachment. He has indicated a wish to marry the lass. And for that, I told them they must appeal to the master."

"Ah." Elizabeth sighed. "And you are hoping I would present the request on their behalf?"

"That has always been the mistress' place at Pemberley, Ma'am. But if you would prefer..."

"No." Elizabeth shook her head. I will speak to Mr Darcy at once. And tell them... Tell Beth that I wish her every happiness."

Mrs Reynolds' smile nearly sparkled with pleasure. "As do I, Ma'am."

WILLIAM ANSWERED HER TENTATIVE knock with his usual "Come."

Elizabeth braced herself, framing a smile on her face, and then discarding it in favour of something more sombre. She tipped her head to the side to view her expression in a mirror hanging in the hall. Dark circles under her eyes, and a sallow appearance to her skin. But he could not accuse her of any inappropriate levity, that was for certain. She cleared her throat and pushed open the door.

William glanced up, and for an instant there was a vulnerable surprise in his eyes, but he quickly schooled his expression and looked back down to the paper upon which he had been writing. "Good morning," he greeted her, in a voice that was both crisp and somewhat formal. "Something amiss?"

Elizabeth slid into the chair opposite his desk and folded her hands in her lap. "Nothing very much. I understand Robert Giles is asking for the hand of Beth Reynolds."

"Yes." He did not look up. "He mentioned that. You disapprove?"

"Not at all."

"Very well, then. The matter is settled."

Elizabeth felt her eyebrow edging upward. "That was... quick."

"I see no reason to meddle in the personal lives of those in my employ. Do you?"

"Of course not. I only thought you might have more to say on the matter."

"I do not." He dipped his quill and scanned down the ledger to find and mark a certain column. "Why anyone would think it necessary to apply to me for my opinions on their relationships seems the height of foolish pomposity."

"You *are* the master of the house."

He dipped his quill again, still refusing to look up at her. "So the family annals declare. In name, at least."

"William, about last night—"

"The wind came up rather loudly, did it not?" He made another note in his ledger. "I shall have to have the shutters on the East Wing repaired this summer. They made a fearful racket."

Elizabeth got up from her chair and came to stand over his desk, placing her hands on the burnished mahogany on either side of his ledger. "I am sorry. There, I have said it again, and I will continue to say it until—"

"Forgive me, my dear, but you are blocking the light. Do you mind?"

She straightened, removing her hands from the desk, and gulped a few times until her voice made some sense. "I did not know it would hurt you so. I hoped to have the opposite effect."

"I would imagine. With a proper man, you most certainly would have."

"William, please. There must be some way I can apologise that you can accept. Some way of making it right—"

"You may spare your breath, my dear. I hold no spite or rancour against you."

Her mouth worked. "No, for that would require you to feel something, and you have closed yourself off from more than one kind of feeling. Will you look at me, William?"

His fist dropped harder than necessary on the desk's surface, and the look he turned up to her was a little short of an indignant glare. "Thank you for explaining so fully your opinions of me and all the ways in which I have failed you."

"I did not say you had failed me! I only asked that you would let me grovel a little. Surely, I owe you some apology. I never meant to hurt you!"

"And as you said, I am devoid of all proper feeling. Logic dictates that I must not, then, be wounded at all. There, does that satisfy?"

"You are simply the most..." She clenched her fists. "Augh! Fitzwilliam Darcy, if I did not love you with every pore and fibre of my being, I would strangle you for being so damnably obstinate!"

For an instant, a slight crack appeared in the granite when the corner of his mouth twitched. But it disappeared just as quickly. "That is certainly language befitting the Mistress of Pemberley."

"Should I go on? You are so bloody impossible to get on with that it is little wonder Giles wants to marry, just so he can have a pleasant person to talk to! Blast and damn your eyes, William, but the only thing keeping me from upending your desk right now and unseating that smug look on your face is the fact that you are obscenely wonderful when you are *not* being a pompous ass! Any normal man would accept his wife's apology, even if he is malicious enough to make her suffer for it some little. But you! No, you bloody well act like you are made of stone!"

She stood, panting, and hoping that little kink in his eyebrow meant she had broken through the ice somehow.

"Are you quite finished?"

She nodded.

He leaned back in his chair, lacing his fingers over his waistcoat. "To answer your question, I *am* made of stone. Or, I might as well be, for all the bleeding good I can do anyone."

Elizabeth swallowed. "You do not mean that."

He barked a caustic laugh. "I assure you, I do. Do you see what I am writing here?"

She let her eyes drop to the page. She had assumed it was a listing of the household accounts, the one they had looked at together the day before, and he said he wanted to return to, for consideration on certain numbers. But when she looked at it again, she recognised that it was not a ledger at all. It was a settlement... Her settlement, with her name on top.

"I have made revisions. This addendum will be forwarded to my man of business in London to be formalised."

She shook her head. "I do not understand."

"You will. I have doubled your allotment and added to it a portion of Pemberley's land that is not subject to the entail, for my father bought the property himself. They will go to you upon my decease... And to any children you might have... someday."

Elizabeth walked around his desk and pulled his chair away so that she could get between him and the furniture. "Now, you listen to me, Fitzwilliam Darcy, and listen well. I do not *want* any of that! Can you understand me? If you sign that blasted paper, I will throw it in the fire grate!"

His features at first flashed in anger, but instantly cooled to calculated impassivity. "You say you want me... *my* happiness, *my* better good. I say, Elizabeth, you do not understand half of what you speak. If you want these things for me, then you will stand aside, and let me be of whatever use in this world I may. So long as I am in it."

She froze, straightening as her hands fell away from the armrests of his chair. "William, what are you saying?"

His jaw worked, and his nostrils flared until the words burst out. "I am saying I am of no use to you. Or to anyone else. And I would rather excuse myself from the party quietly, without fanfare... before I wear out my welcome. Now, please, push me back to my desk like the helpless wraith I am so I can do this one thing, at least."

Her mouth simply refused to work. "You cannot mean..."

He raised his brows. "The desk, please."

Numbly, and quite without even remembering how or why she did it, she complied, wheeling him back up within reach of his writing desk. But her eyes were unfocused, her limbs all watery, and her stomach roiling with a new, quaking fear.

"Thank you." William leaned forward and took up his quill again. "I shall see you at dinner."

Chapter Thirty-One

ELIZABETH WANDERED THE GROUNDS of Pemberley for the third morning that week, her mind roiling with worries for her husband's bleak moods of late. Though spring's tender blossoms and emerald shoots often lifted her spirits considerably, today's melancholy clung stubbornly, despite nature's beauty all around. Ever since *that* night, nearly a month ago, he had been a withdrawn shadow of his usual self. He hardly spoke, he allowed nary a flicker of emotion when he did, and he could not be roused to take an interest in anything.

Anger and outrage were better than this. She would far rather argue with him, shouting hotly across the room at each other as they did a few times when they were first married. At least then, he would speak to her. Now... he would not even permit their former routines, the little things they had always done to find a few moments of quiet intimacy.

If only there was some way to spark some liveliness in him again! He would not allow her to apologise. It did no good to try little acts of kindness—he saw through those and rejected them. Flattery was pointless because he always found ways to refute it. And any thought of physical affection, even something so simple as holding his hand, was flatly snubbed.

He was, indeed, a chunk of granite.

Elizabeth scowled and kicked a pebble along the path as she walked. Colonel Fitzwilliam would know how to liven his vexing cousin. But Richard was in London at the moment, having volunteered to investigate the matter of the entail, and any updates regarding the solicitors' findings. Sometimes, she wondered if the man ever spent any time at all with his regiment because he seemed always to be at the beck and call of Lord Matlock or Darcy.

For now, she had to manage on her own, and one of the first things she had done was to pour out every last drop of William's laudanum, as well as hidden his pistol and even his pen knife. And Giles had strict instructions not to leave the shaving razor unattended. Not that she truly thought he would take matters so far... but the worry still gnawed at her. Would he... *could* he... do that? From the way he had been behaving, she had no confidence in his powers of reason just now.

Pausing beneath a flowering cherry tree, Elizabeth sighed heavily, spreading her skirts to sit atop a nearby stone bench warmed by the climbing sun. She let her gaze travel fondly across gently rolling lawns to fix upon the study's windows, where she knew William passed his days surrounded by ledgers and letters yet separated from life thriving outside. How it must torture him being lord of such stunning vistas, now forbidden their solace! Impulsively, she plucked a delicate pink blossom loose, twirling it idly between restless fingers as she pondered ways to bring hopeful cheer back to their strained rapport.

And that was when it struck her. Spring... *life* was happening all around him, and he was not outdoors to partake of it. How greatly did it frustrate her when she ached to climb distant hills and could not put a foot out of doors? How deeply did her soul drink of nature's well when she did get to go outside? And how much worse must it be for him?

William had been an active man once. That was one of the chief sources of his discouragement, was it not? He could no longer do any of the things he had once enjoyed. But what if she could find a way to change that for him?

Perhaps she might suggest short jaunts in a low phaeton? Surely, Pemberley had such a vehicle, for they were popular with wealthy young ladies. He was able to comfortably sit in his chair for hours together now, so the sufferings he had endured on those first harrowing journeys from London were a thing of the past. If Simmons could guarantee the horses were safe and calm, William could even take his hand at driving them—a thing that would surely give him pleasure.

Wistful yearning squeezed Elizabeth's throat, picturing William's striking eyes alight with some of their former passionate zeal, like that painting that hung in the drawing room of the London townhouse. That painting lived in her mind's eye as the true man she had married—strong and active, full of virility and quiet dignity. She must find some way of restoring freedom's sweet balm to his battered spirit, lest increasing bitterness utterly consume the vulnerable heart she had come to cherish beyond reason.

Would he even let her talk him into trying to go outside? Or had she cut that thread irrevocably, the one that had seemed to tie their hearts until she could tug on it and pull him along to whatever brighter feeling or tenderness she could impart? There was only one way to find out. She surged upright with fresh determination, her steps turned purposefully back across familiar gardens blooming hopeful and new. She must not permit mournful doubts to undermine her courage when William had sacrificed everything so selflessly out of devotion for his sister's welfare. And for hers.

Perhaps, if outings in the carriage proved insufficient to lift his mood, she could suggest something even more of a piece with his old self. She would ask Simmons directly, but perhaps they could devise a way to get him back into the saddle! A few straps for his legs to keep him secure, and he could once again know freedom. Why, with two strong lads to help him astride, and a properly docile horse, why could he not? His upper body and arms were stronger than ever before, and it would only be a matter of finding the right saddle and mount. Surely, Pemberley's stables boasted a wide enough selection of both to choose from, and the weather was only going to start improving more as the weeks wore on.

Yes, that would do. Her steps quickened, and instead of turning toward the house, she hurried in the direction of the stables. She was still some distance from the main drive when a voice called out behind her.

"Ho, there, Madam!"

She stopped and turned around. A lone horseman stood on the grass, his hat gently doffed and his mount showing signs of a good long gallop. Elizabeth pressed her mouth into a smile and curtsied. "Good afternoon."

The gentleman replaced his hat and gave her a peculiar look. "I beg you will forgive my poor manners. I am visiting Lambton with some friends—taking a little air today, as you see, and I did not realise I had ridden so close to Pemberley. Please, pardon me for intruding on your peaceful walk."

She dipped her head. "Not at all. You are to be forgiven, for if you came through the forest, I am told there is no landmark there, and the house is not immediately visible."

He leaned forward in his saddle, resting his hand on the pommel as his eyes travelled up and down her person. "Exactly so. And now, I must crave your indulgence again, but you do not speak as one native to Derbyshire. I have not the pleasure of speaking to the new Mrs Darcy, do I?"

She tilted her head and straightened. "Indeed, you do. How do you know of me?"

"Oh, it was in all the papers. Elizabeth Bennet of Hertfordshire, as was?" He smiled winningly. "Do not look so surprised, Mrs Darcy, for anyone in London with an ear to hear would have heard your name more than once. Particularly if he planned to make the journey to Derbyshire this spring, anyway, he would certainly take notice. May I say, Mr Darcy is a fortunate man."

"That is very kind of you. If you will excuse me, Mr...?"

"Oh! I did not mean to keep you. But, if you will permit me one last impertinence, my friends and I were wondering if the house is presently open for tours. I have heard much of Pemberley's beauty, and we had not yet inquired anywhere."

"I am afraid not. Perhaps later in the season, sir."

"Indeed." He lifted his hat and reined his mount back. "Then I will wish you a very good day, Mrs Darcy, and thank you." A moment later, he was cantering off over the rolling green, and Elizabeth was quite alone.

What a curious visitor! But Mrs Reynolds had already prepared her for that—Pemberley received all sorts. Tourists, some harmless and some hoping to compare their own holdings to those of the Darcy family, seeking some chink in the perfect stone edifice. Well, the man could just go on and try some other time. Even if the gardens were ready to be viewed, the household's occupants were in no spirit to have to avoid certain corridors of the house during visiting hours.

But it did give her an idea. Jane... and Aunt and Uncle Gardiner...

Yes, that was what she would do! She would invite Jane to come stay at Pemberley with her. What better way to soothe her sister's heartache than to snatch her away from all her cares at Longbourn? And if they were fortunate, Mr and Mrs Gardiner could even bring her there, and stay for a fortnight or so themselves.

But only if William approved. For as much as Elizabeth ached to see her sister, the shroud hanging over her husband... their life, and any hope they had of recovering what she had almost broken... that had to come first. Because if she invited Jane now, with things so raw as they were between her and Wiliam, it would become a great ugly mask between them—smiling and meaningless and empty, until Jane felt unwelcome in the middle of it.

No, she had to mend that relationship first. And it would start with a conversation with the coachman.

H E DID NOT ANSWER her knock. But Elizabeth was, if nothing else, at least too stubborn to be sent away by one who simply refused to acknowledge her. The door latch creaked, and she stepped inside.

William was sitting up in his bed, reading. His gaze never left the page, but she saw the tension enter his shoulders. He flipped a page, but from the random, disordered way his eyes were flicking, it looked as if the book could have been upside down, and he would have comprehended it just as well.

"May I speak with you?"

He wetted a finger and turned another page. "When has anyone ever been able to keep *you* from speaking?"

"Then, will you hear my words?"

He looked like he was holding his breath, but then the book lowered fractionally, though his eyes did not yet raise. "I hear everything you say. Even when you do not say it in words."

Elizabeth approached slowly, her footfalls soft on the carpeted floor. His jaw tightened, and the book began to tremble. "If you are come to apologise again, you may consider that apology tendered. I've no need to hear it rephrased yet again."

"No." She sniffed faintly... oh, he was not going to make this easy. The words lodged in her throat, her tongue sticking to the roof of her mouth as her fingers found the edge of the bedpost. "William, I have come to ask you to do something for me."

That brought a response, though a slight one. His shoulders bunched, and his brow tightened down upon the bridge of his nose. "What could a cripple possibly do for you, madam?"

She swallowed a gulp of air, held it, and then plunged ahead. "I have not come to ask a favour of a cripple, but of my husband. The man I love."

His breathing shifted, and his eyes grew hazy as they drifted distractedly up the page. And then, the tell-tale blink. She had broken something. "What," he managed in a harsh whisper, "can I possibly do for you that you cannot manage on your own?"

Enough. Elizabeth closed the distance between them and tugged down the top edge of his book with one finger. His eyes tried to follow it for a second, then closed. When they opened again, they fixed on her face, and the ache and thirst there—for compassion, for understanding... for respect... it was as naked as she had made herself, that night he rejected her.

"I want you to..." She paused, pinching her lips over the words. "No. I just... I want you. I want you back."

"I am right here, madam."

She edged closer. "And I care not a whit for your body. I want your heart back. I want to put your spirit back where it belongs, and I want to see joy in your eyes again."

A sheen, swift as a bitter wind, suddenly clouded those eyes, but his mouth twisted wryly into what was almost a faint smirk. "I cannot think how you propose to do that. Shall you cast your nightgown into my face again?"

Elizabeth had to bite her tongue—physically bite it—until she tasted copper. The saliva filled her mouth, and she had to swallow before trying to speak. "I went walking today, William."

His cheek twitched. "I know. I had you followed."

She stiffened and tilted her head. "When? Who?"

He shook his head faintly and looked away. "One of the gardeners. Do not look so surprised, Mrs Darcy. He did not intrude upon your solitude or report to me of your doings. He was only there to see that no one could accost the lady of the house while she toured the grounds. If you had twisted your ankle, he would have brought word to the stables to send for help. That has always been the standing order at Pemberley for any lady out walking—she is to be protected but left to her own pleasures as much as possible."

"I see. Then you probably know in which direction I walked and the travelling party to whom I spoke."

He blinked slowly. "Is this some sort of test? I already told you; the lad was not there to spy on you. I've no idea where you went once you passed out of the sight of my study window. I may be an antisocial ogre, but I hope I have not lowered myself to *that*."

"If you knew where I went and what I saw, you might have guessed what I mean to ask of you."

He rolled his eyes and blew out a heavy sigh. "Can we cease with the interrogation? I am aware that you walk out. It has always been your way. I've no intention of trying to guess the myriad of things you might have seen."

Elizabeth clasped her hands behind her back and stood up taller. "Very well. Then tell me you are not jealous."

At this, his neck went rigid, and his gaze sharpened. "Of what?"

"Of me. Of the fact that I was out in the fresh air while you were working in your study."

He turned aside again. "You cannot think an estate such as this would continue on if I did not do my work. A gentleman's duty is often to see his affairs put right so that others may pursue pleasures."

"And you cannot think me such a fool that I would believe that."

She stalked closer and grabbed both of his hands, though he resisted somewhat. Apparently, she was not worth putting up much of a fight for because, after a second, he let his hands go slack and passive in hers. "Do you not have a steward who manages when you are away? Have you not spent nearly every waking hour of late in your study? Heaven and earth, Fitzwilliam Darcy, you have worked so much this last month that you shan't need to step back into that study for five years, and Pemberley would not suffer for it."

"Have you a point, madam?"

"The cherry trees are in bloom."

"I... what?"

"You heard me. And the daffodils are hanging on. Soon, we shall start to see spring bluebells and, after that, a few violets."

He shook his head. "Your *point*?"

"My point is you have not seen any of it. My point is you have a fine grey stallion standing in the stables whose thick winter coat is nearly shed out, and a groom who has kept him fit all through the cold months, just in case the master should want him again."

He blinked, his gaze faltering. "Hercules."

"Yes. Your favourite mount, Simmons tells me."

"He..." William's mouth worked. "He was my father's hunter. Quite the elderly pensioner now, but in his day, he was as fine a specimen as was ever seen north of Newmarket."

"And he was one of your few delights after your father died. I know. Simmons told me."

"And what do you want me to do about it now?" His voice hardened, and he pulled his hands from hers. "He is too old to be sold. Too full of himself to be put out to pasture. Shall I have the old sod put out of his misery before he turns rheumatic? Would that please you?"

Elizabeth crossed her arms. "I want you to ride him."

"Ride..." His face froze on a grimace, and he gave a sardonic laugh. "Ride him! You must be barking mad."

"Simmons says it can be done. He is fashioning straps for your legs to keep you secure in the saddle. You needn't fear any tomfoolery from the horse, because he is seasoned and steady."

"That shows just how little you know about stallions, even aged ones, in the spring."

Elizabeth permitted a smile. "And who better to stretch that great stallion's legs than the master who knows him like no other?"

His brows pinched together. He looked... why, he almost looked like he was considering it! A little more, and she would have won him back... but not yet. No, for he was examining the thing, now. Tempted by it. If she pushed too much, he would flatly refuse, and she would have lost more ground than she had gained in this conversation. He had to turn the shiny new thought over in his mind and own it to be his idea before he would be persuaded to it.

"How the devil would I even get on?" he shot at last.

This time, she had to master her smile of victory, lest he sense it and withdraw his interest. "That is simple. For this first time, Simmons and his head lad will help you. But if you make a regular thing of it, I... that is, Simmons has thought of a rope hoist that—"

"I'll not be dangled at the end of a rope like a convict on a noose."

"Then the thing remains simple. A lad on either side, to steady you until you are secure in the saddle... and then, you are free again."

His gaze turned inward, and his chest was rising sharper with each breath. "Free..."

"The horse will be waiting in the stable yard tomorrow morning at half past ten. But the choice to go out to him, William, will be yours."

He glanced swiftly at her face, then back down to his hands, flexing in his lap. "I... I shall consider it. Good evening, Mrs Darcy."

Well, that was as promising as it was going to get. She sighed. "Good night... William."

Chapter Thirty-Two

"**S**TEADY NOW, WE'VE GOT you sir," Simmons coached as he and the stable boy eased Darcy's rigid frame into the modified saddle atop his beloved Hercules.

Anxiety warred with the exhilaration curdling his stomach while Darcy clutched the pommel fiercely. What madness permitted him to attempt this fool's errand, hoping to recapture the fleeting vestiges of his former self?

Yet how could he resist when Elizabeth gazed at him with such tender hope lighting her fine eyes? He could be *free*, she said... Trust her to know the precise word that was the key to turn the bolt deep inside him.

"There now, quite secure, I'd say!" Simmons gave one final sharp tug on the leather straps binding Darcy's thighs and calves safely to the saddle before relinquishing his hold on the bridle. "Hercules has had a brisk gallop already to get the tickle out of his feet. Keep to a steady pace, sir, and all will be well."

Suppressing clamorous doubts, Darcy forced his rigid posture to relax somewhat and gathered the reins loosely. Beneath him, Hercules sidled and tossed his proud grey head, but made no effort to bolt away as Darcy feared. God willing, he might manage more than some feeble hobble about the paddock without toppling ingloriously!

"Are you ready, William?"

Elizabeth slid her hand up the horse's neck, though he could see how she hesitated in coming so close to the great beast. She was ready to grasp the bridle, if necessary, a thing which caused him no small degree of wonder because she had already told him she had no love for horses. But there was certainly something that looked like love glowing in her eyes when she looked up at him.

"I think so." His heart was clogging his throat, and his hands trembled on the reins. "How did I let you persuade me to this?"

Her grin widened... blast, he was done for. He never did have the slightest hope of a defence against her smile. "You never let anyone talk you into anything you did not already wish to do."

"It is sheer lunacy, you know."

She squinted up at him in the sunlight. "It is, that."

"You must be in a hurry to claim your widow's portion. I cannot think why in the world I ever agreed to this."

"Because, Fitzwilliam Darcy, you needed this as badly as I needed to see *that*."

He shifted the reins in his hands and glanced down. "See what?"

"That smile. Yes, that one there, that you would claim is not even half a smile, but to one who knows you, it is your purest expression of pleasure. *That* is what I have been aching to see for weeks."

He studied her, letting his eyes caress the face he loved above all others. Aye, he had been an ass of late. Not unprovoked, it was true. Never had anything crushed him—not even his father's death or everything that had happened to Georgiana—nothing had ever split his heart from his soul like having to refuse his wife. And nothing had seemed so impossible as swallowing what remained of his pride to let her back in, where she might wound him again.

Nevertheless, he had been nearly ready to bridge that divide himself, and he had already been formulating a plan to do so when she had approached him last evening with a hesitant smile and this wild scheme. *Would he try,* she wanted to know.

Bloody bollocks, yes. For her? He would try anything, even strapping himself to half a ton of unpredictable beast, if it could make him feel alive again. If it could give her even just a glimpse of the man he had once been, and wished beyond hope or reason he could be again for her.

Her unhappiness of late was his fault. He knew how she wandered Pemberley's grounds alone, lost in melancholy thoughts after he had tried to close himself off from her. With haunting clarity, Darcy recalled roaming these same fields and forests every spring, but this one. This year, for the first spring of memory, he had been locked away from everything growing and alive, dead to it all.

Until now.

Squaring his shoulders, and longing to show Elizabeth just how pleased he really was with this notion of hers, Darcy clicked his tongue to encourage the stallion to a slow walk. And immediately, the sway and dip of the horse's stride made him grapple for the mane and tug the reins.

"What is it?" Elizabeth asked in alarm.

He swallowed. "This might not be a good idea. I cannot balance as I used to."

"Well, of course, you cannot. Nothing is the same. But William, Simmons has you strapped in so well that I actually worry about what will happen if the horse decides to run off over the hills with you. We would never get you back."

He tried to chuckle, but it only came out as a nervous grunt. "My legs are going nowhere, but there is nothing to keep me from folding in half as I tip over in the traces."

"Then..." She stepped aside and surveyed him. "If you fear toppling sideways, lean back, instead."

"Back? Out of the question."

"Why? Your bent knees and the weight of your legs will keep you from falling all the way back, and your stomach muscles are strong enough to pull yourself forward again."

He experimented with the posture doubtfully and found that while it did prevent him from feeling so unsteady to the side, he was out of position in every classical sense. "No respectable huntsman would sit thus," he proclaimed.

"They would if their only other choice was to ride in the carriage. Come, William, try walking again."

To his surprised relief, it worked. It felt quite manageable indeed, so long as Hercules's steady pace remained unhurried. Nothing remotely akin to galloping freely through wild forest paths, but neither was it an invalid's confinement indoors! Buoying confidence lent Darcy's voice a bit of lightness that had been absent for too many days.

"Well, Madam, I have not overturned the first few paces, at least, thanks to your clever suggestion. Do I seem likely to embarrass myself completely just yet?"

Pleased laughter rewarded his gentle gibe as she easily matched the horse's sedate steps. "Indeed, not! Why, before long, all Pemberley shall remark the return of their Master astride his favourite steed. Does it not recall many fond memories?"

Nostalgic joy kindled bittersweet longing in Darcy's breast. Gripping Elizabeth's proffered hand briefly, he guided Hercules slowly onward. "Yes. Things I... I would like to revisit. God willing, I shall not be alone."

Whether his allusion to tentative hopes kindled unwise expectations, Elizabeth offered no acknowledgement, merely strolling serenely onward with one hand resting lightly upon Hercules's glossy neck. But the brilliant glow filling her expressive eyes needed no words.

Eventually, Darcy reined Hercules to a halt beneath a gently rustling birch canopy, sheltering a sunny clearing. In another month, this field would be carpeted with tiny wild violets. He had often retreated here to this secluded hollow for solitary contemplation in his youth. Now, he wished fervently to watch spring and summer roll into this valley with Elizabeth, hoping its tranquil beauty soothed away the remnants of all their bitter words.

As vivid memories and present realities mingled, raw longing to erase that horrible barrier between them resurged more fiercely than Darcy could withstand any longer.

"Elizabeth I... You cannot know my everlasting remorse over... how I spoke to you."

She lowered her head but said nothing.

His throat garbled his words, but he forced them out. "Your constant consolation and care for my family—for me—you deserve far better. And what did I give you? I... God forgive me, I crushed you. When all you did was to—"

"Stop." Her fingers twined in Hercules's mane as if she was tugging on the horse for support, and she lifted her face. And under the rim of that bonnet, tears shimmered. "Please stop."

"Not until I have said what you deserve to hear. You have shown me nothing but love, Elizabeth. Even when I could not receive it—even when I raged and stormed about *my* feelings, *my* selfishness... Even when you offered the most intimate part of yourself—to *me*, of all people! You found your courage to do what no other woman would, but all I could think of was how *I* felt cheated. When, in reality, I may be the most blessed man alive."

She shook her head, sniffing faintly as tears tumbled down her cheeks, and she had to swipe them away with the back of her glove. "I should not have... I knew it was foolishness. I just wanted... oh, dash it all. You see? There I go, talking about what *I* wanted." She sniffed again, blinking and trying to smile as more tears flooded her eyes. "I am just as selfish as you are."

He reached down and touched her chin until she relaxed and let him tip her face up. A soft blink, and then her gaze was all his. "What you wanted was to give yourself to me. To find a way to bring me happiness. That is not selfish. That is... that is the most beautiful thing anyone has ever done for me." He wanted to smile, but a sob robbed him of breath for a moment. "I only wish I was worthy of you."

She turned her face into his gloved palm, kissing the soft leather and leaning her cheek on it as she fought to steady her breathing. "Stop talking, you stubborn man. You never would listen to anyone, anyway."

He gave a broken laugh. "I think, madam, I have met my match. Will you forgive me, Elizabeth? Please, I beg of you, end this torment—aye, I have done it to myself, I know that. But only you can save me from it. I want us to be... not as we were."

Her eyes opened swiftly. "What was wrong with how we were? I loved us. I was happy, William."

"No, you weren't. You were content enough, but always something hung over us—that wish that things could be different. Some unreasoning hope that we could change what cannot be changed. We—*I* was never satisfied, always looking for some solution to this problem. Yes, that is what I saw myself as, for I *was* the problem. But..." His brow furrowed in thought. "You deserve a man, not a problem."

"William, I do not care about your legs."

"I am not talking about my legs. I am talking about my attitude. Men come of all statures, do they not?"

She looked doubtful. "Yes?"

"All shades of hair and eyes and skin. All pitches of voices and varieties of talents. And some..." He tapped the strap securing his knee to the saddle. "Some are more... athletic than others."

Elizabeth's chuckle was immediate, bringing the light back to her eyes that he loved so well. "That much is true."

"I want to be that for you, Elizabeth. Not your 'problem' anymore, but your partner."

Her smile widened, and she reached up to cup the hand that caressed her face. "You always have been, William. Although..."

"What?"

She lifted her shoulder and gave him a teasing grin. "Well, sometimes not willingly. I did have to learn how to herd you along like a sheepdog... from time to time. But you did always stand up for me."

He arched a brow. "Strange choice of words."

"Because standing is not a physical act. It is a manner. An exertion of your willpower. And if there is one thing you have in spades, Fitzwilliam Darcy, it is willpower."

"Ah... indeed. Sorry about that."

"I am not." She strained her neck to the side and squinted as a shaft of sunlight struck her in the eyes through the tree limbs. "Gracious, what I *am* sorry about was that I never asked Papa for riding lessons, so I could sit on a horse beside you rather than having to stare up into the clouds! You say *you* are stubborn? Why did I not learn that when I had a chance?"

Surprise jolted through Darcy as a bizarre inspiration took sudden root. "Why indeed! No time like the present. Let us walk back to the stables at once and have a horse saddled for you. I shall teach you the basics now."

Elizabeth cocked him a curious look. "You, ah... you can teach me?"

"Doubting me already, are you? After that lovely little talk we just had?"

"No, I am doubting myself. I have to ride with my knee up in my chest and my back all twisted. At least you can have a leg on each side of the horse."

"Georgiana has tried both ways of riding. Does that scandalise you?"

She shielded her eyes and looked up at him. "Not really. What is her verdict?"

"It took her some while, but she eventually said she preferred the lady's way of riding. She says it is quite secure."

Elizabeth grinned wickedly. "Then, I dare you to try it."

Darcy winced. "I am not *that* brave."

"THERE NOW, EASIEST THING in the world! Just grip here and here, see? Gideon shan't let you fall. He taught many a young lady to ride before I bought him for Georgiana."

"Ah... and how do I..." Elizabeth fumbled with the riding crop in her right hand and the twisting reins in her left. "I have to carry all this? I do not plan to beat the horse."

"It is not for 'beating' him, and I do not hold with such practices. But only a very small portion of what you communicate to your mount is actually channelled through the reins. The rest comes from your posture, your body language. You haven't a leg on his right side to guide him with your seat the way a gentleman would, so yes, typically, ladies carry a crop."

She looked pointedly at his hands. "I see you do not have one, and you..."

"Yes, yes, I haven't a single leg at all to guide him. But I also know Hercules, and he wants no urging. Had I a crop, we would be galloping over the next rise by now."

She shrugged and grinned. "You said it, not I. Look, can I drop this for now and just work out what to do with my hands? It is not as if I mean to take any fences today."

"As you wish. Sit tall, my love. Left heel down, right knee tight. That is how you wedge your balance properly. And hold the reins gently—you needn't strangle the poor beast."

Under his patient guidance, Elizabeth gradually relaxed, her back straightening as Gideon plodded on. Seeing her feminine confidence blossom with every successful step buoyed Darcy's spirits beyond reason. Why, this was something they could do together! As she developed her skills, he might re-master his own, and they could once again explore the lands he loved and had always wished to share with his future wife.

And so, onward they ambled. It was hardly an exhilarating gallop, but it was still delicious. Darcy adjusted Hercules's reins, savouring the empowering rush of controlling his magnificent stallion once more. Though securely bound to the saddle, he could almost fancy himself lord of all creation, racing wild and unfettered through verdant forests again. Beside him, Elizabeth picked her way cautiously across gently rolling lawns, sunlight glinting warmly off the curls that peeked from under her bonnet.

"Shall we wander down to the lake?" he asked. "I think you would admire it."

"I already do... have... yes." She bit her lips together and flopped her left foot uncertainly. And Darcy's heart melted even more than it already had, watching her try to brave something that clearly intimidated her... just to be with him.

"We used to swim here, Georgiana and I," he mused as they walked toward the water. "I taught her when she was five. Father never learned of it—or, at least, he never let on that he knew." Darcy smiled up at the heavens. "Now that I think of it, he had to know. Someone would have told him."

Elizabeth's lip popped free from between her teeth. She was breathing a little easier now as Gideon's hooves slowed, sinking in the marsh at the water's edge. "Do you like swimming?"

"I did. I suppose I still would, if I..." He stopped, refusing to let himself dwell on yet another thing he could no longer do. "Well. A gentleman has not always his leisure, does he?"

"I think you should swim again. When the weather warms, that is."

He laughed softly. "I would sink like a rock. I cannot kick to keep myself afloat."

"But your arms are strong. We could fashion a sort of raft... or I could help you," she added, almost shyly. "Further evidence of my rather nontraditional upbringing, but I know how to swim, and if it is only a matter of keeping you horizontal... surely, you could float on your back. What do you think?"

He turned in the saddle and cocked a grin at her. "I think you are mad. Utterly, reprehensibly and unforgivably mad. But I love you for it."

A grin as wide as the sunrise split her face. "Then I shall keep suggesting these outlandish things, for by no means would I suspend any pleasure of yours."

Darcy held his hand out to her as their horses inched closer to the water, squeezing her fingers. Yes, indeed... he was the most blessed man alive. And for a few minutes, as his horse plunged his nose into the water's edge for a drink, Darcy was content merely to soak in that.

"We ought to be going back," he said at length, as Hercules lifted his dripping muzzle from the water. "It is still quite early in the year, and I would not wish for you to take a chill."

Elizabeth lifted her hand, almost looking as if she knew what she was doing, and gently turned Gideon back toward firmer ground. But Hercules's attention had been caught by a bird twittering in the boughs of a nearby tree. Still a stallion, even at the age of one and twenty, the old horse was no doubt feeling the nip of spring in the air like no gelding ever would. Darcy had to give the rein a sharp tug to draw the horse's attention.

Before Darcy grasped the potential danger, Hercules snorted in surprise, plunging sideways into sucking mud at the water's weedy edge. "Whoa... steady, my lad!" he called.

But the horse was floundering as the slick earth gave way on the muddy bank. There was an incline there—why had he not noted *that* before?—and the grey's hooves slipped and clambered and, eventually, lost purchase altogether.

"William!" Elizabeth cried.

And then the great body slammed downward. Darcy's head struck the earth—mercifully squishy muck—and his shoulder was pinned. His left arm, his leg trapped, and white-hot agony speared through Darcy's side as the stallion's frantic efforts to right himself instead just crashed his rider's helpless body into the marsh. Fighting nausea, he reached as far forward as he could and clung fast to the bridle, gasping hoarsely.

"Hold Hercules still! My leg is trapped beneath him in the mud."

The horse froze for a moment, still pulling at Darcy's hand to free his head and plunge his feet forward in an attempt to rise, but he was no longer panicking. He was too seasoned an old soldier for that, thank heaven.

Wordless terror widened Elizabeth's eyes as she scrambled with her skirts, trying inexpertly to free herself from her own saddle, then finally flung herself over the side with a little squeak of terror. She flew to him in the next instant, but hovered helplessly over Hercules's heaving flanks, trying to keep clear of the horse's thrashing hooves.

"What should I do? Oh William, you cannot move at all, pinned so. But neither can I lift the horse!"

"I might be able to let him up if he can steady himself. After all, it is not as if I am going to fall out of the saddle," he retorted grimly.

But Elizabeth was shaking her head. "The earth under his feet is shiny, it is so slick. I can hardly stand myself. Surely, he will only fall on you again. Oh, stupid, this was a *stupid* idea! It is all my fault!"

"It was my idea to walk to the lake," Darcy grunted, still holding Hercules's bridle fast. "Unfasten the straps on my right leg. Perhaps I can get free."

Elizabeth bent over him and did as he asked, her fingers clumsy on the thick leather, but as she freed the last buckle, she gasped. "Why, now you are worse off, for you are still buckled fast to the left side, and I cannot get to those. Oh, what if he has broken your leg? Or what if he gets up and you topple..."

Darcy could hear the shouts from the stable lads now, all running toward them. "Help is on the way. Just help me keep him down, and—"

Before Darcy could say more, another shout rang above all the other voices. A shout he would recognise anywhere. Darcy groaned.

Elizabeth had been leaning over the horse's neck, covering his eye and speaking soothing words to him when she jerked about, her mouth wide in surprise. "It is Richard! His carriage is in the drive—he is running from it now, and..."

"Oh, bloody hell," Darcy swore.

She blinked back at him. "Why do you say that?"

He grimaced. "You will see."

Colonel Fitzwilliam was charging full speed down the path, waving and shouting orders at the stable lads—one to bring a knife, another a litter to carry Darcy, and another a gun in case the beast had broken his leg. Darcy rolled his eyes and just gritted his teeth.

Barely had Elizabeth a chance to jump out of the way before Richard flung himself bodily against the stallion's muddy withers.

"I shall roll him forward. Elizabeth, on three, help pull Darcy's leg out."

"Colonel, you cannot pull his leg. He is buckled to the saddle. If you will only—"

"Buckled!" Richard stared, aghast between them, but shook his head and put his knee into it, bracing Hercules's shoulder and Darcy's torso by main strength as Darcy kept hold on the horse's head. "There, Elizabeth. I bloody well hope that is all the straps."

Elizabeth dove in, her fingers nimbler this time as she unfastened both buckles. "There! I got it!" An instant later, a stable lad was dragging Darcy clear, and Richard stood back to let Hercules recover his footing.

The groom helped Darcy to firmer ground and laid him out on the grass. Elizabeth was at his side in an instant, and Richard was only half a breath later, feeling down Darcy's left leg for any signs of a break.

"What the devil what you were about?" he spat. "A merry little jaunt? Strapped to the saddle, of all things! Darcy, any fool knows—"

"I was doing quite well until the horse slipped," Darcy shot back. "No one could have foreseen that."

"Anyone with any sense would have! What possessed you two harebrains, taking such risks? Shall I even ask whose idea that was?"

"It was mine," they both blurted together.

Richard curled his lip. "What, did you rehearse that? Knowing you would have to explain yourselves?"

"We do not have to explain anything, Richard. My wife contrived a way for me to experience something I had long regretted. Had I simply been content to walk along the path, no ill would have come to me, but I had to press the matter and go to the water."

"Darcy, you have no business riding a horse at all! What the bloody blazes—"

"Is the horse well?"

Richard broke off his sputtering to glance over his shoulder at Hercules, standing placidly on the bank, snatching mouthfuls of grass. "He appears to be. And by some miracle, you did not snap your leg like a twig, but I shouldn't wonder if you are black and blue from waist to toes."

"Then it is no bother." Darcy grinned. "The bruise shan't pain me at all."

Chapter Thirty-Three

"**C**ONFOUND YOUR RECKLESS STUBBORNNESS, Darcy! Have you learned nothing this past year?"

"Calm yourself, Richard. I told you, I am in no pain." Darcy folded his hands across his lap and watched his cousin stalking across the room, pacing as he had always done—as Darcy once did himself—when he was frustrated.

"You have a morbid sense of humour, you know. That leg is—"

"Yes, yes. Black and blue. I shall ask Elizabeth not to massage it tonight."

Richard stopped pacing. "*Mass*... Egad. No! I shall not ask. I do not want to know, but Darcy, when are you going to learn that you are, in fact, breakable?"

"That was the first time I have left this chair in an age. Give a man allowances for stumbling once or twice as he finds his feet again—and yes, that was meant to be a jest as well."

Richard pointed a finger. "I blame Elizabeth for that one, you know."

"Well! I say, my joke was not *that* bad."

"Darcy, has it ever occurred to you that people need you? You matter profoundly to the lives of hundreds of people, and that is no exaggeration. Here I have come all the way from London to speak with you about something important, and I learn that you seem to have developed a death wish while I was away!"

"You do exaggerate. No real harm was done, and you see before you a man content enough with his lot."

"Content..."

"I *am*," Darcy repeated firmly. "Many men haven't half my blessings."

"That is not what I..." Richard paced away, covering his mouth before he hissed and turned around. "There is a difference between contentment and blissful ignorance."

"Oh, doubtless. Out with it, then—what dire tidings make you especially waspish just now? Surely, a simple mishap hardly warrants such blistering reproofs without deeper cause?"

With a muttered oath, Richard swung away to glare out the darkened window, hands locked behind his rigid spine. The reluctant confession emerged terse and bitter. "I come straight from London with unhappy news. George Wickham sidestepped justice once more. A legal technicality."

"What?"

Richard turned around. "You heard me. He is supposedly free as a bird. No transportation, no fines levied... and from what I have been able to find out, his gaol sentence—which was short—is already served."

Fierce outrage surged with Darcy's guttural snarl. "Damnation take that blackguard and inept militia buffoons both! By God, I should have shot him dead that day, and saved everyone the trouble." He unclenched white-knuckled fists. "How can this be? You swore the court-martial condemned him beyond reprieve."

"A miscarriage all around. The presiding officers were green. Turns out they mishandled his enlistment requirements from the start when Wickham lied outright about graduating Cambridge to claim a higher rank."

Darcy snorted. "He was expelled in his second year. Father got the matter 'cleared up,' he re-enrolled, but he dropped out again just a month before Father died."

"Yes, I recall. But he claimed on his enlistment documentation that he graduated, and that detail was missed until they were sentencing him for desertion. They say it was Wickham himself who confessed, knowing full well that the false claim invalidated his enlistment. Therefore, with charges of desertion technically unsupportable, they instead charged him with fraud. A much lighter sentence, of course."

He walked away from the darkened window, frustration carving deep lines upon his craggy face in the flickering firelight. "The blackguard deserved shackles and hard prison rations before being remanded for court martial properly. Instead, he received thirty lashes for 'dishonesty' and a month incarcerated in the stockade before walking free as you please. My contacts report Wickham boasted of visiting several fashionable gaming hells just days after release."

Agonised fury ignited Darcy's veins, helpless fists twisting bed linens as impotent rage scalded bitter through his chest. God almighty! Would earth or heaven never justly punish such wilful desecration of innocence and virtue? How arrogant to imagine divine justice merely delayed—more like denied forever whilst snakes like Wickham wandered free.

But a harsher thought was yet to fall. "Then... he remains my heir beyond all efforts. Another innocent shall likely fall helpless prey to him soon."

Richard surged forward, gripping Darcy's shoulder. "You've got to get a son on your pretty young wife there. Why, with a son who bears your name, what need to fret about old Wickham anymore?"

Outraged disbelief widened Darcy's eyes. "Have you lost all vestige of reason? What part of 'paralysed utterly below the waist' eludes your comprehension regarding my ability to father children?"

"Well, I only hoped that with you doing insane things like horseback riding, perhaps you might be feeling... better. I do not suppose you have made any attempts..."

"There is nothing to be done."

"I see." Withdrawing slightly, Richard dragged agitated hands down his haggard face.

"What happens if Georgiana marries and bears a son?" Darcy asked quietly.

Richard blew out a sigh. "Heaven knows. Wickham's grandfather was actually the elder Darcy, whereas yours was the younger. His claim would be stronger because yours is only the collateral line, and he is the direct descendant. And let us remember that Georgiana is not close to marriage, nor is she guaranteed to be able to bear a child, either."

"Yes... particularly after... Well, I suppose it is no use. Unless and until Wickham's crimes catch up with him, he stands to gain everything." Darcy snorted. "One would think such a man would find it within his means to live up to his prospects."

"Wickham does not know about your..." Richard cleared his throat. "If he paid attention, he has probably heard rumours about your marriage and will be assuming you are about the business of setting him back in line. He would not know that there are... difficulties, nor how close he really is."

"And how close is he? Tell me, Richard. Am I as fragile as you seem to believe?"

"Oh, blast, Darcy, how should I know? You look well enough. If you would stop risking your neck..."

"I am determined to act in a manner that considers first the happiness of my wife and myself."

"And I am not proposing to interfere with that. I only suggest we must secure your lineage and these lands against that reprobate by any means. If you cannot manage the duty yourself, then..." He trailed off suggestively, jaw set stubbornly.

Revolted comprehension speared Darcy with such force that renewed agony blazed through his bruised ribs. With blistering contempt barely leashed, he enunciated each word precisely. "You overstep egregiously, sir. My wife is no broodmare for hire, nor will I casually disregard my marital vows. Besmirch Elizabeth's honour at your peril—even in seeming jest."

"Oh, blast propriety, and consider the circumstances! Do you imagine it has not crossed her mind that her own security depends on having the matter settled? She is no fool, Darcy. She did her duty by her family once. Surely, she will see the sense of it a second time. Shall I discreetly raise the notion?"

"You shall not! Nor breathe a word repeating your offensive suggestion." Darcy nearly shouted hoarsely before mastering his fraying temper. "By what depraved logic do you justify soiling my wife's reputation? "

"I like it as little as you do, Darcy! But you have not the leisure of options. Unless you think Wickham will mend his ways? Do you think he will be less monstrous if he should ever step into such an inheritance? Few men can keep their principles intact when given power, and he never had any to start with."

"You speak of principles, but you suggest compelling Elizabeth to lie with a stranger just to get a child?"

Richard swallowed, and his hands twitched at his sides. "Not a stranger."

Darcy's lip curled, and if he had anything to hand, he would have thrown it at the blighter's head. "You offer yourself, then? How noble of you, Cousin! What a sacrifice!"

"I do not think of myself, Darcy!" Richard shot back.

"Oh, indeed, you are selfless. How long have you been scheming this? Since you first saw her?"

"Scheming? Darcy, you always used to be a sensible man. Do not give in to paranoia and jealousy."

"I do not call it paranoia. It all makes sense now. You saw a handsome woman with no power to refuse. You knew I could keep her in comforts, but no more, and you could—"

"Darcy, stop! I am not lusting after your wife!" Richard's shoulders were heaving, and his face mottled with rage. "Lord have mercy, I thought you would appreciate the fact that I would never hurt her! That I would never hurt you!"

Darcy clenched his jaw. "You thought wrong."

Richard stalked away, throwing a punch at a decorative pillow from the sofa by the hearth before he whirled. "You are so sanctimonious—you in your fine house and padded chair with your sweet little wife. What about your tenants? What about the serving girls? Hell, I will put a face to them. Mrs Reynolds and Mrs Hodges, Giles and Beth and a dozen others I could name. How many pretty farmer's daughters would he ruin? Think you of them, as you sit here in your ivory tower, calling *me* the offensive one? You are not guaranteed tomorrow, Darcy. The one thing your father asked of you was to look after those in your care."

He was panting, still pacing, and he had started toward the door before he stepped back. "You are running low on options, Cousin. Unless you mean to simply stand aside and give a mongrel the keys to the estate."

Darcy's fingers were ripping into the cloth on the armrests of his chair. What did he mean to do? Push up out of it and launch himself at his cousin's head?

But at that instant, the door to Elizabeth's room opened, and she stood at the threshold, her eyes flicking between them. One sweep of that icy glare confirmed she had overheard far more than either of them intended. *Blast*, he thought she was downstairs! He ought to have known she would stay close to him.

"Are you two aware that you are shouting?"

Mortified heat scalded Darcy's face. What she must have heard! His cousin—a man she trusted—proposing such indecent bargaining, like she was livestock at market.

"Elizabeth! Pray, excuse Richard's astonishing lapse in propriety, my love." Darcy cleared his throat. "His... frustration over Wickham's undeserved freedom briefly caused him to forget himself."

Richard raked a hand through his disordered hair before addressing Elizabeth directly. "Elizabeth—Mrs Darcy," he amended when Elizabeth stiffened, "forgive my indelicacy. Desperation, I fear, drove me to overstep. I swear, I only meant to help."

"It does not sound as if Mr Darcy appreciates your 'help,' sir."

"I did not expect him to be pleased. But neither did I expect him to be a fool. You haven't the luxury of sentiment, either of you."

Elizabeth studied Richard for a moment—her creamy throat working and her lips softly parted. By thunder, she was not... *considering* it. Was she?

Darcy's pulse was thrumming wildly. She could not... she would not! Images of what that decision would entail—of *her*, and Richard—blasted through his mind until he wanted to carve his own eyes out. It could not be!

Richard's voice broke Darcy's anguish, making him hold his breath for what new infamy his cousin had to express. And it all came down to Elizabeth, really. What she would do, and just how much "duty" she could countenance.

"Mrs Darcy, you know better than anyone what is at stake. You have it in your power to do something about it. What say you? You know—I hope you know—that I speak with utmost respect and compassion for the situation in which you find yourselves. Is the possibility... something you would consider?"

Elizabeth tilted that elegant chin proudly, her delicate jaw visibly clenched. "You presume much, sir. What 'possibility,' specifically, do you suggest I embrace?" Arctic chill frosted each pronounced syllable. "Pray, enlighten me. Say it out loud."

Richard shifted uncomfortably beneath her glacial stare. "I intended no offence. Yet surely, as two reasonable people, we must acknowledge obstacles... which unconventional arrangements could resolve, if you follow my meaning." He flushed before proceeding delicately. "Naturally, I would offer any assistance required. Discreetly, of course."

Prolonged silence reigned until Elizabeth turned deliberately to search Darcy's downcast features. After an endless moment, her solemn words fell softly into the room's thick atmosphere. "You have talked me into some rather significant decisions. Life-altering decisions, none of which I have cause to regret."

Richard lowered his eyes and let go a sigh, relief straining through the lines of his face. "Yes."

But Elizabeth was not finished. She stepped closer, fully into the room, until she stood beside Darcy's chair. "This, however, is something you will not persuade me to. And I think you should go. Now."

Discomfited awareness blossomed across Richard's countenance. With belated contrition, he nodded acceptance before quitting the room. Once alone, facing Elizabeth's compassionate gaze, scarcely-contained emotions overwhelmed Darcy completely. Humiliated tears long denied finally released in bitterly cleansing torrents.

Her hand was in his hair, brushing it off his face, and then she was sliding into his lap, into his arms, and sobbing herself from the shock of it.

"I am sorry you had to hear that," he groaned into her hair as he pulled her close. "Sorry he could ever conceive such a thing... and sorry that once again, I cannot—"

"Shh." She put her fingers to his lips, long enough for him to still. "Just hold me, William. That is all I want, and all I shall ever want. Hold me."

His breath gushed from him, and he nodded as she shuddered and buried herself into his chest. "Forever, love."

Chapter Thirty-Four

ELIZABETH HURRIED OUTDOORS, SHIVERING slightly in the early morning chill. She had risen at first light, hastening to dress and quietly slip outside before the rest of the household stirred, hoping to avoid another awkward encounter with Colonel Fitzwilliam. His outrageous suggestion still scalded her conscience nearly as much as William's devastated expression afterwards.

Was it selfish, escaping outdoors while her injured husband endured fresh humiliation, facing his cousin again this morning? Perhaps... But they had talked and held one another long into the night. She perfectly comprehended his feelings on the matter, and he hers. At the moment, Elizabeth desperately needed soothing solitude to clear her head.

Heedless of the dew-drenched grass soaking her hem, she wandered slowly over softly rolling lawns edging Pemberley's woods. What a comfort it would be to have Jane's gentle companionship now! Seeking relief in action, Elizabeth had already penned an impassioned letter, urgently inviting her elder sister to visit. If the missive rapidly reached Longbourn and Jane promptly arrived, hopefully, her wisdom and empathy might bolster Elizabeth's flagging courage.

The horrible truth of it—and she and William had both acknowledged this—was that the colonel was not wrong. Not from a practical standpoint, at least. Morally, the idea was reprehensible. And the ramifications of the twisted, tangled knot such an alliance would weave... why, it would poison all of them. William could never again look at her without shuddering from *that*, Richard could never see the child without a certain pang of truth, and she... she would come to resent both men.

It was unthinkable. It was the sort of mess her father had warned her might await, and thank Heaven for that warning because her eyes had been opened early.

Pausing beneath a flowering cherry tree, Elizabeth sighed heavily, spreading her damp skirts to sit atop a nearby stone bench warmed by the slowly climbing sun. She let her troubled gaze travel across gently undulating lawns towards Pemberley's imposing silhouette etched against the brightening horizon. Fresh heartache squeezed her throat, knowing that William would also be awake by now, and worrying inside those shadowed walls. Probably having another argument with his cousin... if they were still speaking at all.

And that might be the worst of it. For all his faults, Colonel Fitzwilliam was a good man. William held him dear, and she had early learned to trust him, for his goodness, his loyalty, and his wise counsel. And now, William was robbed of his closest ally.

Light rustling amidst sheltering shrubbery made her sniff and quickly swipe the moisture from her face. Probably only a hare or... no, for two small forms burst forth towards her. Relief briefly lifted the oppressive weight as she recognized the tenant children from a nearby farm.

One of her first "duties" upon returning to Pemberley this spring was to tour the local farms with Mrs Reynolds, being introduced to all the tenants. And, just as she had at Longbourn, she had started bringing baskets when anyone was ill or sitting for a quarter-hour with an elderly widow whose son tended the farm all day.

And these children, she knew, were Benjamin and Sarah Jacobsen's four youngest. Their guileless enthusiasm always refreshed her spirit since that first day, when they had discovered their new mistress most willing to play simple games or hear youthful concerns without condescension. Gripping plump hands outstretched in greeting, she managed a genuine smile.

"Well met, young sir! Pray tell me, Tom, what adventures have you rascals been about this fine morn?"

A jumbled chorus of piping voices overlapping with laughter provided ample answer until the toddler clinging to his sister's patched frock whimpered fretfully. The little maid Lily whispered her mother's instructions that her little sister must not be jostled.

"Jostled! Of course not, Lily. We shall see that she is not disturbed." Elizabeth slid a compassionate arm round her thin shoulders until the anxious spell passed.

But there was something odd in the way their elder sister Hannah hovered. Should she not be home helping her mother and elder sister, instead of minding the children?

Hannah was too old to care for a romp in the fields, and Tom and Lily were more than capable of getting about on their own.

"Hannah, is something amiss?"

The girl, who was about thirteen, Elizabeth thought, tucked her hands behind her skirts and shook her head. But she would not meet Elizabeth's eyes as she did so.

Something was clearly troubling her. Elizabeth frowned. "How is your mother today? Your sister is well, I hope?"

Ah, there it was. Tom's eyes widened and he held his breath, blowing his cheeks out and sealing his lips, looking very much like the frogs he liked to catch. Beside him, Hannah paled and looked down, scuffing one worn shoe over thick moss.

"Are they at home?" Elizabeth asked.

"Aye, mistress," Hannah confessed.

"Well! I shall have Cook ready a basket and—"

"There's no need for that," the girl interjected. "She's not poorly. There isn't so very much wrong with her, but—"

"She's scared of that man," Tom put in.

Elizabeth blinked, her eyes shifting between the two. "Which man?"

Hannah hissed a command for silence to her brother, but Elizabeth held up a hand. "No, do not answer. I will pop by and speak to your mother myself, then, shall I?"

The children began to protest, but Elizabeth would not hear of it. She went on ahead of them, across the freshly ploughed fields and over the stile until she was knocking at the door of the Jacobsen's cottage.

Inside, Mrs Jacobsen greeted her with a quick curtsey—if a little clumsy, as she was already heavy with her sixth child—as Lily hid behind her mother's skirts. "Mrs Darcy, Ma'am! 'Tis a right fine day, Ma'am. I hope my young'uns haven't been a bother."

"No! Of course not. I only thought to stop in and ask after you and Mr Jacobsen. I am sure your husband is readying for the spring planting. And Jenny? I... I do not see her. She is not unwell, I hope?"

The children shifted anxiously until Mrs Jacobsen attempted a tremulous, reassuring smile that failed to reach her eyes. "Oh nay, Ma'am, Jenny is well enough." Her work-reddened hands twisted an apron corner as she briefly hesitated. "Truth is hard telling what ails the lass."

Behind the woman, Elizabeth saw the twitching of a curtain that walled off the sleeping areas of the house. Cold fingers closed round Elizabeth's throat as fragmented puzzle pieces shifted. Quietly she tried keeping rising hysteria from her tone. "Did something happen to your daughter, Mrs Jacobsen?"

When the stoic tenants remained mute, Elizabeth crossed swiftly to draw back the faded curtain. Behind it lay the trembling form of Jenny, face averted, and slender frame curled tight amidst bed linens. At Elizabeth's soft query, the girl only hunched tighter as if wishing to disappear entirely.

"What happened?" she asked in a low voice.

"Nothing much," Mrs Jacobsen hastened to explain. "Only a fall in the fields. Her ankle, Ma'am."

Elizabeth was no stranger by now to the vagaries of lower limbs, and a quick glance over the girl's stockinged legs yielded no signs of swelling. But her stockings were ripped and muddy to the knees.

"And *who* made her fall?" she prodded.

Mrs Jacobsen went quiet, but Hannah piped up. "That man grabbed her. He ripped her dress, too, and—"

The woman shushed her second daughter, but not before Elizabeth had risen to her feet and beckoned Mrs Jacobsen outside. The door closed on the house, and Elizabeth rounded on her.

"Jenny was attacked?"

"It weren't nothin'," the mother said, her face averted. "No harm done, Ma'am. Just a ripped dress."

"Nothing else? I find that... difficult to believe."

"It's true." Mrs Jacobsen clenched her jaw and tried to force a smile. "My Hannah scared him off, she did. Jenny's just frightened because the fellow kissed her and tried to put her on his horse, but—"

"*Which* fellow? Someone from Lambton?"

Mrs Jacobsen shook her head. "I didn't see him, Ma'am, but Jenny said it was no one from the village. Spoke gentle-like to her, asking questions like a visitor from London, and then made for her."

"And you did not report this to the steward? Mrs Jacobsen, this man may try to harm someone else. The matter ought to be investigated."

Mrs Jacobsen only shook her head and looked down. "Beggin' your pardon, Ma'am. Naught but ill comes from a girl's shamin'. We'd be ruined. Please, Ma'am, don't say a word to Mr Darcy. We'll keep our troubles to ourselves and not make more for the master."

Elizabeth thinned her lips. "I very well *will* say something to him, but you need have no fear. Mr Darcy will want to see that your family is safe, and you may be assured of his discretion. Meanwhile, I shall send a basket round with some fresh stockings and dress material for Miss Jenny. She cannot possibly go around in those."

Mrs Jacobsen swallowed and nodded hesitantly. "I... I thank ye, Ma'am."

"Of course. Good morning, Mrs Jacobsen."

She hurried back to the manor, her mind tumbling with dismay. To think, someone bold enough to make a grab for a respectable young girl, almost within sight of her own house? One of Pemberley's tenants!

One thing Elizabeth had early noted was how well William saw to his lands and the people who lived there. To meddle with one of the good families who lived on Pemberley's farms was to invite retribution from the master. Surely, the man must have been a stranger to the area and did not know.

Or... perhaps word had got out that Mr Darcy was not so strong as he once was.

But the thing that troubled her even more was this physical evidence, impossible to ignore, that William's position... well, it mattered to people. He had the power to do something to protect girls like Jenny, as well as the goodness to see it done.

How miserable must it be, then, when the master was not a good man? When he was as much a predator himself as the wolves nipping at the borders of Pemberley's lands?

And that was exactly what Colonel Fitzwilliam had been saying last night. Elizabeth stopped and pressed a hand to her stomach. She... she *did* have the ability to do something... but that something would cost her everything.

E LIZABETH TUGGED OFF HER bonnet and pelisse and looked anxiously up the stairs, hoping to find William without another awkward encounter with Richard. The footman informed her William was in his study, and that he was alone. What luck! Relief eased her quick steps towards the solid oaken door.

She tapped lightly before peering inside the still chamber. William sat silhouetted beside tall, open windows, overlooking a copse of newly leafed trees. Several plump wood thrushes flitted amidst quivering branches as a light breeze ruffled William's dark hair in echo. He appeared years younger just now—perhaps as he had looked before his injury. He turned his head at her entry, and there was that half-smile she loved. She moved to take his hand, lowering her face to his to kiss his cheek.

"Good morning," he greeted her.

"*Is* it a good morning?"

"I suppose that depends on what you mean." He glanced significantly beyond her toward the door. "Our guest has departed."

She blinked. "He has? So soon?" Well! That... that answered one question. She would not be confronted with the temptation to revisit her opinions of yesterday, at least. Not yet, anyway.

William laced his fingers through hers and nodded, his gaze returning to the window. "I spoke with him briefly before he went."

"And does he depart with or without your blessing?"

William hissed, and his shoulders lifted. "He left a letter addressed specifically to you, which he dared not deliver in person. Quite right—I was in no fit state for charitable partings." He studied their joined hands rather than meet her eyes directly. "But we did settle one point between us before he went, and at least his foolish suggestion died a swift death. You need not entertain fears on that score."

"I am relieved to hear it." Sudden tears burned Elizabeth's eyes, despite her fervent intentions otherwise. She was relieved—relieved that William was not still boiling in wrath this morning. That might bode well for future relations with his cousin. "Surely, in time, you will be able to forgive him. I cannot believe he meant any insult. He cannot have thought the thing through, surely."

"Likely not, though nothing excuses dishonouring my wife's integrity." William drew her palm gently to his lips before relinquishing their clasped hands to slide a folded vellum square from his waistcoat pocket. His arm trembled faintly, extending it towards her. "You should read Richard's apology. He deeply regrets discomfiting us both."

"Are you certain?" Hesitantly, she accepted the creased letter. "We need not revisit everything."

William shook his head firmly, jaw visibly clenched. "No, you deserve to understand my cousin better. By Heaven, you've endured trenchant diatribes by everyone connected to this cursed disaster, and most particularly me, and you managed to see some good in me yet. Pray, read it."

With mounting trepidation, Elizabeth straightened the crackling page, hardly know-ing what to expect given the fiery Fitzwilliam temper so akin to her husband's. But fervent contrition marked every line scrawled across the page. The colonel clearly ag-onised over shaming them all. He feared they could never be in company again without that fracture remaining between them. The words could not be unsaid... but the sen-timent that caused him to utter them was as heartfelt and genuine as it had ever been. He implored Elizabeth not to think too unkindly of him, despite fully deserving her resentment.

She swiped a few stray tears aside to glimpse William staring silently at the dancing patterns of light and shadow beyond the window again.

"Shall you write back to him? There must be some way of mending what was broken."

William tapped a finger on the armrest of his chair in thought. "Richard meant that vile scheme to somehow secure everyone's future, although I am damned if I understand his logic." His voice dropped lower. "He is not half bad, as scoundrels go. I believe I can forgive the old rogue... a lifetime of looking to my right hand and always seeing him there—I know him too well to think he meant everything that scheme implied. Though you needn't feel likewise after he placed you in an intolerable position." He passed a shaking hand over weary eyes. "*For you have I toiled and wrought; for you, I have sinned, many's the year and oft...*"

"What do you mean by that quote?"

He reached for her hand again, twining their fingers together. "When I was first injured, still in outraged denial about all the doctors were telling me, Richard scarcely left my side. He said something... he said he would do everything under Heaven to help me. And..." His brow furrowed. "... One or two things under Hell."

Elizabeth squeezed his fingers but said nothing—just waited for him to continue.

"I thought little of that at the time. More histrionics, I thought, and I had enough angst for the whole world at the moment. But later, I began to realise that he truly meant it. He could find a justification for almost anything, if he felt it was for my benefit."

She chuckled softly. "Just like he rode to Hertfordshire and browbeat a stubborn girl who was slighted by everyone who knew her into coming to London to marry a man she never met."

"Yes..." He smiled a little. "And I am forever in his debt for that."

"As am I. So, we are agreed? Your cousin is to grovel a little, and then be forgiven?"

"So long as we make a point of drawing out that 'grovelling' part."

She snorted. "I, for one, am grateful for a bit of distance for now. Much as I would like to see it all forgotten in good time, I am quite a little too spiteful to forget it today. But William, there is something very serious I must tell you."

"Hmm?"

She wetted her lips, then forged ahead, telling him about Jenny Jacobsen. He listened, his brow darkening by the moment as he asked more details of what she had learned.

"I shall speak with the local magistrate, and I shall also have Thompkins have a discreet word with the tenants about guarding their daughters," he decided when she had finished. "An opportunist like that will not be deterred by a single failure."

"William, what else can we do? I hate to confess it, but as I was returning home, I... well, I started to wonder if the colonel did have a point. What happens if..."

He turned to gaze steadily at her. "If?"

She swallowed. "Are we being selfish, refusing what options are available to us?" She scooted her chair closer to his and squeezed his hands. "Are we thinking only of ourselves, and what *we* want, lamenting that things are not as we wish and wilfully putting others in a precarious position because we will not... do everything possible?"

A heavy sigh lifted his shoulders, and he frowned. "I have asked myself the same question."

"And? Tell me you have an answer."

"None, save that I have searched my soul, and I have discovered that I cannot protect the whole world. Even should I desire to."

She pressed her lips into a weak smile. "The whole world is not yours to protect, but Pemberley is."

"No. You are. Pemberley is people—good and decent people, who look to me to do my best. God has apparently dictated the limits of what that is to be, but He also gave me you. And you are my highest responsibility. If I fail to protect you, Elizabeth, what am I?"

She laughed brokenly, finding it necessary to mop her face again with the heel of her hand. "You are a fine one for the speeches. Now, what am I supposed to say in return to measure up to that?"

"Love has no measure, Elizabeth. You show yours in everything you do."

"Oh, now, I truly am a puddle, Fitzwilliam Darcy. Bloody unfair of you, I say."

"I never claimed to play by any rules." He grinned and touched her chin. "I do love that you care for Pemberley as I do, Elizabeth. While I cannot say what will happen beyond my tenure, at least I know one thing. My home has a fine mistress."

She caught his hand and pulled it from her face with an arch look. "Oughtn't we think at least a little about the future? Surely, there is something we could do to prepare—"

"Oh, as to that, I shouldn't worry," he replied lightly. "In order to inherit, Wickham would have to outlive me."

She glanced hesitantly down at his legs, and for an instant, her mind filled with all the things she had heard about invalids, and how his injury would inevitably compromise his health as a whole. "That... that is true," she confessed.

"I see you doubt me. Have you not heard what is said about married men, my love? They live much longer than those who live in vice. The saying is thought particularly true when the man is happy in his marriage. Now, who, I ask you, has more cause for happiness than I?"

She was laughing by now, helpless before those dimples he would display from time to time when he was truly smiling. "Who, indeed?"

Chapter Thirty-Five

D ARCY SMILED SOFTLY DOWN at the open estate ledger spread across his desk. The orderly columns of figures blurred at the edges of his vision as Elizabeth's lilting chatter drifted in from the entrance hall. Even the familiar sounds of her cordially directing the maids as they attended to their duties filled his breast with contentment lately. She had become a warm ray of sunshine gracing Pemberley's halls, one he vowed solemnly never to take for granted again.

A fortnight had passed since Richard's awkward departure, and he and Elizabeth had, after some days, extended an olive branch, of sorts. A letter written by the both of them, requesting distance enough for time to work its healing potion, but still speaking of their hopes for reconciliation. And a reply had come today—words that went some distance toward breaking down what remained of Darcy's indignation over the affair.

But it was not Richard's letter that had set Pemberley astir this afternoon. Elizabeth had also received word from her eldest sister. Jane Bennet would arrive in less than a week, escorted by Mr and Mrs Gardiner. And Darcy had never heard Elizabeth laugh quite so gaily as she had when she clasped that letter to her heart and danced around his chair earlier.

An expanding warmth suffused his being as he listened to all the preparations taking place in the hall. His wife deserved the full measure of joy that the reunion with her family would certainly bring. Heaven knew, she had risked and sacrificed too much by selflessly joining her future with his over these last painful months. He owed her this, a thousand times over.

How ardently he yearned for her to want nothing at all, and to be able to surround her continuously with pure felicity for choosing a fate bound to his. Why, now that Georgiana was very nearly her old self and so many of the fears of the winter had passed, he was ready to throw open Pemberley's doors and invite the remainder of Elizabeth's lively Bennet contingent to descend *en masse*. Her initial gently amused demurrals at such a lavish prospect had not deterred him from envisioning far grander hospitality.

Only that morning, he had repeated the notion, only to have her blush and roll her eyes. "William, I tell you again, you do not know what you are saying. Truly, to have Mama and Lydia under this roof? You would never speak to me again!"

"Nonsense! Surely Pemberley's halls will prove more than commodious enough," he had declared.

Elizabeth's warm laughter had subsided into wry acknowledgement. "Indeed, your magnanimity outstrips your good sense at times, husband. I expect you shall quickly repent of such sweeping permission once my mother descends amidst her fluttering handkerchiefs and overflowing opinions. Even my father's biting sarcasm may not balance her, ah... *enthusiasm* for every aspect of your home and life generally."

"I know what it is. I embarrass you. Is that it?" This, he had said with a smirk and a fond touch to her cheek, softening the little quip, but if he confessed it to himself, there had been a touch of earnestness to his question. *Was* she embarrassed by him? As far as he knew, only her father and elder sister knew of his injury. To the rest of the family, he remained an imposing enigma—the strange, wealthy man who had, for reasons unknown, carried their daughter and sister away to a reclusive "wedding tour" on another continent. Perhaps Mrs Bennet would be the sort of mother to mock him when she learned the truth, or lament over her daughter's poor misfortunes in such a husband.

But Elizabeth swatted his shoulder playfully, vibrant mirth transforming her fine eyes into lambent pools of old brandy that set his sluggish blood ablaze. "No, I am afraid *they* will embarrass *me*! But what is family if we cannot endure a little humiliation at their hands, now and again? Do not say I did not warn you, though."

"Nonsense. I have spent eight months shackled to you. How much worse can they be?"

Elizabeth had set her hands on her hips to lower her face to his and issue a mock laugh, just before kissing his nose. "Very true! Well, then, since your stout manly nerves have already endured the most wayward of the pack, surely the remaining Bennets shall pose no undue imposition. Very well, husband, I shall extend the invitation. But do not be surprised if your serene country life rapidly transforms into ongoing chaos under our collective whirlwind."

He was still chuckling about that conversation this afternoon, hours later, as he tried to accomplish something worthwhile at his desk. But all he could think was to wonder what Miss Bennet and Elizabeth's aunt and uncle would think of his wife, now that she had been his wife for some while. Would they find her changed?

Hopefully. But not diminished—heaven forbid they should find that. He prayed instead they would find her flourishing, blossoming into all she had been meant to become. He, at least, suffered no end of pride, watching her growing confidence with every passing day commanding Pemberley.

He should send her to London for a modiste who could dress her with the sort of elegance she deserved. Perhaps he would write a letter to Lady Matlock, asking if she would escort both Elizabeth and Georgiana to—

Absorbed in this new idea, Darcy was leaning forward to reach for a fresh sheet of paper when his body jolted suddenly with a sharp tingling sensation, spearing into his left thigh. Sudden shock froze his breath, half exhaled from his lungs as if a dagger had lanced through his flesh. His quill dropped to the desk, forgotten as it bled an unsightly pool of ink all over the page.

"What the devil?" he muttered. He pressed his hand into the top of his thigh... nothing. Gently, he smoothed down his trousers, his breath still ragged in astonishment. Could he be going mad?

That was the leg Hercules had pinned, and the bruising had been deep and ugly, so much so that it looked worse after a week than it did when it was fresh. Now, it was a green and blue mottled nightmare, and indeed, had he been able to feel it, it would have been excruciating. Even the healing process would have been unbearable, bone-deep itching that probably would have kept him awake at night. Elizabeth had been optimistically rubbing arnica over the bruise, but he had been sceptical of any benefit. Time was the only healer he had ever known for a great purple swelling like that.

Darcy's heart was still pounding as his hand squeezed his numb thigh. "Just my imagination," he assured himself. "There, see? Nothing." Good heavens, what if anyone saw him twitching and slapping at ghost sensations in his legs? They would think he had gone dotty in the head.

And now he had a mess of ink to clean up. Darcy sighed and picked up the corners of the ruined paper, then rolled the whole thing in upon itself to toss it in the dustbin.

He was just reaching for another new sheet of writing paper when it happened again. This time, he yelped and lurched back in his chair, gasping with panic. Sweet merciful God, was his own mind now taunting him? Silence shattered as his pounding heartbeat roared against his eardrums. He gripped his thigh fiercely enough to leave fingerprint bruises through the fabric of his trousers. Then... nothing.

Crushing disappointment bore down as the phantom agony receded as swiftly as it had struck. Throat cinching shut, he let his forehead drop into both trembling hands with a guttural groan that was half anguished laugh, half bitter sob. Was he to start fantasising about odd pains now, after more than six months of deadness?

He had just accustomed himself to this strange new existence. Had he not made his peace with matters? Why, then, would his mind be playing such tricks?

But... what if it was *not* his mind? What if...

Experimentally, Darcy shifted forward again. Both times, he had felt the sensation when he was in a specific posture. What was it? A little stretch from the rib cage, a bow of his spine and a firm reach of his arm...

Nothing.

Well, so much for vain optimism. He scowled faintly, but what did he really expect? He might as well return to his tasks so he could rejoin Elizabeth all the sooner.

After dragging the nearest volume straight once more, he cleared more blotched and scattered papers aside to select a fresh sheet before reaching again for the nearby quill. Keeping busy was the best way he knew how to put his mind back on an orderly path, as it had been. Heaven knew he had fought hard enough for that little ribbon of peace, and he was not about to let some cruel figment of his imagination snatch it away now.

But attempting to resume his abandoned task proved unusually difficult, as his still clumsy fingers and palms were sticky with drying perspiration. The cursed quill twitched and splattered fat, erratic inkblots across the paper's pristine surface before he could begin committing any coherent line of thought.

He stretched his neck up and back, trying to work out a knot in his shoulders from too long already bunched over his desk. What had he even been doing before he got distracted? Oh, yes! A letter to Lady Matlock. But now, he had made such a hash of his desk's surface that he would almost have to call a footman in to help him reach what used to be a neat pile of sheets on the far left corner of his desk.

Hoping to spare himself at least that little embarrassment, he pushed up in his chair a little and stretched as far as he could go. The bloody front wheel of the thing swivelled slightly, almost ready to roll away and topple him, but Darcy caught the edge of the desk and, with the strength of his forearm, pulled the nose of his chair back where it belonged...

And there it was again. Stronger, even, than before—like a knife plunging into his hamstrings, followed by a tingling itch that shot straight through his marrow. And never in his life had pain felt so blessedly rapturous.

Darcy's hammering heart rapidly outpaced his thinning rationale as a heady mixture of terror and intoxicating exhilaration flooded his veins. His dazed mind grappled to comprehend these bizarre, contradictory sensations assailing his battered nerves. What did it signify, that thrilling spectral agony that fled rapidly as phantom mists at dawn?

The salient fact remained that for the first time in more than eight empty months, he had *felt something* below the waist besides humiliating helplessness! What new devilment or fresh miracle transpired here?

Wildly spinning thoughts trailed off into aching silence, broken only by the ornate longcase clock ticking atop the distant mantle and his own ragged inhalation resounding harshly in the empty study. The familiar chamber seemed to dissolve into a surreal swirling dreamscape until Darcy swayed dizzily, panicked euphoria clenching his chest.

Was this bizarre phenomenon merely further indication that all rational thought had, indeed, fled his mind completely? Had the relentless trauma he had endured these many torturous months finally shattered his reason beyond recovery? Surely, he must already hover on the brink of plunging irrevocably into full frenzied madness! Darcy shuddered violently, ice flooding rigid veins while his head dropped weakly into his hands. Perhaps at long last his overwrought mind, unable to fully process all it had been forced to face, had simply splintered reason beyond repair.

But this... this felt too real to be a product of a deranged mind. Gradually, his juddering heart rate slowed, and he began to tick through remembered conversations, little snatches of phrases he had heard from this doctor or that. There existed possible logical explanations, far removed from lunacy, for these mysterious flickering agonies shooting through his deadened nerves. Could it be... possible? Could his body be mending, after he had at last given up all hope?

"No," he gritted through his teeth, grasping the edge of the desk and clenching his eyes. "It makes no sense." This was probably just a fleeting thing—a curiosity of the moment that might become a torment, bringing occasional pain but no real healing. Would not that be just his luck?

Had not the most skilful London surgeons unanimously declared his paralysis irreversible? And who was he to argue against their learned consensus? Darcy snorted derisively. As if his paltry, stubborn clinging to tenuous optimism bore any weight whatsoever in countering generations of established medical doctrine, or the laws of Almighty God!

Thus, he passed a long moment, sitting immobile behind his expensive carved desk until he loosed a shuddering breath and straightened his slumped shoulders once more. He was lord of Pemberley still, and long practised in mastering unruly moods.

Willing his heart to slow to its typical steady rhythm, Darcy dragged at the corner of his desk to turn his Bath chair slightly sideways. Once more, he began redistributing the scattered papers and quills lying higgledy-piggledy across his normally fastidiously organised desktop. How mortifying if Elizabeth discovered this dishevelled chaos and deduced his temporary lapse into maniacal folly! She would never be satisfied with a simple untruth about forgetting what he was about. No, she would force him to talk until she knew all. Lips twisting wryly, he reached to straighten the nearest inkwell back into place and wipe splattered shining black droplets marring freshly sharpened quills.

Elizabeth must not learn of this. That much, he vowed to himself. Not until he knew what there was to tell her, at least. He would not shatter the peace they had worked so hard for by igniting false hopes in her.

But... His hand stilled on the quill he was cleaning. What *could* this mean?

Would he ever feel her hands on his legs? Oh, Lord, please yes. Was it possible he might become master of those sensations he had long ago lost? Even... egad, what if he could walk again someday?

No, no, that was asking too much, surely. Just a tingle of feeling now and then, that was miracle enough.

But what if... if he did recover somewhat... even a very little would do... Was it possible?

Intense, deep yearning blazed as an impossible vision swarmed his mind—a child with his chin and her nose, the Darcy curls over his head and Elizabeth's bewitching dark eyes, cradled at her breast as she smiled up at him. If only Providence permitted some miracle, granting them children of their shared blood! Then he and she truly would be one in flesh, as they were in spirit.

That, surely, was a bit too much to hope for. He pressed his hands into his leg, hoping for yet another spasm of pain to prove the reality to his doubting mind. There was no response, not even when he twisted and stretched in all the ways that had provoked something before.

Perhaps it was not to work that way, appearing and disappearing at his pleasure. But he would be damned if he did not try to find out what more could be done. He needed to ask some questions and have some direct answers. And he needed to do it without alarming Elizabeth.

Finding fresh paper, he began scribbling several urgent missives, including a startlingly thick one addressed to Richard with candid recent developments for his cousin's perspicacious insight. The next, he dispatched to that Scottish oddity, Doctor Douglas—the only doctor to ever say anything to him resembling hope. By heaven and earth, he would thrash out the mystery, and God willing, he might, one day, have a surprise for the woman he loved.

Chapter Thirty-Six

"**T**HEY ARE HERE!"

Elizabeth flew down Pemberley's imposing front steps into the courtyard just as the Gardiners' carriage pulled up the drive. She was a flurry of billowing emerald skirts, already standing by the carriage by the time footmen opened the doors.

"Jane! Oh, my dearest Jane!" She threw her arms wide as Jane rushed into her eager embrace.

"Lizzy! It has been an age—"

"Two ages, and a half!" Heedless of her dignity as the mistress, Elizabeth squeezed her taller sister's neck, nearly dangling from her and possibly even choking the life out of her in her exuberance. They embraced for long moments, tearful laughter mingling with happy exclamations until Mr Gardiner gently interrupted, smiling indulgently.

"Well now, do I not deserve more than a cursory glance after enduring your aunt's mounting excitement each mile from London?" He winked playfully at his wife's little teasing scowl before enfolding Elizabeth into an affectionate bear hug. "Let me get a good look at you! Why, I do declare our Lizzy here looks absolutely radiant as Mistress of Pemberley!"

"Edward, really!" Mrs Gardiner hustled both sisters aside, clucking her tongue. But she quickly drew Elizabeth into a fierce maternal hug, whispering emotionally. "Oh, my dear girl, we have missed you so! Letters were woefully inadequate to truly know your daily trials..."

Sudden tears burned Elizabeth's eyes as she returned her aunt's embrace just as fervently. The loving familial intimacy she had sorely missed these many months welled over, momentarily loosening the formidable Mistress of Pemberley into Lizzy Bennet again.

"Dear Aunt, there were certainly bleak moments when I wished you had been near! But come inside, away from the chill wind." Eagerly, she shepherded them all into the entrance hall as the footmen began unloading their trunks. "You must be famished from your travels, and I have ordered rooms made up for you in the family wing. Oh, Jane, you will adore Miss Darcy. Uncle, Mr Darcy was sorry he could not come down the steps to greet you, but he is waiting in the hall."

Elizabeth turned slightly to lead them in, but a soft tug at her elbow made her pause. "Lizzy," her aunt whispered, "You must forgive my indelicacy last autumn. We did not know... Jane told us on the journey, about Mr Darcy. How... ah... are you certain we are not a burden to him? And are you... well?"

She tucked her aunt's hand under her elbow and smiled. "Mr Darcy is very well, and he is looking forward to meeting you. You shall see, Aunt, we are quite the happiest couple alive." She leaned close to whisper, "I *have* missed you all, though. We shall not be parted for so long again, shall we?"

Jane had taken Elizabeth's other arm, hugging it close as if unwilling to let her go for even a second as they walked. "I am so dearly pleased to hear Mr Darcy is well. I felt so for the poor man! You must have been a great comfort to him, Lizzy, but I confess to an indecent amount of jealousy that he could lay claim to your time and affections while I must do without."

Elizabeth laughed. "Jane Bennet! That is as close to a reprimand as I have ever heard from you. Brava! Come, we will get you to your bath, then have all manner of scandalous talk and cry an abundance of tears, after which we shall be merry once more. Oh, and there is Mr Darcy waiting for us. Do try not to let him know how impudent and headstrong I am. I nearly have him convinced that I am quite the fine lady."

They were climbing the steps by now, and William had overheard every word of her last two sentences, for he was laughing and extending a hand for her to take. "Not a bit of it, Miss Bennet. I suffer no illusions regarding your sister's irreverence." He bowed his head to Mr Gardiner. "Fitzwilliam Darcy, at your service, sir. We are pleased you could make the journey."

Elizabeth's uncle made her proud in the way he doffed his hat and returned William's greeting—respectfully, as one greeting an equal, rather than grovelling before William's consequence, as she was certain many did, or disdainfully, as one looking down on a man in a Bath chair. "Mr Darcy, we are honoured by the invitation. May I present my wife, Mrs Gardiner? And my niece, Miss Jane Bennet, you already know."

William squeezed Elizabeth's fingers as he inclined his head to her aunt and sister. "Indeed. Welcome, ladies. My sister, Miss Georgiana Darcy, is eager to make your acquaintance. She is in the music room and will greet you after you have refreshed yourselves."

Elizabeth was not blind to the subtle lift of Jane's brows, but Mr and Mrs Gardiner's faces reflected only serene pleasure. So, Jane was curious about Miss Darcy's recovery—for Elizabeth had written certain specifics to her—but apparently that was a detail she had kept from their aunt and uncle. So much the better, for Georgiana's sake.

Elizabeth glowed with burgeoning delight as she led the procession towards the upstairs bedchambers. William's little signs of thoughtfulness toward her family showed in the way he had invited her uncle to join him for cigars in an hour, the kind way he had asked after her aunt's relations in Lambton, and the gentle familiarity he showed to Jane, whose former acquaintance with him had been less than promising. Aunt and Uncle were already complimenting her on her husband—his kindness, obvious intelligence, and pleasing manners as they were shown to their rooms.

At that, she did have to chuckle. Elizabeth knew enough of her husband by now to be assured, with absolute conviction, that his manners might not have always been declared "pleasing," even before his accident. But he was so very pleasing now.

"Lizzy, what luxury!" Jane's wondering voice echoed in the enormous room to which Elizabeth led her. She wandered in some awe near the ornately canopied bed, draped in embroidered silk counterpanes and fat down pillows. She caressed the intricate velvet bed hangings, astonishment softly lighting her delicate features taking in the space appointed specially for her visit. "Why, everything looks so elegant I fear even breathing, lest I disturb the perfection."

"As if your very presence does not make any room more wonderful!" Elizabeth hugged her sister impulsively once more before busying herself opening the nearest trunks. "But come, let us find you a fresh gown after those dusty roads. The maid is drawing your bath, and Mrs Reynolds prepares a small nuncheon downstairs once you have refreshed yourself a bit."

"Lizzy, there is..." Jane paused, nibbling her lip and holding up a staying hand. "There is something I wanted to ask you."

Elizabeth straightened from the trunk. "What is it?"

Jane tugged at one finger with her opposite hand, her eyes shifting. "I meant to ask you before, but I could not put such a thing down in a letter. I know that... that is to say, Miss Bingley often spoke of coming to Pemberley in the summers..."

"And you fear that the Bingleys will come here during your stay? You need have no fear of that."

"No, do you see, that is precisely the opposite of what I had hoped. I shan't wish to see them again—any of them—but neither do I wish for Mr Darcy to deny his friend simply because I am here. I shall keep my visit short if they are already making plans to—"

"Jane." Elizabeth closed in, cupping her beloved sister's cheeks in her hands. "I cannot say how sweet and dear you are for even thinking of such a thing, but you see, Mr Darcy is even better. He has written a rather scathing letter to his friend for the abominable way he treated you. And as a result, I regret to say, they are friends no longer."

Jane's brow creased, and she sank down on the counterpane. "Oh, dear. I never meant to break up a friendship of such long standing."

"Nor did Mr Darcy." Elizabeth sat down beside her sister and took her hands in her own. "He was as indignant as I when he read your letter, but he wrote to Mr Bingley fully expecting that the matter required only a simple explanation. I regret to say he was dissatisfied in the gentleman's response."

Jane swallowed. "Tell me, Lizzy. I suffer no illusions that he ever means to come back for me, but tell me all, so that I may know that I have lost nothing of great worth."

"I am not certain you will find it of much comfort. Mr Bingley wrote that he did fancy you—quite ardently, in fact. But there were other complications that, in his mind, prevented him from declaring himself."

"Ohhhh." Jane lowered her eyes. "I think I know what it was."

"Our sister, of course."

"And his own sisters, who held us in no regard." Jane sniffed and raised a shoulder. "'Twould take a powerful attachment to overcome society's disdain for us all."

"But he had the power to do it, had he but the inclination. That was what enraged William so—forgive me, but I scarcely ever call him Mr Darcy, as we are so little in company. William was irate that Mr Bingley was of two minds in his dealings with you. If he could not endure the world's censure for taking an interest in you, then he ought to have guarded himself better. As it was, I would warrant he made matters worse when he left for London than they ever were before he arrived."

"Very much so." Jane sighed. "But it is in the past now. And Mama will not let anyone forget how advantageously you married, most particularly the Lucases."

Elizabeth chuckled. "How is Charlotte?"

Jane sniffed and fumbled in the pocket of her travelling gown. "She sent a letter for you. I think she was ready to stow away in the carriage boot when I left Longbourn."

"Then I shall be sure to invite her soon, as well." Elizabeth took the letter and could not help smelling it, as if it could imbue all the fragrances of Hertfordshire between the lines of ink. "Come, darling. I am sure the maid has your bath drawn now, and we can talk more of how disappointing men are in general after you are warm and comfortable."

Jane permitted Elizabeth to tug her to her feet but then stayed for a moment, squeezing Elizabeth's hands. "I know that for a pretty little falsehood, Lizzy. You are happy with Mr Darcy. I can see it in your eyes. You cannot know what a relief that is to me!"

"And a surprise, I warrant."

"Yes, indeed! I thought one of you two would have thrown the other out of the house long before now."

"It was a near thing, once or twice! But I love him now, so very dearly. I only wish there were another such man for you."

"No, for I see your radiance. I think you could give me forty such men, and I would still not be as happy as you are. Until I have your determination and your dignity, I could never—"

"Say it properly, Jane. My *stubbornness,* and no small measure of cheek. And it has, by some miracle, stood me in good stead. Now, come, for your bath is getting cold."

E LIZABETH DESCENDED THE STAIRS slowly, not wanting to cut short the delightful laughter still lingering between her aunt, sister and herself. What a pleasure to be with them again! She would have to make the most of the next few days before Aunt and Uncle left for London again.

As they passed the study, Elizabeth overheard her husband conversing within and slowed her steps to listen. She was surprised to make out not only his mellow tones, but also the laughter of a handful of others. There was her uncle's laugh—she knew that sound well. Then, an unfamiliar voice that certainly did not belong to any of the footmen.

But it was the bark of laughter that followed it that almost made her quake out of her slippers.

Richard?

Elizabeth halted with a faint gasp, drawing a curious look from her aunt before she remembered herself and resumed her pace. What could have brought *him* back to Pemberley so soon? Indeed, they had reconciled in the form of letters, but she would never have imagined that William would welcome the man back already, and without even warning her. Curiosity mounting, she determined to investigate once her relations were comfortably settled.

"Do allow me to introduce my new sister Georgiana first," Elizabeth offered brightly, steering them towards the music room. "She can be rather shy with strangers, but I know you shall put her at ease."

Aunt Gardiner smiled encouragingly. "Of course, we should be delighted! From your glowing letters, I feel as though I know the dear girl already."

As soon as introductions were made, Georgiana did, indeed, warm to her new acquaintances with gratifying swiftness. Watching her tentative smiles blossom, Elizabeth felt it safe to take her leave after only a quarter-hour or so. She was too eager to discover what unexpected reunion was occurring down the hall to linger longer.

Making her excuses, she retraced swift steps to the study and tapped lightly before entering without waiting for a response. Four heads turned in unison to greet her—William's with a smile of welcome crinkling his eyes, her uncle's with a pleased, "Ah, there she is!", and an unknown greying gentleman who promptly turned to acknowledge her with a polite bow.

Colonel Fitzwilliam, however, looked as if he would prefer to crawl under William's desk. He stood back, his hands clasped behind him and his eyes scarcely daring to lift to hers as she drew near.

She glanced at William, for his manner would inform hers. He inclined his head slightly, raising his brows as if to beg her, *"Be polite,"* and offering a faint smile. Well, that was enough for now. She would wring an explanation out of him later.

"Welcome, Colonel," she greeted him softly, extending her hand.

A great sigh of relief rushed from him, and he stepped forward to place a gentlemanly endearment on her fingertips. "Mrs Darcy. I beg you would forgive me for taking you by surprise like this, showing up unannounced."

"No forgiveness necessary, I assure you, but what brings you from London?"

"Business," William interjected before Richard could form a word. "My dear, allow me to present... Mr James, from London. Mr James, my wife, Mrs Elizabeth Darcy."

She offered the man a smile and dipped a curtsey as he bowed. "Charmed, sir. I do beg you would excuse me, but I have other guests awaiting me in the blue salon. I only wished to offer my greetings."

"One moment, my dear." William held up a hand, and as if reading his mind, Richard was at the rear of the Bath chair, pushing him forward to speak to her. "I was hoping you would invite Mr Gardiner and my cousin to join the ladies in taking refreshments. Mr James and I have... a rather important matter to discuss."

She felt one eyebrow climbing her forehead, but she smothered the dubious expression as quickly as she knew how. "Of course. Colonel, you will remember my aunt, Mrs Gardiner, and my sister, Miss Jane Bennet, I believe?"

Was it her imagination, or did the colonel's expression soften ever so slightly on the mention of Jane? He smiled politely. "With pleasure. I would be delighted to see them again."

"And I am sure they will be equally pleased to meet you."

But before they could go, William caught her attention once more. "My apologies for the lack of forewarning, my dear. Truly, I believed it would be some days before I had word of... the affairs at hand. My cousin is swifter than the post, it seems. I am only honoured that Mr James could attend him as well."

He shared another meaningful glance with the two gentlemen that piqued Elizabeth's curiosity further as to what mysterious business was so pressing. But she knew better than to pry openly in mixed company. Oh, she would most certainly pin him down later for a full and complete explanation.

For now, however, she smiled invitingly. "Well, I am certainly pleased to meet any friend of yours, Colonel, even unexpectedly. I hope Mr James' stay proves enjoyable and productive for you both." Glancing between them, she added politely, "Shall we all remove to the blue salon and see if there remain any refreshments after we ladies have made free with them?"

Richard's soft chuckle as he followed her from the room... well, it was everything. Everything that it used to be—cheerful and ready to be entertained, easy and yet discreet enough that it did not even begin to make her uncomfortable.

And that was as it should be. She still meant to have words on the matter, but this was a promising beginning, at least.

She offered him one quick smile as the footman opened the door to the blue salon, and that was the last that he looked at her at all, for at least half an hour. For it seemed he did remember Jane with pleasure... a great deal of pleasure.

Chapter Thirty-Seven

D ARCY'S FINGERS DRUMMED AN anxious rhythm on the armrest of his chair as he watched Elizabeth escorting Richard and her uncle from the study. The surprise of his cousin's arrival just on the heels of Elizabeth's family had caused Darcy a moment of panic, but the fact that Richard had brought with him Doctor James from London, the surgeon who had examined him upon his first injury... well, his cousin could have conceived of no more effective ticket to buy his way back into Darcy's good graces.

Elizabeth might be harder to convince—by the look in her eye, she still meant to exact her pound of flesh from the man who had humiliated her. But even at that, he could see by the swift way that she composed herself that there was still hope for Richard in Elizabeth's opinion.

Now, to find out if there was any hope for himself.

"Doctor James, thank you for coming on such short notice," Darcy said, gesturing for the man to take a seat nearby. "I apologise for not properly introducing you to Mr Gardiner and Mrs Darcy earlier. I hope you understand my desire to prevent any speculation on their parts regarding the matters I wish to discuss with you today."

"Of course, Mr Darcy. Discretion is paramount in my profession," Doctor James assured him, setting his satchel down and taking the proffered chair. "Now, shall we begin the examination?"

Darcy nodded, a flicker of apprehension crossing his features. "Yes, please. But first, would you mind locking the study door? I would prefer complete privacy for this conversation."

The doctor obliged, securing the lock before returning to Darcy's side. "Very well, Mr Darcy. Please describe to me any changes or sensations you have experienced in your lower limbs since we last met."

As Doctor James began his methodical examination, Darcy recounted the intermittent shooting pangs in his left leg, drawing attention to the faint green hue that lingered from the deep bruise sustained a month prior. "And there is something else," Darcy added hesitantly. "In the past few days, I have detected a faint sensation, no larger than a thumbprint, on my right hip. It is a new development."

"Is it? Most intriguing." The doctor's brow furrowed in concentration as he carefully tested Darcy's lower limbs for signs of returning sensation. Darcy watched the man's face intently, searching for any glimmer of optimism, but found the doctor's expression frustratingly inscrutable.

"The circulation appears excellent. I must say, Mr Darcy, I rarely see such health in legs that have been unused."

"I have Mrs Darcy's excellent care to thank for that," Darcy murmured, unable to keep a hint of pride from his voice. He leaned forward as far as he was able, watching the doctor carefully and almost afraid to breathe, lest it disrupt the man's findings.

As the examination concluded, Doctor James cleared his throat, his demeanour sombre and clinical. "Mr Darcy, it is not uncommon for individuals recovering from traumatic spinal injuries to believe they are experiencing occasional flickers of sensation, such as those you've described."

Darcy leaned forward still more, his heart pounding with a mixture of hope and trepidation. "What does this mean, Doctor? Will I regain the ability to walk?"

The doctor's apologetic gaze met Darcy's, his words measured and cautious. "Mr Darcy, while these sensations are encouraging, assuming they are genuine, I must advise against harbouring unrealistic expectations. In my experience, the likelihood of a full recovery, particularly the restoration of ambulatory function, is not optimistic."

Darcy felt the weight of disappointment settle heavily upon his shoulders, a crushing realisation that he had unwittingly allowed himself to hope for the impossible. Swallowing past the lump in his throat, he pressed on, his voice strained. "What about other faculties, Doctor? Might I at least recover those?" With a delicate pause, Darcy added, "Mrs Darcy and I... we wish to have a child."

Doctor James hesitated, his expression a mixture of compassion and professional reserve. "While I cannot say it is impossible, Mr Darcy, I would be remiss in inciting false hope. The extent of your recovery is difficult to predict with certainty. It has, after all, been several months, with no signs further than these."

Darcy's heart sank further, his excitement crumbling to dust in the face of the doctor's measured words. He nodded, not trusting his voice to remain steady.

The doctor, sensing Darcy's despair, attempted to inject a note of cheer into his tone as he packed up his medical satchel. "Mr Darcy, I must say, I am pleased to see how well you have mended, given the circumstances. It would not surprise me if you continue to experience occasional odd sensations, but I caution against expecting a full recovery of your ability to walk. Such cases are exceedingly rare—in fact, I have never seen it personally."

Mustering his well-practised facade of composure, Darcy forced a smile. "Thank you for your candour, Doctor James. Might I offer you some refreshment before you depart?"

The doctor's apprehension was palpable as he declined the offer. "That is very kind of you, Mr Darcy, but I believe I shall retire to the inn in Lambton. Colonel Fitzwilliam has generously provided ample payment for my return journey to London, and I intend to set out first thing in the morning."

Darcy nodded, his smile not quite reaching his eyes. "Very well, Doctor. I wish you a safe journey, and thank you again for your time and expertise."

As the doctor took his leave, Darcy turned his gaze to the window, his vision blurring with unshed tears of discouragement. He had so desperately wanted to share good news with Elizabeth, to offer her hope for a future unburdened by his limitations. But perhaps it was a mercy that she had not been riding the same wave of optimism, sparing her the crushing disappointment that now dragged upon his soul.

Drawing a steadying breath, Darcy closed his eyes, seeking solace in the knowledge that Elizabeth's love for him transcended the boundaries of his physical condition. Whatever else might set him down, at least he had that.

L ATER THAT EVENING, DARCY sat in his room in pensive silence, his thoughts a tumultuous whirlwind in the wake of Doctor James's discouraging prognosis. The creaking of floorboards beneath Richard's agitated pacing served as a staccato accompaniment to the crackling hearth, but Darcy had not the heart to lift his eyes to his gesticulating cousin.

"Blind or inept, I tell you!" Fitzwilliam sputtered, his voice rising with each emphatic step. "The symptoms you described in your letter, Darcy—there's simply no way they don't indicate healing. That doctor must be a fool!"

Darcy's gaze remained fixed on the dancing flames, his cousin's words echoing the desperate hopes that had taken root in his own heart. He certainly would have thought the things he was feeling were more than promising, but if they were to flicker out and lead nowhere... well, what was the point in denying reality? He would perhaps not be quite so numb to all sensation, but in a practical sense, the improvement meant nothing of import.

"Darcy?" Fitzwilliam's pacing slowed, concern etching his features. "You seem very quiet. Are you still angry with me? If so, I invite you to speak your mind. I'll gladly bear whatever chastisement you deem necessary. By Jove, it would be better to have you scorching my ears than to look at you sitting there in misery."

A heavy sigh escaped him, and he shook his head, finally meeting Fitzwilliam's gaze. "From me, at least, there is nothing more to forgive, Richard."

A wry smile tugged at Fitzwilliam's mouth. "Ah, but Mrs Darcy might be another matter entirely, I suspect."

Darcy's own lips twitched in response. "Indeed. I suggest you practise your compliments and mind your manners in the lady's presence."

"Mind my manners, indeed." Fitzwilliam's laughter held a wistful note. "Funny, isn't it? Not so long ago, it was I cautioning *you* to mind your manners before her."

Darcy acknowledged the irony with a silent smile, his thoughts drifting to those early days when Elizabeth had effortlessly unravelled his carefully constructed defences. Richard's admonishments regarding currying the lady's favour were hardly necessary beyond that first uncomfortable meeting. It was not long before he had considered her the most remarkable woman of his acquaintance and craved her good opinion.

As Fitzwilliam's pacing resumed, albeit at a more sedate pace, he ventured cautiously, "At least I was right about one thing, Cousin."

Darcy's attention snapped back to the present, his brow arching in inquiry. "And what might that be?"

"Bringing you and Mrs Darcy together," Richard replied, a touch of pride colouring his tone. "When I first encountered her, I had high hopes that she could be just the sort of encouragement you so desperately needed. But even I am pleasantly surprised by how far she has exceeded my expectations."

A soft smile graced Darcy's features, his voice filled with quiet conviction. "Richard, if I had to do it all again—every moment, even my injury—I would, without hesitation, if it meant having Elizabeth in my life."

Fitzwilliam nodded, satisfaction evident in his manner as he finally settled into a chair, leaning forward with an altered expression that could not help but signify a shift in topic. Darcy straightened in his own seat, curiosity piqued by his cousin's shift in demeanour. "Oh, dear. This looks serious."

"It is. I've been considering retiring from the army," Fitzwilliam confessed, his words measured and deliberate. "Mother has deeded me the estate in Scotland. A ruin, I know, but I plan to sell the land and, combined with a small fortune set aside by Father, establish myself in a modest home somewhere, leaving military life behind."

Darcy's eyebrows shot up in surprise, a genuine smile spreading across his face. "That is wonderful news! If there is anything I can do to assist you in this endeavour, you need only ask."

Relief washed over Richard's features, his shoulders visibly relaxing. "I had hoped you would not be displeased."

"Displeased, why would I be?"

"Because a very short time ago, you would have cheerfully seen me taken down by musket shot in Spain, I am sure of it."

Darcy scoffed. "You had not been gone an hour before I was persuading myself to forgive you. We... We have been through too much together for me to doubt your intentions. Your delivery, however..."

"Aye," Richard sighed heavily. "And that is why I hesitated. I mean to continue to give Mrs Darcy a wide berth—"

"Not too wide, I hope, or she will think you despise her."

"Good heavens, how am I to know what to do? Too familiar, and the lady will be made uncomfortable, too distant, and she will feel disdain even if it was unintended."

Darcy chuckled. "You know her too well to believe that she will leave you any room for doubt. Had she been unwilling to grant you a second chance, we would not now be having this conversation."

"That much, I am sure of. I am glad of it, for if I do leave the army, I anticipate our paths will cross all the more often. And Darcy, there is something you should know, now while the thing is fresh. After... that conversation and my removal to London, I spent a great deal of time reflecting on things."

"Such as?"

He lifted one shoulder. "Duty and honour and sacrifice—you know, the soldier's bit. And perhaps there is one thing all my training has overlooked. I believe I've come to understand your unwillingness to disrupt the harmony of your home and marriage for the sake of duty alone."

Darcy nodded. "'Tis a rather cold comfort, is it not? I would far rather honour those dear to me than hypothetical generations in the future who will never even recall my name."

"Well put." Richard shifted in his chair, his eyes drifting to the floor as he made himself more comfortable. "You have found something worthwhile, at least. I can only hope that someday, I might find the same happiness you have, Darcy."

Darcy's grin widened as a mischievous thought struck him. "You know, Richard, it might be wise for you to make a concerted effort to ingratiate yourself with Mrs Darcy."

Puzzlement creased Fitzwilliam's brow. "Why is that?"

Darcy's smile turned enigmatic. "Perhaps it is within my power to return the favour you once bestowed upon me, by bringing you into company with a lady who might prove to be your perfect match."

Richard blinked, confusion momentarily clouding his features before realisation dawned, and a hearty laugh escaped his lips. "Mrs Darcy's sister, Miss Jane Bennet! Darcy, you sly devil!"

"Sly? Or just more clever than you? Take care to mind your manners, Richard."

D ARCY RECLINED AGAINST THE plush pillows, his eyes fixed on the door as he awaited Elizabeth's arrival for their nightly ritual. It swung open only a moment later, and Elizabeth swept into the room, her musical laughter filling the air. Darcy's heart swelled at the sight of her, his lips curving into a smile. "What has you so amused, my love?"

Elizabeth grinned, her eyes sparkling with mirth. "You will never guess who I just encountered in the hall, down on his knees with a bouquet of spring daisies."

Darcy's eyebrows shot up in mock surprise. "Richard? On his knees?"

"The very same," Elizabeth confirmed, settling herself on the edge of the bed. "I thought for a moment he looked as if he was about to propose marriage, but the poor fellow looked so contrite that I had to ask what he was about."

"And what was he about?" Darcy asked, trying to hide a smile.

"I suppose 'someone' has let it be known that he has not quite yet redeemed himself in my opinions, and he is now going out of his way to win my favour again."

Darcy tsked. "If he wins too much of your favour, I shall have to call him out. I think I am still a fair shot with a pistol."

"Cheeky fellow! I believe he is quite too afraid of either of us to make a single wrong step. At any rate, he was most friendly and easy, and I no longer despise him. You may tell him he can stop tiptoeing around me."

A smug expression settled on Darcy's features. "He will be pleased to hear it. I have a guess as to why he's working so diligently to regain your approval."

"Because of Jane, is it not?"

Darcy did not even have to feign his surprise. "Why, how did you know?"

She scoffed. "Oh, please. The colonel has been staring at Jane whenever they are in the same room since his arrival. I am not blind, William."

"Has Miss Bennet noticed his attentions?"

Elizabeth pondered for a moment. "I do not believe so. She has been rather preoccupied. Aunt Gardiner noticed, though."

Darcy's brow furrowed slightly. "Is she still nursing her disappointment after Bingley's defection?"

"No, I am quite certain that is not the case," Elizabeth replied confidently. "Jane is thoroughly disillusioned with Mr Bingley and determined to think of him no more. But with such a disappointment still so fresh, that might make it more challenging for another man to win her favour."

A glimmer of satisfaction flickered in Darcy's eyes. "Perhaps Richard deserves to work for a lady's favour. Some might say you let him off too easily."

Elizabeth leaned in, pressing a playful kiss to his lips. "In the interest of harmony between cousins, I am willing to overlook a great deal. But I must admit, I was rather gratified by the flowers, even if I know he plucked them from my own garden."

Darcy chuckled as Elizabeth began her nightly massage, her skilled fingers kneading his legs with practised precision. As she worked, a startling sensation bloomed beneath her touch—a new prickle of awareness, like the gentle caress of a feather, on his left thigh. Darcy's breath caught in his throat, his heart pounding with a heady mixture of excitement and disbelief. He could feel her hand, the warmth of her skin seeping into the cold space of his muscle, in a palm-sized patch that had previously been numb!

The urge to share this revelation with her surged through him, but the doctor's warnings about false hope echoed in his mind, tempering his enthusiasm. No! Better to wait, to see if the sensation persisted before igniting her expectations.

Elizabeth's voice broke through his reverie. "What business brought Mr James to Pemberley today, William? And why was it so important that Richard dragged him all the way from London?"

Darcy schooled his features, aiming for nonchalance. "What makes you think he came at Richard's pleasure?"

She fixed him with a sarcastic look and an arched brow.

He cleared his throat, drumming his fingers on the counterpane as he searched for a plausible explanation. "It is related to the entail, I'm afraid. No new information, unfortunately."

Elizabeth hummed in disappointment, her fingers continuing their gentle ministrations. Each time she brushed over the spot where sensation had returned, Darcy's heart leapt with barely contained elation. Yet, the fear that this newfound feeling could vanish as quickly as it had appeared kept his excitement in check. He couldn't bear the thought of raising her hopes, only to have them dashed if the sensation proved fleeting.

But it was there, clearly. And the certainty of it, the conviction that his skin would keep sensing her fingers with each repetition, only grew.

Later, as Elizabeth finished the massage and curled into his arms, Darcy held her close, pressing a tender kiss to her forehead. "I do not believe I have ever properly thanked you for the way you've faithfully tended to my legs these past months," he murmured, his voice thick with emotion. "I am certain your care is the reason I'm as healthy as I am."

Elizabeth's sleepy reply warmed his heart. "You make the duty a pleasant one, my love."

As she drifted off to sleep in his embrace, Darcy marvelled at the incredible woman he had the privilege to call his wife. Her unwavering devotion and the renewed sensation in his leg filled him with cautious optimism, a glimmer of hope for a future even brighter than he had dared to imagine.

Chapter Thirty-Eight

"I AM SO PLEASED that William has taken to riding Hercules again," Elizabeth said, shifting the basket she was carrying as she and Jane set out across the spring lawn. "And what a relief that Colonel Fitzwilliam now rides with him instead of scolding him for leaving his chair. It brings him such joy—both being on horseback again and having his cousin's company. I can see the improvement in his spirits each time he returns from a ride."

Jane smiled, squinting slightly into the afternoon sunlight. "It is wonderful to see Mr Darcy so active and engaged, Lizzy. I know how much it means to you both."

"And I've no doubt it must be restorative for his body, as well. I did not tell you, Jane, but I quite think my husband is keeping secrets from me."

"Oh?" Jane's feet slowed. "Surely not. Why, I think I have never seen a couple more devoted to one another, or a husband who so freely shares his confidences with his wife. What could he be keeping from you?"

"Well, this past week or two, I have noted a sharp increase in the strength of his arms. Now, that alone might not be much, particularly as they were already quite strong. But the more I thought about it, the more I realised that when he holds me close, he is able to twist his body to my comfort in a way he could not before."

Jane's ears reddened, and she fixed her eyes woodenly on the path. "Lizzy, you probably ought not to tell me—"

"But do you not see? He could not reposition himself like that after his injury. It required some measure of control over his lower body to anchor itself so his upper body could move freely. I have to wonder how much his riding has to do with that because he has had to find some way to keep himself stable in the saddle."

Her sister still looked vastly uncomfortable with all this talk of body parts and holding and such, but she wetted her lips and ventured, "I daresay that *does* sound promising. Have you made no mention to him of your observations?"

"No, for the last time I tried to compliment him by saying how well I liked the way he had his arms about me, he cut me off by tickling me soundly in the ribs and kissing my neck until I could only laugh."

Jane gulped. "Oh, Lizzy, I feel I oughtn't hear—"

"Clearly, he is hiding something," Elizabeth broke in. "He would never interrupt that sort of talk unless he had a reason to distract me from asking questions." Elizabeth gave a jerk of her head, a determined glint in her eye. "And I mean to get to the bottom of it. If riding is what has done it, then I have a mind to truly master the skill myself."

"What a lovely idea!" Jane exclaimed. "I am certain Mr Darcy would be delighted to teach you, and it would be something you could enjoy together."

"Yes, yes," Elizabeth said, waving a hand. "But more importantly, I must learn this secret of his. I want to see the magic happening for myself. And he has most obligingly already offered to teach me."

"Then what are you waiting for? I hope it is not because of me that you have not joined Mr Darcy on his outings."

"Do not be silly. No, the last time I was on a horse with him, I thought I had accidentally killed him when the horse fell. Let me forget the terror of trying to unfasten us both from those vexing saddles and all those wretched straps, and I will give it another go. For now, I am content knowing he is out riding with his cousin. It does my heart good to know that Richard can see for himself how well William is truly doing."

"The colonel is a good man," Jane murmured.

Elizabeth raised a brow to survey her sister before answering lightly, "He is not terribly contemptible."

"Lizzy! One might think the colonel had offended you." Jane's steps stopped. "Has he?"

Elizabeth puckered her mouth. "Not truly, no. The only thing Colonel Fitzwilliam has ever been guilty of is trying to do too much. And even in that, he saw his error and repented swiftly. No, Jane, you are right. He is a good man, and I wish him every happiness. And I hope that happiness proves not too elusive."

Jane's mouth tugged sideways, and she shot Elizabeth a wry look. "You are not trying to play matchmaker, are you?"

"Me? Heavens, no. I am sure Mama has that well in hand. I was only referring to his intentions to retire from the Army." Elizabeth hooked her basket over one arm and tugged her sister's elbow until they resumed walking. "William was terribly happy about it, you know. There was talk of Richard's regiment being sent to the Continent this spring or summer, but he has already taken measures to ensure that he will be at liberty before that happens. I am glad—as much for the colonel's sake as for William's."

As they walked, the conversation turned to their family back home. Jane pulled a letter from the pocket of her walking gown. "I received a letter from Papa just yesterday," she said, unfolding the paper. "I know he wrote to you, too, but he specially charged me to show this to you. He sends his love and asks after you and Mr Darcy. And would you believe it? He had some rather generous things to say about your husband."

"Uncle and Aunt Gardiner must have given Papa a glowing account, indeed, when they stopped back in Hertfordshire last week. Either that, or Papa just wants to earn an invitation to plunder Pemberley's library for himself. Let me see." She put down her basket and reached for the paper.

"Such stuff! Papa can read your letters as well as any of us, and I believe he is relieved that all has come right."

"He was right to worry," Elizabeth confessed, biting her lip as her eyes scanned the page. "I did not know how any of it would turn out. I am only blessed that it has."

"But you knew something from the first, did you not? There was something about your face after that second time you spoke to Mr Darcy. I knew nothing could shake you after that, though I confess, it did terrify me. How *did* you know, Lizzy?"

Elizabeth glanced up from her father's letter, and her eyes grew unfocused for a moment. "Truly, I cannot say. It was just a... a surety, I suppose. A moment when I glimpsed him with his guard lowered, and I could see the man beneath. That is the man I fell in love with, almost from the first moment I knew him. But the rest—learning to get on, to meet each other where we each needed the other most—I suppose it came on so gradually that I hardly noticed. There was just a day when I discovered that he was the one person in the world I could never wish to be parted from."

Jane's face had grown tender and broken as Elizabeth spoke, and she sighed gently. "I had rather hoped it was something like that."

"Like what?"

"Like... an old friend, coming along beside you and slipping his hand into yours. Not the useless thrill and theatrics Mama makes it out to be."

Elizabeth braced an arm around her sister's shoulders. "I think it can be many things, but for you? Yes, I have a feeling it will be very much like that."

"I CANNOT BELIEVE YOU have not told her." Richard scoffed and shook his head as he drew his horse back to a walk. "Look at you, Darcy. You just took a splendid gallop, and did I not see that leather strap around your boot, I would not know a thing. I think you could even take a fence!"

Darcy patted Hercules' neck in satisfaction. Fancy that, he could bend forward at will now and still have the balance to sit upright again. His balance side to side was improving almost daily as well, and never more markedly than when his feet were secure in the irons. "Having a steady horse helps, I am sure."

"Poppycock. You, Cousin, are mending. Hah! Wait until I see that worthless Doctor James next time I am in Town. I shall have a thing or two to tell him. But you! Egad, you cannot be serious, that you have not said anything to your wife."

"Because I still do not know what there is to tell her." Darcy frowned and tightened the reins, slowing Hercules even more. "I still feel almost nothing."

"'Almost nothing' is not the same as 'nothing.' Come, out with it. What more have you noticed?"

"I..." Darcy furrowed his brow. Did he dare mention the most recent sensation? No, surely, that was not... well, it was not decent. But it *was* promising. "There have been more pinpricks," was all he would say. "Random, and not predictable, but occasionally strong enough to wake me from a sound slumber. Richard, I thought it was impossible. All the doctors, every ounce of common sense dictates that a man with a broken back shall always have a broken back."

"Perhaps your back was not actually broken. Perhaps it was more of a... a shock and deep bruising in your nerves. So much swelling and chaos that everything simply closed down until it could recover. Is such a thing possible?"

"I've no idea. Would that there were some way of looking at the depth of a man's bones through his flesh." He drank in a sigh. "All I know is that each day, I can hardly keep up with what is to come next. Perhaps it is time to say something to Elizabeth."

"You bloody well should! You ought to be letting her experience all the novelties with you! Unkind of you to rob the lady of that pleasure."

"I had not thought of it that way." Darcy rode on for a moment in silence. Richard was right. There were simply too many signs now to be chalked up as anything but the very best news. Where would they lead? That was why he had not told her... he could not know. But if there was one person in the whole world who should have the right to ride the highs and lows with him... well, it was not his provoking cousin, that was for sure.

Richard let the peace settle for several minutes, then broke it with a sigh. "While you ruminate on that notion, I've another to put before you. When I called on Mother at Matlock last week, she introduced me to someone."

"Oh?" Darcy asked disinterestedly. His mind was far more agreeably engaged—on what he would do tonight, when he told Elizabeth. How she would squeal in delight and kiss him and—

"Young chap. Seventeen, I think she said. But a nice fellow—unaffected and handsome. Ruddy, you know, and broad-shouldered, how some of those Scots are."

"He was Scottish?" Darcy returned mildly. Perhaps Elizabeth would settle in his lap and toy with his hair, and if she were *very* pleased, she might—

"Oh, yes. You did know that Mother has some relations still there, I expect?"

Darcy rolled his eyes. Richard was not going to let him have his little fantasy. "It stands to reason. What are you on about?"

"Well, this lad is a... I think a second cousin of hers, two or three times removed. Douglas is his name. Archibald Douglas."

Darcy pulled the reins. "Douglas, as in..."

"There it is. Now I have your attention. Yes, it seems he is the son of that doctor and his wife. Enlisted last year and was promptly sent to Spain... then sent back home again with a wooden peg for his leg."

"That is dreadful. How does he do?"

"Well, apart from a bit of a limp, quite well. But he is trying to discover what to do with himself now, and Douglas had the notion of sending him to Mother to see if he might suit as a clerk and meet some different people. Clever chap, well educated. Only waiting to come into his inheritance."

"Wait." Darcy shook his head and put out a hand. "You said he was the doctor's son. What inheritance?"

"Why, his father's estate. Did you not know?"

"How should I have?"

"Ah, it is not much—the house, that is. But the land, now... and the title—I do not care how poor a man is, if he has 'lord' or some derivative of the word in front of his name, he will have Mother's attention quick as a flash."

"Title!"

"Of course. Laird Ewan Douglas of Glencairn. Egad, Darcy, did he never tell you? He and Mother's great-grandfather were cousins or... Oh, I cannot recall the exact relationship. But you keep distracting me from my point."

"Which is?"

Richard stopped his horse and turned to Darcy. "Why, I think I have seldom met with a more winsome youth. Mother is impressed by him, and so is Father. But he thinks far too little of himself, particularly where the ladies are concerned. That leg, you know. He can no longer dance, which, for some reason, is the highest merit a gentleman can attain in the eyes of some ladies."

Darcy narrowed his eyes. "You cannot be saying what I think."

"And why not? All I am saying, Darcy, is that the lad could use a bit of cheer. A little time spent in the company of a sweet young lady ought to liven his spirits. What do you think?"

"I think..." Darcy urged his horse forward again, his gaze fixed on the ground before his horse. "I think you could put any number of scheming Society mamas to shame with your conniving, that is what I think."

"So, you approve?"

Darcy groaned and shook his head, then shrugged. "You are asking the wrong Darcy. Put the notion to Georgiana. Her fate is her own to decide."

Chapter Thirty-Nine

"HERE IS THE HOUSE," Elizabeth announced. They had finally got round to the true purpose of their outing, which was to bring a basket to Mrs. Jacobsen. She and Jane had walked some distance from the lane proper before wending their way back, mostly because the day was so fine that Elizabeth was unwilling to return to the house yet. William would be out enjoying his ride for some while longer, so why should she and Jane not take advantage of the day?

But the basket *was* growing heavy, what with all the cream and cheeses from Pemberley's larder. This was Cook's traditional basket when any of the tenants' wives was brought to bed with a new babe, and yesterday, Mrs Jacobsen had delivered a strapping young lad they named William, after Pemberley's master.

"You will like Jenny and Hannah," she told her sister as they turned in the little wicket gate. "Watch that Tom and Lily do not try to put a frog on your shoe, though."

Jane laughed. "I will watch my toes. How many children do they have?"

"Six now, with young William. A rather full house, though they were talking of sending the eldest daughter to the main house as a maid." Elizabeth frowned. "William spoke to Mrs Reynolds on her behalf already, and her mother thinks she might be safer there."

"Safer? Whatever does she need to be protected from?"

"Oh! Nothing. It is only that Mr Darcy is known to look after his... Oh, look, there is Hannah now, waving at us from the door. And that tall girl behind her is Jenny." Elizabeth raised her hand in a friendly wave, a warm smile on her face.

"Jenny, Hannah!" Elizabeth called out, quickening her pace. "It is so wonderful to see you both."

"Mrs. Darcy! Good afternoon." Hannah and Jenny both bobbed deep curtsies, and Elizabeth introduced them to Jane.

"Thank you for coming to visit," Jenny said shyly. "Mother will be so pleased."

"Of course," Elizabeth replied. "I trust she is recovering well? Forgive me, I know we ought to have come later, but I could not wait a day longer to meet little William and bring a basket from Pemberley."

Hannah stepped forward, reaching for the basket. "Oh, Mrs. Darcy, you shouldn't have! But thank you, truly. Mother will be delighted."

Elizabeth waved a hand dismissively. "Of course, Hannah. Cook tells me she packed something special for the younger children. Now, I do not suppose I might be able to meet your new brother? I've been so eager to see him!"

Jenny grinned, her eyes dancing with pride. "He's just inside with Mother. Would you like to hold him, Mrs. Darcy?"

"Hold him? Oh, yes, please!" Elizabeth exclaimed, her heart leaping at the thought.

"Just a moment, Mrs Darcy. Mama is resting just now, but I think little Willy is just waking. Shall I bring him out to you?"

"Oh! He shall not take a chill?"

"Nay, Mrs Darcy. He's a fine, strong little fellow. I'll not be a moment." Jenny disappeared into the cottage, returning almost immediately with a tiny bundle cradled in her arms. Elizabeth's breath caught in her throat as she gazed upon the baby's peaceful face, his rosy cheeks and delicate features absolutely perfect.

"Oh, Jenny, he's beautiful," she whispered, gently taking the baby into her arms. A wave of emotion washed over her as she held him close, a bittersweet longing for a child of her own mingling with the pure joy of this precious moment.

Jane leaned in, cooing softly at the baby. "Look at those little fingers! And how much hair he has already. I imagine your father must be so proud, Jenny."

Jenny smiled, taking the basket from Jane. "Thank you, Miss Bennet. If you'll excuse me, Hannah and I will just put these away before the littler ones wake Mama. I know she will be sorry to miss you, but Papa gave us strict instructions because Mama had a hard time of it..."

"Oh, by all means. This little gentleman and I will become better acquainted while we wait, shall we not?"

As Hannah and Jenny disappeared back into the cottage, Elizabeth found herself lost in the wonder of the tiny life in her arms. She swayed gently, humming a soft lullaby as the baby yawned and began sucking his cheeks in and out, turning his head as if rooting for something to eat and fussing softly when he did not find it.

Jane watched with a knowing smile, reaching into the blankets on occasion to let the little lad grasp her thumb. "Lizzy? I hope you are not..."

Elizabeth only smiled as she danced a little waltz with the bundle. "Am not what? Absolutely smitten? Too late, Jane. But I shall not make myself unhappy for what others have that I do not. I have my own William, remember?"

Jane chuckled. "So long as you are content, Lizzy."

"Perfectly so." Elizabeth blew out her cheeks and made a face at the child, dazzled by the way his eyes tried to track her face already.

The sound of approaching hoofbeats drew Elizabeth's attention, and she glanced up to see a gentleman astride a tall chestnut horse cantering down the lane. As he drew nearer, he slowed to a trot and doffed his hat in greeting, a charming smile upon his handsome face.

Elizabeth's brow furrowed slightly, a flicker of recognition sparking in her mind. She had met this man before, during one of her walks on the grounds. Why, it was the same fellow who had introduced himself as a visitor from London, holidaying in the area with friends, but try as she might, she couldn't recall his name.

Shifting the baby gently in her arms, Elizabeth made her way to the wicket gate, determined to greet the gentleman properly. As she neared, he brought his horse to a stop, his eyes falling upon the bundle in her arms.

"Good day, Mrs. Darcy," he said, his voice smooth and pleasant. "I see congratulations are in order."

Elizabeth smiled politely. Rarely had she ever seen a gentleman stare so openly at a baby. How very touching! Far from discouraging him, she rewarded him by tugging back the blanket a little.

"Good day, sir. Indeed, they are. Is he not a fine, stout little lad?"

The gentleman nodded, his eyes still fixed on the child. "Indeed. Very fine." He cleared his throat. "Lovely weather for an outing, Mrs Darcy. And who might your fair companion be?"

"This is my sister, Miss Jane Bennet. Jane, this is a gentleman I have had the pleasure of meeting during one of my walks."

Jane curtsied, her manner reserved but polite. The gentleman inclined his head in acknowledgement, his gaze lingering on Jane for a moment before returning to Elizabeth... or, more precisely, the child in her arms.

"I trust you are enjoying your stay in Derbyshire, sir?" she asked. "You are returned from Town again, I see."

The gentleman waved a dismissive hand. "Oh, indeed. The countryside is quite charming. I never can stay away from dear old Derbyshire. But tell me, Mrs Darcy, how fares your husband? I heard a rather distressing rumour when I was back in London about an accident last autumn. Something about a grievous injury that left him... incapacitated?"

Elizabeth stiffened, her eyes narrowing slightly. While news of Darcy's injury must have spread over time, she was certain it was not common knowledge among London society. Lady Matlock would have told her if it was.

"Forgive me, sir, but I do not believe I ever caught your name," she said, her voice calm but firm.

The gentleman's smile faltered for a moment, but he quickly recovered. "Ah, how remiss of me! Do you know, I am quite old friends with Darcy. And Bingley—why, yes, I believe it was he who made mention of Mr Darcy's mishap. I trust he is mended after his ordeal?"

Elizabeth exchanged a glance with Jane, noting the anger that flashed in her sister's eyes at the mention of Bingley's name. Turning back to the gentleman, Elizabeth shook her head.

"I am sorry, sir, but I do not think it proper for you to be speaking to me so informally. Now, if you will excuse us..."

She took Jane's arm, intent on leading her towards the Jacobsens' cottage and away from the unsettling conversation. As if on cue, Jenny emerged from the cottage, her eyes widening in horror as she caught sight of the man. A scream tore from her throat, the basket tumbling from her hands and spilling its contents across the ground.

A sickening realisation dawned on Elizabeth. Could this man, with his evasive manner and probing questions, be the same one who had attacked Jenny two months ago? Her heart pounded in her chest as she glanced back over her shoulder, her suspicions growing by the moment.

And the hardening look in his eye at the sight of Jenny told her all she needed to know.

Elizabeth turned to run, but the man was too quick. He leapt from his horse, his hand catching the back of her gown and sending her sprawling. She twisted as she fell, shielding the baby from harm, but the stranger's hands were on her in an instant, wrenching the child from her grasp.

Panic seized her heart as she watched him dashing towards his horse, the baby clutched tightly to his chest. "No!" She scrambled to her feet, lunging at him with a desperate cry, her fingers clawing at his back as she tried to stop him.

Jane, who had been frozen in shock, sprang into action. She raced forward, her hands outstretched, and somehow managed to grab the baby from the man's arms. Cradling the child close, she ran back to the cottage, shouting for one of the girls to take him inside.

But the man had Elizabeth now, one hand knotted in her hair and the other twisting her by the arm.

"Not so fast, Mrs Darcy," he hissed. "I know Darcy's little secret now. By thunder, it all makes sense! The timing of your marriage, the hasty departure from London... It's all too convenient."

Elizabeth's mind raced, trying to make sense of his words. What did he mean by Darcy's secret? "I don't know what you're talking about, sir," she rasped. "Please, unhand me at once!"

The man's grip only tightened, his fingers digging painfully into her arm and yanking it behind her back until she cried out. "Come now, Mrs Darcy. We both know the truth. You married Darcy to pass off my child with Georgiana as his heir, thus cutting me out of the line of succession."

Elizabeth's breath froze. "Mr... *Wickham?*" she hissed. "Let me go!"

Jane, who had frozen in shock at the man's initial assault, found her voice. "How dare you speak such vile lies about my sister and the Darcys!"

The gentleman barely spared her a glance, his focus entirely on Elizabeth. "Lies, you say? I think not. Darcy would never have married so far beneath him unless he had no choice. Now, bring my child back out, and I will refrain from snapping your neck. I know it's mine, the one Georgiana was carrying. With Darcy an invalid, it is only a matter of time before he succumbs to his frailties and—"

Elizabeth clawed at his hand, gasping for air. "You're mad!" she choked out. "That child is not yours, nor Georgiana's!"

"Aye, you have mettle, Mrs Darcy. Your blood tells—I would know that Bennet spunk anywhere. A pity you are wasted on a cripple! Oh, yes, I read the papers. I know who you are. Sister of that little bit of fluff I had the pleasure of knowing last autumn. You and

Darcy were both ruined, I daresay, and you took up together. Tell me, Mrs. Darcy, do you taste as sweet as your sister?"

Elizabeth's stomach churned at the implication of his words, and she renewed her efforts to break free, twisting her arm. Oh, where was the gardener that William always dispatched to look after her? "Help! Someone, please help us!"

From the corner of her eye, she saw Mrs. Jacobsen emerging from the cottage, a broom clutched tightly in her hands. The woman's face was set in a determined scowl as she advanced on the man, ready to defend her mistress and, no doubt, avenge her daughter's dignity. But she was barely on her feet after recovering from childbed and could not hope to rally a serious attack. Jane hesitated, then swirled around and found a heavy rock by the door that she hefted over her shoulder as a ready weapon, and she dashed forward with Mrs. Jacobsen.

Wickham, however, was too quick. He yanked Elizabeth closer, his free hand coming up to grab her chin, forcing her to look at him. "One more step, and Mrs Darcy suffers for it," he snarled, his breath hot against her face. Jane and Mrs Jacobsen hesitated, their eyes darting between Elizabeth and Wickham and their weapons still raised in a defensive stance. He was distracted for half a pulse—long enough for Elizabeth to swipe a vicious kick at his kneecaps with the heel of her walking boot, but he had her spun around to face him in a flash.

"You think to take what is mine? Bring me back the babe!"

"There *is* no babe!" she shot back. "No child, no son for you to try to claim is yours! Leave us be!"

But Mr Wickham only twisted his hands harder into the hair at the nape of her neck. "You think me such a fool? Darcy cannot sire a child, so he tries to claim mine—ah! See, your face gives you away. I might have known Darcy would marry an honest one. You should take some lessons from your younger sister. There was a strumpet and no mistake."

Elizabeth jerked and dipped her weight, trying to break Mr Wickham's hands free of her hair and gown. If she twisted hard enough, she might just loosen his grip enough to...

With a sudden, violent motion, Wickham yanked Elizabeth towards him, crushing his lips against hers in a bruising kiss. Elizabeth struggled, revulsion and fury coursing through her veins. She managed to raise her free hand and deliver a stinging slap across Wickham's face.

He reeled back, his eyes blazing with anger as he shoved Elizabeth away, sending her stumbling to the ground. Jane rushed to her side, helping her to her feet.

"You'll pay for that, you little whore," Wickham snarled, advancing on them.

Elizabeth grabbed Jane's arm and turned to run, her heart pounding in her chest. But Wickham was faster, his long strides eating up the distance between them. Just as he was about to grab Elizabeth once more, a commanding voice rang out across the grounds.

"Wickham! Step away from my wife, or by God, I will put a bullet through your black heart!"

Elizabeth's head snapped up, relief flooding her body at the sight of William astride Hercules, a pistol levelled at Wickham's chest. Colonel Fitzwilliam rode up beside him, his own weapon drawn and ready.

Wickham froze, his eyes widening in shock as he took in the sight of Darcy, sitting tall and proud upon his horse. "Darcy? But... but I heard you were bedridden, a cripple!"

Darcy's gaze remained steady, his voice calm and controlled. "As you can see, Wickham, I am perfectly well. Your information, like so many things about you, is sorely lacking."

Wickham's face contorted in confusion and anger, his fists clenching at his sides. "Impossible! I was told—"

"You were told wrong," Darcy interrupted, his tone brooking no argument. "Now, I will not warn you again. Step away from Mrs Darcy, or I will not hesitate to end your miserable existence here and now."

For a long, tense moment, no one moved. Then, a figure emerged from the fields, running towards them with a pitchfork in hand. It was Mr. Jacobsen, his face etched with concern and determination.

"I heard the ladies screaming for help, Mr. Darcy!" he called out, his eyes darting between Wickham and his master. "What would you have me do?"

Darcy, his pistol still trained on Wickham, spoke calmly but firmly. "Mr. Jacobsen, do you have any rope in your barn?"

The tenant nodded, understanding dawning on his face. "Aye, sir. I'll fetch it right away."

As Mr. Jacobsen hurried to his barn, Colonel Fitzwilliam leapt from his horse, moving to snatch Wickham by the front of his cravat. He was not gentle, nor did he show any restraint when he slammed his right fist into Wickham's jaw, then plucked his staggering form back from the earth to do it again. Elizabeth watched in some strange detachment as Jacobsen rushed back from his barn with a length of rope, and the two men worked together to bind the rogue, their movements precise and efficient.

In the midst of the chaos, Elizabeth's gaze drifted to Jane, who stood a short distance away, her eyes fixed on Colonel Fitzwilliam. There was a look of admiration and something more in her sister's expression, and Elizabeth couldn't help but notice the way the colonel's eyes kept drifting to Jane's in those beats between breaths, as if assuring himself that she was unharmed before he turned his attention back to the task at hand.

"You can't do this, Darcy," Wickham spat, struggling against his bonds. "You have no proof of any wrongdoing."

Darcy's eyes narrowed, his voice cold and unyielding. "I have the testimony of Mrs Darcy, her sister, and the Jacobsens, whose newborn son you tried to kidnap under some false apprehension. You will face the magistrate and answer for your crimes."

Wickham lurched against the colonel's grip, straining at the rope binding his wrists. "At least let me have the satisfaction, Darcy! What, afraid I will trounce you again? Afraid to get your hands dirty?"

Elizabeth was watching him as William flicked his eyes to her. They lingered on her for the faintest second before returning to Wickham. "I have no need to soil my hands with you ever again. The law shall do quite satisfactorily."

With that, he nodded to Richard and Mr Jacobsen, who hauled Wickham onto his horse, preparing to escort him to the authorities. As they rode off, Elizabeth stumbled forward and sagged against William's horse, pressing her face into his right thigh as his hand dropped to caress her cheek.

"It's over, my love. You're safe now."

She turned her face up to him, smiling at the way the sun splintered through the trees and over his broad shoulders and strong presence. "We all are."

Chapter Forty

"So... HE IS GONE?" Georgiana shook her head as if she could not believe it. "Finally arrested?"

Darcy squeezed his sister's hand. "He is. This time, there is no ambiguity—we have respectable witnesses who can attest to an unprovoked attack on a woman and a child. And I shall be stating my case in person at his trial."

Her face relaxed, but her eyes remained unfocused. "I started this, William. Is there nothing I can do to help see it finished? Anything more wanted?"

"There is. You can become who you were born to be, defying any attempt to diminish or distract you. You can extend care and grace where you may—perhaps you could begin by finding the courage to attend Elizabeth as she calls on the tenants. And you can learn to truly smile again, enjoying your life and showing me the girl I once knew, and I pray I have not lost."

Georgiana's mouth tightened, her lips trembling a little as her eyes glistened. After several pained seconds, she broke into a smile, then even dipped her head in bashful laughter. "I think I can manage that. Anything else, William? Please, tell me. Is there... anything?"

He sat back slightly in his chair, letting his gaze travel over her features—the face of a young woman, no longer a child. "One thing. Lord and Lady Matlock feel it is time for you to begin considering a discreet courtship with some carefully chosen young gentleman."

She blinked... and blinked again, and then she drew a shaky breath before opening her mouth. But he held up his hand, staying her protests before she could panic.

"I have rejected their efforts at pressuring you. As far as I am concerned, the choice is yours. I would not have you ever again manipulated into a situation you did not desire of your own accord, no matter how well-meaning the intentions."

Her cheek flickered. "But? I can see it, William. There is something else you mean to say."

He chuckled and dipped his head in defeat. "Indeed, there is. There is... someone. A relation of Lady Matlock's you may like for his own merits. Or so Richard tells me. If and when you feel ready, we may call at Matlock and greet this fellow. If nothing else, I would like to make his acquaintance merely out of respect for his parents."

Her eyes narrowed. "And who are they?"

"Why, you know them already. The very doctor and midwife who snatched you from the jaws of death and brought you back to us."

"Doctor Douglas?" Georgiana's face brightened. "Truly?"

"Truly. I—"

"No, no, that reminds me of something!" Georgiana jumped up from her chair and ran to Darcy's desk to snatch something. "Pritchard brought these in while you were out. He was asking when you might return, and I happened to glimpse the seal on the letter. It was not one I recognised, so I asked to see it, and he obliged, and..." She thrust the letter into his hands, and Darcy clasped it loosely, trying to make sense of the seal. A "D" with a thistle embossed behind it, for Scotland.

Darcy's heart began to pound, and before he had even thought twice, his thumb was under the wax, breaking it open and flattening the page. Georgiana hovered for a moment but then seemed to sense that he was too much diverted even to look up at her. Her hand touched his shoulder, and she went out. He barely felt a hitch in his breath when he tried to acknowledge her departure, and then his eyes were all for the paper spread between his hands.

Dear Mr Darcy,

I hope this letter finds you well. It was with great pleasure that I received your recent correspondence, detailing the remarkable improvements you have been experiencing in your condition. I must apologise for the delay in my reply, as I have recently returned from a journey to London, where I had the opportunity to consult with a highly esteemed colleague of mine, a preeminent surgeon at one of the city's most respected medical colleges.

During my visit, I took the liberty of discussing your case with him, and I am delighted to share that he confirmed what I had long suspected. Though it is rare, in some instances of spinal trauma, patients can, in fact, make significant recoveries over the course of a year or two. While there may be some lingering nerve damage, if the spine itself was not fractured, it is not outside the realm of possibility that what you are describing is indeed the beginning of a genuine recovery.

I must confess, Mr. Darcy, that I had harboured this suspicion from my earliest examinations of your condition, given the elasticity you retained in your affected limbs. However, without further evidence, I was hesitant to raise your hopes prematurely.

My colleague and I also discussed several therapeutic activities that may aid in your continued progress and help improve your overall strength. Swimming, when the weather permits, can be an excellent way to engage your muscles without placing undue strain on your body. Additionally, horseback riding, with proper precautions and support, may provide both physical and emotional benefits. And naturally, as we had discussed before, the efforts of Mrs Darcy at maintaining the circulation have done wonders. No doubt, it has expanded the possible limits of what nature has already dictated.

A chuckle escaped Darcy's lips, even as his body began to thrum with elation. As if he needed more confirmation of what remained possible to him, Douglas's letter was everything he could have wished for! The irony of the doctor's suggestions was not lost on him. It seemed that his wife's wisdom surpassed medical knowledge in timing and zeal, at least, if not experience.

Douglas's letter went on to speak of more personal matters—his son, he mentioned, and he asked after the Darcy ladies... but Darcy had no patience for that much just now. He creased the paper between hands that suddenly ached with nervous joy and tried to measure his breaths lest he hyperventilate and fall out of his chair.

"Parker!" he barked to the footman waiting outside the room.

The young man snapped to the summons, rounding the doorway. "Yes, sir?"

Darcy folded the letter and stuffed it into the breast pocket of his jacket. "Call for Giles. I wish to retire early tonight. Will you have word sent to Mrs Darcy, as well? There is something I desire to speak to her about."

T HERE WAS A CERTAIN confidence inspired in the heart of a man, Darcy had always thought, when he has the honour of defending his own.

For too long, that confidence and honour had been stripped from him. Though Elizabeth had worked for months to demonstrate that so much of his fancied insufficiencies were all in his head, there was truly nothing to that moment when he had been able to address wrongdoing himself. The chance to prove that he could protect his wife—truly protect her—and do his duty by all concerned, had kept his colour high and his spirits in a euphoric jumble all afternoon.

What to do with all this feeling? How to make sense of it without learning to believe that it was only due to the strength of his body that he was able to act? For a strong arm was nothing—more harm than good, even—if it was not wielded by a faithful mind and stout heart. And how could he keep the proper sort of humility, in the face of today's dizzying triumphs?

But soon, he would be able to apply to the one who made his thoughts and feelings come to order. He had but to look to her, and he would be right.

As the door creaked open, Darcy's eyes fixed on the shaft of light from the hall until her figure broke the emptiness. Sober... patient... that was the way to greet her. Let her speak all that was surely on her heart before gushing about his own elation.

She crossed the room, her skirts swishing softly as she settled beside him on the bed. "Good evening, handsome man of mine," she teased as her fingers hooked under his chin. "How is my dashing husband this evening?"

Darcy grinned, capturing her hand and bringing it to his lips for a gallant kiss. "Lonely and sad."

Elizabeth laughed. "Liar." She inched further up his chest until her nose was touching his. "How did your conversation with Georgiana go? Is she relieved?"

He nodded, his thumb tracing gentle circles on the back of her hand. "Yes, but no more so than I. I can hardly believe it, though... after so long of waiting for some chance to make things right, I—"

"William?"

He stopped, letting his protests die as he studied her eyes. "Yes, love?"

"I do not want to talk about that... any of that... tonight. I do not even want to hear his name, for he has taken up far too much space in our lives already. Perhaps there will be matters still requiring your attention concerning him, but for tonight, can we speak of something else?"

"That may be one of the best ideas you have ever had," he said, writhing under her weight a little to permit him to pull her a little closer. Yes, he liked that idea very much, for he certainly had better things to talk about than gaol for a criminal.

"Excellent!" Elizabeth pushed off of him, somehow missing the way he had been trailing his fingers along her lower back and waist. Blast... if he was going to try to seduce her, or at least try to talk her into seducing him, he would have to work a little harder.

For now, though, she had retrieved her little jar of lotion and flipped back the covers to commence her nightly ritual. Except tonight, her posture seemed less practical and more intimate than usual. Her hip rested along his right thigh, her knee hooked suggestively under his, and her upper body was half-turned so she could speak to him more easily... allowing him to admire her figure in the firelight.

And there was something now that he had not permitted himself to believe before. The sensation of general pressure under her hands—not specific, and the skin itself was mostly insensitive. But he could no longer deny the sensation of his muscles being manipulated—thready and faint, but persistent.

"Elizabeth?"

"Hmm?" She leaned forward, exerting a little more pressure as her hands closed around his calf and swept downward and upward again together.

Darcy's throat clamped down on his trachea like a vise. Heavens above... Had she any idea what she was doing to him?

"Do you think that might be too hard?" she asked in concern. "I thought I might try something different tonight, but if you feel the other way might be better—"

"No, no, that is not it," he choked. "I..." He closed his eyes and tried to swallow. "Give me a moment."

She shrugged and continued with what she was doing. "Perhaps I will speak, then, until you gather yourself. It seems that listening to my endless chatter tends to help you overcome whatever is tying your tongue."

He cupped her shoulder with his hand, for she was sitting in such a position tonight that he could reach it. "I like your 'endless' chatter. By no means would I ask you to suspend it."

"Well, then, I shall not. I noticed something odd today, and I think Jane might be developing feelings for Colonel Fitzwilliam."

Darcy smiled. "Is that so, my love? What makes you say that?"

Elizabeth sat up straighter, her hands stilling on his legs. "Well, today, when the colonel was dealing with Wickham, I couldn't help but notice the way Jane was watching him. Of course, it would be natural for her to look at him with admiration at such a moment, but after the things she said while we were walking, I think it is more than that. He may have won her regard after all."

"And you are only just seeing this now? I have suspected as much for a month."

"You have?" Elizabeth asked, her eyes widening. "But I have never noticed any particular symptoms of attachment on her part before today. She has always been so reserved in his presence."

Darcy's smile grew. "That is just it, my darling. Your sister is a shy creature, much like someone else you know." He tapped his chest, earning a little grin from her. "She is not likely to wear her feelings as openly as you, or even Richard for that matter. But that does not mean she is immune to his good qualities. And he *does* have them."

"I never said he did not!" she protested. "I just thought she would make him work harder."

"Has he not done enough? Surely, you have seen the way she watches him when she thinks no one is looking, the softness in her eyes when he's near."

Elizabeth leaned into his touch. "Look at you, Mr. Darcy, defending my sister's shy nature. I never thought I'd see the day. He will have to go to Hertfordshire, you know, to speak to my father straightaway. And Mama was denied the pleasure of attending our wedding, so Jane will surely not want to cheat her out of that. If Jane accepts him, that is, and I hope she does, Mama will be making plans for throwing Mary and Kitty into the paths of other rich men. Who should we... oh, I shall have to ask the countess for advice on that."

Darcy chuckled. "Elizabeth Darcy, are you turning into a matchmaker like your mother?"

With a playful swat to his left calf, Elizabeth gasped in mock indignation. "Fitzwilliam Darcy, how dare you compare me to—"

Her words were cut short by Darcy's sudden yelp of surprise. Elizabeth froze, her hand hovering over the spot she had just touched.

"William," she whispered, her voice trembling with a mixture of shock and hope. "Did you... did you *feel* that?"

Darcy nodded slowly, his heart pounding in his ears so loudly that he could scarcely hear his own voice. "I did, Elizabeth. I felt your hand on my leg."

"But... but *how?*"

He reached for her cheek, and she came willingly, letting her hand trail up his thigh. He had to suck in a gasp as her fingers incited random prickles and even a muscle twitch that he was helpless to deny.

"There it is again! Did you feel that?" she cried. "Fitzwilliam Darcy, you *have* been keeping secrets from me!"

"Only because I could not be sure. But I am sure now, Elizabeth. It started slowly, but these last few days have been like a rushing waterfall of new feelings. I am mending—*you* have mended me, I daresay."

"I could not possibly! Can it be true?" Tears sprang to Elizabeth's eyes as she began to rub and gently smack her hands up and down his legs, watching his face intently for any sign of sensation. While most areas remained numb, there were a few precious patches of skin where he could feel the warmth and pressure of her touch.

"Elizabeth," he breathed, joy and wonder suffusing his voice. "I can feel you! I can feel your hands!"

A laugh bubbled up from her throat, a sound of pure, unadulterated happiness. She continued her exploration of his legs, each touch a revelation, each sensation a miracle. "You fiend, you! You have been feeling this for weeks, at least, and yet you said nothing!"

"Not like I can feel you tonight. Here." He grabbed her hand and placed it on a spot she had not yet explored, where he was sure of at least some measure of sensation. And instead of blushing and withdrawing, she gasped in awe and let him guide her fingers.

"Can you *feel* that?" she whispered, her eyes growing wider by the instant as her warm hand learned what to do under his touch.

He nodded. "I feel you in my soul, Elizabeth. The rest... well, it will come with time, but yes. I can feel you."

Elizabeth Darcy was never one to do anything by half measures. If she had appointed herself as his nurse, his confidante, protector and friend, she had excelled in every measure. But this night, she became his lover.

And in that, too, he had no cause to repine.

Epilogue

T HE SUMMER SUN DANCED through the windows of the grand drawing room at Pemberley, casting a warm glow over Elizabeth's skin as she stood, her heart full to bursting. Beyond the glass, a dozen of her favourite people gathered on the sprawling lawn for an early summer picnic, their laughter and chatter floating on the gentle breeze. Two years had passed since William had felt the first flickers of life returning to his body, and he had grown stronger almost daily, ever since.

She was waiting for him now to finish his business with his solicitor—something to do with a man she no longer cared to grant the dignity of a name, who was presently languishing in a debtor's prison. William had gone to some lengths in the last year or better, amassing the sum of the man's misdeeds and ensuring that he stayed where he was for a good long while. Long enough that he would be too grey and frail to harm anyone if he ever did get out.

Elizabeth tugged at the little cross pendant at her neck as her gaze grew hazy over the lawns out the window. Hopefully, her husband would hurry his business along so they could walk out to their guests together.

Walk... indeed, he was walking now, a thing they had both once accepted as impossible. He used a cane still, for he never had fully recovered all his balance and agility, but he was fully the master of his limbs, for all that.

"There you are, love." Warm arms closed behind her, and William's hands framed a precious heart shape over her stomach as he kissed the nape of her neck. "I thought you would have gone out without me."

"And field all Mama's questions by myself? You overestimate my fortitude, husband."

"And you underestimate your impertinence. You know why your mother flutters and preens so, do you not?"

She turned in his embrace, kissing his chin and leaning back a little. "No. Tell me."

"Because she is afraid of becoming obsolete. Your sister Lydia married and gone to Newcastle—a thing that did not come one day too soon—Mary now settled in Hunsford with Mr Collins, and Jane finally happy with Richard... she has only Catherine left, and it seems that, too, may be soon taken out of your hands if what your aunt said in her last letter is true. What is the poor woman to do?"

She wrapped her arms around his neck. "Not bragging about my husband's wealth and consequence to anyone who will listen would be agreeable enough for me."

"Oh, let her have her fun." He squinted out the window. "She must have some means of giving herself purpose. You intimidate her, love, and I wager you always have. So, let us go out and make ourselves agreeable so your poor mother's mind may rest easy this afternoon."

"Is it my mother who excites your sympathy, or Georgiana?" Elizabeth turned him to face the window, and she pointed to a couple strolling on the lawn.

William leaned over her shoulder, and she heard a low chuckle in his throat. "Sympathy for her? She looks perfectly content. It is young Archibald I pity. Do you suppose he has made his proposal yet?"

"If not, I am disappointed. They have known each other for two full years! You proposed to me after two *minutes*."

"Come, now, they were not ready. We promised to give her time, and so we have, but I am growing impatient. What were the terms of our wager again?"

"The end of July. If he works up the nerve to ask you for her hand before then, you claim the forfeit. If he waits until afterwards, I win."

He quirked a brow. "Who are we kidding? You will ask the same thing in forfeit as I will. Why did we even make that wager?"

Elizabeth smiled serenely. "My dear husband, would you miss your chance to be compelled to please your wife or be pleased by her? Tsk, tsk. We simply must work on your sense of humour."

"No, thank you, my love. Your father has me wrung out quite enough already. Let me bask in a moment of peace, and then you may make free with me however you wish." He pulled her close and simply leaned his face into her hair. Elizabeth waited, thrilling to the tickle of his breathing over her skin and feeling the way his pulse calmed, just in holding her. It always did.

Eventually, they made their way out to the lawn, with William leaning less on his cane even than he had earlier in the spring. Perhaps by the end of the summer, his dependence on it would lessen still more.

Her gaze drifted to Jane and Colonel Fitzwilliam—Brother, as she now called him—strolling arm in arm, their faces alight with the glow of newlywed bliss. They had just returned from their wedding tour in Scotland, for Jane had been slow and cautious in letting herself be romanced again. The waiting, it seemed, had been worthwhile, for they were very nearly walking in the same pair of shoes wherever they went, and they had an eerie habit of finishing each other's sentences. And Richard, for all his good intentions, finally had something besides Darcy and Elizabeth's affairs to turn his hand to.

With the newlyweds had come Doctor Douglas and his wife, but Elizabeth had yet to greet them. She had been preoccupied upstairs when they arrived from the carriage, but now she steered William toward the doctor and Mrs Douglas, eager to offer the proper greetings.

"Well, Darcy!" Douglas boomed, extending one hand while the other clapped William's shoulder with a familiarity that almost no one would dare. "You did not say you owned half of Derbyshire, lad! I'd no idea Pemberley was such a grand affair."

William smiled and glanced back at Elizabeth, silently leaving her to Mrs Douglas's company as he walked off with the doctor. Elizabeth watched him go, then turned to smile at that good lady...

The lady who was, even now, helplessly staring at Elizabeth's cheeks... her figure. Her eyes scanned all the way down to Elizabeth's toes before lifting again with arched brows and a little puckered smile. "Am I to offer congratulations, Mrs Darcy?" she asked in a low voice.

Elizabeth pressed a finger to her lips. "Oh, I might have known *you* would see it right away! I have told only Mr Darcy so far."

The woman dipped her head and smiled. "Then no one shall hear it from me. Oh, I am so pleased. Another Darcy for Pemberley's nursery! How old is young Richard now?"

Elizabeth offered Mrs Douglas her arm and led her a little away from the others, who were already gathering on the blankets spread on the grass. "Just a year last week, which is why I was so surprised when... Well! That is to say, Mama always said a nursing mother had no fear of that sort of thing again so soon."

"Oh, I assure you, Mrs Darcy, the only thing that prevents a second occupant in the nursery is the lady keeping her door locked. But as you and Mr Darcy appear to be quite uncommonly attached to each other, I expect you will have to build another wing onto the house."

Elizabeth laughed. "I doubt Mr Darcy will object. Oh! I beg your pardon, Mrs Douglas, but I see my father looking as if he is very full of something. No doubt a crisis in the library or some such. Would you mind if I...?"

"Not at all. I believe I will join Miss Darcy and see if I may become reacquainted with her."

She squeezed the woman's hand. "A capital idea."

Elizabeth hurried across the lawn to her father, who was standing under an oak tree with his pocket watch in one hand and a book in the other and looking expectantly around. "Ah, there you are, my dear. I was beginning to think you'd forgotten about your poor old father, what with all the excitement around here."

"Not a bit of it. Why do you look as if you are counting down the minutes until you can return to the library without giving offence?"

"That obvious, is it? No, no, I am only setting my watch."

"Oh?"

He nodded toward Elizabeth's mother, who reclined on the picnic blankets beside Lady Matlock with her hands dancing animatedly in the air. "Indeed. Did you know, Lizzy, that your mother has said the phrase 'ten thousand a year' eight times already, and with such startling regularity to the minute that I was able to discern where the second hand on my timepiece is inaccurate?"

"Oh, Papa," she scoffed. "At least Mama likes my husband."

Her father studied his watch for several seconds, not looking up. "I like him, Lizzy." He wetted his lips and slipped the watch back into his pocket. "I like him far better than I like myself."

Her brow creased, and she stepped closer, resting a hand on his arm. "Papa, surely you do not mean that."

"I do, Lizzy." He looked up, his eyes rheumy and red, and nodded toward where William walked on the lawn with Doctor Douglas, and now Richard. "I have had a deal of time to study him and discover his qualities, and I daresay he is as fine a fellow as ever breathed. You took your measure of the man in a matter of moments. You saw what I did not, and Providence has blessed you for it."

She squeezed his arm. "But you were not wrong to worry. Your cautions were warranted, and had I not heard them, I might have made... several wrong steps."

"Well, well, then I can claim at least some credit there, I suppose. Heaven knows, little enough of my daughters' fortunes is because of my doing. But enough sentiment. Mrs Bennet will see me looking dewy-eyed and start thinking I am ready to expire from some malignant disease. I would rather spare Mr Darcy that sort of scene."

Elizabeth laughed, shaking her head in fond exasperation. Some things, it seemed, would never change.

Just then, a nurse hurried across the lawn, her steps aiming toward Elizabeth as she toted a fussing toddler in her arms. "Begging your pardon, Mrs. Darcy, but the young master is asking for you."

Elizabeth's heart leapt, and her feet were scarcely slower. Their son, Richard, named for the colonel who had brought them together, had become the centre of their world, apple of his father's eye, and she cherished every moment spent with him.

"If you'll excuse me, Papa," she said, a smile playing at her lips. "Duty calls."

Her son reached for her neck and pillowed his head on her shoulder. Elizabeth stroked his back, cooing into his thick nest of curls that looked just like his father's. "Did you have a good lie down?" she asked him.

He only had a handful of words so far, but he knew how to use them well. He rubbed his eyes and asked, "Papa?"

"Ah, you want Papa. I am afraid he is busy, but—"

"Too busy for my son?" William's voice rumbled behind her. Elizabeth turned, and as she did so, her son twisted from her embrace to reach for his papa.

"William, are you..." Elizabeth could not help the way her hand hovered, as though she could catch her much taller husband if the act of holding his child caused him to lose his balance on the uneven turf. But she bit her lip and forced herself to subside.

"Doubting me, are you, my love?" he asked teasingly.

She let him wrap one arm around her waist as he bounced Richard in his other, then leaned into his chest to watch the smiles bubbling from their son's face. "Never. I had full faith in you from the first day I met you."

He leaned down to press a kiss to the top of her head, heedless of anyone who might have been watching them. "And I in you, Elizabeth."

N OT READY FOR THE story to be over? Keep reading for a preview of *The Measure of Trust* and swoon along with our favourite couple as they find the love they were destined for!

The Measure of Trust

"**B**LAST THIS INFERNAL MUD!" Elizabeth Bennet muttered under her breath. She tried to wipe a slimy splatter of it off her riding gloves as her horse trudged through the soggy autumn fields, its hooves heavy with the weight of the mire.

Hertfordshire had not even been experiencing any extraordinary measures of rain this autumn. But the fields had become irredeemable marshes—a complaint Elizabeth had largely ignored, when she heard anyone speak of it, until *she* became the one to accidentally try wading through the quagmire.

"You should have stayed home, Lizzy," she grumbled to herself. Jane had warned her, but no, she simply *had* to call on Charlotte, even though her ankle was still tender from the day before, when she had slipped most ingloriously on the path back from Oakham Mount. So, what was her solution?

A horse. A bloody *horse*.

And as the carriage horses were wanted on the farm that day, the only alternative had been her father's riding horse—a temperamental beast with a penchant for putting his head between his front legs and pitching his tail in the air, whenever the fancy suited him.

Which it had earlier… Thus, the muddy gloves.

But for Charlotte, Elizabeth had been willing to put up with a little discomfort, perhaps even a little danger. Charlotte had been suffering from what Elizabeth could only describe as low spirits this autumn. Indeed, that was a generous term for the way poor Charlotte had been feeling, and she found little comfort in her mother's admonishments or her younger siblings' carelessness. And so, Elizabeth had been making the trek nearly every day of late, with the hope of lifting her friend's spirits even a little.

The horse's hooves squished into another soft bit of earth, and being as displeased by the notion of slogging through another swamp as his rider was, he lodged his feet in the ground and refused to move forward. Elizabeth uttered one or two indelicate phrases about the horse's parentage, but rather than fight with him again, perhaps it was best if she turned back and found firmer ground. Just... Where was that? She leaned slightly forward, inspecting the earth below for a promising path.

That, however, proved to be an ill-judged notion. The moment her weight shifted, the horse tossed his head and snorted, then his front feet popped a few inches off the ground in a menacing threat to rear, if she tried to make him go where he did not wish to go.

"Easy now," she coaxed. She would get nowhere by telling the horse exactly what she thought of him, so perhaps gentle manners might prevail. "Just a little further, and we'll be back on solid ground."

Another rabid-sounding snort, and the horse subsided long enough for Elizabeth to pull him away towards firmer footing. There, now they were getting somewhere. Just a little farther on, and they would be on the road. And she would be hanged before she tried to cross these marshy fields again before next summer. Shortcut or not, her petticoats were already several inches deep in mud, and she was starting to shiver. Just a few seconds more...

But fate, it seemed, had other plans. As they approached a particularly waterlogged section of the field, the horse's feet seemed to just... stop. He splashed up to his knees, and then his head went down, his body wrung to the side in a slithering hop... and Elizabeth felt, just for an instant, what it would feel like to fly like a bird.

A pity she could not land like one. Elizabeth hissed when she splashed into the wet grass and rolled to her side, then surveyed herself with a groan. Good heavens, she was a slimy wreck! There was another gown ruined.

But that was not the worst of it. Pain shot through her already injured ankle as she struggled to sit up, her hands sinking into the cold, wet mud. The horse, its eyes wide with panic—or malice, she could not decide which—thrashed against the sucking earth and splattered her with more of the infernal stuff. Not that it made any difference now, though.

"No, no, no!" Elizabeth gasped. "Don't you dare try to run off. You got me here. Now, you shall... Ooh!" She grabbed whatever leather was within her reach and pulled herself to her feet, wincing as she put weight on her throbbing ankle and trying to reach for the dangling rein.

Where was she? Elizabeth steadied herself by resting a hand on the pommel of the saddle and sought her bearings. She should never have taken the shortcut.

"Let me see... There is that stand of oaks, and the lane wrapping around, and oh, drat. Had I not got farther than that?" She shaded her eyes and turned about one more time. There was the marker for Netherfield, just around the bend. And that meant that she was still three miles from home.

There was nothing else for it. She would have to climb back on that pompous, twitchy beast somehow. She certainly could not walk home in this condition, but just now, hobbling three miles back to Longbourn on one good ankle seemed a great deal more appealing than getting back on that recalcitrant brute. He had done nothing today to earn her regard.

With a heavy sigh, Elizabeth gathered her skirts and braced one arm over the saddle to keep herself from falling as she tried to walk. And thus began the long, painful trek back to Longbourn.

Fitzwilliam Darcy fingered the brim of the hat in his lap as his friend, Charles Bingley, strained to look out the carriage window. The autumn air was crisp, carrying with it the promise of change and new beginnings—that was the poetic way Bingley had described the weather. He had hardly ceased chattering since they left London, and now he was busy pointing out every building with which he had already become acquainted in the little village of Meryton.

Darcy obliged by glancing out the other window and nodding agreeably, whenever Bingley seemed particularly enamoured of something or other. "That there is the bookseller's," Bingley informed him—as if the sign in the window was insufficient to the task. "You recall that fine first edition I showed you the other day? Well, that is where I found it. Odd thing, too, for I should never have thought to... oh, and there is the haberdasher. I was a little concerned there would be few options outside of going to London—you know, small village like this. It is a very respectable shop for all that. And there is the milliner. They had a very fine beaver that I admired immensely, and I think I shall look in on it again after we have concluded our business."

"We are not here to purchase a hat," Darcy sighed. "In fact, we are very nearly late for your appointment with Mr Philips. We shall not have time to make ourselves presentable at the inn before we are expected."

"I suppose we ought to have left when you recommended," Bingley confessed. "But I thought surely it was not so very critical, as I thought the roads would be quite good. A real shame about that downed tree we had to go around. Fancy, a two-mile detour just to go around a tree!"

"Would you rather drive off the road and get the carriage wheels stuck in the mud?"

"No, no. It is only that it seems like it should not have been such a bother. But Mr Philips seems an easy chap. I doubt he shall mind so very much."

"I always mind when people waste *my* time," Darcy grumbled. But the complaint was lost on Bingley.

Some minutes later, the carriage pulled to a halt directly outside the legal office of one Mr Walter Philips, solicitor. Darcy gave his jacket a cursory dusting, wishing he did not feel so badly on account of their tardiness that he refused to stop at the inn first, as planned. Well, Mr Philips was a solicitor from a small village. Surely, he had seen gentlemen arrive with creases in their trousers before.

They entered the office and were asked to wait a moment, but before they had even taken seats, Mr Philips himself came to greet them. "Mr Bingley, Mr Darcy," he began, his tone heavy with regret, "I am afraid I have some unfortunate news. The lease for Netherfield has been taken by another party. I sent a letter to inform you, but it appears it did not arrive in time. I do apologise, sirs."

Bingley's face fell, his enthusiasm draining away like the colour from his cheeks. "But... How is that possible? We were in negotiations, were we not? I had hoped to establish myself in a house before winter."

"I am very sorry, Mr Bingley, but another presented himself only two days ago and was willing to offer far more generous terms if the owner would agree to consider leasing to another."

"We had a contract, man!" Bingley's ears were starting to turn red, and Darcy drew himself up in some surprise. Bingley was not the man to lose his temper, but his looks now bordered on very vexed, indeed.

"In fact, Mr Bingley, we did not have a contract. That was the purpose of our meeting today. Thus far, we had only discussed details, and you have performed your due diligence, but there was nothing legally binding on either party. I truly am sorry, sir, but I am merely the one managing the contract. The decision was Mr Northam's, as Netherfield property belongs to him. And once the other contract was signed, he departed for Bath, as he means to make his residence there. I am afraid there is no possibility at this point in asking him to reconsider."

"But... Well, this is dashed indecent. Shoddy business, I should say! Who is this other party? Was he made aware that the property was under consideration?"

"I am afraid it is not within my purview to disclose any private matters, but indeed, he was made aware of your interest. Thus the reason for his... exceeding generosity toward Mr Northam."

"I should have been at least given the opportunity to match his offer!" Bingley protested. "I daresay, most indecent. I shall make a formal complaint, I shall, and—"

"Mr Philips," Darcy interjected firmly, "we thank you for your time." Darcy held an arm before Bingley, inviting him to extricate himself.

Philips nearly sagged, such was his evident relief, but Bingley was not quite prepared to surrender. "Well, I... I shall write to Mr Northam myself, I suppose. This should not have been carried on in such a way."

He continued posing similar remarks, more to himself than anyone else, as Darcy ushered him out. His expression bordered on broken, and in the short span of time it required to descend the stairs, he had gone from blaming Philips and Northam to questioning himself.

As they stepped into the carriage, Bingley turned to him, his brow furrowed with confusion. "Darcy, what more could I have done? I was prompt to answer all correspondence. My man in London looked over everything and said nothing looked out of the ordinary. Is it not irregular for a property to be let out from under one's nose in such a manner?"

Darcy nodded. "Indeed, it is. These transactions usually take weeks, if not months, to complete. The last letter you showed me, a mere four days ago, gave no indication of any other interested parties."

Bingley sighed. "That was what I thought, too. It is a shame, Darcy. Netherfield had everything I'd hoped for. I dearly wish I had been able to show it to you."

"A pity," Darcy agreed. "You will show me the next one."

"Of course, but..." On impulse, Bingley leaned out the window, and called out to the coachman, "Take us along the North Road before we turn back, would you? I would like to catch a glimpse of Netherfield, even if it is no longer to be mine."

Darcy studied Bingley's profile, noting the sharp disappointment etched in his features. Bingley was a chap whose every emotion played loudly across his face, but Darcy had never seen such extreme peevishness over a simple missed opportunity. He was not without sympathy, but surely, the matter did not warrant this level of disappointment. "I do not think it advisable to drive by the property. You only torture yourself needlessly."

Bingley lifted his shoulder. "It is a lovely prospect, Darcy. I did want you to see it if for no other reason than that, once you do, you will not doubt my taste."

As the carriage rolled along the country lane, Netherfield came into view, its stately façade rising majestically against the backdrop of the Hertfordshire countryside. Indeed, it was a property worthy of admiration, and he could understand Bingley's attraction to it. They did not drive directly up to the house, rather, taking a road that ran parallel to the property from which they could see most of the manor.

"It is a fine estate, Bingley," Darcy remarked, his tone measured. "But there will be others."

Bingley sighed, his gaze fixed on the retreating image of Netherfield as the carriage rolled on. "I know, Darcy. It is just... I had such high hopes for this place. The promise of a new beginning, a chance to establish myself."

Darcy nodded, his mind already turning to the practicalities of their situation. So, it was not the loss of this particular house that had Bingley so crushed, but the delay in all the things he had looked forward to. To become more like Darcy—that had always been Bingley's unstated desire, and though flattered, Darcy often wondered if he was the proper standard by which Bingley ought to be measuring himself.

Well, there was nothing else for it now. They would need to redouble their efforts, to seek out new opportunities for Bingley to secure a suitable property. Just as he was about to voice these thoughts, a flicker of movement in the distance caught his eye.

"Bingley, look there," Darcy said, pointing towards a figure on the side of the road. "Is that a young lady? And... is her horse lame?"

Bingley squinted, following Darcy's gaze. "By Jove, I think you're right, Darcy. She appears to be in some distress."

Darcy rapped on the roof of the carriage, signalling for the driver to stop. As the carriage rolled to a halt, he alighted, his long strides carrying him towards the lady in question. The young woman was covered in mud from head to toe, her skirts caked with the stuff. She stood beside a horse that looked equally worse for wear, its chest and legs mired in bog that was beginning to dry.

"Miss, are you in need of assistance?" Darcy inquired.

The lady had continued walking with her head bowed, as if meaning to pass him by, but when he spoke, her eyes lifted to his, flashing with a mixture of frustration and embarrassment. "Unless you have a magic wand to turn back time and prevent me from ever getting on this wretched beast, I am afraid there's little to be done, sir."

"Well, I have no wand and I never met one who could work such arts, but it looks to me as though an injured ankle and a rather awkward state of discomportment are your chief troubles at the moment. Please, is there anything that may be done for your assistance?"

"Oh, I should think not, for that in itself would create further complications. Think what would be said of me if I accepted a ride from a stranger?"

Darcy turned about, scanning the road in each direction. "Do you happen to see anyone about with whom you *are* acquainted?"

One of her eyes narrowed faintly, and a corner of her mouth turned up. "Someone will be along eventually. Or I will simply hobble home as I am. As you see, I am not entirely lame, and I have already managed half a mile in this... state."

"Miss, I have no intention of arguing with you, but it is clear that you cannot continue much further. Look here, permit me to introduce myself, and we shall not be strangers."

Her mouth turned up even more. "That silly line only works in children's books."

"Naturally, but as there is no one to overhear me, I had dearly hoped you would not call me out on my lazy reasoning. I am Fitzwilliam Darcy of Pemberley, and my friend—" he gestured over his shoulder and saw Bingley walking toward them after having a word with the coachman— "back there at the carriage is Charles Bingley. We would be happy to offer you a ride back to your home, Miss...?"

"Bennet," she supplied, her voice clipped. "Elizabeth Bennet of Longbourn. And while I appreciate the offer, Mr. Darcy, I couldn't possibly impose. I am not fit to be seen, let alone to soil the upholstery of your fine carriage."

Bingley, who had joined them during the exchange, chimed in. "Nonsense, Miss Bennet! We insist. It would be our pleasure to see you safely home."

Miss Bennet hesitated, her gaze flickering between Darcy, Bingley, the carriage, and the muddy road ahead. "I suppose I am not quite so well off here as I would like to appear. But the upholstery in your carriage...."

"No bother at all," Bingley interjected. "For, you see, I had a picnic blanket in the boot, as the weather is fair, and I had already intended on an afternoon of celebration on the lawn of... well, that is not to be now, but I had my coachman cover the seat for you."

She wetted her lips and looked down at herself, surveying her gloves, her gown, the boots that were so thick in mud it was a wonder she even kept her footing... and swallowed. "I suppose the usual fears of a lady who finds herself suddenly dependent upon the aid of two gentlemen whose characters are unknown to her are abysmally lacking in this case."

Dacy stepped marginally closer. "I do not follow, Miss Bennet."

She held up one hand, spreading the fingers of it to display the crusting mud over her gloves. "You would have to be desperate, indeed, to try to take advantage of me. It would ruin your expensive coat."

Darcy nearly choked on a laugh. Had she meant to be impertinent? Or was she simply so out of sorts that the words and thoughts jumbled together in her mouth until they came out sounding gloriously amusing? "I assure you, Miss Bennet, you will be as safe with us as in your own father's carriage."

She frowned, a crease appearing under the cracks of mud over her brow as she deliberated. "Well, what about my horse? Frankly, I do not mind leaving the brute here to rot, but my father seems unaccountably to like the rogue. I think he just likes being contrary."

"The matter of the horse is quite simple," Bingley replied. "We can fasten the reins to the back of the carriage and lead him. What say you, Miss Bennet?"

She swallowed, her eyes flicking to Bingley, then back to Darcy. "It *does* sound better than walking, but you do not know what you are offering. Are either of you gentlemen single?"

"Single?" Bingley chuckled a little. "Whatever does that have to do with..."

Darcy put a hand up. "We both are. I can guess at your concern, Miss Bennet. We shall be discreet, but I cannot, in good conscience, drive away without seeing a lady safe on the road. I could never look my own sister in the eye afterwards."

She shot one more caustic look back at the horse, then nodded wearily. "Oh, what is the use? I am a tragic enough sight as it is. Perhaps no one will recognise me."

Darcy doubted that very much. Miss Bennet was already fixed in his mind as one of the most unique creatures he had ever encountered, and those who knew her well could not help but spot her at fifty paces, even if she was covered in mud. But he kept this thought to himself as Bingley tugged the horse's reins from her hand, and Darcy offered his arm to help her hobble to the carriage.

"Oh, I do not think..." She drew back, eyeing his coat. "Sir, I cannot possibly..."

"Your concern is touching, Miss Bennet, but what you 'cannot possibly' do is walk unaided. Without leaning on your horse for support, how do you mean to make the carriage?"

"With a great deal of stumbling and more mud on my knees, I should imagine." She made a wry face. "Very well, but I will touch only your glove, sir."

Darcy, fighting back a smile at her frank words, offered his hand to assist her to the carriage. "I assure you, Miss Bennet, a little mud is of no consequence."

Miss Bennet's lips twisting into a droll smile, accepted his hand and limped away, leaning on him even more than he had anticipated. After some torturous distance, she climbed into the carriage, taking great care to keep her skirts from brushing against the plush velvet. Bingley and the coachman had secured her horse to the back of the carriage, and a moment later, they were underway.

"You will have to give some direction to the coachman. Which way is your home?"

Miss Bennet sat ramrod straight, her hands clasped tightly in her lap, her gaze fixed resolutely out the window. "Two more miles to the southeast, I am afraid."

"Two *miles*?" Darcy repeated. "However did you mean to walk that distance?"

"One step at a time, sir," she retorted, but not without a sweet little smirk that took the bite out of her words. "I imagine that is the way most people walk."

"You must have been enjoying quite a long outing. I take it your ride did not go as planned, Miss Bennet?" Darcy ventured.

"What gave it away, Mr. Darcy? The mud, or the fact that I was trudging along the road like a vagrant?"

Darcy, feeling a flush creep up the back of his neck, stammered an apology. "Forgive me, Miss Bennet. I did not mean to pry."

Miss Bennet's expression softened slightly. "No, forgive me, Mr Darcy. It has been a trying day, and I am afraid my temper has gotten the better of me—not least in the matter of the horse. I might have still been mounted, had I made some little effort at getting along with that ill-mannered cad."

Darcy permitted another small smile, but hid it away immediately, lest Bingley should see it. "I was not aware that it is ever incumbent upon any lady to make herself agreeable to a... a cad, did you say? Some creatures are better left alone, lest you injure yourself in trying to redeem them."

The mud on her cheeks somehow faded, when compared to the brilliance of a genuine smile from her. Egad, the lady *did* have fine eyes, that sparkled just so in the light from the carriage window. "Well said, Mr Darcy. And now, you and I may be friends. There, I have not done such a wretched thing in accepting a ride from you, after all."

That might be the first time a lady had ever evoked such an easy laugh from him. Darcy forced himself to look away, for it would not do to wonder what she looked like, properly cleaned up and turned out for... oh, say, a ball. No, it would not do to imagine that at all.

"I say," Bingley asked, "how did you come to be so..." He cleared his throat and gestured to her person. "... besmirched?"

"I tried to take a shortcut," she sighed. "And I did not realise that nearly every field around here is doing its best to join the ocean."

"Yes, that is a deal of mud. Has Hertfordshire suffered more rain than London this autumn?"

"No, that is just the shock of it. No one can discover why it is so, but the irrigation channels have all flooded over and broken down any earthen dikes set up to divert the water."

Darcy narrowed his eyes. "Interesting. I wonder where the water has come from, if it is not raining overmuch yet this season."

"The lake, I suppose, but it does not bode well for winter..." Miss Bennet's brow furrowed again. "Or next spring, when the farmers must harvest winter wheat and plant new crops."

Darcy had begun to let his eyes wander over those very fields out the window, but at her words, they snapped back to her. What a... singular thing for a young lady to mention, or even think about.

They rode in relative silence for a little while, until Miss Bennet straightened, her eyes on something out the window. She bit her lips together and tried to restrain a sigh. "Mr Bingley, I beg your pardon, but did you say this was your carriage? Pray, ask your coachman to let me out just over the ridge there, behind the stand of trees shielding the road from the house beyond."

Darcy leaned to look out the window. There was a cluster of young ladies walking on the path ahead, with much giggling and tomfoolery between them. One of them pointed at Bingley's carriage and squealed in some delight, and Darcy was certain he caught the phrase "rich men from London."

Miss Bennet groaned and sank back into the corner, looking away.

"Friends of yours?" Darcy asked.

"My sisters," she hissed as a hand covered her cheek from the window's light. "I only hope Jane does not look up and recognise Papa's horse. Lydia never would pick up that sort of thing, but Jane... oh, please beg the driver to slow down and let them pass before we reach the turning of the road! I would rather not make a scene."

Bingley gave a short command, and they heard the feminine chatter dying away as the girls passed on. Miss Bennet gave a great roll of her eyes and released a shaking breath. "Well! There's a relief. If Lydia had spotted me in your carriage, I am sorry to say that Mama would have shackled me to one of you unfortunate creatures before sundown."

Bingley laughed. "Oh, surely, you jest, Miss Bennet. Nonsense, for it was only a matter of helping a lady in distress. No one could fault you for accepting, what with an injured ankle and all. I should like to present myself to your father and assure him that your safety and reputation were properly seen to."

Miss Bennet cast a weather eye over him, then her gaze shifted to Darcy, and she raised a brow. "You understand, sir. I can see that much."

Darcy dipped his head. "Unfortunately, I do, Miss Bennet."

"Then you will understand that I mean what I say when I beg you to let me out before we are quite in sight of the house."

Darcy nodded. "Indeed, Miss Bennet. Bingley, have the carriage stop just there." He pointed to the place she had indicated.

"Oh, very well. It seems rather ungallant, though." Bingley rapped on the roof and said something to the driver.

Miss Bennet shifted on the cloth Bingley's coachman had laid down as she gathered her skirts and prepared to disembark. "Thank you again, gentlemen. With any luck, I shall not have to endure the embarrassment of meeting you again."

"Why would that be an embarrassment?" Darcy asked as he disembarked and reached to hand her down.

"Because I shall never have any credit in your eyes, after such a miserable first impression! It would take me months to redeem your opinion of me, and I daresay there would be little reward in it for either of us. No, sir, far too much effort. I shall bid you a good day, and you shall return to London or wherever you are bound, thinking that all Hertfordshire ladies are accident-prone and barely civilised."

His mouth turned up a little more—dash it all, he could not help it. "And what will you think of gentlemen from London?"

She turned her face up to him with a thoughtful expression, puckering her mouth. Darcy almost chuckled aloud at how the drying mud on her cheek stretched and caked and cracked as her features moved. "I think they are not all cads, sir. Some of them, but not all."

"Well, that is a relief. I would hate to have such a remarkable lady alive in the world and thinking ill of me."

She looked away long enough to take the reins Bingley passed to her, then shot him one final, impish look. "I believe you are assured of my good opinion, sir. Little as that matters, I can at least grant you that. Good day, and thank you again for your kindness." With that, she turned and made her way toward the house, disappearing around the bend without a backward glance.

Bingley sighed. "It truly is a pity about Netherfield, Darcy. With neighbours such as Miss Bennet, I am certain I would have been quite happy there."

Darcy shook his head. "With neighbours such as her, Bingley, you would have found yourself wed before Christmas."

ELIZABETH WINCED AS SHE stepped out of sight of the gentlemen's carriage, her ankle throbbing with every movement. Oh, if Mama ever heard of this...

If Mama ever heard of this, Elizabeth would find herself bundled in a fast coach for London with her mother and a clergyman trying to chase those poor gentlemen down.

But they truly had been kind. Certainly, there were worse ruffians a lady could find herself compromised by. She glanced back over her shoulder, ensuring that the gentlemen were well out of sight before letting out a long, painful sigh. The horse, drat him, was all friendliness now, and he nuzzled her hand. She patted his shoulder absently.

"We dodged a bullet, you miscreant. It seems no one saw our little misadventure."

Limping towards the house, Elizabeth braced herself for the inevitable confrontation with her family. Mr Hill saw her in the drive and immediately came to take the horse. "Shall I help you inside, Miss Elizabeth?" he offered. "I shall call Mrs Hill to attend you."

"No, no, that will not be necessary." She sucked a breath between her teeth and hopped a little on her good foot to make it up the steps to the house. No sense in exciting Mama more. Let her believe it was no more than the same sore ankle from yesterday.

"Lizzy!" Jane, her eldest sister, exclaimed as she caught sight of Elizabeth's at the door. "What on earth happened to you? Why, you are covered head to toe!"

Elizabeth grimaced, holding up a hand to halt her sister's concern. "I know, Jane. It's a long story. Could you help me get cleaned up before Mama sees me? I'd rather not have to explain myself just yet. Or ever, really."

Jane nodded and quickly ushered Elizabeth upstairs. Together, they worked to remove the mud-caked clothing and tidy Elizabeth's appearance. It would take a full bath to get some of the slime out from under her nails and the roots of her hair, but hopefully, Mama would not have cause to look too closely. That walking dress, though... she would have to sneak it out to the stream behind the house before Hill had a look at it.

Once presentable, Elizabeth descended the stairs, her breath caught in her throat as she noticed the muddy footprints she had tracked into the hall. Oh, dear... perhaps Mama would be too preoccupied with asking her sisters what they had done in town to notice before Elizabeth could get it cleaned up.

But Mama was not in the sitting room to notice. Nor was she upstairs, or even in the kitchen talking to Hill. Guilty conscience, perhaps, but Elizabeth could not be easy until she knew precisely where her mother was, and if there was any chance the details of her little afternoon outing might have been discovered.

She did not have to look long, however. Elizabeth was just returning to the hall when her mother burst through the door, both hands framed in the air.

"Girls!" she cried, her voice echoing through the house. "Netherfield is let at last!"

Well... This was... fortuitous timing. There was no better way to distract her mother from the fact that she had just ridden home alone in a carriage with two wealthy, single gentlemen than for her mother to have something better to gossip about.

Elizabeth knotted her shaking fingers behind her back, willing the nervousness to remain at bay while she smiled serenely for her mother. "Is that so, Mama? How thrilling."

"Aye, and do you not want to know who has taken it, Lizzy?"

Elizabeth sighed. Mama would not rest until she had divulged every last detail of the new tenant. She nodded, resigning herself to the inevitable gossip that would follow. "I am all anticipation."

"The man has come from the north, with a large fortune," Mrs. Bennet proclaimed, her voice filled with barely contained glee. "And his name, girls, is Wickham."

Dive into The Measure of Trust and swoon along with our favourite couple as they find the love they were destined for!

From Alix

T HANK YOU FOR INDULGING with me and spending a little time with Darcy and Elizabeth.

I hope you've had a delightful escape to Pemberley. I'd love it if you would share this family with your friends so they can experience a love to last for the ages. As with all my books, I have enabled lending to make it easier to share. If you leave a review for *The Measure of Love* on Amazon, Goodreads, Book Bub or your own blog, I would love to read it! Email me the link at **Author@AlixJames.com.**

Would you like to read more of Darcy and Elizabeth's romance? I have another rich tapestry for you to try next! *Dive into The Measure of Trust* and swoon along with our favourite couple as they find the love they were destined for!

And if you're hungry for more, including a free ebook of satisfying short tales, stay up to date on upcoming releases and sales by joining my newsletter: https://dashboard.m ailerlite.com/forms/249660/73866370936211000/share

Also By Alix James

The Heart to Heart Series

These Dreams

Nefarious

Tempted

Darcy and Elizabeth: Heart to Heart Box Set

The Sweet Escapes Series

The Rogue's Widow

The Courtship of Edward Gardiner

London Holiday

Rumours and Recklessness

Darcy and Elizabeth: Sweet Escapes Box Set

The Sweet Sentiments Series:

When the Sun Sleeps

Queen of Winter

A Fine Mind

Elizabeth Bennet: Sweet Sentiments Box Set

The Frolic and Romance Series:

A Proper Introduction

A Good Memory is Unpardonable

Along for the Ride

Elizabeth Bennet: Frolic & Romance Box Set

The Short and Sassy Series:

Unintended

Spirited Away

Indisposed

Love and Other Machines

Elizabeth Bennet: Short and Sassy Compilation

The Mr. Darcy Series:

Mr. Darcy Steals a Kiss

Mr. Darcy and the Governess

Mr. Darcy and the Girl Next Door

Mr. Darcy: Swoonworthy Collection

The Measure of a Man Series:

The Measure of Love

The Measure of Trust

The Measure of Honor

Christmas With Darcy and Elizabeth

How to Get Caught Under the Mistletoe: A Lady's Guide

North and South Variations

Nowhere but North

Northern Rain

No Such Thing as Luck

John and Margaret: Coming Home Collection

Anthologies

Rational Creatures

Falling for Mr Thornton

<u>Spanish Translations</u>

Rumores e Imprudencias

Vacaciones en Londres

Nefasto

Un Compromiso Accidental

Reina del Invierno

Una Mente Noble

Cuando el Sol se Duerm

A lo largo del Camino

Reina del Invierno

Una Mente Noble

El señor Darcy se roba un beso

<u>Italian Translations</u>

Una Vacanza a Londra

About Alix James

Short and satisfying romance for busy readers.

Alix James is an alternate pen name for best-selling Regency author Nicole Clarkston.

Always on the go as a wife, mom, and small business owner, she rarely has time to read a whole novel. She loves coffee with the sunrise and being outdoors. When she does get free time, she likes to read, camp, dream up romantic adventures, and tries to avoid housework.

Each Alix James story is a clean Regency Variation of Darcy and Elizabeth's romance.

Visit her website and sign up for her newsletter at AlixJames.com

Made in the USA
Columbia, SC
05 November 2024

45726859R00228